AHRIMAN:
SORCERER

JOHN FRENCH

A hint of a smile formed and faded on Ahriman's face. It was the most terrifying thing Silvanus had ever seen. The clouds of dust were shifting, the winds pulling the drab curtain back again. The Rubricae still stood there, but now all of them were staring up at the fortress.

'In time this place will change. Others will find it, and their hands will remake the fortress we stand on. Then, in that future, one person will come here. Her name will be Iobel, and she will have something I need. This is what I have been seeking – a point of intersection in the threads of time, a point where I can be certain where she will be. We are not here for what this place is now – we are here for what it will be.'

Silvanus followed Ahriman's gaze down to the plains at the foot of the fortress. Drifting dust was burying the Rubricae. Already their feet and shins were beneath the surface, as though swallowed by a rising tide. The light in their eyes was dimming.

'Sleep, my brothers,' said Ahriman softly. 'Sleep in dust, and wait.'

More Chaos Space Marines from Black Library

• **AHRIMAN** •
John French
Book 1 – AHRIMAN: EXILE
Book 2 – AHRIMAN: SORCERER
Book 3 – AHRIMAN: UNCHANGED (2015)

THE TALON OF HORUS
A Black Legion novel
Aaron Dembski-Bowden

NIGHT LORDS: THE OMNIBUS
Contains the novels Soul Hunter, Blood Reaver
and Void Stalker, *plus additional short stories*
Aaron Dembski-Bowden

THRONE OF LIES
A Night Lords audio drama
Aaron Dembski-Bowden

STORM OF IRON
An Iron Warriors novel
Graham McNeill

IRON WARRIOR
An Iron Warriors novella
Graham McNeill

THE SIEGE OF CASTELLAX
An Iron Warriors novel
C L Werner

CRIMSON DAWN
A Crimson Slaughter novella
C Z Dunn

DARK VENGEANCE
A Crimson Slaughter novella
C Z Dunn

BLOOD GORGONS
A Chaos Space Marines novel
Henry Zou

PERFECTION
An Emperor's Children audio drama
Nick Kyme

A WARHAMMER 40,000 NOVEL

AHRIMAN: SORCERER

JOHN FRENCH

BLACK LIBRARY

For Alan Bligh.

A Black Library Publication

First published in Great Britain in 2014 by
Black Library,
Games Workshop Ltd.,
Willow Road,
Nottingham, NG7 2WS, UK.

10 9 8 7 6 5 4 3 2 1

Cover illustration by Fares Maese.
Tzeentch icons by John Blanche.

A CIP record for this book is available from the British Library.

UK ISBN 13: 978 1 84970 700 8
US ISBN 13: 978 1 84970 701 5

See Black Library on the internet at

blacklibrary.com

Find out more about Games Workshop
and the world of Warhammer 40,000 at

games-workshop.com

Printed and bound by CPI Group (UK) Ltd, Croydon, CR0 4YY

It is the 41st millennium. For more than a hundred centuries the Emperor has sat immobile on the Golden Throne of Earth. He is the master of mankind by the will of the gods, and master of a million worlds by the might of his inexhaustible armies. He is a rotting carcass writhing invisibly with power from the Dark Age of Technology. He is the Carrion Lord of the Imperium for whom a thousand souls are sacrificed every day, so that he may never truly die.

Yet even in his deathless state, the Emperor continues his eternal vigilance. Mighty battlefleets cross the daemon-infested miasma of the warp, the only route between distant stars, their way lit by the Astronomican, the psychic manifestation of the Emperor's will. Vast armies give battle in His name on uncounted worlds. Greatest amongst his soldiers are the Adeptus Astartes, the Space Marines, bio-engineered super-warriors. Their comrades in arms are legion: the Astra Militarum and countless Planetary Defence Forces, the ever-vigilant Inquisition and the tech-priests of the Adeptus Mechanicus to name only a few. But for all their multitudes, they are barely enough to hold off the ever-present threat from aliens, heretics, mutants – and worse.

To be a man in such times is to be one amongst untold billions. It is to live in the cruellest and most bloody regime imaginable. These are the tales of those times. Forget the power of technology and science, for so much has been forgotten, never to be re-learned. Forget the promise of progress and understanding, for in the grim dark future there is only war. There is no peace amongst the stars, only an eternity of carnage and slaughter, and the laughter of thirsting gods.

*Abandon the limitations of what you think is possible
and you are left with a universe that is truly infinite.
That realisation is the root of all power. Cage your mind
with the possible and you have stolen your own future.*

– Rumination of the primarch Magnus the Red,
recorded in the Athenaeum of Kalimakus.

PROLOGUE

The old man was close to death. The attendants watched the quill tremble in his fingers as it scratched across the page. They did not move. There was an order to this moment, an order that stretched back to before any of them could remember, so they waited and watched as the old man shivered and shook in the last moments of his life. They called him the Remembrancer, though none knew why. Ultimately the reason did not matter, only the fact of him, and those who had come before him.

The Remembrancer took a wheezing breath. The quill stopped moving. Ink began to bloom across the parchment. The cloak of cables, which fell from his skull and back, trembled. He raised his head and turned it from side to side, as though looking around the domed chamber, as though the metal visor riveted to his skull was not there, as though he could see. His mouth flapped silently, lips trying to form words without a tongue. The hooded and cloaked attendants waited. The only sound was the rasp of the old man's breath, and the *gulp-hiss* of the tubes linked to his body.

The brass and iron lectern holding his shrivelled frame quivered. The blue flames of the candles that ringed the lectern and man spluttered and then stretched high, burning brighter and brighter. The Remembrancer's back arched. Tubes popped from his flesh and sprayed blood and fouled water into the air. The liquid boiled before it hit the floor. The man screamed in silence. The cables and pipes began to glow with heat where they connected to him. Smoke rose from his body. His hand spasmed, smearing the ink on the parchment. The visor covering his eyes blazed with heat and began to melt.

The attendants moved forwards as one, unfolding from niches which ringed the chamber. There were nine of them, all robed in grey, the face of each hidden behind silver masks that left only one eye uncovered. They closed on the old man in a circle. He was still screaming, but now something was moving in his mouth, something that thrashed as it grew from inside his throat. He began to croak out sounds that might have been words, but which popped and gurgled like breaking cartilage and bubbling pus. The circle of attendants closed in further. When they were two paces away, the Remembrancer went still. The candles went out. The sounds coming from his throat became a simple whimper of agony. He went utterly still, and then slumped forwards, his face wiping across the still-wet ink of his life's work.

The attendants worked quickly. All but one of them had done this before, and all of them knew that they did not have long. They lifted the smoking body of the Remembrancer from the lectern, pulling the cables and tubes from their plugs as they did so. The iris hatch in the domed roof of the chamber opened. An unconscious figure was lowered through the ceiling on a hoist. The plug ports for the waiting cables and tubes already dotted his body, and a visor of silver covered his eyes. Of his limbs only his left arm remained. The attendants met him as he descended, attaching the cables and web of pipes before he settled into the lectern.

One of the attendants glanced towards the ink-blotted page of the book; it had begun to char at the edges. The others had noticed this too and began to work faster. Finally, they put the quill in the man's hand, and walked backwards to the chamber's edge. Smoke was rising from the book.

The man awoke. The new Remembrancer's mouth moved as though he still had a tongue, and then became still. Slowly he turned his blinded gaze to the page in front of him. The candles lit one after another, their flames burning blue. The Remembrancer's arm jerked and the quill began to move across the parchment. At the edge of the chamber the attendants watched, and waited.

PART ONE

WAR OF PROPHECY

I

DREAMS

Soon it will be done.

Grimur Red Iron closed his eyes, feeling the growl of the boarding torpedo around him as it cut through the void. He ran his tongue across his teeth; they had grown long. He shifted, feeling the knot of mis-grown and damaged muscle twist on his hunched back. The hunt had been long, but it was almost done. *Soon*, he thought again and opened his eyes.

His pack waited beside him, their armour and weapons stained red by warning lights. Thirty figures of grey iron filled the narrow space. The marks of time and battle were on all of them: in the scars on their war-plate, in the worn handles of their weapons, but most of all in their silence.

A scream of tearing metal filled the air. The torpedo shook, and shook, with the roaring shriek of metal grinding past its hull. Grimur felt his muscles tighten against his bones, and braced. The torpedo slammed to a halt, and its tip exploded outwards. Smoke and molten droplets blew back into the hold. Grimur launched out of his seat and his pack kin rose as one to follow him.

He came out of the smoke at a run. A human stood before him, eyes wide in a face of stitched and scarred skin. Grimur noticed the filth-spattered overalls and the barbed iron collar around the human's neck. His axe cut the man in half, from head to groin. Blood and bowel fluid flooded onto the deck. Another figure appeared, a ragged outline at the edge of sight. Grimur straightened and fired. The bolt shell turned the figure to red tatters and bone shards.

He could smell the warp's sweet reek even within his helm, like the taste of rotting meat and honey. But it was the other scent that drew him on through the smoke and the strobing detonations, the scent of a soul that had walked these decks and touched this vessel's skin. The one they sought had fled long ago, but his spoor remained. Sycld and Lother had followed the scent through the Underverse of the warp, and led them to this ship orbiting a dead star at the Eye's edge. Half crippled and skeleton-crewed, the ship was almost a corpse, but it had still croaked its name in defiance as Grimur's ships had run it down: *Blood Crescent*, it had hissed across the vox. That it would die was a certainty, but that did not matter, not truly; what mattered was that it spoke its secrets before the end.

Grimur ran through the hammering of gunfire and

ducked into a wide passage mouth. His pack kin bounded forwards behind him, chainblades growling to life, teeth and bone amulets rattling on scarred grey armour plate. They moved without words or howls, like wolves that had seen many winters and lost their hunger for blood. More of the ship's ragged and mutilated crew died, their bodies burst and hacked apart, their blood slicking the rusted metal of the decking. The thunder rhythm of bolters filled the air as the pack swept on through the murk, deeper into the rotting ship.

Crowds of slave crew fled before Grimur, choking the passage with screams and bodies. He cut his way through them without slowing down. Dark red blood drooled down his armour, pooling in its dents and matting the black fur of his cloak. He killed with every step – cutting, trampling and crushing. He killed in silence, his mouth closed over his long teeth, weapon and body moving as one. He felt only the smack of his axe hitting meat, and the judder of the haft in his hand. The rest, the blood slapping his armour, the cries of the dead, meant nothing. The joy of battle had left him long ago. This slaughter was just what it was, what it had always been: a means to an end.

A roar filled the passage as Grimur broke through the crowd of dead and dying crew. He looked up. A creature of twisted muscle stared back at him with bloodshot eyes. It stood head and shoulders taller than a Space Marine, its face hidden by a plate of hammered metal. It had no hands, just stumps fused with blades. Chains hung from hooks in its pale skin, clinking behind it as it paced forwards.

A blade-tipped arm punched towards him. Grimur saw the blow unfold. He kicked from the floor, twisted past the killing point, and buried the curve of his axe in the mutant's head. The axe wrenched free, blood fizzing to smoke in its power field. The mutant began to fall. Grimur landed and kept running. Behind him the mutant's body hit the deck in a shudder of dead muscle and fat.

The bolt-round exploded across his chest before he had taken another step. He stumbled, his helmet visor suddenly bright with warning runes. Pain spread across his chest. He caught his balance, and pivoted to face the direction of fire.

A Space Marine was advancing towards him, bolter held in one hand, a hooked chainaxe in the other. Flaking layers of red covered its armour and tatters of skin hung from the spikes studding its pauldrons. Severed human hands flapped from chains at its waist. It wore no helm, and it grinned with hooked iron teeth from a face of flayed muscle. It had a name for its own kind. A name which, like every other part of its fallen life, was a lie – a vile daubing covering the colour of its sins. The Harrowing, they called themselves.

Grimur leapt, his axe spinning low, old muscle unwinding into the cut. The Harrowing warrior almost killed him then. The chainaxe spun to life as it hacked forwards. Dried blood and skin scattered from the turning teeth. The cut was fast, very, very fast. Grimur just had time to half twist aside. Chain teeth chewed across his right shoulder and the snout of his helm. His helmet display blanked out in a flare of static. He lashed out with the butt of his axe, felt it hit armour and rock the Harrowing warrior back. He kicked out, still blind. His boot crashed into something solid, and a snarl of rage filled the air. His vision cleared in time to see the warrior's chainaxe descending towards his head. He fired his pistol then, holding it low. The rounds took the other warrior's legs out from beneath him. Grimur brought his axe around and down, and the warrior's grinning head fell away in a wash of black blood.

Grimur straightened above the kill. Carefully, he clamped the pistol to his thigh, and reached up to pull the ruin of his helmet from his head. The foetid air met the bare skin of his face. He ran a bloody hand across his scalp, mottling the tangle of faded tattoos with blood. An old habit, but one he kept even here, even when the blood smelled of ruin. Around him the tunnel had become quiet, the sounds of battle a distant rumble. His pack kin were swift, and the rest of the murder-make would be done with soon.

The stink of the Harrowing warrior's blood rose to fill his senses as he breathed. He could taste the tumours seeded in its flesh, and the dead meat of its body. He wondered whether he would one day be the same, if the light of the Eye would sink deep enough into his bones that he would no longer be a Lord of Fenris, if he would end his thread of life a beast walking in the frost-night of the Underverse.

Fenris. Could he even remember it? Sometimes it seemed just a name, a word to conjure faded memories of starlight glinting on the sea, the roar of cracking pack ice and the sight of blood clotting on snow.

'He was here.' Sycld's voice broke Grimur's thoughts, but he did not turn. He had known the Rune Priest had entered the passage without needing to see or hear him. He did not need to answer, either. Instead he bent down, dipped the tip of his armoured finger in the spreading pool of blood and then touched it to his tongue. For a second he just tasted salt and iron, then the blood memory came, a shimmer of half sensations, smeared with madness and corruption. He saw the decks of the ship he stood on sluiced with blood as sacrifices were impaled on altars, he saw a figure in power armour with a helm shaped like a hound, and he saw a fading image of a banner with a silver sword held in a black fist on a field of red.

The dead warrior had once been called Elscanar, but he had forgotten that name long before Grimur's axe had cut his thread. The blood and flesh remembered, though.

Grimur straightened, aware again of the curve in his back and the hunch of his shoulders. Sycld's frost-blue eyes looked back at him. Unconsciously Grimur's hand went to the shard of red iron hanging on a cord around his neck. The Rune Priest had also removed his helm, and the plait of his white hair had uncoiled from the top of his shaven head to hang to his waist. Skeletal crow's wings spread across his chestplate and pauldrons. Bird skulls, and dead eyes set in amber hung from the edges of his battleplate, clicking against the storm-grey ceramite as he moved. Pale, almost transparent skin pulled and creased over the sharp bones of Sycld's face as he bared teeth that were long and needle fine, closer to those of a feline than a wolf.

He was young, at least young in the company of Grimur's pack. When the hunt had begun Sycld had been newly blooded, his face full, his eyes golden and his laugh quick. Time and the hunt had changed that. He had found the wyrd was in him. His body was shrunken, flesh seeming to suck back into bone even as the wyrd bloomed in his soul. Now he rarely talked, and the rest of the pack turned their eyes from him as he passed. He was a nightwalker, a hunter of the underworld, and while he was still their kin, he stood apart even from the other Rune Priests.

'Ahriman was here,' said Sycld again, his voice low and dry. 'I can feel his steps on the floors, his touch on the bones of the *Blood Crescent*. Time has passed but the scent is still strong.'

'Strong enough for you to lead us to him?'

Sycld's eyes fluttered closed, and his tongue ran across his teeth.

'Perhaps,' he said, after a pause.

'We must have the scent,' growled Grimur. They were close, he knew it in his bones and breath. The wyrd was not in him, but he knew. They could not fail now. They had given too much to fail now. 'Take it from this one.' Grimur inclined his head to the dead Space Marine at their feet.

Sycld held Grimur's gaze for a long moment. Then the Rune Priest bowed his head and stepped forwards, strings of finger bones clacking against the haft of his staff.

'By the edge of your axe, my jarl,' he said. The seals on his gauntlet released with a hiss of pressure. Sycld knelt and ripped a handful of meat from the corpse. Blood oozed between his bare fingers. He brought it up to his face, and inhaled. The pupils in his pale eyes almost vanished. He breathed out. White mist filled the air. Grimur felt his skin prickle. His right hand tightened around the throat of his axe.

Sycld nodded once, and tilted his head back. His mouth opened wide, cartilage cracking, skin stretching. Grimur felt his hand close on the red iron amulet around his neck. Sycld's jaws opened wider and wider. He dropped the meat into his mouth and his teeth closed. He swayed where he knelt, face still upturned, blood running down his distorted cheeks. There were no pupils in his eyes now. Frost bloomed across his armour. He began to shake.

Grimur lifted his axe, his eyes fixed on the Rune Priest. The warp had touched them all. It had wound its way inside their bones and bred with the beast that lurked beneath their skin. They were all one step from abomination, and when the Rune Priest ran the path of dreams he touched that fate. Sycld roared, the sound echoing and repeating, rolling with pain. Black blood and bile vomited from between his teeth. Grimur brought the axe up to strike.

The silence halted his blow. Sycld had slumped to the deck, his eyes and mouth closed, his fingers twitching.

'Brother,' said Grimur, but did not lower the axe. Sycld

did not move. A whine and hiss of armour drew Grimur's gaze upwards. Halvar and ten of the pack stood beside him, their weapons and armour sheened with blood. All of them had removed their helmets. Fresh blood marked the mouths and jaws of some.

This must end soon, or we will be lost.

'We are clear to the central core on this deck,' said Halvar, his gaze flicking to the beheaded warrior, and the slumped form of Sycld.

Grimur opened his mouth, but as he did so, Sycld's eyes opened. The Rune Priest's face had returned to its normal shape, and his eyes were hard as he stood. He reached up and picked a shred of meat from his teeth with a bare hand.

'I have it,' he said, his voice like wind murmuring across an ice field. 'I can see the path he took, his shadow body dances on the edge of the netherworld, seeking some fragment of the past. We have the scent, we can hunt.'

Ahriman ran and the wolves ran after him. His breath panted in his lungs, and his bare feet bled into the dust. The night was a silver-scattered dome of sable above him. Tattered strands of light trailed from his left hand. He clenched his fist tighter, feeling the threads squirm against his fingers. Behind him howls rose to the moon. He looked back; the wolves were close, black blurs of movement near to the ground. Their eyes burned coal red and molten gold.

Too close. Far, far too close.

The howls came again. He looked ahead to where the cliff

rose before him, close, so close. He leapt for the face of pale rock. Scree slipped beneath his feet, and suddenly he was tumbling back, and the howls rose in triumph.

This is not real, he thought as he fell. *This air in my lungs is just a memory, the light just an idea.*

He hit the ground. Air gasped from his lips, and he rolled to his feet. The wolves came out of the night, jaws wide, tongues of fire lapping from their throats. A stink of blood, smoke and matted fur was thick in the air. He stood.

This is not real. His eyes met theirs. *It is a dream, a painting created by scraps of experience and imagination.*

The wolves leapt, burning droplets of spittle falling from teeth of ice.

But a dream can still kill you.

Ahriman jumped up the cliff face. Jaws fastened on his ankle. He screamed and kicked down. His grip slipped, and he was swinging by one hand, feet scrabbling on the rock face. The golden threads of light writhed in his left hand, struggling to break free. The wolf bit deeper. Words bubbled up in his mind as blood scattered from the wound.

'We have come for you,' hissed a voice. 'We will never tire. We will open your belly to the crows, and feed your soul to the serpent at the world's heart. We are your oblivion, Ahzek Ahriman. Your soul will sing to the night forevermore.'

Ahriman felt his grip on the cliff begin to give. He looked down at the wolf hanging from his leg, its shadow-furred body seeming to swell. His eyes met the pits of fire in its skinless skull. Beneath it the other wolves scrambled at the cliff, their mouths smiles of flame.

No! He twisted to crash his right foot into the wolf's snout. He felt its hold give, and he ripped his leg from its jaws. It fell to the ground, yelping in pain and rage. Blood was pouring from his leg down the face of the cliff. He gasped. Numbness was spreading up his body, ice crystals forming on his skin, his blood boiling. He looked up at the moon and sky at the top of the cliff, but the cliff was stretching up, growing taller even as he looked at it. He reached for the next handhold. The fingers of his right hand hooked onto the rock and he began to haul himself upwards. The wolves howled in frustration. He thought he heard voices in the cries, old voices shaped by hatred.

I must not fall. Not now. If I can only reach the top I will be safe. Beneath him the wolves were circling, watching, silent now that they had tasted his blood. He leant against the rock face, reached up with his free right hand, found a handhold and pulled.

The rock beneath his hand broke apart even as his grip tightened. He screamed as the burning in his muscles fought the coldness spreading from his leg. He looked down. The eyes of the wolves looked back.

A hand grasped his arm.

His head snapped up. He had an impression of a hooded face outlined against the stars. Hard fingers clamped tight on his flesh, and he had a fleeting sensation of wrinkled skin moving over whipcord muscle. Then he was being pulled up the cliff, and into the mouth of a cave.

He lay still, breathing hard, not caring that it was not real air filling his lungs. Firelight flickered against cave walls. The howls of the wolves were a distant murmur. He could hear logs crackling and popping as they burned. Wood smoke filled his nose. He flexed the fingers of his left hand. They were empty.

Ahriman's head snapped up and he began to rise.

The figure standing above him straightened. A tattered robe the colour of rust hid its form, but could not hide its bulk. Muscled shoulders slumped under the worn cloth, and Ahriman saw scarred arms vanish within wide sleeves. A shadow-filled hood pointed briefly at him, and then back to the golden threads hanging from its fingers. The threads twitched and squirmed like snakes.

'A long way to come for such a fragment of knowledge,' said the figure, in a voice that crackled like the logs on the fire.

'Give it back,' said Ahriman softly, but there was a sharp-ened edge in the words. The figure shrugged, and held the threads out to Ahriman. He took them, noticing the pale skin stretched over the long bones of the figure's hand. The threads folded back into his grasp again, warm and writh-ing against his skin. The robed figure began to shuffle away towards the light of the fire.

'You will live,' said the figure, bending and folding until it sat on the cave floor. Ahriman remembered the wound to his leg, looked down, hands reaching to clamp shut over bloody scraps of flesh. He stopped. His leg was whole. No blood marked the cave floor. He looked closer, probing with his fingers. As the firelight shifted he saw it: a pale mark on his skin, like a ragged white scar. It was cold when he touched it, but there was no pain.

He looked up. The figure was watching him. 'The marks of their teeth will linger for a while, but they will fade in time.'

Ahriman ignored the words, his eyes scanning the cave, taking in the texture of the rock, the glint of crystals in the water-worn walls, the smoke-darkened roof, and the patch of night sky beyond the cave mouth. He understood the symbolism of each part of what he saw, but he was still surprised his mind had led him here.

'You are thinking this is still a dream,' said the cloaked figure.

Ahriman said nothing, but looked into the dancing heart of the fire. The wolves had almost had him, had almost pulled him down. No matter whether he felt the pain here and now, he would feel it later. They were getting closer each time he came to this land.

'Perhaps it is still a dream,' chuckled the figure. Ahriman tried to ignore it. 'But perhaps not.'

'It is,' said Ahriman, and looked up at the hooded figure. The firelight caught the glint of a blue eye within the tattered hood. 'This cave is a refuge, a metaphor of a sanctuary built from memories and scraps of imagination. It is a reaction of my mind to danger, nothing more.' He reached down, lifted a handful of dust from the floor, and let it trickle slowly through his fingers. 'This cave is like one in the mountains of Prospero. The stars and moon of the sky outside belong to Ullanor, and this dust is the dust of the land of my birth.'

'What then am I?' said the figure.

It was Ahriman's turn to laugh.

'A hooded stranger who asks questions, but hides his face?' Ahriman pointed at his own bright blue eyes. 'You are part of me, a part of my subconscious, which has broken free because of the trauma.'

The figure nodded slowly, stirring the embers at the edge of the fire with a blackened stick.

'But the wolves...' said the figure softly, and shrugged. 'They were real enough to kill you, weren't they?' Ahriman looked up, his senses suddenly tingling. The stranger's voice had changed, had become something he had not thought to hear again. The figure turned his head slowly to look at Ahriman, the hood hiding all but a single blue eye. 'Tell me, why does Ahzek Ahriman run from wolves through his own dreams?'

Ahriman had become still. Somewhere far off his twin hearts were beating faster.

'Father?' he said. *No*, he thought even as the word came from his lips. *This is not real, this is a dream, and your father is lost to you.*

The figure gave a dry laugh, and turned its eye back to the fire. Slowly it reached up and lowered the hood. The head beneath was a lump of bone and glossy scar tissue. The right side of the face was warped and ravaged, the eye swallowed by malformed flesh. The lone eye glinted sapphire blue in the ruin of his face. Suddenly the figure looked like a colossus shrunken by time and twisted by pain.

'You are wondering how this could be,' said the scarred figure. 'Whether the wolves bit deep enough to bring the idea of me to the surface, or if it is because of what you seek.' The figure paused, drawing the tatters of his robes closer around him as though cold. 'But part of you wonders if this is not your dream any more. Part of you can't help wondering if your father knows what you seek, and has come to stop you. Part of you can't help wondering if I am really here.'

Ahriman did not move. He should have anticipated this. His questing, and the flight from the wolves, had drained him. He had gone too far, and taken too much from the well of his unconscious. Slowly he extended his mind beyond the mouth of the cave, searching for the thread of physical sensation which would lead him out of this dream. Somewhere far off he could hear the rising drum of his hearts, and the sea surge of blood in his veins.

'I am not here to harm you, Ahriman.'

'No,' said Ahriman. 'You are not here at all.'

'Is that a fact, or a hope?' The figure stirred the embers again. 'You seek the Athenaeum, don't you?' The question hung in the air, and the fire crackled in the silence. 'All my thoughts and all my *dreams*, recorded and hidden away – a treasure trove of knowledge, a window into the past. That is why you are here, seeking the threads to lead you to it.'

'My father does not even know that the Athenaeum exists. Only a few know it is real, even fewer know that I seek it now.'

Ahriman stood up, and took a pace towards the cave mouth. Somewhere he felt real breath fill his lungs; it tasted of incense and static. He looked out into the night, and placed his hand on the lip of the cave.

'It will not give you the answers,' said the figure. Ahriman looked back over his shoulder. The hunched and one-eyed figure was looking directly at him. Behind it a shadow danced on the wall, growing and shrinking, as it blinked between impressions of horns, wings and claws. 'You followed me in war and treachery. You followed me over the precipice into hell, you believed me, and betrayed me, and yet still you wonder if you ever knew your father at all.'

'I knew him,' said Ahriman softly.

'Then why seek the Athenaeum?'

'For the future.'

'A good answer, my son.' The figure looked away, and Ahriman saw a smile struggle to form on the ruined face.

Ahriman frowned. Something in that smile was familiar, yet it did not remind him of Magnus but someone else, someone he could not place.

'Speak your name,' demanded Ahriman. The fire dimmed at the words, and the walls of the cave seemed to press closer. The one-eyed figure prodded the glowing logs again.

'Go,' said the figure. 'The wolves will return soon.'

Ahriman took a step back into the cave. The figure raised a hand, and the fire became a white-hot pillar. The shadows grew on the walls, snaking into the light, swallowing it. Sparks, embers, and ash tumbled through the air. Heat stung Ahriman's skin. Darkness embraced him, and the burning pillar of flame was all he could see. He tried to take a step forwards, but he was tumbling through lightless space, the light of the fire a single distant star that dimmed as he fell.

'Wake, Ahriman,' said a voice that seemed to be carried on the wind. 'Wake.'

II

BROTHERHOOD

Ahriman's eyes opened, black pupils shrinking to pinpricks in the bright light. The chamber was quiet, as much as any part of a ship the size of the *Sycorax* could be quiet. The only noise was the distant slow throb of engines and power.

The chamber sat at the summit of a kilometre high tower that rose from a forest of lesser towers which ran down the spine of the *Sycorax*. It was small, its roof curved into a peaked dome like the inside of a closed flower. Symbols, each one finer than a hair, crawled across the walls in endless patterns, interlinking, flowing together, but never repeating. The symbols glowed with white light. Beyond the walls Ahriman could hear the murmur of minds, hundreds of thousands of minds, their thoughts pattering on the chamber's wards like raindrops. And beyond the clouds of thoughts, the cold void cradled the ship's hull.

31

He took a breath, allowing himself to feel and remember what it was to have a real body again. A red weal grew across the bare skin of his left leg even as he looked at it. Pain spread in its wake, as though he had been burned by ice. He hardened his will, isolating the pain and containing it at the edge of his awareness. His mind could defeat normal pain and heal normal wounds, but neither the mark on his leg nor the pain it brought were normal. Both would take time to heal. He coughed and tasted iron on his tongue. He touched his lips and his fingers came away red.

Close, far too close.

He had pushed too far for too long in the dream sending. In his chest he felt the shards of silver shift and cut a little deeper. The slivers were a remnant of an encounter with the Imperium he had forsaken, an encounter that had almost killed him. The part of his mind that perpetually hardened and healed the flesh around the shards in his chest had faltered as he had tired, and the poisoned slivers of silver had slid a little closer to his hearts. Even now his mind could not touch, feel or grasp them. They were unreachable by his powers. Had they been mundane metal he could have pulled them from his flesh with his will, or could have broken them down into atoms.

But they were not mundane. In fact, every time anyone had tried to remove them by any means they had slipped deeper into his chest. So he had contained them, wrapping them in flesh which hardened and healed as quickly as it was cut. Awake, dreaming, in trance or battle, part of his mind spun on, keeping the silver from his hearts, keeping him alive.

He focused, rebalanced every level and thought process of his mind. His heartbeats slowed. He tasted the blood in his mouth, saw the molecules spinning in its substance. He touched the silver, felt his mind slide away, like water from a sheet of glass. A part of his thoughts became like stone. The bleeding stopped, and the silver shards were still again.

Slowly he let out a breath, tasting its texture and scents. For a long moment he listened to the slow beat of the blood in his ears. A feeling of isolation and spreading calm. For now he was alone, watching the present become the past, allowing the moments to just form and vanish without care. He let the illusion of freedom last for nine double beats of his hearts.

Only then did he turn his inner eye to focus on the thing that he had brought from the dream. It sat in his awareness, a golden thread leading off through the churning storm of space and time. It was tattered by paradox and possibility, but it was enough to lead them true.

Without moving he extended his mind, touched the symbols worked into the walls of the chamber around him, and collapsed their barrier to the world beyond.

A tide of consciousness broke over him.

...it pleases, does it not... nesun'nth'agara... gods of the abyss let me live... what can I do... I will kill them... five thousand at least... I serve... sentun ushur... two by five by ten... in this instance impossible... what is this... how can that be... now

will be best… where are we bound… the pillar… where will I get food… it is a good knife… ametrica… magir ushul'tha… what is it to you… sleep… I won't… death for certain… system subroutine…

Hundreds of thousands of thoughts boiled around him, buffeting his mind like a spiralling wind. It was disconcerting, like plunging into water after years spent in a desert. He allowed them to wash over and through him, listening for meaning formed by their tides. He had been in the dream for longer than he had intended. The *Sycorax* and its fleet had been still in dead space for almost a month. It did not matter, of course, not given where they were going.

He blanked out the storm of voices, and reached out for a mind that he knew would be waiting for him.

+Astraeos,+ he sent.

+Ahriman,+ answered a thought voice, strong and clear above the clamour.

+We have it. Join me here.+

+As you will.+

The palace began in the distance. Astraeos watched the silver and marble towers rise on the black horizon. Darkness separated him from it, so that it seemed as though he were seeing it through an aperture cut into the wall of a lightless room. Slowly the image grew larger, though whether it was moving closer, or if he floated towards it, he could not tell.

It was not in the distance, of course. The palace was a mental construct, crafted from memory and imagination, and it held the knowledge of many mortal lifetimes. Each corridor and staircase led to a door through which another part of the past could be glimpsed. They were not Astraeos's memories, though. The palace was part of another mind, Ahriman's mind. In reality both he and Ahriman sat in a tower chamber, the light of oil lamps casting shadows over their still faces. More and more they met this way, within the architecture of Ahriman's psyche, rather than in reality.

The Circle, Ahriman's council which led his army of fractured warbands, met face to face. Ancient signs and formulae kept those gatherings safe from prying eyes or minds. Under the sign of that assembly all spoke with their true voices. He had asked Ahriman why they did not meet the same way. Ahriman had not answered, and left Astraeos to draw his own conclusions.

Even after all this time, walking into his master's mind still made Astraeos's skin crawl. High-pitched whispers rose around him. Invisible hands touched and tugged at his skin. He kept walking, holding on to the idea of having limbs, of there being a ground beneath his feet even though he could see none. Technically he could have appeared in any form he chose, but he always came as an image of him-self as he was in the real: unarmoured, his skin scarred, and his right eye a glowing green lens in a metal setting. The tabard of red and black cloth he wore was the image of the clothing he had worn long ago in a different life. A sword hung at his waist, its pommel the head of a serpent.

He took another step and suddenly the palace was rising

above him. The darkness was gone, replaced by the bright heat of a noon sun in a clear sky. He looked up at the palace walls. They had changed since he had been here last. Towers had grown from the upper wings, and new spire tops shone bright in the sun. Covered bridges of white marble now spanned wings that had been unconnected before. Complex geometric designs in azurite and porphyry winked from roofs and doors. To Astraeos the palace looked like a mass of coral grown in sunlit seawater.

He began to climb the steps. No matter which way he walked in the palace he would reach Ahriman – after all, this was Ahriman's domain.

Summoned to my master, he thought, and felt a twinge of the old bitterness, but the feeling was tired and the fire it raised weak. *It was my choice. No one else made it for me. Ahriman is right, we make our own fate. Even when we think we are bound to another it is a choice to bend the knee to their will.*

The dry wind followed him as he passed through the doors and down the first corridors. Sealed doors lined the walls, each door different: some made of riveted metal, some of blank stone, some of etched glass. He passed windows which looked out on plains of sand dunes, spirals of dust rising from their crests in the wind. After only a few turns he had lost the sense of where he was within the palace, whether the windows were the same as he had seen from the outside, or if they looked out on somewhere else. Wooden shutters carved with birds hid the view from some openings, though he occasionally caught glimpses of other landscapes, of cities under red setting suns and lush jungles in twilight. He kept walking, following no path, making choices of which corridor or staircase to take without consideration. At last he emerged from a spiral staircase and found himself on a wide platform of black marble.

Ahriman stood before him. He wore no armour, but his robes were white silk. Tiny ivory amulets in the shapes of animal skulls hung from his shoulders and waist on tapers of blue silk. A table of polished wood and beaten copper stood before him. A stack of crystal cards sat on the table, flicking into different arrangements like leaves turned by a breeze. Ahriman turned to look at Astraeos.

'I have it,' he said, without preamble. He held out a hand. A strand of golden light hung in the air above his fingers, coiling and squirming into knots as Astraeos looked at it.

A thread of destiny, Astraeos thought. *Plucked from the loom of time.*

'Is it enough?' he said, stepping closer.

Ahriman gave a brief smile that did not reach his eyes.

'Almost.'

'There is no other way?'

Ahriman closed his hand and the strand of light melted into his skin.

'Many, but all with greater risk.'

'Tracking an individual's destiny to one point in the future is not a risk?'

Ahriman turned back to the table. The crystal cards rose into the air before him, forming an orrery of images, each one turning and changing in relation to one another. A king in red looked from the face of one card, his right eye hidden by his hand. A priestess in burning robes glided past, her face changing to a skull as the card moved.

'Knowledge is power,' said Ahriman softly. 'But the greatest knowledge is how to find more. There are too many uncertainties in what we attempt already, introduce more and...' He extended a finger and tapped a card. It spun away, tumbling wildly end over end. It struck another card. Suddenly the delicately rotating arrangement was tumbling in chaos, collapsing into a fluttering storm of changing images: a blind crone, a man with a wolf's head, a hunched scribe writing red letters on white parchment. Then two cards hit each other and shattered. Rainbow fragments expanded out, hit other cards, and soon there was just a sphere of bright crystal splinters.

'I seek the lost book of my father,' continued Ahriman, 'penned by the remembrancer Kalimakus, and Inquisitor Iobel knows where it is and how it is protected. For that knowledge we fight a war. Others make the earth their battlefield, or space, but we are doing more – we are making war through time. The person we seek is unique. Perhaps there are others who know what we need, but Iobel is already linked to me, and that link allows us to see the paths she may take in the future. Knowing this we look for the points of intersection in time, the points of certainty. We choose one point and go to find her.'

'So simple,' snorted Astraeos. He had learnt many things

from Ahriman. He was no longer what he was when he began, but there were things that still remained beyond his understanding. Most of them he had little desire to grasp.

Ahriman gave a sad smile, his eyes suddenly bright.

'It is both simple and not,' he said. Beside him the tumbling shards of crystal spun together. A tree of crystal dust grew in the air, reaching into the sky above them. Ahriman continued, his eyes turning to look up at the growing sculpture. 'To *see* the future is like looking up at the branches of a tree. From the ground the trunk is visible, but after a while the tree begins to branch. Suddenly something that was one becomes several. Those branches in turn divide again, and again, and again. The further up you look the more the tree branches, the more the lower branches hide those that grow higher still.'

A broad canopy of crystalline foliage hid the sun above the tower now, each leaf a different colour. Astraeos thought he glimpsed the face of the red-robed king, high up and far away, just one shard amongst many.

'And now we see that the tree is a living thing, its every inch moving between new growth and death. Leaves bud, wither and fall. The tree grows higher, and a wind rises. New branches spread above you. Some branches die, and become dry limbs creaking as they scrape at the sky. Sometimes the wind is just a breath that only stirs the thinnest twigs. Sometimes it is a gale. The tree sways, the branches thrash. And all the while, through every change, every stir of the air, every new growth, you are looking up, seeing the pattern of branches change, glimpsing its heights only to then have them hidden again. We see what is closest most clearly, what is further away perhaps not at all.'

Ahriman stood still, staring up, and then he looked down. The crystalline tree crumbled, glittering leaves falling through the sunlight with a sound like the ringing of a thousand glass bells. The pieces began to spiral as they fell, rotating like a dust devil around the table to coalesce at its centre. The cascade of crystal vanished, and a stack of crystal cards sat on the beaten copper surface of the table.

Ahriman reached down and picked up the topmost card, and held it out towards Astraeos. The priestess in the robes of fire looked out from her crystal prison, her face flickering between skull and flesh.

'To predict the future is not to try and see one leaf on the tree – it is to see a forest, and find one tree, and on that tree to find one leaf.'

'Is it even possible?'

Ahriman placed the card back on the pile.

'It is, but it is not the easiest way to know the future.'

'What is?'

Astraeos thought he saw something harden in Ahriman's expression.

'To destroy every other possibility except the one that will occur.'

Astraeos shivered, despite the heat of the sun.

'The Athenaeum,' he said softly. 'Is it worth it, Ahriman?'

Ahriman looked away, but said nothing.

He has promised salvation to his Legion, thought Astraeos. *What else can he do but try to understand what went wrong, to see if there was an error that could have been corrected.*

'There is something I must ask of you.' Ahriman looked around again. Astraeos held the cold blue gaze.

'Ask,' he said.

Ignis stepped from the gloom of the gunship into the bright light of the *Sycorax*'s hangar bay. He paused at the bottom of the ramp. It had been a long time since he had been on board the ship, and longer still since he had breathed her air or walked her decks. Centuries had passed for him and in that time he knew that he had changed, but it seemed both time and change had touched the *Sycorax* more deeply. Blooms of verdigris crusted the recesses of plates and rivets. Geometric reliefs in bronze and lapis crawled over the decks and walls. Some of them looked as though they had grown from the ship's bones. Figures in billowing yellow robes moved on the margins of the hangar, clicking with machine noise. All of them seemed to either be skeletal and tall, or bloated and squat. They were watching him. He could feel their eyes and curiosity prickle his mind.

Ignis began to count and calculate as he watched. The numbers and geometries of this situation were not good, but then what should he expect given what this ship was, and who commanded it? He turned his head, and saw the other craft in the hangar bay. Gunships, assault boats and shuttles of every mark he knew, and several that he did not, lay on the tarnished bronze deck. Groups of warriors hung close to each craft. Most were Space Marines, but each group was as different as the craft that had brought them. There was a warlord and his entourage, their armour glistening with an oily rainbow sheen, their helms curling with crowns of carved horn. There were others shrouded in grey, standing in a perfect circle, hands resting on the hilts of bared swords. There was a cohort in off-white battleplate, the eyepieces of each warrior weeping silver without ceasing. They all noticed him at last. Eyes turned slowly, a few weapons were touched. He watched questions and pride flicker in the auras of each.

And well they might look, Ignis thought. They were the leaders, emissaries, and chosen of the warbands that Ahriman had drawn to him or inherited from Amon's Brotherhood of Dust. Here they waited to see the sorcerer lord who led them all, but Ahriman had left them like dogs waiting outside a feasting hall. Slighted pride and petty superiority foamed close to the surface of the watching warriors. All of them wanted favour, or fortune, or secrets. Ignis could read the desire in them without having to sense it in their thoughts. Each of them wanted to rise higher in their own schemes, but all believed that only the Thousand Sons could ever hope for Ahriman's true favour. They hated that, as much as they feared the sorcerers and their Rubricae warriors.

And into this pattern of discord Ignis had walked; a lone figure, a newcomer to the sorcerer lord's court. He could feel the aggression seeping into the air as his eyes skimmed the vast chamber. Even in his furnace-orange Terminator plate, he was a weakling in their eyes, another lost warrior drawn to the flame of power.

A hulking warrior in pearl-white battleplate broke from a cluster of identically armoured figures. Ignis watched the warrior out of the corner of his eye. He sighed inwardly. It was always going to be like this, and it was only going to get worse. He had not wanted to come, he really had not.

The white-armoured warrior was five strides away now. He had a hook-headed sword in his left hand. Symbols spidered the blade. Ignis wondered if the warrior really knew what they meant, or why they did precisely nothing.

The warrior halted two and seven-eighteenths of its blade length from Ignis. A vein twitched in Ignis's temple as he noted the imprecision of the distance. He really should not have come.

'I am Augustonar, first blade of the hundred that serve Iconis of the Broken Gate.'

Ignis let a breath out slowly, but did not look at Augustonar. The warrior tilted his helm, waiting.

'My lord, whose word lives in eternity, wishes to know your name.'

Ignis flicked his eyes upwards. He could feel familiar minds in the vast structure of the ship, but all of them were distant.

My brothers, he thought. Then he frowned, sending the black electoos on his face into a dance of reforming patterns. *Brothers* – he had not used that word in a long time.

Augustonar's voice growled out again.

'I am Aug–'

'You are Augustonar, first blade of a mongrel set of traitors, culled from a Legion of credulous scum.' He looked directly at Augustonar. The warrior's aura was a red blur of rage. 'I am sorry – do these facts offend?'

Augustonar lunged forwards.

Credence came out of the dark hold of the gunship behind Ignis with a thump of extending pistons. The automaton made the deck in a single stride, weapons arming as it straightened to its full height. The orange lacquer of its body plating gleamed in the stablights. Geometric patterns etched down to the black metal spiralled across its every inch in lines no thicker than a blade edge. It was an echo of the colour and marks on Ignis's own Terminator armour; not identical, of course, never that.

Credence hit Augustonar across the shoulder with a machine-clamp hand. The warrior lifted from the deck and slammed down ten paces away.

Ignis watched Augustonar try to rise.

The automaton coughed a stream of machine code.

'No, the threat still seems to be present,' said Ignis.

Behind Augustonar, the rest of the white-armoured warriors surged forwards. The cannon on Credence's back rotated towards them.

Ignis closed his eyes. It was inevitable that it would come

to this; the patterns and alignments would not allow for anything else.

+Enough!+ The telepathic shout snapped Ignis's eyes open. He was in time to see the first three white warriors fall, the weapons of each tumbling from their hands. The rest halted.

A figure stood in front of Ignis. His armour was the blue of a sea beneath a noon sun. He had a sword in each hand, one sheathed in a crackling power field, the other in pale ghost light. Two jackal heads snarled in opposite directions from the high crest of his helm, and when he turned to look over his shoulder at Ignis the blank silver of his face-plate glinted beneath green eyepieces.

Ignis met the stare, feeling surprise roll through his mind. Credence rotated towards him, and clattered a query.

'No,' said Ignis. He paused, as he tried to select words. 'No, it is not… a threat.'

The swordsman glanced back at the white-armoured warriors, who were backing away.

+Sanakht,+ sent Ignis. Credence clattered as the swordsman stepped closer. Ignis could see Sanakht's aura harden with control, but there was something wrong with it, as though it was a flame cast by a broken lamp. +It has been a long time.+

Sanakht just stared at him, then turned away. +Not long enough perhaps,+ sent Ignis as Sanakht strode away across the deck.

Credence's gun mount tilted upwards with a hiss of

releasing pistons. The automaton gave a low rattle of questioning binaric.

'That,' said Ignis carefully, 'is the first of my brothers I have seen in eight hundred years.'

Sanakht sheathed his swords as he walked from the hangar deck. The power sword with the hawk pommel went across his left hip close to his right hand, the jackal-capped force sword across his right. His fingers tingled as he broke the connection to the blade's psychoactive core. Around him slaves, servitors and machine-wrights made way and lowered their gazes. He felt the breath held unreleased in his lungs.

Ignis had seen the weakness in him; it had been there, clear in the bastard's eyes.

He had last seen Ignis on the Planet of the Sorcerers, staring at the circle of Ahriman's surviving cabal from the cordon of those who had not been part of the Rubric conspiracy. Sanakht could remember looking between eyes filled with shock and anger, and amongst those looks there had been Ignis's cold gaze. The Master of Ruin had not looked shocked, merely curious. Sanakht had been barely conscious, his broken soul leaking strength into the aether, but that cold, calculating stare had penetrated into his awareness, and had followed him through the centuries.

You are crippled, it had said. *You are nothing.*

Sanakht let out his held breath, and pushed his mind out into the aether. Behind the mirror plate of his helm, his face twitched at the effort.

+He is here,+ he sent.

+Alone?+ It was Astraeos who answered, the sending thick with raw power. Sanakht blinked. So Ahriman was still secluded.

+Yes, apart from an automaton bodyguard.+

+You are escorting him to the citadel?+

+He can make his own way,+ snapped Sanakht. +He is here. That is enough.+ He broke the mental link. A mote of pain pulsed at the corner of his eyes. He shook himself, careful to make sure that his discomfort did not show. All use of his abilities took effort. What once would have been like breathing to him, was now a matter of deliberate focus.

Why had Ahriman brought Ignis, one-time Master of the Order of Ruin, to him? The question pulsed in Sanakht's mind as he ascended back up through the *Sycorax's* decks. The Order of Ruin had been the masters of the sacred numerology of destruction in the old, long dead structure of the Thousand Sons. By their arts the Legion had levelled cities, arrayed armies for sieges, and determined patterns of attack. They had always been a strange breed, and Ignis more so than any. He had not been part of Ahriman's cabal, nor part of Amon's Brotherhood of Dust, but he had also left the thrall of Magnus. He was an outcast by his own choosing, a breaker of fortresses and worlds with no loyalty to anything. Yet here he was, called by Ahriman to stand with them in whatever was to come.

And where are we going that we need his kind? wondered Sanakht.

* * *

Kadin looked up into the daemon's shark grin.

'Can you hear me, brother?' he said. The daemon hissed, and stirred in its web of chains. Kadin took a step back, his mechanical legs squealing as they cracked the ice from their joints. The chamber was small. White frost covered the silver of its eighty-one walls, ceilings, and floors. The glow of the sigils cut into every surface diluted the dark. The daemon hung at the chamber's centre. Its flesh was moon white. The body of a Space Marine, which was now the creature's host and prison, could still be glimpsed in its form, but only just. Its hands were sharp cradles of bone, and black quills had pushed from the skin of its torso. It looked at Kadin with eyes of glistening night.

'I…' began Kadin again, but the rest of the words drained from his mouth. He did not like coming here; it made him feel something he did not understand. However, he came anyway. The thing hanging in the chamber was not his brother any more, though it was as a brother that he talked to the creature. Cadar had died on the *Titan Child* many years ago, and even if a spark of his life had survived, the daemon bound into his flesh would have consumed it. At least that was what Ahriman said. Kadin hoped he was right. 'We are still waiting,' he said at last. 'The fleet is ill at ease. Ahriman has said nothing of what he is doing, or where we will go next, or when. Astraeos and the rest of the Circle hold things together, but…' He paused again. The daemon's head had twitched around at the mention of Astraeos's name. Its chains clinked, as though it had tensed against their grip. Kadin licked his lips.

He should not have mentioned Astraeos. That had been a mistake. The daemon was bound here because it could not be allowed free and it could not be destroyed. It was a creature of raw hunger, but it was strong. Astraeos had bound the creature to him to help save Ahriman, and the two remained linked. Astraeos had never called on the daemon again, but as long as Astraeos lived so the daemon had to remain shackled. Kadin himself had shunned the daemon's cage for years, but recently he had felt himself drawn to it, and so he had come once, and then again, and again. He came and talked to his dead brother.

'I can't remember the home world any more,' he said at last. 'I can't even remember how it was destroyed. What does that mean, Cadar?' He shook his head, and a double set of eyelids closed over his eyes. 'I think I used to be able to remember before the dead station, before… I was changed. But sometimes I am not sure. Does that matter, brother? Does it even mean anything?'

He shook his head, and turned towards the silver door out of the chamber. The daemon hissed behind him. Kadin raised his machine hand and tapped the door. The sigils flared, and he felt heat itch around his skull. Then the sigils dimmed and the door opened. He paused, one foot on the other side of the threshold.

'It's going to get bad,' he said over his shoulder. 'I don't know why, but I think it's going to get very bad.' The daemon remained silent. Kadin nodded to himself, eyelids briefly closing over his green, slitted eyes. He stepped from the room and the silver door sealed behind him.

Maroth waited for him in the passage beyond. The broken and blind sorcerer was crouched on the floor, the tatters of his robes hanging over his dented armour. He raised his head as the door sealed.

'The answers of silence are pleasing?' chuckled Maroth. His hound-shaped helm tilted up as though to emphasise the question. Kadin did not bother to look at him or reply. Maroth always followed Kadin when he visited the daemon in its gaol, as though he liked to be close to it even if he was never allowed to see it.

Kadin walked away from the silver door. His vox-link popped and crackled back into life as the door receded into darkness behind him; things were happening. It was as though the whole fleet had woken from sleep while he was not looking.

'The war on fate, it is beginning, is it not, yes?' breathed Maroth, as he scrambled to follow.

'Yes,' said Kadin. 'Yes, I am afraid it is.'

III
CONCLAVE

The seer was blind, and old, and shuffled at the centre of her web of chains. Two steps into the chamber she stumbled, and hung for several seconds. She spat on the floor.

From her place on the lowest of the encircling tiers Iobel watched the thick yellow phlegm splatter on the flagstones. Candlelight glinted from the thick liquid. The seer gave a moan and tried to stand. Iobel blinked, and felt the muscles of her face tighten. The attendants holding the chains did not move, but just pulled the restraints tight, their slab muscles strained under their tattooed skin. The eye holes of their hoods did not turn towards their charge, in fact they did not move at all. The figures standing on the stone tiers shifted quietly, waiting. Eventually the seer found her balance and began to shuffle towards the centre of the chamber again.

'This will be unpleasant,' murmured Cavor, and Iobel could tell he was grinning. Across the chamber eyes flicked at Iobel and Cavor, then away. Without thinking she stabbed a mental rebuke at Cavor, only to feel the deadening effect of the null fields steal the thought. Instead she turned her head and favoured Cavor with a stare. Clad as she was in layered plasteel and leather, she was smaller than him by far. Dark hair folded and set by silver pins topped her pale face. She met the green glow of his bionic eyes with her own clouded, grey gaze. The rayed disk of the Solar cult tattooed on her left cheek twitched as she raised an eyebrow.

'Sorry, my lady,' said Cavor, and then tried a grin. The skin of his lips twisted to show the filed bronze of his teeth. The green light in his eyes widened. He took a step back, bandoliers of rounds and pistols clinking softly. Iobel gave a short shake of her head and turned away.

After a second of silence she heard Cavor step back to his appointed place.

I should have brought Linisa, she thought. *Or even Horeg*. The ex-gang boss might have the decorum of a dying grox, but at least without a tongue he would have been quiet. She pursed her lips as the seer came to a halt at the centre of the chamber.

The chamber was the deepest in a fortress which sat under a blue sky, in the centre of a desert on a world that had been dead for centuries. The fortress was a spike of stone built into a mountain, which jutted from the dry plains like a rotten fang. Iobel had seen it from the lander as she had descended from orbit, and had walked through the dust-cloaked halls and passages on the way to the council chamber. It looked as though it had been made by human hands, but you could never be sure. Timeworn gargoyles had watched her pass, and the stones had last seen the tread of feet long ago.

But of course it was not deserted – the servants of the Inquisition had claimed the dead fortress for this conclave. Thick trunks of cable snaked down the sides of corridors, and vanished down openings in the floor. Glow-globes hovered close to the high ceilings, suspensor fields buzzing in the dry air. Hooded serfs moved in tight groups, and soldiers in gloss-red armour walked the walls under the spitting light of void shields. And everywhere the hot wind blew, and the dust rattled across the floor stones.

In the sky above, over a dozen warships glinted like stars. Some had brought Iobel and her peers, but most simply hung still above the fortress like guards mounted over an open grave. It was not a permanent occupation, but a place selected for its isolation and made temporarily strong.

If she was being honest she would have said that she felt the whole thing rather daunting. She had attended a conclave once before at the side of her mentor, but that had been on Luna, in sight of hallowed Terra. It had been a grand gathering filled with a sense of coming to the centre of things, of ascension. On this dead and dry world, it felt like coming to the margins and looking over the edge into the drop beyond.

In truth Cavor was right, what was to come would be unpleasant; there was no avoiding that fact. But then what else were the duties of an inquisitor but an unpleasant necessity? Iobel glanced at the two other inquisitors who stood beside her with their attendants. Erionas shifted but did not meet her eyes. He was tall, his face smooth, hairless and its features so bland that they looked as though they had been pressed from a mould. He wore a grey bodyglove, and cables extended away from his spine to the trio of hooded followers who stood behind him. The old crone Malkira was still, her chromed exoskeleton whining with a gum-aching purr. Before the seer had entered, the eyes of every one of the figures in the higher tiers had been watching the three of them, judging, assessing, calculating...

That is what you get for calling a grand conclave of your peers, but what choice did we have?

They had journeyed into the Eye of Terror and returned bearing knowledge, and that knowledge was beyond the power of the three of them alone to address. The seer held a portion of it. She was the last of the astropaths they had taken with them to sift the Eye for truth, and what she had seen was burned into her mind. That fragment of knowledge, and what had happened as they had tried to leave the Eye, was why they were here, in a forgotten fortress on a dead world.

The seer stopped at the centre of the chamber. She swayed, and the chains clinked. The chamber doors closed. Quiet filled the gloom, and then a rustle of fabric and whispers rose from the audience. A figure stood on one of the higher tiers. Silence fell again. He was thin, and clad in an unadorned black robe with a pale face, which reminded her of a sharpened axe head. His name was Inquisitor Izdubar, and he was the other reason they were here.

No, not just Inquisitor Izdubar. *Lord* Inquisitor Izdubar. The silence in the chamber as he looked around him left no doubt as to that status.

'Still looks young,' Cavor had muttered when he had first seen Izdubar take his place in the chamber. That was true as well, of course, but if anyone knew how old the lord inquisitor was, Iobel was not one of them. He had always looked the same, even when they had first met. It had been a decade since she had last seen him on Sardunas, and he had not seemed to age a day, except perhaps in the stillness of his eyes. She was grateful that he had come, but the weight of his name meant this was now his conclave, and by standing now he had just gathered it into his hand. Part of her wondered how much he already knew; he always had a habit of knowing more than you thought.

Slowly he moved his eyes to Iobel.

'So,' he said, his voice soft, 'what do you bring to us?'

Just like that. No ritual phrasing, no high booming oratory, just a question.

Erionas spoke from beside Iobel, his monotone voice rising in the still quiet.

'We return from the Eye, with matters of profound and broad importance.'

'Enough to draw us all here? I would hope nothing less.' Izdubar smiled a brittle smile. 'What did you see?'

I saw hell made real, she thought. Memories opened in her mind, scratching against the emotional dams she had built around them. *I saw nightmares walking the spaces between stars. I saw reality torn open, and carrion swarm to its blood. I saw the doom that awaits us all if we fail. That is what I saw, what I still see when I can sleep.*

They had gone into the Eye of Terror, where the physical realm and the warp overlapped, and the laws of reality danced to the laughter of madness. They had found what they sought and more, and returned alive... barely. Another great outpouring from the Eye was coming, they all knew it. It waited there just beyond the horizon of the future. The old seer, who stood weeping in silence before them, was the last of their psychic auspices who had survived to tell of what else they had found.

'The mission was a limited-duration operation,' said Erionas, his voice clipped and clear. 'Psycho-synthesised impressions were taken from a volume that extended at least into the tertiary zone of reality breakdown. The quantity of data was considerable despite losses among the auspices. We–'

'Of course such a mission gathered much of extraordinary value.' Izdubar broke through the monologue with another smile. 'But even such learning would not cause you to call us all here.' He glanced around the chamber, leaving the statement hanging between an accusation and a question.

'We found the remains of a war,' said Iobel.

'Yes?' asked Izdubar, turning his gaze back to her.

'A war that had scarred the warp itself.'

'Such things are–'

'Something was, or will be born out of it. A storm that will come for us.' She laid emphasis on the word storm, and saw a flicker in Izdubar's eyes.

'The Despoiler…' began a voice from a lower tier.

'No,' said Iobel. 'The name carried on the aether was that of another.' She looked at Izdubar. He met her gaze, his face impassive and unreadable. *He must know already. He would not be here otherwise. And besides us three, he is the only one who will know what the name of the storm means.* She gestured towards the seer at the centre of the web of chains. 'Hear for yourself.'

Izdubar held her gaze for a second longer and then nodded.

'Light,' she said. The word was soft, but it carried up the stone tiers with complete clarity. A second later a low grinding filled Iobel's ears and she felt the stone beneath her feet tremble. Iobel braced herself. She, like the half-dead seer held in the web of chains, was a psyker. Ever since she had entered the fortress, null fields had shut the warp out from her mind, blunting her ability. It was uncomfortable, but so would be the sudden return of her psychic senses.

A crescent of light appeared at the apex of the chamber's domed roof. Every eye in the chamber turned upwards. The crescent became a widening smile of sky. The Eye of Terror looked down through the open hole, visible even in the noon light.

The seer twisted in her chains, hiding her blind eyes in her hands. She began to moan.

The null fields vanished.

The warp flowed back into Iobel's senses, fragments of thoughts and sensations carried on it like driftwood on a floodtide. She gritted her teeth as the psychic reality of the chamber settled in her awareness. She was not powerful, not in the sense of some that she had met, but even so she heard surface thoughts and emotions bleeding from the minds around her. There was curiosity, excitement, fear even, all focused on what would happen next, on why they were here. Only Izdubar's mind stood clear and calm.

The old seer began to unbend, spine popping as she straightened. Her hands fell away from her face. The soiled emerald of her robes hung sheer against her skeletal body. Her head turned upwards, lank hair falling away from her face. Empty eyes met the rays of the sun. Her mouth opened a crack. Air rattled from her lips. And then, as though it was nothing, as though she was a fallen flower lifted by a breeze, she floated into the air. The web of chains clinked, and the masked attendants tensed.

Iobel waited, half watching with her eyes, half feeling the invisible tide of the warp spiral through the chamber. It pulled at her thoughts. Sweat began to bead Iobel's forehead, and ran into her eyes. Heat was spreading through her flesh. A taste of lightning and metal ran across her tongue.

Izdubar was silent and utterly still, his eyes focused on the seer. The silence extended beat by beat.

The seer spoke.

+Ah-zek-mag-nus-oh-there-wyrd-make-kall-is-ta-er-is…+

It was a whisper at first, a low murmur of sound that rose out of the waiting quiet, overlapping and echoing. Iobel strained to hear, and then realised that she was hearing the same sounds twice, once with her mind and once with her ears.

+…cam-illes-hi-vani-ah-muz-emekh-he-ru-me-aph-ael-au-ri-es-fu-er-za-ra-mse-h-ett…+

The sound rose, rolling along with a rising rhythm. Beside her, Erionas had closed his eyes, light glowing through his eyelids.

'Names,' mouthed Erionas to himself, his head nodding in time with the wash of syllables.

+…hor-kos-haa-kon-oulf-ca-r-me-n-ta-gz-rel…+

Iobel knew the names. They were names she had found in dried scraps of lore, in what remained of a forgotten and secret history.

+…ph-o-sis-t-k-ar-ha-th-or-maa-t-u-th-iz-aar-kha-lo-ph-is-a-sh-ur-kai-dj-ed-hor-jai-k-el-ka-ra-ja-hn-ru-tat…+

The seer spoke the names in a continual flow without break or pause.

+…ra-ho-tep-ph-ae-l-to-ron-au-ra-ma-g-ma-an-khu-an-en…+

She frowned. She had heard this mind impression before,

but each time the names were different, some added, some gone.

+…Xiatsis Cottadaron Maroth Karoz Kadin Thidias Cadar Ohrmuzd Lemuel Gaumon Amon Magnus Tolbek Hagos Egion Helio Isidorus Mabius Ro Pentheus Nycteus Memunim Menkaura…+

The seer was shouting now, spit flying up to meet the sunlight. The warp was singing, a chorus of whispers scratching against her will.

+…Amon Zebul Ketuel Silvanus Yeshar Jehoel Midrash Arvenus Kiu Zabaia Siamak Artaxerxes Calitiedies Iskandar Khayon Ignis Sycld Grimur Sanakht–+

The seer went silent. Her withered face twisted, creases forming and shifting around the empty sockets of her eyes. Her lips trembled as though she was trying to cry. She looked utterly terrified.

'Nine suns,' whimpered the seer, turning her head as though looking around her. 'Nine suns above towers of silver and sapphire. It is here, it is all of us. It is burning. I am burning. It has fallen – the sun has fallen and the entire world is light.' She paused and shook her head. 'What have we done? Failure has no answer. There is dust, dust rising on the wind so that I cannot see. The eyes of the dead are all around me… Is this the redemption you sought?'

The seer hung her head, her shoulders shaking.

'The swirl of stars. A figure burned onto the horizon. I am fate come round at last. I see lines of choice vanish into darkness, and I cannot see their ends. The broken king remade. Vortices of destruction that scream the names of those who created them. The netherborn scavenging the remains of worlds split open like soft fruit.' The seer stopped suddenly, her breath coming heavy, fuming with cold in the shaft of sunlight. Frost was spreading across her face from her mouth. 'They rise,' she breathed. 'The dreams of enslaved worlds scream. The storm calls them. It stands on the horizon. It is the void defined by fire.' The seer breathed out the last word, swayed, and her head lolled to her chest. Ice had crusted her robe now, and crawled across her skin.

'And what is the storm's name?' said Izdubar. His voice was low, but its sound made Iobel flinch.

The seer did not answer.

'Speak its name,' said Izdubar, and the command cracked like a whip.

'Ahriman,' gasped the seer. 'Ahriman.' She was shaking, the web of chains holding her creaking and glowing with heat. The ice was thickening across her body.

Izdubar stared at the seer for a long moment, and then nodded slowly.

'May the Emperor reward your service.'

His hand moved so fast that Iobel only saw the pistol in the instant before the shot rang out.

The seer fell. The chains rang as they caught her weight. She hung at the centre of the web, limbs slack and hair falling over her face. Ice began to fall off her body. The chains creaked as they cooled to a dull red. A dribble of blood began to splatter the floor under her feet. Izdubar's hand dropped to his side, and the pistol vanished back beneath his robe. For a second there was no sound beside the slow patter of blood on stone.

The *Sycorax* pushed free from the hole she had punched between the real and unreal, and settled into the vacuum. She was truly vast. At her forgotten birth she had been one of the greatest ships of her age, and her time in the Eye had only added to her bulk. Seen from above she resembled a spear blade, its edge waved and curled like a rippling flame. A city of spires and domes glittered on her back, and her belly hung with inverted towers. The muzzles of her guns were as wide as hab-blocks. The citadel of her bridge was a mountain of glinting metal and pinpricks of light. Arcs of lightning crawled across the tops of her towers as the power which had guided her dissipated.

More ships appeared, tearing the sheet of stars into tatters as they left the warp. Some had once been ships of the Thousand Sons, but most had been made for different masters. Some had been captured, and made to serve Ahriman's brothers. Others served the herd of warriors and sorcerers that had been drawn to follow the Exile. There were the three sister ships of Zelalsen the Wanderer, their hulls crawling with growths of bronze and bone, trailing luminous smears of light as they slid through the dark. The *Pyromonarch*, Gilgamos's split-hulled barque, coasted to station beside squadrons of gunboats clad with sapphire-stained brass.

Even the smallest of ships held the population of a small city, and the largest swarmed with life. Thousands laboured on each vessel. Many of those souls had never known another life, had been born into the dark, and had only ever known the metal growl of the beast they lived within. Strange creatures stalked the dark of many ships, things that might have once been flesh, or might have walked from nightmare. In the deep holds of each ship masked prophets, redeemers, oracles, machine abominations, and petty kings rose and fell, and went unnoticed by the Space Marines who called themselves lords of realms they never saw and had no care for.

The fire-darkened *Word of Hermes* was the last to emerge from the warp, the spear tip of its prow trailing lightning from its re-entry to reality. Together, the assembled fleet settled into position around the *Sycorax*, and waited.

At the summit of a spiral-sided tower above the *Sycorax*'s bridge, Silvanus Yeshar vomited. His head was pounding, and his flesh felt as though he had been boiled in oil. Vision echoes of the warp lingered inside his skull, like neon bruises. The fading sound of screams still rang in his ears. He took a deep breath, almost vomited again and then managed to steady the sense of being spun around while not moving. He was fairly sure he was lying on the floor. He could feel and smell his vomit pooling around the side of his face. Slowly he pushed himself up to his knees, and wiped his hand across his face. He began to open his mundane eyes.

+Silvanus,+ growled Astraeos's thought voice inside his skull.

Multi-coloured stars exploded inside his head. He screamed, as the pain rushed out to every corner of his awareness. After a moment the screaming just ran out, and the pain began to fade back to a dull ache.

'Yes,' he croaked.

+You are alive,+ sent Astraeos.

'Yes, thank you for your concern.'

'Concern?'

Silvanus shook his head. The bare lines of the pyramidal chamber were forming slowly around him. He scrambled to tie the strip of blue silk back over his third eye, then looked up. A giant in sapphire-blue war-plate looked down at him, its eyes an impassive green in a blunt helm. A swirl of gold marked the helm's faceplate beneath the left eye, like the memory of a molten tear. A golden serpent coiled on the shoulder guard, its jaws eating its own tail. Silvanus shivered despite the fever heat in his flesh.

'You are correct,' he nodded. 'I am alive.'

+It was successful.+

Successful, thought Silvanus as he blinked away the fading smudges at the edge of his sight. Successful in that they had found the Antilline Abyss. Successful in that the Circle had managed to burn through the storm spill at the Eye's edge. Successful in that Ahriman had managed to guide Silvanus, and through him the fleet, to this place. Wherever *this place* was; Silvanus was not even sure how they had got here. It had felt more like a dream than a navigation, following a path that was not his own. Of course, that was true; it had been Ahriman's. He had just been an eye, an additional sense organ grafted into Ahriman's awareness.

+Ahriman wishes you to be there when it comes to planetfall.+

Silvanus shook his head, holding his hands against his eyes. When he took them away, he noticed again that the fingers looked longer, the skin more translucent and clammy. It was getting worse and worse. He looked at his hands for a long moment.

+Silvanus.+

'Yes, I heard.' He got to his feet, swayed and then took a step, but had to stop to steady himself. Astraeos just watched. Silvanus felt a stab of annoyance as he trembled under the cold green gaze. 'Tell me, Astraeos, why are you here?'

+I watch over you, Navigator.+

Silvanus snorted, and wiped a trailing string of sick and spit from his chin. He was angry, the navigation had been... a nightmare, and he felt as though part of the warp's fury had soaked into him as they had passed through it.

'The Circle of Ahriman's closest lieutenants is formed, and you are sent to watch me?' He shook his head. 'An honour rather than an insult, I am sure. Tell me, why does Ahriman keep others close, and send you away? He gathered eighty-one slave acolytes for each stage of the passage here. Eighty-one, to aid him and the Circle, but you are sent to watch over me while human witches lend their strength to him. You are called his lieutenant, but is any other lieutenant so favoured with scorn?'

Astraeos was perfectly still. The skin-itching hum of the blue power armour was the only sound.

+You should rest, Navigator.+ The telepathic words were brittle-sharp, and sent a stinging blizzard across Silvanus's scalp. He bit off a bark of pain.

'Just speak with your voice, for Terra's sake!'

The armoured hand was around Silvanus's throat before he could breathe in. Astraeos lifted him from the floor. He gasped, his own fingers scrabbling at the hand locked around his neck. His lungs were empty. Beneath him his legs and feet thrashed the air. Panic flooded him, overwhelming every thought and instinct. He had to break free, had to breathe. His eyes blurred, washing out of focus. He felt his nails and skin rip as they pulled at the ceramite digits. He could not breathe, he could not get free. His vision fogged to black at the edges. At the end of the narrowing tunnel of sight the green eyes of Astraeos's helm watched him with still indifference.

The fingers suddenly opened, and he fell to the floor. He lay sucking in air, feeling the relief at still being alive flood over him. Astraeos looked down at him, and then turned and walked from the chamber.

'So,' said Izdubar. 'The first son of the Crimson King lives.' He paused as though measuring the weight of his words.

Iobel was not looking at Izdubar; she was watching the muscled attendants drag the dead seer from the chamber. A wet, red trail smeared the grey stone floor behind them.

'Unpleasant indeed,' muttered Cavor from behind her. Above them the aperture in the domed ceiling ground shut. A scowl flickered across Iobel's face as she looked back to Izdubar. His expression was grave, but she thought she saw something else flickering in his eyes. Excitement? Anticipation? Triumph?

'Yes, Ahzek Ahriman lives, and this psychic impression tells us much more,' said Erionas, and smiled with his eyes closed. 'Its meaning–'

'Does it really mean anything?' The voice was acidic and came from a sour-faced girl in a red bodyglove and black velvet cloak on one of the higher tiers. Izdubar looked at her. Everyone looked at her. The girl looked around, and gave an open-handed shrug. 'Come now, the warp is littered with patterns of thought, dead dreams, and storms of lost meaning. This *prophecy* could mean nothing.'

'It means something,' said Malkira. The old crone's voice cut the air like broken glass. 'Of that there is no doubt.'

'Then you had better tell us what and how.' The sour-faced girl met Malkira's cold gaze with her own.

'Ahriman?' said a dry voice on the other side of the chamber. Iobel turned to look at the speaker. His eyes were sunken dots in a fat and age-folded face. Worn robes of purple and silver silk hid his bulk, and rings glittered from a heavy hand as he gestured stiffly to Izdubar. 'Ahriman is not a name or formulaic that I have encountered before. What does it signify?'

'Not what, but who,' snapped Erionas. 'Ahriman was a son of the Fifteenth Legion, a traitor from the great time of betrayal, a son of one of the fallen fathers of the Imperium.'

'The Fifteenth are gone,' said the old man, his voice a slow creak of sipped breaths. 'Swallowed by the Eye. If any survive, then…'

'They are not all gone,' said Iobel, and felt the eyes of the assembly swivel to her. She felt her mind sting as it sensed the thoughts of the assembled inquisitors point at her, assess her, judge her. 'Not all of the Fifteenth are gone, perhaps not even most. The signs are there, in the warp and those that touch it – a girl born on Marius Nine with one eye blue and one white, a girl who screams of the Crimson King before she dies in the Black Ships, the accounts of the attacks on Cadia nine centuries ago, the tales told by the Wolves of Fenris when they believe they are not heard. The signs are there, but each age forgets more, and becomes a little more blind. Perhaps one day we will not remember or recognise the truth at all.'

'Poetic,' croaked Malkira. 'But true.'

Izdubar cut through the silence before it could form.

'There is more than that even, but Iobel speaks the truth.' Izdubar flicked a glance at Iobel, and she could read the message in that glance without needing to see his thoughts. *Do not mention the Athenaeum,* said that look. *Do not speak of what we have both seen.* He turned his eyes back to the others and carried on smoothly. 'The Fifteenth lives, and now we know that Ahriman, who was once its greatest son, lives too.'

'Very well,' said the sour-faced girl, 'but without more we are floundering in prophecy and symbolism.'

Iobel noticed the twitch of a smile at the edge of Izdubar's cold eyes.

'You are right, we do not know what these words may mean, or how they may play out, or even if there is a way of preventing what they do tell us. But discovering such things is what we do, is it not? What we exist for?'

He knows what comes next, thought Iobel, and felt a shiver scuttle across her skin, the early guess now a certainty. He had just set the stage for the final piece of evidence, the last fact that they had brought to the conclave. *You knew what we would say, and what evidence we brought. You always were the showman, Izdubar. It's all been an introduction, a setting of the stage. This is not our moment – it is yours.*

'But we have one more thing,' said Iobel, feeling as she said it as though she had spoken a line on cue. The grinding of stone and machinery filled the chamber again. 'We have the means to find answers.'

The floor of the chamber started to break apart. The flagstones cracked along hidden lines and hinged downwards. A circular shaft yawned wide. Red-orange light glowed in the unseen depths. Iobel blinked as the null fields snapped back into force again. The chamber became dark to her mind, the warp and the whispers of minds held back beyond a barrier of silence. A whine of engines and a clatter of gears echoed from the gloom beneath.

A circular platform as wide as a battle tank ascended from the shaft. A vertical black casket rose from the centre of the platform, fuming steam and wisps of energy. A warrior stood beside the casket. The light rippled across the silver of his armour. Blue light burned in the eyepieces of his plough-fronted helm. Bronze amulets in the shape of swords, lions and eagles hung from chains beside parchments crowded with script. The warrior held a sword as tall as a man, its tip resting point down.

Iobel found she could not look away from the silver-clad warrior. He was utterly still, as only something carved from stone or cast in metal should be. Her eyes stayed fixed on him, her pulse racing despite her fighting it down. She had seen the warrior before, but those previous encounters did not stop her reaction. The silver-clad figure was not human; it was a weapon from ages past, created to face the enemies that no others could. The very existence of such a creature was a secret that would have killed all those in the chamber had they not been on the left hand of the Emperor. It was a son of Titan, a Grey Knight.

The platform stopped when it was level with the floor. The Grey Knight remained silent and unmoving. Izdubar inclined his head.

The Grey Knight reached up and unsealed his helm. A tight-fitting leather caul framed the broad features beneath. Dark eyes glittered above a mouth set in a line.

Flesh-bonded silver wire spiralled across iron-black skin, gleaming like the lost tracks of tears. Iobel's first thought was that it was the face of a troubled king remade as a demigod. The Grey Knight knelt on one knee, but did not bow his head.

'Sires,' he said.

'Cendrion,' said Iobel with a nod.

The Grey Knight called Cendrion stood, and turned to the black casket at the centre of the platform. It stood taller than him, and was a little wider. The oily shell of a shield surrounded it, distorting its dimensions. Cables linked to sockets in the casket's black surface snaked down into the platform. Transparent tubes sucked and bubbled with viscous liquid: arterial red, neon blue, polluted yellow. Two hunched tech-priests lurked behind and to the sides of the platform, the green light of their machine eyes glowing in the caves of their cowls. Machines ringed the casket's base, thrumming with a low bass note. Iobel's teeth ached as she looked at them: null-generators, shrouding the casket in a second layer of psychic deadness.

Cendrion gestured. Steam vented as a wide crack formed in the black metal. The front of the casket broke into a hundred pieces which folded back into its sides. A figure lay within.

He was not human, but like the Grey Knight, he had begun as human. He was a Space Marine. Thick bands of silvered adamantine looped around his wrists, waist, ankles and neck. Stitch scars ran across his bare skin – faded with age, but still visible – telling the story of the process which had changed him from a child into a weapon. The marks of war were there too, twisting the flesh in knots and ridges. The skin of his hands was glossy, as though it had once been stripped away and regrown. A halo of black iron and silver cables circled his head. Iobel could see the dried blood from where it had been riveted to his skull. Old marks showed that this had been done many times before. Wires hung from the empty socket of a bionic eye. His face was lean, proud and strong even in sleep. He had been like this when they found him, caged in ice and locked in the wreckage of a ship drifting close to Cadia.

Murmurs ran around the chamber, growing in volume.

'What is he?' asked the sour-faced girl. Izdubar remained silent, and just looked at the bound Space Marine.

'Wake him,' said Iobel. The murmuring faded to a hush.

Cendrion nodded to the tech-priests. They bent to the machine with a sigh of clockwork. A few moments later the colour of the liquid in the tubes began to change. The bound figure stirred. His lips twitched, gums peeling back as muscles contracted. One of the tech-priests reached out with a hand of tarnished bronze, and tapped a control on the pillar's side. The halo of cables jerked, sparks running over the black iron clamp as it dug into the prisoner's skull. Muscles spasmed as blue sparks spread across bare flesh. A smell of ozone and cooking meat rose to Iobel's nose.

The figure's one eye opened. His muscles became still as though at a command. Arcs of electricity continued to play over him. He did not make a sound. His head moved slowly, his one-eyed gaze holding on Cendrion for a long while before it moved to Izdubar, and then to Iobel.

'You will answer me,' said Izdubar in a level voice. The bound Space Marine just stared back. 'Who do you serve?'

'No one,' said the Space Marine, and Iobel heard the hate rolling in the words.

'But who did you serve? You have already told my comrades this, have you not? So, as you did before, tell us who you served.'

The edge of the Space Marine's mouth twitched. On another face, belonging to a different species, it might have been a smile. To Iobel it looked like a predator baring its teeth.

'Ahriman,' said the prisoner. A murmur of sound ran around the room. Iobel realised that she had been holding her breath. Izdubar looked up at the tiers of faces nodding in agreement, before turning back to the prisoner.

'Tell us, what is your name?'

'My name…' said the prisoner, his jaw chewing the words slowly. Then he shook his head. The silver cables linked to his skull rattled. 'My name is Astraeos.'

IV
WORLD MURDER

Ahriman watched the fleet gather around the *Sycorax*. Engine fires and the dispersing energy of warp wake flickered across the depths of the crystal sphere which hung in the high dome of the *Sycorax*'s bridge. He shifted the direction of his thought, and the view widened, pulling back until the *Sycorax* was just one island of light amongst many. Beyond them a single star burned bright against the distant void. It was not a large star, but seen from the edge of the system it was clear and bright.

Like a candle, thought Ahriman. *A lone flame to guide the lost through a storm-lashed night.* His mind flickered and the crystal's bound vision glided closer, until the star's planets were dots of visible light, and it had become a disc of raw white. *Or like a ghost light, dancing out of sight, leading the traveller to their grave.*

The bridge at the summit of the High Citadel was a pile of armour and architecture which rose like a mountain at the stern of the *Sycorax*. The bridge itself was half a kilometre long, its armoured shell clad in bronze and supported by spars and pillars of black metal. Blue-green light shimmered up the walls and across the floor, as though the chamber were far beneath the ocean. A swarm of crew filled the bridge, webbed into machine cages by fleshmetal cables, or muttering over consoles. These were the Cyrabor, a sect of machine-wrights bred in some warp-soaked corner of the Eye of Terror, who had taken the *Sycorax* as both their goddess and nest. The air smelt of cinnamon and machine oil, as it did everywhere that the machine-wrights went.

He liked it here; of all the places that existed in the *Sycorax*, it was one of the few where he felt at peace without having to impose that state on his mind. The hum of the machines washed through him, and above it the clicking and hooting of the Cyrabor calling to each other, the mingled sounds rising and falling like the break and retreat of waves on a seashore. Above him the sphere of crystal hung like a great pearl of night.

He closed his eyes, and dipped his awareness into the web of telepathic voices stretched across his fleet. All had arrived, all were ready. They were a fusion of disparate renegades, traitors and outcasts, bound to his will by oaths, by hope, by the desire for power. Some were his brothers by blood, Thousand Sons like himself. Others were simple warrior bands whose only loyalty was to the promise of power. Of these he trusted few, liked even fewer, and found most vile, but they were a distasteful necessity; for what was to come he would need every weapon no matter the hand that wielded it.

'Overkill,' the voiced rasped behind him, its human tones riddled with static.

He did not answer, but watched the Cyrabor machine-wrights scurry through the bridge, yellow robes rippling around their bloated or spindle-thin frames. The image in the crystal sphere dissolved into blackness. Behind him his ears picked up the whisper of fabric as the figure on the great brass command throne turned her head. Metal-sheathed cables clinked as they shifted against each other. He heard the *click-hiss* as air sucked into metal lungs.

'Are you ready, mistress?' he asked.

'Have you told them what you intend?' asked Carmenta, electronic clicks wheezing between each word.

'No,' said Ahriman. 'Not all of it, not yet.' He turned to look at her. The green light of her eyes gleamed from the cracked red lacquer of her face. Crimson velvet swathed her, and cables swarmed over her like strangling vines. The brass and brushed plasteel of the throne rose around her like the setting for a queen of a forgotten age.

'Do you tell any of us the whole truth, Ahriman?'

He watched her but did not reply.

She looks smaller. Every time I see her she always seems smaller.

'You should trust them,' said Carmenta. 'At the least you should trust Astraeos.'

Ahriman shook his head.

'That would be unwise,' he said.

'Trust, Ahriman. It is the only thing you do not have, and cannot buy or take by force.'

'I trusted you,' he said, and let the words hang in the heavy air.

'You did,' said Carmenta, and her machine gaze was steady under Ahriman's blue eyes. 'And we know where that led us. So why is it that you tell me things you keep from those bound to you by oaths and blood?'

'It is necessary.'

'Necessary that you keep secrets from them, or necessary that you tell some of those secrets to a dying traitor?'

'You are not dying,' he said.

A cough of distortion and clicking code came from Carmenta's hood.

'A good lie. The *Sycorax* is older than I am – older, stronger, and an unkind child. As much as I have made it mine, it has taken from me, and it takes more with each passing cycle. One day I will be gone.' She seemed to nod, and breathed a stream of machine code to herself. 'But of course you know this – you are Ahriman.'

He did not answer. She was right; he did know. He could feel the shape of her mind changing, breaking apart into islands of awareness and madness. Damaged long ago by the attempt to become one with a machine the size of a warship, the bond with the *Sycorax* was now pulling the old cracks wide. The ship was not only vast, but had grown ancient swimming the tides of the Eye of Terror. The warp was in its bones, chuckling in the fires of its reactors and whispering in its data links. Its spirit was corrosive and pernicious. Carmenta could not leave the embrace of the *Sycorax*, not now, but every day she lost a little more of herself. Sometimes – times like this moment – she would seem as she had once been, but more often she would not respond at all, or if she did it was only to look at him in confusion while she burbled in mangled machine code.

Her head began to loll towards her chest.

'Are you ready?' he asked again.

Carmenta's head came up again. The light of her eyes fluttered, brightened, and became hard and steady.

'To destroy a world?' Somewhere far beneath the bridge, the *Sycorax* began to tremble as breeches swallowed shells, landing bay doors opened to the void, and the engines began to push the ship towards the lone star burning brighter than the rest of the heavens. 'Yes, we are ready.'

'Sire.' The voice was close and insistent. Hemellion, 251st Bearer of the Regency of Vohal, heard the voice, shook his head, muttered, and rolled over in his bed. He had been up well after sunset, trying to persuade that old cur Setar that it was best not to march south as soon as high summer came. The discussion had not been successful, and there had been a good deal of soured wine before Hemellion had finally given up and withdrawn. 'Sire,' said the voice again, louder now. 'Sire, please wake.'

Hemellion opened his eyes. His chatelaine Helana was leaning over him, her scaled and lacquered armour looking as though it had been donned in haste. He blinked, trying to clear the fog of sleep and wine from his eyes. Helana waking him rather than one of his bondsmen: that was odd. He sat up. The fire had burned low in the hearth, but the wicks of the oil lamps were alight. It was still night then. That was not good, not good at all.

'Have the Western Clans begun to march?'

Helana shook her head.

'No, sire.'

She looks shaken, thought Hemellion. *No, not shaken, frightened*. That was bad; that was very bad. He pulled himself out of the bed, and felt the cold air wrap around him as he reached for a fur-edged robe.

'Well, what–'

'There are lights in the sky,' she said. He stopped still, hands tying the robe around his neck. His flesh prickled, and cold sweat formed in the creases of his skin.

'You are sure?'

Helana did not answer, but walked to one of the high windows and pulled the heavy shutters open. The night sky was a star-brightened strip across the horizon. In the east the curdled light of the Eye of Woe waxed against the darkness.

Hemellion stepped forwards, forgetting the coldness of the flagstones beneath his feet. He stopped before the window and stared. New stars burned in the night, pulsing with ragged light, moving even as he watched them.

They have returned. After all this time, the Imperium has returned to us again. The thought fell through him, spreading cold fear and elation. The Imperium had not come to Vohal since the time of the 203rd Regent, and now they came again during his stewardship.

Vohal was a world of the Emperor, a seat held in trust as part of His realm amongst the stars. Long ago mankind had found it, and those few desperate settlers had given their new home a name from their species' ancient past: Vohal, they called it. Wrapped in wind, cloud and clear blue skies it was much like the world the settlers had left, but though they came in a ship from across the stars, they found their new home was not a kind master. When the Great Crusade had discovered Vohal, its population was small, its cities few, and despots ruled its scattered cultures from fortresses of stone that stood on the horizon like broken teeth. The Imperium claimed Vohal, recorded its name, and left an official to ensure that it remained compliant. That official, remembered only in the pages of books, had been Hemellion's ancestor, and his line had borne the stewardship of Vohal ever since.

Hemellion let his eyes dip to the fortress beneath the window. It had been built into the side of a mountain, and the result of hundreds of generations of stonecraft descended from his tower to meet the plains at the mountain's foot. The outer walls were thick enough that three carts could drive abreast along their tops. Within those walls chambers extended back and down into the mountain itself, held safe behind iron-bound doors. The fortress's purpose was to dominate a world in the name of the Emperor. Hemellion looked back to where that Emperor's servants now filled the night with strange stars.

'Light the signal fires,' he said, his breath misting in the cold air. 'Send riders to the near holds.'

'Yes, sire,' said Helana, and he heard the question left unspoken at the end of her words.

'Yes?'

'Why do they come now?'

'Who knows?' he said with a shrug. 'They come when they will.'

'What do they want?'

'The same as any ruler wants from his lands and vassals – they come for tribute. The records speak of them taking armies to serve in wars across the stars, or coming to cull those with the witch-sight.'

'And we…?'

He rubbed a hand across his face, feeling the stubble that had accumulated on the wrinkles of his face. He suddenly felt very tired. Forty years of life, twenty since his mother had died and left him the regency, and in all that time, in all the decisions and crises, nothing had made him feel as burdened as those small points of light shining in the sky.

'We give them everything they ask for,' he said. He was about to say something else when Helana gave a cry. He looked up. The stars were falling. As he watched they birthed smaller stars, until a net of fire fell through the night. Cries rose from the fortress, and more stars fell.

Ignis began to count time after the first salvo. The numbers streamed through his mind, forming shapes and patterns in his consciousness. Triangles became pyramids, spheres became circles, and spirals danced in his awareness as time sliced into ever thinner slivers. Beneath his feet the *Word of Hermes* shook as its guns added to the second salvo. Fresh streaks of fire began to reach for the world laid out in front of his eyes. This salvo had begun seven hundred and twenty seconds after the first. Two hundred and forty tonnes of active agent filled the warheads in each salvo. There would be three salvos.

The first shells would already be breaking apart in the lower atmosphere. The defoliant-agent would reach surface saturation within nine hours. Even if some of the other ships did not attain his level of precision it was still certain that every blade of grass, tree and leaf would be dust within twenty-seven hours. Once he would have considered that symbolism beautiful, or profound, or perfect. Now, watching the warheads begin to glow as they cut through the doomed planet's atmosphere, he simply considered it a relief.

Clusters of falling shells formed a pattern in his mind's eye. His subconscious caught the pattern, and multiplied it into spreading designs of fire, each part of the whole identical to every other part. He felt the pattern slip into the warp, and continue to grow. He let it multiply to the point that he could no longer control it, and then blanked it from his mind. He took a deep, slow breath.

Ahriman had commanded Ignis to engineer the planet's end, but Ignis knew that the calculations of obliteration mattered little to his one-time brother. Only the result mattered to Ahriman, and Ignis could give him that. It was a simple task, and it let him touch the pattern even if only for a brief time. It was not much, but for now it was enough.

He blinked, eyelids closing for five seconds while he followed the progress of his design one more time in his mind.

He turned from the viewport, and found the blank mask of Credence staring at him.

'All is well,' Ignis said, and gave a small nod. The towering automaton clicked, and the gears in its shoulders cycled. Credence clacked another binaric query with its metal insect voice. Ignis thought that there might have been a tone of concern in the machine's inquiry, but he knew that inferring genuine emotion to a capsule of silica in an armoured shell was madness. But then he did not understand expressions of emotion in humans either. He shook his head and replied anyway.

'Yes, all is well in a personal sense too.'

He closed his eyes again, and let the voice of his mind slip free.

+Ahriman,+ he sent, feeling the thought reach across the void to the *Sycorax*.

+Ignis.+ The sending was delicate, but to Ignis it sounded

like the low rumble of a rock slide. He flinched, and felt the counting and calculations slip from his focus. He bit off an angry mental retort, as he tried to pull the threads of number and pattern back together. +Ignis,+ came Ahriman's thought voice. +What do you have to tell me?+

Ignis had no choice but to let go of the calculations.

+It is done. The world will be dust in twenty-seven hours.+

+The third salvo–+

+Is to be sure, though the outcome is now a certainty. Twenty-seven hours, not one minute more. Beyond that, one thousand and eight hours should see the majority of the population depleted, and the rest incapable of impeding us.+

+My thanks, brother. You will join me on the surface once it is done.+

'Astraeos.' Izdubar echoed the bound Space Marine's name into the silence, as though he was weighing it on his tongue.

Astraeos remained silent, his lone eye steady on Iobel.

'He was recovered from a ship found drifting close to the Cadian Gate,' said Iobel. 'The ship was wrecked and warp damaged. Only he was found alive, his life processes in suspension.' A ripple of glances ran around the chamber.

'Really?' It was the girl in the red bodyglove, again. She leant back, shrugging, her face composed into a superior sneer as she looked at Iobel, Malkira and Erionas. 'Please tell me you have something other than this? A lone traitor, spat out of the Eye, with a name and a claim to serve another traitor who has not been heard of since the dark times? What else do you know of him?' She turned her sneer to Astraeos. 'Of what world were you born? What Chapter did you betray?' She cocked her head to the side. The gesture reminded Iobel of a bird of prey. 'What was the cause of your treachery?' The girl smiled as no answer came. 'Your *evidence* seems reluctant to answer.'

Iobel looked at Izdubar. The lord inquisitor was still smiling.

'Why now?' croaked another inquisitor from the folds of his robes. 'Why summon a conclave now?' continued the dry voice. 'You venture into the Eye, you find an echo that speaks of Ahriman, and then a traitor to a traitor falls into your hands with the same name on his lips. A coincidence?' He left the word hanging like a curse. 'Or is something hearing your desire and answering? And if so,' his fat, pale lips parted to show emerald teeth, 'why now?'

'Why does it matter?' Iobel said.

'Diplomatically done,' muttered Cavor from behind her.

'You missed a question,' said Izdubar. 'All of you should also ask "why us?"' He nodded again. 'The answer to *why now* is meaningless. It is a confluence of time and events. Coincidence, yes, but each of us knows that there is no such thing, not in the world we see. We are all here because we know of the Fifteenth Legion, the warriors of the fall called the Thousand Sons. We have seen the footsteps they left in the ashes of worlds, heard their sins whispered from dry pages. Even if you did not know all of it, you have all seen the scars they have left. We are their enemies.' He turned his head to the girl in the bodyglove. 'And while you are correct to challenge this evidence, mamzel, there is of course another way to get answers to questions.'

Cendrion glanced up at Izdubar, then to Iobel. She met his eyes, held his gaze, and then slowly nodded. The Grey Knight moved forwards, his hand rising. The gauntlet on his right hand released, and unfolded from his fingers with a stutter of metallic clicks. He raised his bare hand; the fingers were long, and seemed delicate despite their size. Cendrion closed his eyes.

Iobel braced herself a second before the null field generators shut down again. The warp rushed in like a razor-laden wind. She almost fell as it scored into her mind. The two figures on the platform burned in her senses: Cendrion with bright white brilliance, Astraeos with coiling red flame. Neon swirled across her eyes. Heat prickled her skin, and the smell of cold iron filled her nose.

A storm of oil-black shadow and blue lightning was gathering around Cendrion's hand. His armour glowed as the script etched into its plates lit. Astraeos was tensing against his bindings, veins writhing under scars. Blood beaded and clotted at the corners of his eye sockets. Iobel could feel the Traitor Space Marine's mind trying to gather the winds of the warp, trying to shape it. Ectoplasm misted the air, glistening and glowing with sickly light. Cendrion reached out, his hand seeming to push against a great weight. Astraeos bared his teeth. His skin was deathly pale, the veins black worms writhing under his skin. Cendrion pushed his hand forward. The tips of the Grey Knight's fingers pressed against Astraeos's skull.

V

INTERSECTION

Silvanus coughed. The dust was everywhere, sucking into his mouth with every breath. He pulled the black silk of his robe closer around him. The wind glided through the fabric, its cold fingers touching his flesh. A shiver took him and his whole body trembled. He really had no idea why he was here. In fact he had no idea why any of them were here, but it was his own presence that troubled him most. He spat and tasted the gritty chemical taste of the dead world mixed with the scent of smoke. It had been called Vohal, and the figure sitting on the cracked stones of the tower top was called Hemellion, and was apparently its ruler.

Had been its ruler, corrected a voice in the back of Silvanus's thoughts. The world the man had ruled was gone, and its people were dead or would be soon enough. Hemellion looked exhausted, and old, and broken. Dust coated his balding head, matted his beard, and had turned the colour of his rich clothes to dull brown. Ahriman stood above the broken king. His armour was blue, but the diffused light blurred it to aquamarine. Horns curled from the brows and cheeks of his helm, and thin pennants of cloth and parchment snapped in the wind. To his left, Kadin stood, the pistons of his limbs creaking as they clogged with dust. The warrior was bareheaded, the glossy scar tissue of his face set into a frown. The rest of the Circle stood around Ahriman. Sanakht was just behind his master, gleaming in polished blue plate; he seemed stooped even though he stood tall, his jackal-crested helm tucked under his arm, his face a carving of focused calm. Ignis stood further away, flanked by a hulking automaton which clicked to itself.

Silvanus did not like being so close to all of them at once. Their presences crackled against each other like storm clouds; his teeth were itching and he could taste ozone. That was never a good sign.

Hemellion looked up at the Space Marines. Silvanus saw green eyes glitter in hollowed sockets. There was still strength there, more strength than Silvanus would have believed anyone in such a position could possess at such a moment.

'Why?' said Hemellion through cracked lips.

Ahriman reached up and removed his helm with a hiss of releasing pressure. His blue eyes settled on the human. Silvanus's teeth trembled. Hemellion's stare did not waver. There was hate there, Silvanus saw, a hate that could overcome even the fear of standing at the feet of a demigod who had just destroyed your world and everything that you cared for.

Out beyond the walls of the stone fortress, the dry plains extended away to meet a horizon lost somewhere behind the clouds of dust. Now and then the cries of a starving animal drifted up to Silvanus's ears from the distance. At least Silvanus hoped it was an animal. The defoliant-agent had done its work quickly, killing all the plant life and reducing it to dust. When the winds allowed the dust to settle the entire planet would be dry and stripped of life, a desert with the broken remains of its civilisation sticking up from the desolation like dry bones.

'This is how fate is shaped,' said Ahriman. His voice was low, calm, the voice of rationality, the voice of reason. Hemellion spat. Silvanus watched the dust-clogged saliva drool thickly down Ahriman's armour. Part of him, a part he did not often listen to now, felt envy of the man's defiance. Kadin made a noise that might have been a chuckle. Ahriman nodded carefully.

Silvanus looked away. Out beyond the tower's parapet the rest of the fortress fell away. Fires burned in its broken stones, fires which flickered with green and blue-edged tongues. They had needed to take the fortress by force. It had not taken long, not for the forces that now waited beyond the walls, hidden by the murk. The billowing dust parted as he gazed beyond the parapet. Rank upon rank of motionless Rubricae stood on the plains around the fortress, the dust turning the green glow of their eyes to haloes. Static discharge crackled across their blue and gold battleplate. The clouds shifted and the Rubricae became smudges in the ochre gloom.

Silvanus still wondered why it had been necessary, why they were even here on the surface, why he was there standing amongst Ahriman's inner circle. The rest of the planet was to be allowed to die slowly, but the might of Ahriman's fleet had descended on this primitive fortress like an executioner's axe.

Ahriman moved away from Hemellion, his armour purring as he turned to Sanakht.

'He comes with us,' said Ahriman, and nodded at Hemellion. 'He may hate us, but his mind is strong, and he will serve.'

'Master?' said Sanakht, his dry paper voice an echo of the wind.

'He lives. He has earned that much.'

Sanakht must have nodded, or spoken in thoughts, because Silvanus heard no reply.

We kill a world for a king who will now be a slave, thought Silvanus. *Is that what we did this for?* He paused, suddenly aware that he had thought of the sorcerers and the fleet, and their chattels, not as *they*, not as traitors who were different from him, but as *we*, as something of which he was a part.

Ahriman turned to face Silvanus. The Navigator felt his hairless skin prickle. He did not look up at his master.

'Ask your question, Silvanus,' said Ahriman, his voice low and resonant. 'They all wish to know as well, so ask.'

Silvanus swallowed in his dry throat.

'Why am I here?'

'So that you can be here, so that you can touch this place, breathe the air of its death. So you can find your way back.'

Silvanus shivered again.

'My way back?' he said and looked up at Ahriman. Clear blue eyes looked back at him without blinking.

'Yes,' said Ahriman. 'We will leave here soon, but we will return. It may be many years, but we will return. You are our eye into the warp, so you must see clearly where I guide you.' He looked away from Silvanus, his gaze passing over Ignis, Sanakht, and the other sorcerers. 'Let this place touch your mind, hold its memory clear inside you so that you can stand here again by closing your eyes. We must all be ready to return.'

'Return?' Silvanus realised he had spoken a second too late. The gaze of every eye on the tower top turned to him. Even the bitter gaze of Hemellion was locked on him. 'Return for what? Why are we here? Why have we stripped this world of life to then return?'

A hint of a smile formed and faded on Ahriman's face. It was the most terrifying thing Silvanus had ever seen. The clouds of dust were shifting, the winds pulling the drab curtain back again. The Rubricae still stood there, but now all of them were staring up at the fortress.

'In time this place will change. Others will find it, and

their hands will remake the fortress we stand on. Then, in that future, one person will come here. Her name will be Iobel, and she will have something I need. This is what I have been seeking – a point of intersection in the threads of time, a point where I can be certain where she will be. We are not here for what this place is now – we are here for what it will be.'

Silvanus followed Ahriman's gaze down to the plains at the foot of the fortress. Drifting dust was burying the Rubricae. Already their feet and shins were beneath the surface, as though swallowed by a rising tide. The light in their eyes was dimming.

'Sleep, my brothers,' said Ahriman softly. 'Sleep in dust, and wait.'

Astraeos felt the Grey Knight's fingers touch his skin, and a sun exploded in his soul. The tiered chamber vanished. He was blind to everything except the light that was burning inside him. Somewhere far away he screamed. He tried to close his mind off, to contain the star forming in his thoughts. For a second his will held, hardening over his mind. Then the light grew, and his will broke apart. The light was blue with soul fire; he felt his surface thoughts peeling away like charred skin. Memories surfaced, fragments of time spooling backwards through his mind's eye.

'…we are here for what it will be,' said Ahriman on a dust-blown tower.

The wind rattled against his armour.

'This is how fate is made.'

Dust swirled around the waiting dead.

'Why?' asked a man through cracked lips.

He tightened his grip, and the Navigator's face began to bulge and gasp for air.

'Why does Ahriman keep Sanakht so close, and send you away?'

'I watch over you,' he had said.

'Tell me, Astraeos, why are you here?'

Stillness filled him, sudden and complete. He sat with Ahriman on the floor of a high tower. He looked around. The floor was lapis, the roof bronze. Silver sigils spiralled across the floor. It was very quiet.

'I am sorry, my friend,' said Ahriman. He wore a pale blue robe and his head was bare. 'There must be something to draw the inquisitors together, a cause to create the future. They will be seeking me, and only answers will make them gather to learn the truth. That gathering must happen. You understand why it must be you?'

'I am not one of you.'

Ahriman's face remained as still as stone.

'They will try to take secrets from you, first by crude methods, but then they will try to take them from your mind.' Ahriman paused, and drew a slow breath. 'They might even have the strength to do it.'

Astraeos did not move. Part of him knew that he could not, that this was not real – it was a memory of something that had already happened, sealed off and buried within his mind.

'You must keep a part of yourself separate from the rest, a part that they cannot reach unless your entire mind falls, a fortress hidden from the rest of your thoughts. I will be there, this memory will be there. Remember then what must happen. You will not have long, perhaps a fraction of a second.'

'How can you be sure that Iobel will be there when this happens? How can you be sure that any of it will intersect as you predict?'

Ahriman gave a tired smile.

'I can't.'

The memory began to fade, the lines of the chamber blurring.

'Remember you will have an instant,' said Ahriman's voice, its tones seeming to reach from a long way away. 'Remember, Astraeos.'

Astraeos's eye opened. Cendrion stood before him. Ice sheathed the Grey Knight's arm from fingers to shoulder. Silver-blue fire crackled and flickered over the stretched fingers. The world was slow, separate, like the crash of water beyond glass. Cendrion's hand began to close. Astraeos felt the power boring into him change.

You will have an instant...

His thought form leapt into the air. It had the shape of a tattered eagle with feathers of smoke and red flame. The warp broke into storm winds that shrieked past him. The eagle soared through the chamber, searching the souls of the figures gathered there. Some were moving, reaching for weapons. He could feel the shock flicker down the pathways in their minds. Slow, so slow. He saw Iobel's mind haloed in an aura of confused red. He dived towards her, claws extending.

Iobel's mind flared to white as it tried to form a defence. It was a strong mind, but it was not strong enough. His claws met aetheric flesh, and his mind ripped into hers.

Iobel. He tasted the name; it tasted like forged steel and fire. It was her, without doubt. The one they needed.

The crowd on the stone tiers rose, weapon breeches swallowing rounds, blades scraping free, shouts forming in a hundred throats. Cendrion's sword was rising. Astraeos could feel the distant beats of his hearts.

Time, there was not enough time. Astraeos ripped free from Iobel's mind. The Grey Knight's thoughts blazed even as his body moved, so slow but faster than an eyeblink.

Cendrion's mind form roared into the aether as he charged forwards. Lion-bodied and reptile-winged, it was the echo of myths from mankind's past. Silver fire fell away from its scaled wings as its jaws opened wide. The two thought forms collided. Ice flashed into existence across the platform. Astraeos's claws raked Cendrion's flanks, scattering smoking blood into the warp. Aetheric teeth ripped into his mind. He could hear voices, a choir of voices singing deep within the Grey Knight's soul. It was beautiful, and terrible, like rage turned to bitter grief. They tumbled together, falling through nothingness, jaws and claws raking at each other. Cendrion fastened his jaws around Astraeos's mind and bit down.

The chamber and platform were a distant tableau moving with stopped-clock slowness. Only Cendrion's sword was clear, a bright line in Astraeos's sight as it cut towards a body he was only distantly aware of.

I am going to fail. I am not strong enough, not for this, not against a creature like this. They had not predicted that such a warrior would be here.

Astraeos felt his thought form tear under Cendrion's aetheric jaws. He bit back, but his strength was failing. Cendrion's thought form was all around him, jaws closing, claws hooked deep.

I cannot… he gasped to himself. *I cannot fail. If I fail I end here, it all ends here.* He thought of Thidias, dead in the cold void, of Cadar grinning with the hunger of a daemon, of the skies burning above his home world so long ago. The silver warriors had come from that sky, the inferno staining their armour black and crimson. *All my dead brothers,* he thought. *All my murdered pasts end here.* In the real world he felt the heat of Cendrion's blade. It was a finger span from his neck, slicing in fast. *This is it – the last stretched moment of a life of broken oaths and failed revenge.*

+No.+ The word roared from his mind as he ripped his thought form free. Chunks of emotion and tattered thoughts tumbled in his wake. He could feel wounds open on his body as his mind bled into the warp. But he was free.

+Ahriman,+ his soul screamed.

He slammed back into his body. His kine shield snapped into existence just before the sword struck. Light sheeted through the chamber. Shouts cut the air. Astraeos split his will into pieces and called the warp. It answered.

The metal of the bindings around his body exploded in a shower of liquid metal. A wave of telekinetic power ripped out from him. Cendrion staggered, recovered and cut again. His silver armour glowed, sucking the invisible force into its core and dissipating it into the warp. His sword spun up and cut down. Astraeos ducked. The blade sliced into the empty casket in a shower of sparks. Someone was shouting for the null shields to be activated. Gunfire began to hiss through the air. Screams and babbling roared at the edges of Astraeos's mind. He ran for the edge of the platform, blood sheeting down his skin from the stigmatic wounds in his flesh.

The Grey Knight moved just as fast. His hand came up, the barrels of his storm bolter wide open. Astraeos reached the edge of the platform and leapt. Rounds hammered after him. He hit the lowest stone tier and bounded up. A burst of shells turned the spot where he had landed to rock dust and spinning fragments. A figure in a red cloak swung a mace at him. He swerved, rammed his shoulder into the figure and heard bones crunch. Above and around him a hundred weapons and eyes turned towards him. His mind became fire. He roared. A sphere of white heat exploded outwards from him. Figures vanished, became ash, became heaps of cooking bone and fat, became shadows flash burned onto the grey stone. He leaped on, feeling his skin burn. He could hear voices talking to him in the flames. At the edge of sight figures were rising, half blind, weapons aiming.

Behind him Cendrion's mind was expanding and reshaping. Astraeos could feel its heat and brilliance burn into the back of his skull. He leapt up another tier of stone. Hard rounds whipped around him. He was almost across the chamber, the ashes of the dead rising from his running feet. A round hit him in the shoulder. He staggered.

A human jumped down in front of him, layered plasteel armour ringing at the impact. The human raised a fork-headed spear. Astraeos rammed his will forwards and the human pitched into the air with a crack of shattering bone. He took another step. The chamber around him was a cauldron of movement and sound, people scrambling, drawing weapons, shouting. Somewhere beyond the sealed doors an alarm was screaming. Above him Iobel looked down from the higher tier. Blood was running from her eyes, nose and mouth. She raised a pistol, its fluted barrel fuming blue light.

The air went ice cold. The warp was suddenly calm, flat, like a frozen lake surface. On the platform Cendrion had paused, his head turning as though trying to hear a distant sound. Astraeos felt the blood thump once in his veins. Somewhere, far off yet just behind him, he heard the call of an unkindness of ravens.

VI
CIRCLE

Cradled in the iron of her machine, Carmenta looked towards Vohal's star. Ahriman's fleet surrounded her, clinging close around the bulk of the *Sycorax* like pilot fish around a leviathan. They had dropped from the warp far beyond the system's edge, fired their engines once, and then cut power and become almost invisible. For four months they had drifted through the night in silence, wrapped in cold, sipping energy from their reactors. Now they were within the outer boundaries of the system, and she could see the planet of Vohal as a disc of dirty yellow hung against the black. It had been two years since she had helped kill it; at least two years as she had lived them. Ahriman said that longer would have passed for Vohal and the Imperium, much longer. The planet had changed in that time, desolation settling over it as though it had never lived. As she looked at it, she saw that other things had changed too.

Squadrons of Imperial warships lay scattered all the way to the system edge. Any ships wishing to reach the dead planet would have to pass through this corridor of guns. It would take the *Sycorax* and the rest of the fleet days to reach the planet, and every second of that would be a battle. But they did not need to reach the planet; they just needed to be closer.

Her engines roared to full life. She felt the vacuum kiss her void shields. Blast hatches peeled back from guns along her flanks. The rest of the fleet woke an instant later. They accelerated out of the dark.

The Imperial fleet noticed them, and a trio of frigates broke away to intercept them.

She smiled. She would enjoy this.

The frigates fired. She felt the shells hit her shields, felt the shudder as explosions danced across them. It was like hail scattering against a stone roof.

Suddenly her thoughts stopped dead.

Pain cut through her. Her head came up, hood falling away from the cracked lacquer of her mask. She was no longer the *Sycorax*; she sat in a brass throne beneath the roof of a vast chamber.

Where am I? she tried to scream, but her mouth was droning in clicks and whistles. Cables were strangling her body. Her eyes swam with green static. *What is this? What has happened? Where am I? Father? Mother?* Breath sucked from the slot of her mouth. She tried to stand. She could not. She saw figures come towards her. They had the faces of metal birds. Hands reached for her, touched her; she felt long fingers grip her, metal pincers lock around her wrists. She did not know who they were. They babbled at her, hooting and clicking like broken vox-casters. She tried to fight them off but they were all around her, holding her and pushing her down. They smelt of cinnamon and burned wiring. *What has happened to me?* She tried to scream again.

The void snapped back into place around her. She was part of the ship, but she was still trying to breathe, trying to scream without lungs. The *Sycorax* shivered, its engines spluttering, its shields sparking. She could hear something laughing at the edge of her thoughts – it sounded like the roar of a reactor and the pulse of power cables. It sounded like the ship.

+Mistress?+ came Ahriman's voice in her thoughts. +Mistress, we are close now. Astraeos calls, we do not have long. We must be closer.+

'Yes,' she said in her mind, and somewhere she knew she was muttering on a throne. *'I… It will be.'*

Her engines coughed to fresh life, and the ship shot towards the inner system. The Imperial frigates were closer, their auspex dancing over her hull as they grasped for a firing solution. She reached out with her own sensors, tasted the range to each of them, and laughed with the voice of a thousand guns. The frigates vanished in clouds of growing explosions.

More Imperial ships came to meet her. A plough-fronted

cruiser spilled bombers from its flanks as it closed. Beside it a silver-hulled strike ship came around, bombardment cannons hammering her. Carmenta felt her shields fail one after another. She replied in kind, her pulse shaking in time with the rhythm of the barrage. The rest of the fleet was firing, but she was blind and deaf to everything but the roar of her own guns. Explosions danced against the stars. The Imperial ships were burning, but they still fought.

A handful of Imperial destroyers spiralled towards her and loosed their torpedoes. More and more ships were turning to face her, even as she felt the distance to the planet close. The last of her shields collapsed in a silent thunderclap. A macro round hit her hull. She felt her skin crack, felt armour become molten tears. The scream of enemy range-finders filled her sensors. There were at least twenty ships closing on her. All of them had now turned towards her. Even those ringing Vohal had pulled away from the surface, their guns and auspex turning towards the system edge and her fire trail of approach.

A torpedo hit her upper hull just behind her prow. A sphere of white light blinked into existence. Towers ripped from their roots. Crystal domes shattered. Within her guts she heard the chattering cries of the slave crew, pleading with the ship not to take their lives, to spare them. She kept firing at every target that she could see. Fires licked from their hulls, and some were bleeding warm atmosphere and plasma into the black. They were dying, but so was she. She would die here and she would die soon. Her hull would break open. The city within would choke in silence and she would become nothing.

'Now, there is no more time,' she said in her own mind, and the message sang through the ship's systems.

A storm was gathering on her upper hull. Arcs of light ran, snapped and tangled between the tower tops. A cloak of shimmering energy coiled over her hull. She could hear the mind voices of Ahriman and the Circle spiralling together.

A beam of plasma hit her prow. It bored into her. Molten stone and bronze bubbled from the widening hole as the *Sycorax*'s momentum drove it onto the beam.

A spill of damage data rose through her awareness, became pain, became agony. She cried out. In the bowels of the *Sycorax*, chained slaves that had never seen the light of stars clamped their hands over their ears as the walls shrieked.

'Ahriman!' she snarled, and the storm of sorcery forming around her broke.

Bright blue and pink light began to arc from the towers across her back. Deep in her hull, human and once-human crew fell to their knees, wailing prayers to their uncaring gods. And from their high towers Ahriman and the Thousand Sons loosed their minds. Frost and fire spread in sheets and plumes across her hull. Green ghost light spun in her wake. Her hull creaked, straining as the warp tugged on it. And through it all she could hear Ahriman, the focused pressure of his thoughts pushing into the realm beyond.

* * *

It began to snow in the desert. Clouds bubbled up across Vohal's blue sky, hiding the sunlight behind iron grey. On the parapets of the fortress the sentinels looked up as the snow began to spin out of the sky. Sirens began to scream. Shouts echoed in the half-deserted corridors. Autoweapons armed and rotated to face the blizzard. Interference screamed across the vox. In orbit, the warships stationed over the fortress saw the clouds spread across the world beneath them. Some ships began to turn back to the planet, scrambling to turn their guns on the surface. Others rose to face the attack from the system's edge.

The snow carpeted the desert. On the fortress walls men and women pressed their eyes to their heat sights but saw nothing. Then the first of the soldiers fell, hands clamped over her head. She shrieked over and over again. Those close to her turned, some made to help her. Then the tide of ghost calls struck. On every parapet soldiers staggered and fell, as the waking cries of hundreds of dead souls filled their heads.

Out on the plain beneath the fortress the first awoken Rubricae pulled itself from the ground. Dry dust and powdered snow fell away from its blue armour as it stood. Green light burned in its eyes.

An automated gun fired first. Las-bolts spat from the fortress's high towers, hammering fire into the white wall of the storm. A line of las-fire hit the Rubricae, slamming into its high-crested helm, making it stagger. It fell to its knees, a molten hole showing the void within. The light in its eyes dimmed. The snow fell faster, tumbling in the rising gale. The Rubricae stood slowly. Light crawled over its armour. The gash in its helmet armour closed. It looked up at the fortress, its eyes bright holes into a furnace. It began to walk forwards. A second later another figure rose from the snow and dust, then another, and another.

Gunfire sheeted from the towers and parapets. Bolts of lightning fell from the clouds, thunder blending with the shout of the guns. The void shields surrounding the fortress blazed under the storm strikes. The Rubricae began to fire. Bolts shrieked as they cut through the blizzard, and smacked into the fortress walls. Kaleidoscopic flames sprang up where they struck, dancing across stone, leaping into the lungs of defenders as they opened their mouths to scream. Falling snow flashed to steam as it met the blaze.

The outer walls began to crack, stone shattering under dozens of impacts. More troops began to recover their senses and ran to the firing steps. Cyborgs with eyeless, gloss-red visors clanked from where they had stood guard deep within the fortress, breaking into piston-driven runs as storm winds and gunfire howled outside. They reached the walls and began to pour multilaser fire down onto the attackers. The Rubricae advanced, their armour rippling and glowing under the deluge, firing without pause.

A tower on the outer wall fell, sloughing away as though it were sand undercut by water. The Rubricae reached the slope of rubble that had been the tower and began to climb.

Ahriman saw every detail of the assault as though his

eyes were the falling snowflakes. The minds of his brothers surrounded him, adding to his awareness, sharpening his focus. Eight minds unequal in strength, but perfectly balanced, perfectly unified. He was all of them, and they were all him. Together they were the Circle. Beyond them the human acolytes knelt, hands linked, white vapour pouring from their eyes as they fed the Circle with power.

The moment was here, the moment he had prepared for. It would not last long. What they did now was a near impossibility, a miracle created through knowledge and foresight. They had created a bridge between two points in space from the High Citadel of the *Sycorax* to the surface of Vohal. As the Rubricae advanced the Circle would appear within its walls. Astraeos's mind was the beacon, the thread drawing them through the night.

The human acolytes shrieked as Ahriman pulled the strength from their minds and broke reality with it. The ghosts of stars rushed past them as they streaked through the warp towards the beacon of Astraeos's call, towards the fortress on Vohal, towards Iobel. Time stretched out without end, and then reality snapped into place with a roll of thunder.

Sanakht's eyes opened. For a halted heartbeat of time he stood still, weapons undrawn at his side. The Circle had manifested in a high vaulted hall of stone. The storm had ripped the roof open, and the light of gunfire and lightning blinked down through the ragged holes. Snow spiralled in the air.

Ahriman stood a pace away from him, his aura roaring like a blue and white flame above the horns of his helmet. Sanakht felt the heat and focus of the rest of the Circle. Once his mind had burned like theirs. Not any more; his power was a candle beside the inferno of Ahriman and the rest. He wondered, as he had many times before, if it would not have been better if Khayon had burned out all of his psychic ability; at least he would not have been able to see what he had lost.

Better to be broken than to be the weakling amongst the strong.

The first gunshot shattered his thoughts. A pulse of las-bolts smacked into Sanakht's chest and shoulder. Blue lacquer blistered from the impacts. Thirty humans stood in the chamber, all clad in gloss-crimson armour. Sanakht kicked forwards. His swords slipped into his hands. Both were curved, their blades inlaid with lapis and copper. A black jackal head capped the pommel of the blade in his left hand, a white hawk head the right. Power shuddered through the jackal blade as he sent his will into its crystal core, and a blue power field sheathed the hawk blade.

The crimson-armoured humans were moving, scattering into firing positions. Blast shutters began to slam down across the door out of the chamber. The air sang with the buzz of las-bolts. Sanakht covered the gap in a single double beat of his hearts. Red threat runes covered his helmet display.

The humans tried to pull back while still firing. They were fast and disciplined, but they were still too slow. He took the first one across the neck with the jackal blade. The human exploded. Fragments of cooked meat pattered off Sanakht's armour. He spun forwards, power and force swords weaving through limbs and bodies. He lifted the intentions from his opponents' minds in the instant before they became action. Shots and blade thrusts reached for him, but touched only air. Here in the dance of blades and the spiralling of cuts he was still something of what he had been; here he was still a demigod of war.

The blast door shut and sealed with a metallic ring.

+Move, brother,+ shouted Ahriman's thought voice. Sanakht ripped the hawk blade from a split torso as he felt the psychic pressure wave building behind him. Another human stood in front of him, its plasma gun levelled at his face. +Move now!+ Sanakht dived to the side. The human fired. A bolt of plasma flashed through the air above him.

The psychic shockwave ripped through the chamber. The armoured humans lifted from their feet, spinning through the air, screaming for the second before their bones exploded. Threat runes blinked out inside Sanakht's helmet display as he rolled to his feet. The blast door was gone. Rock dust filled a ragged hole where it had been. Blood pattered on Sanakht's armour as he ran through the breach.

Torn pieces of flesh lay amongst the rubble. He saw severed hands still clutching twisted lasguns. Blood seeped into the powdered rock as it settled. Targeting runes spun across his helmet display in search of a threat, but he had already seen the enemy that waited for him.

A tall man stood amongst the rubble, his mind shining in Sanakht's awareness like a fire on a dark night. A spherical kine shield surrounded the man, glowing where debris had slammed into its surface. A coat of grey leather hung from his thin frame. An axe's haft projected behind his head from where it was sheathed between his shoulder blades. Augmetic eyes shone from beneath the smooth skin of his scalp. A battle psyker.

Sanakht charged. A ball of lightning rose like a halo around the psyker's skull. Sanakht threw the jackal sword. It blurred through the air, psy-fire clinging to its edges. The ball lightning catapulted from the psyker's mind. Sanakht's sword met the sphere, and a sheet of white light bleached the chamber. The human psyker reeled, and fell to his knees. The jackal sword was falling, its edge smoking. Sanakht caught it as he leapt into the air. The sword blazed at his touch. The human psyker was beneath him, still trying to rise. Sanakht descended, twin swords trailing fire and lightning above his head.

The psyker moved at the last instant, his mind hardening even as he spun to the side. The hooked axe was suddenly in the man's hands, its edge oiled with warp light, its crystal cores shrieking with fury. Axe and swords met.

The force of the psyker's mind slammed through Sanakht as the weapons kissed. Once Sanakht would have simply pushed his mind across that link and crushed the human psyker's mind inside his skull. That, though, had been long ago, before the Rubric, before everything had changed. Now victory had to take a different, more mundane form.

Sanakht scissored his two swords through the psyker's axe. Its core exploded. Metal and crystal fragments rang against Sanakht's armour. The psyker screamed, his arms truncated stumps, his face a shredded lump of meat. He was strong, though. He tried to rise, tried to find balance in his mind even as it boiled with agony. Sanakht spun the hawk sword through the man's neck. Behind him he felt the minds of Ahriman and his brothers rush past him into the rest of the citadel.

They were close, very close. All they had to do was reach Astraeos and–

A psychic cry rose up from beneath his feet, sharp with pain, bright with anguish.

Astraeos gasped and stumbled. The shockwave spilled across his mind, shrieking in dead voices as the storm broke and the Rubricae woke. Across the chamber men and woman reeled, and some fell. He suddenly smelled blood, vomit and faeces. He leapt up the stone tiers. Plasma screamed over his head. Iobel stood still, burst blood vessels blooming red across her eyeballs, her arm steady as she aimed at him.

+Ahriman,+ he shouted to the warp. Only the thunder roar of the storm answered him.

Behind him Cendrion leapt from the platform to the chamber floor with a crack of stone. Astraeos was a pace from Iobel. She began to step back, the pistol still raised, gas fuming from its vents.

+Cavor,+ Iobel's mind roared, her thought faster than her muscles. Astraeos struck her just below the elbow, and Iobel's arm shattered as she pulled the trigger. Plasma sprayed into the air. Astraeos looped his arm under hers.

The ground shook as Cendrion landed on the lower tiers and charged. Astraeos felt the warp take shape from the Grey Knight's thoughts. Fire kindled and stabbed towards him. He focused his mind to meet the inferno.

The explosive round hit him from behind, and ripped away a bloody chunk from his thigh. Astraeos turned as he began to fall. Blood was pulsing down his legs. A las-bolt clipped his shoulder.

A figure stood three tiers above him. Astraeos had the impression of a sour face, and a whip-thin body beneath a ragged coat; that, and the silver of the guns in the man's hands. Iobel twisted in his grasp, still conscious. He heard the gun cylinders turn, and the hammers cock. His mind flicked out to crush the rounds in the chambers.

The guns fired. Astraeos saw the tongues of flame lick from the muzzles. Slow, so slow. He tried to turn aside, to refocus his mind into a shield. Something hit him in the chest. It felt soft and warm. Blood misted in front of his eyes. He felt his control of the warp falter, and the processes of his mind slipped free. He began to fall again. He still could feel nothing. The second round hit an instant later, and blew the front of his skull away.

I am truly blind now, he thought as he hit the stone tier. Still there was no pain. Just a sense that somewhere locked behind walls of pain suppression there was a world of blades and razor edges waiting for him.

+Ahriman.+ The sending was weak, almost a croak. His awareness was fading, his body and mind closing down to the barest essentials. Everything had become a slow surge of sound and movement behind a window of numbed pain. His will scattered into fragments. The warp crashed in. Memories and half-formed thoughts whirled in the tide.

It was never going to work.

Trust me, my friend.

He was on the ground, slumped on the blood-slick stone. He tried to rise, tried to focus his will. There was a centre of calm within his mind, a pool of utter control that would save him if he could reach it. He would be able to heal himself, to see, to fight. It was there, just there, he could feel it in his grasp…

His will slipped, and he felt the tangle of occult formulae bleeding out of his thoughts.

Now, thought part of him. *Ahriman will come for me now. I do not end like this. As I came for him, he will come for me. He gave me his oath. He is my master, my brother. He will–*

Darkness came down across his mind like a closing gate.

Someone far away was screaming. As the dark took him he realised that he recognised the screaming voice. It was his.

* * *

+What was that?+ Ahriman heard Sanakht's voice rise out of the sea of thoughts. +Ahriman?+

Ahriman did not answer. He had felt it too. A shift in the warp, like a wind suddenly changing direction. He could see the whole design in his mind like a cage of spun glass, each filament a connection between the real and the warp. Each one and a thousand more had created this moment, had brought them here, and had raised the Rubricae from the ground. And it was slipping out of control. The vital beacon of Astraeos's mind had blinked out like a snuffed candle. And they were running out of time. He could feel uncertain futures branching ahead of him with every step.

This must not fail. I must not fail.

They were one level above where they needed to be. They would break through to the conclave chamber in one hundred and thirty-five seconds, but that would be too late.

He felt time unravel around his mind like fraying rope. The glowing storm pattern fractured. Ahriman poured more of his will into it. The minds of his brothers shuddered as he drew on them.

He felt all sense fall away. Everything became distant, just another pattern spinning through the quiet stillness. He could see the possibilities of the next nanosecond, multiply and collapse. He saw the Rubricae climbing over the walls, the molten stone squashing beneath their feet. He saw Astraeos fall. He saw a figure of fire waiting at the end of a billion branching futures. He was the storm, the still point around which the warp turned.

He straightened, felt his muscles relax as he lowered his weapons to his side. Sanakht and the rest of the Circle moved closer, though he had given them no command. Their wills were his will, all their power his. The chamber vanished.

High above them a thunderhead of force broke from the summit of the fortress, staining the cloud of the storm red.

The stone floor beneath Ahriman's feet became a void into nothing. He fell, he and his eight brothers with him, like angels from a burning heaven.

'Mistress.'

Iobel tried to focus on the voice, but there was blood in her eyes, and her thoughts felt soft and unfocused. She felt hands begin to lift a weight pinning her legs. She blinked, and looked up. Cavor knelt above her. His mouth twitched to show his broken-toothed smile. Behind him the silver mountain of Cendrion was turning, his head tilted upwards to the domed ceiling. At his feet lay the body of Astraeos. Blood was pumping from what had been the Space Marine's face. She could hear shouting, running feet, the sounds of panic.

'Stay still, mistress,' said Cavor. She frowned. Her head hurt a lot. She rolled onto her front, pushed herself to her knees. Purple and black spots bloomed in her vision. The ground felt like it was spinni–

...*A web of light and colour spinning into a storm, growing, filling her sight. Ashes and ice and...* The vision snapped from her awareness.

She bit off a yell of pain, blinked away the afterglow of the image.

She felt hands trying to steady her. She flicked them away and stood, her teeth gritted. Smoke was bubbling through the chamber. All around her people were moving. Thunder and gunfire rolled overhead. Cavor was at her side, chromed guns drawn, his head twitching. She could see shapes moving through the smoke, clusters of people with weapons drawn.

'Did you see that?' she said, feeling her mouth struggle to form each word.

'Mistress?'

...*A web drawing tighter, each strand a line of fire in the night*...

She was breathing hard, sweat prickling her cold skin.

No one was moving. Her eyes flickered over them. *Can't they feel it? Can't they–*

...*The web drew around her, drawing tighter, and she was alone with just the sound of her own rising pulse*...

She blinked and found Cendrion's silver-grey eyes on hers.

+Inquisitor?+ he sent, but his voice was distant as though he was moving away from her, as though she was falling. She could feel herself shaking now.

+Can't... you... see... it?+ she sent. Cendrion's brow flickered. Then he looked up, and then back at her. He nodded once as though in apology. His mind punched into hers. It was like being stabbed by a crystal knife.

...black stillness, and beyond the stars spinning in a blur...

+Run,+ he sent, as his mind withdrew. He raised his sword: its edge was suddenly burning. He looked upwards as thunder echoed through the castle's stones. +Run. Now!+

Iobel took a step, her hand moving to draw the hand cannon from her second holster.

The ceiling vanished. Her vision flashed white, each person and object becoming a black shadow. It was still, silent, like the image of an explosion burned onto the retina before the eye could close.

Figures of shadow stood around her, looming taller and taller, their edges blurred, their shapes without depth. Iobel realised that she could not feel her own heartbeat.

+Iobel.+ The voice was all around her, holding her in place.

A shriek rang through the chamber. A tongue of white flame cut through the growing dark. One of the shadows was falling, its shape twisting and shrinking like a burning scrap of paper. Colour and shape blinked back into place. She was at the centre of a circle of giants armoured in sapphire blue. She had an impression of blood flicking across white silk robes, of a figure falling with a whine of armour. Cendrion was there, moving faster than she could track. She saw his sword rise and come down.

One of the blue warriors moved to meet him, slashing out with a blade-tipped staff. Cendrion sidestepped the blow, and cut down. Another sapphire warrior fell. She felt the force holding her weaken. Other shapes moved in the glowing cloud of dust. She dipped her gun in her good hand.

She saw him then, one figure amongst the ring of warriors. His armour was silver-edged blue, and his eyepieces glowed red beneath his horn-topped helm. He nodded once as though in greeting.

+Now,+ called a voice in her head. +It must be now or the alignment will pass.+

Cendrion was a pace away, his sword a sheet of blinding light.

+What of Astraeos?+ said another voice.

Iobel raised her gun, until the muzzle was pointing at the red eyes. Her finger tightened on the trigger.

+Now.+

The world vanished, and there was just the rushing of a storm wind and the spinning of stars.

PART TWO

ALL THE SONS OF ASHES

VII
LOYALTY

The jungle of his dreams closed over Ahriman. The leaves stirred around him as he slid between them. He paused, cocking his head to listen. The creak of insects and the murmur of the wind in the canopy answered him. Heat pressed close to his skin. Sweat beaded across his body and dribbled down his muscles.

The fatigue of the real following me into the unreal, he thought, as he took a heavy breath. The efforts of the battle on Vohal still clung to his mind and body like a fever. Out in reality, he sat in the *Sycorax*'s High Citadel as it cut through the warp. The ship and the rest of his fleet had broken off their attack and run back into the warp as soon as the Circle and the Rubricae had materialised on the *Sycorax* again. The diversion the void assault had provided had cost them a handful of vessels. There had been other costs, though. Here, in the landscape of his dreams, he had no doubt that the oppressive heat of the jungle was his mind's way of expressing his weariness.

The jungle had once covered Sarlina, a world which had been conquered by the Thousand Sons in a different age. The shadows were different, though; something within his psyche had touched them, and made them grow until they seemed to flow around him like black oil.

He began to move forwards again, feeling the mud ooze around his feet. A flat-bodied insect emerged from beneath a leaf, its carapace a luminescent blue, its fringe of waving antennae tapping at the heat-thickened air. Ahriman watched it move across the leaf.

'Are you here to find me?'

The voice came from just in front of him. Ahriman leapt back, muscles whipcord tense, eyes scanning the darkness in front of him. A pool of shadow split to reveal a one-eyed face beneath a ragged hood. The lone eye glowed red within the cowl.

'You are looking for me, aren't you, my son?' The figure's voice rattled dry from cracked lips.

Ahriman straightened. The figure shuffled forwards to where the luminescent insect still sat on a leaf.

'You were the best of my sons,' said the figure.

'The memory of Magnus's last words to me,' said Ahriman, and turned away.

'Quite right. I am not here. I am just an idea, a cyst in your memories formed around the idea of your gene father. You are tired. Your mind is allowing things to manifest that it would normally not. This is a form of conversation with yourself. I am not here. I am a dream. Why break with the simplest explanation? Unless…' Ahriman turned. The twisted figure was smiling at him, and the flat insect had crawled to sit on the palm of the figure's hand. 'Unless it is wrong.'

'Why would you be here?'

The figure looked back at the insect, raised a long finger and brushed one of the waving antennae.

'Because you are looking for me. You are looking for me in the past, wondering if there were more secrets that I kept from you even before Prospero burned.'

Far off a distant howl shivered through the dark. Ahriman's head came up. The leaves were rustling, rubbing their edges together like wet teeth.

'Then why not answer me now?' said Ahriman as he looked around again.

The figure had gone.

Another howl rose through the night, closer this time. Ahriman stood, eyes moving across the shadows, and then he began to slide through the dream again, running towards wakefulness.

Grimur watched the stars. His axe rested in his hand, and the hunched muscle of his back twitched in complaint at his stillness. Beneath his feet the chunk of the broken star ship turned over again. Sealed in his armour, his boots mag-locked to the metal, it seemed as though he was still and the universe turned around him. He stood on the largest piece of wreckage they had found: a half-kilometre-long chunk of plasteel, blackened and torn by explosions. Smaller pieces of debris spun in the distance, all slowly drifting away from the point where the ship they had been part of had died. To Grimur they looked like burned splinters of bone.

The vox clicked, and Sycld's breathing wheezed from the static before cutting out. The Rune Priest had climbed down into the crushed and broken passages that ran through the wreckage. He would be crawling over the girders, baring the flesh of his hands for a few seconds to press them against the scorched plating. He needed to touch the bones of the dead ship to connect with the spirits, and hear the echoes of the past.

Grimur shivered, and touched the red iron shard hanging around his neck. He had never liked the ways of the wyrd. He had liked Sycld once, but that young warrior had disappeared a long time ago. They were pack brothers and always would be, but that did not alter the fact that they stood apart. Sycld walked the paths of the dead, and nothing could alter that. Long ago, during Grimur's few human years on Fenris, he had seen a woman in a cloak of crow feathers freeze the sea around five of his blood-father's ships. The waves had become white mounds, the black depths bowls of dark ice. The woman had made a sign and the frozen sea had crushed the ships. Grimur's father had turned the rest of the war fleet back from the attack after that. The woman had laughed, and the sound had carried on the wind that had filled his father's sails. Even now, many lives of men later, Grimur could still hear the crow-cloaked woman's laugh, and the screaming of warriors as the ice sea ate them. To him that sound was the voice of the wyrd.

The vox clicked again. Grimur waited for the Rune Priest to speak.

'The trace is here,' panted Sycld.

'Enough?'

'Yes. It was not his refuge for long, but it carries his soul-spoor even now.'

Grimur nodded, though there was no one to see. He looked up. Slowly spinning islands of debris winked back with reflected light. His helmet display flickered with runes, bracketing the pieces of wreckage with data, framing them with projected arcs of movement. Out beyond the debris field his ships waited, five dark shapes sliding against the void on comet trails. The ships had not started in the service of the Wolves. Grimur had taken them from slain enemies, and given them names that reflected their new purpose. *Hel's Daughter*, *Storm Wyrm*, and *Crone Hammer* were the largest, three scarred sisters of war. Beside them ran *Death's Laughter* and *Blood Howl*: smaller, faster, their twin spirits like murder daggers. Behind the ships, the Eye of Terror spread across the heavens. Folded wings of glowing gas flickered between colours as he watched, the darkness at their centre a malignant pupil staring back.

For so long the Eye's tides have been our home, he thought. *What will become of us when the hunt is done? All those who have fallen, who have died with an axe in their hand and wounds to their front – Oulf, Haakon, Inge, and the rest – will be forgotten. Our tale is a saga that can never be told.*

'What can we be after it is done?' he said to himself.

'Lord?' came Sycld's voice. Grimur blinked his helmet display back to a standard view, and looked down again at the twisted metal beneath his feet.

'What was its name? The ship, what was its name?'

'*Titan Child* – a renegade ship fleeing from retribution.'

'So are all that come to this place.' The vox crackled, but Sycld said nothing.

Grimur shook his head. He brought the curve of his axe up, and clinked its edge on his helm. His twisted back twinged as the muscles woke. He remembered making the same gesture under a burning sky once before. The axe he had held then was broken, and the remaining shard of its red blade hung over his chest like an iron tooth, but then, as now, the vow in the gesture remained.

If we die unremembered, but with great deeds done, it will be enough. He felt the previous bleak mood shake free from his mind like snow from fur. *Time will remember us even if men do not speak our names.*

'We return to the ships,' Grimur said into the vox. 'You will guide us.'

'I can see the way. I can feel the scent pull at my waking,

calling me into the paths of dream. I know the course we must steer.'

There had been a cold note in Sycld's voice, as though he were speaking a warrior's doom, or talking of an unclean death in battle. Grimur paused, suddenly aware that he did not want to ask the question which was forming on his tongue.

'Where?' he asked at last. The vox rasped and clicked.

'Out of the Eye, into the Allfather's realm.'

Grimur nodded to himself, his fingers resting on the red iron shard hanging from his neck.

Of course – the prey returns to the lands he betrayed. And we… He smiled inside his helm, baring a yellowed fang at the Eye above him. *We follow.*

'Failure,' said Ignis. The word hung in the High Chamber. Ignis looked around the circle, his eyes lingering on Ahriman. Hard blue eyes met Ignis's stare. He suppressed a shiver. Ahriman's face was unmarked by time or battle. Except the eyes; they shone with a controlled insight that made Ignis's skin crawl inside his armour. *What are you beside me?* they seemed to say. *What can you claim to know that I do not already know?* Ignis held Ahriman's gaze and repeated his judgement.

'It was failure,' he said. Behind him the looming bulk of Credence clicked and shifted as though uncomfortable. Ahriman's eyes twitched to the automaton then back to Ignis. 'There is no other way of seeing it.'

The Circle remained silent. There were five of them now, each unarmoured and robed in white. Beside Ignis stood Kiu, Gaumata, Ctesias, and, of course, Sanakht. Even here the crippled swordsman wore his twin blades. Ahriman stood at their centre, his bare feet resting on a serpentine sun spread in silver across a floor of obsidian. The whole chamber sat at the apex of the High Citadel of the *Sycorax*. The light of the stars glimmered from beyond the crystal pyramid which formed the chamber's roof. Scented resin burned on brass tripods close to the walls. Shadows hung at its edges, hemming in the small circle of figures with emptiness and silence. The warp lapped at the chamber walls, held back by the incantations woven over the gathering. Ignis normally did not like being separated from the Great Ocean, but under Ahriman's gaze he was suddenly glad that this moment was confined to the real.

'It worked,' said Sanakht, from across the circle.

Ignis felt his jaw muscles tighten involuntarily. Sanakht was frowning, his handsome features creased in puzzlement beneath his ash-blond hair.

'It did.' Ignis bit the words off with brittle care. 'But not without cost.'

'Success always has a cost,' said Sanakht, shaking his head slowly, as though stating a simple truth to a child.

'A platitude,' said Ignis, blinking once.

'A fact.'

'Ah,' said Ignis carefully, making his face smile. 'You, of course, are best placed to tell us about the cost of failure.'

Sanakht's frown flickered, and Ignis was suddenly aware that the swordsman's hands were resting upon his weapons. He had not even seen Sanakht move.

He is still fast, thought Ignis, *even if his inner strength is broken*. Part of him wondered if Sanakht could reach and kill him before being stopped by the rest of the Circle. Then he wondered if any of them *would* stop him. He was an outsider here, even if he shared their blood. He decided that it was irrelevant. Credence gave a dull binaric click, which sounded like agreement. Ignis let his false smile fade. Sanakht took his hands from the pommels of his swords.

'Three of our number gone,' Ignis gestured at the gaps in the circle. 'Three. For one human soul. If the salvation of the Legion is our aim, how can this calculation have any other answer?'

'Four,' said Ahriman quietly. They all looked towards him. He met each of their gazes, and then looked at the empty space where Astraeos would have stood. 'We lost four, for one human soul.'

'One soul who has what?' asked Ignis. Around the circle the others shifted in discomfort. They all wanted to ask the same question, had wanted to ask it ever since Ahriman had begun this endeavour, of that Ignis was certain; he could feel the hunger in the air.

'Secrets, brother.' Ahriman looked up at Ignis. All of the Circle had gone completely silent. All of them had followed and obeyed Ahriman at every step, but Ignis knew they had all asked what Ahriman intended before and received the same reply. Now, at long last, it seemed they would get a different answer. 'The answer is secrets. Or rather one secret that the Imperium has buried deep.' They were all still now, all of them watching. 'The inquisitor we captured knows this secret, and we have bought that knowledge with the lives of our brothers.' Ahriman paused, nodding slowly as he looked around the circle. 'Her name is Selandra Iobel. Our paths have crossed before.'

'How?' Gaumata's slow voice rose into the silence. Ahriman looked into the pyromancer's wide face. Red and black eyes glittered back.

'She was on the ship I took Silvanus from. The silver in my chest is from her weapon. She almost killed me,' said Ahriman. Surprise rippled around the circle. 'And in that moment our minds connected. In that one instant she knew me, and somehow recognised me. She did not think that meeting chance – she thought that I had come for her because of what she knew, because of Apollonia.'

'What is Apollonia?' Sanakht spoke. The swordsman's eyes seemed to have sunken into his ageless face.

So even Sanakht has been kept in the dark. Ignis felt a twinge of pleasure at the thought.

'A place the reborn Imperium has hidden from itself. It is a planet, or perhaps a system, but in Iobel's mind Apollonia has another name linked to it. When she thought of Apollonia, she thought of an Athenaeum, a library of knowledge.' His gaze stopped once again at the circle's centre. 'She called it the Athenaeum of Kalimakus.'

Stillness and complete silence formed after the words.

Inside his mind Ignis slotted the fact into calculations which he had not been able to complete since Ahriman had summoned him. Kalimakus had been Magnus the Red's personal remembrancer, psychically bound to the primarch so that he was not a scribe but a conduit. He had not been seen since Prospero had burned, and his fate had never been known. Until now.

'The words of the Crimson King.' Sanakht broke the silence, his voice dry with awe. 'You are seeking our father's secrets…'

'Yes.' Ahriman nodded, his face grim as his eyes moved between the empty spaces in the circle. 'That is what four lives bought. The Rubric failed, but its seeds came from our father's work, from the Book of Magnus.' Ahriman paused, and when his voice returned it was lower, edged with sadness. 'But what if there was a flaw in that work, an error which tainted all we built on it? In the source we may find the flaw, and from the flaw we may find a cure. Sanakht is correct – there is always a price, and we have only begun to pay for what we have done, and what we will still do. We do not bow to fate, not now, not ever again. Tell me which of you would not pay for such freedom?'

Silence was his only answer.

Hemellion did not look up as he moved through the *Sycorax*. It was best not to look at the others that walked the metal city; he had learnt that truth within hours of being brought aboard.

The first time he was set free he had tried to run. The silver chains around his ankles had turned his strides into a limp, but he had run until his lungs were burning. As he scrambled through the bronze and iron caves he had found a tall figure robed in saffron and yellow, its face hidden by a hood. He had called for help, for a way out of this iron city. The saffron-robed figure had ignored him. He had hobbled after it, calling, and had grasped its robe. At that moment he had realised that he had made a mistake. He had pulled his hand back, but it was too late. The figure had turned. Hemellion had looked up into the shadow of the hood before he could stop himself.

He had woken later, his clothes matted in his own vomit and blood, head and ears ringing, face resting against the crystal view of stars glimmering in the distance. That was how his new master had found him.

'You will not try to run again,' Sanakht had said, and he had been right. In that view of the stars Hemellion had found another truth; there was no escape from the iron city besides death.

The silver chains jangled as he quickened his step past a group of yellow-swathed Cyrabor. The machine-wrights hissed and clicked in his wake like cogwork birds. No one ever tried to stop him; some even bowed as he passed by, as though the scarlet of his robes were a mark of favour rather than slavery.

Scarlet, he thought, the colour of the slave serfs; of those who were permitted into the close presence of the Thousand Sons to tend their armour, clean their weapons, and do their bidding. The white robes of the acolytes were a higher honour, but when Hemellion thought about the withered men and women, some of them drooling with madness, crawling with the witch-touch, he was pleased it was an honour he could never obtain. For him it had been six months since he had left his dead world and gone up into the city in the sky, six months of learning a new life and unlearning an old one. How long had passed in the realm he had left, though? He could not know. Sanakht, his master, had explained the paradox of time in the warp to Hemellion once, but it had been an explanation that seemed closer to insanity rather than truth. He had not asked to have it explained further.

He stopped before he reached the passage leading to his master's chamber, sucking breath through his teeth. He ran a hand over his shaven scalp, and it came away slick with sweat. It had taken him two hours to come from the lower passages to this place. On Vohal he could have walked from one side of the largest city to the other in half an hour. His sense of scale was one of the most minor of things that had changed since he had seen his world die.

He felt the hate rise up inside him as he tried to catch his breath. They had taken everything that he knew, had made it nothing without a thought. They had not even put his people to the sword. They had just killed everything that could support life, and let nature wield the scythe. A whole world had died in the dust, children crying in thirst, old women eating the dry earth from hunger. He had been there when the last well had run dry, and the desperate had tried to storm his fortress walls. The Thousand Sons had created a hell, but from the moment he had looked up into Ahriman's eyes, Hemellion had known that it had not been for malice. No, it had been as part of a process. That truth had kept him alive, had kept the hate beating in his heart as they had shaved his head, robed him in scarlet and told him that he would serve the murderers of his world until he died.

I will see them dead. I will see them die in the ruin of their star city. I will find a way.

He looked about him, suddenly aware of the hate in his thoughts. He pushed the emotion down, waiting until his heartbeat slowed and his thoughts were calm. They were witch-kind, all of them. They could see his thoughts, and if he was not careful they would smell the treachery in him. He turned a corner and limped towards the entrance to Sanakht's chamber.

A Rubricae stood to either side of the sealed doors. Green corpse light burned in their eyes beneath high-crested helms. Hemellion averted his gaze as he approached the entrance. He did not look into the Rubricae's eyes; even being close to them made him feel dizzy. He had only to wait a heartbeat before the doors split open, and pulled back into the bronze walls.

The chamber beyond the doors would have been large if it had not been for the figure standing at its far end. Even without armour Sanakht made the room feel small. Flocks of golden birds rose across the sky blue of his robes. His face was thin, and reminded Hemellion of a youth just grown to manhood, his features unmarked by scars, ash-blond hair cut short against the dome of his scalp. He held a curled parchment in his hands, and more parchment lay scattered across the chamber, heaped in corners and hiding the black stone of the floor.

Hemellion bowed slowly.

As kings and warlords once did to me, said a whisper in his mind.

Sanakht tilted the parchment so that the light of the hovering glow-globes fell across it from a different angle. Hemellion waited, still bowed.

'Fill two cups,' said Sanakht after a long moment. Hemellion straightened from his bow. A silver jug and a trio of silver cups sat on a stone plinth at the side of the chamber. Most often his master called on him to clean his armour, or to take some artefact to another part of the ship. Sometimes Sanakht called Hemellion, and then dismissed him as soon as he arrived. But the legionary had never asked Hemellion to fill cups before.

Sanakht looked up. The parchment dropped from his fingers and fluttered to the scroll-strewn floor. Hemellion met his master's gaze, and quickly looked down. Red blotches covered the white of Sanakht's right eye, and the pupil was a ragged hole, like a broken yolk in a bloody egg. The left eye was clouded white. The corner of Sanakht's mouth twitched, but if it was in humour it did not show on the rest of his face.

Hemellion shuffled to the silver jug and filled two cups. The liquid that came from the jug was a red so dark that it looked like clotted blood. Hemellion carried both cups back to Sanakht, and held them up.

Sanakht laughed, the sound so sudden and deep that Hemellion almost dropped the cups. The legionary reached down and took one cup.

'Sit,' said Sanakht. Hemellion looked at the cup still in his hand, and then back up at the demigod. 'Sit.'

Hemellion looked around before folding slowly to the floor. A second later Sanakht mirrored the movement.

Like a tiger curling up under a tree, thought Hemellion. Sanakht's mouth twitched again. He raised the cup to his mouth and took a delicate mouthful.

'Drink,' said Sanakht, and tilted his cup.

Hemellion looked down at his own cup. Slowly he raised it to his lips and drank a sip. The liquid was thick on his tongue and tasted of hot sun and spice. He coughed, blinked, and glanced back up. He could feel sweat prickling his skin. Something that would have been a smile on a human cracked Sanakht's face.

'Unpleasant, is it not – having your will bound to another?' said Sanakht, his voice low and measured. 'Having another creature command you?'

'It is…'

'I know this,' said Sanakht. 'And I know that you know this, Hemellion, King of Vohal.'

Hemellion watched his own reflection in the still surface of his cup. He was trying to think of something to say. He felt as though he had walked into a dream made from a child's story; the man talking to the smiling serpent.

'I…' He felt his mouth go dry as he tried to speak.

'Do you know why Ahriman gave you to me?'

Hemellion shook his head without looking up. In fact he was not sure why he was having this conversation.

'He gave you to me because he thought that of all my brothers I am the one who needs another serf. The others can break apart their armour with a thought, remake the atoms in the air, unmake the light that meets their eyes. I…' Hemellion looked up. Sanakht was turning the cup in his hand, watching the liquid cling to the silver. 'I cannot. Not without great effort, not any more.' He looked back at Hemellion with the cracked pupil of his eye. 'I am *of the Circle*, but I am a child by comparison to my brothers. In battle their minds carry me. A brother in name but not in kind. When they use their hands it is because they choose to. I need serfs to carry my scrolls and clean my armour, not because it is my right, but because otherwise I would have to do it with my own hands.'

Hemellion looked down from Sanakht's face, and took another sip from his cup. A fire spread through his chest. He felt soft tongues of warmth run through his thoughts.

'What happened to change you so?' The question slipped from his lips before he could stop it. He realised what he had done a second later. 'I am sorry, I did not... I...' The words dried in his throat.

Sanakht was just looking at him, eyes unblinking in a carven face. Hemellion felt his own flesh become very still, the adrenaline hammering in his veins telling him to run now, to run and not look back.

'A fair question,' said Sanakht, at last. 'You were a king once, or as good as, a man used to questioning as he saw fit. I will not take that from you. A mind that sees and questions is worth more than the adoration of a million crawling fools.' Hemellion felt the race of his pulse slow, but he still did not move or speak. 'What changed me? Loyalty, Hemellion, loyalty made me like this.' Sanakht took a longer drink from the cup. 'All our kind were... on a path that would see us become monsters. Ahriman had a way of stopping it, a way to save all of our brothers. We, many of my brothers and I, were his cabal. We all agreed that we could not allow our Legion to fall any further.' He paused, his gaze sharpening on a point somewhere in the distance. 'But not all were with us. One of our brothers tried to stop us. He came for us, for Ahriman. Some died. Ahriman survived.' Sanakht's gaze dropped, his eyes seeming to pull back into his skull, the hollows of his face deepening. 'And that had a cost.'

'Where is he now?' asked Hemellion. 'The one who tried to stop Ahriman, what became of him?'

'Khayon?' Sanakht shivered, then shrugged. 'He was remade in another way.' Hemellion took a swig from his cup, allowing the liquid to steal a little more of his fear. Sanakht was watching the ripples settle to stillness on the surface of his own drink. 'For a long time I thought the Eye had taken Ahriman, that he was gone. But Amon believed him alive, and we followed Amon. He was right – Ahriman lived, and now we follow Ahriman again. Now we give him our loyalty, and we trust that he can change us again. We are what we were once again, falling into the same abyss. Whatever he intends will fail, and even in failure it will have a price that he will pay without a thought.'

Hemellion went very still, his eyes watching Sanakht for a movement, for a sign that the treachery he had just spoken was a test. Somewhere, far off at the back of his thoughts, he remembered looking into Ahriman's eyes, blue and cold as winter stars. *'Because this is how fate is made,'* the sorcerer had said. Sanakht looked up, and Hemellion thought he saw understanding mirrored back at him.

'They were right,' said Sanakht softly. 'All those who tried to stop us: the Emperor, Khayon, Amon. We follow lies and pay the coins without thinking, believing that we are right, and that only we see clearly. Those who challenge us we condemn as ignorant, and we run on into darkness, trying to reach a false light. We are the heirs of blind kings, ruling a kingdom of ashes.'

Sanakht nodded back at Hemellion's wide stare. The air in the chamber seemed heavy and still. He was suddenly aware of the taste of the liquor on his tongue, the smell of parchment, and the buzz of the glow-globes.

'It must end,' said Sanakht. 'He must end.'

Hemellion felt the fires of hate kindle in his guts. They spread through him before he could stop them. He felt his heartbeat rise even as he tried to slow it. The corner of Sanakht's mouth twisted, but the rest of his face remained as still as before.

'This is not vengeance, Hemellion, not of the kind that you clutch close in the night.'

Cold spread across Hemellion's skin. He thought of the dreams which filled his sleep, and the anger he hid inside.

'How do…?' he managed

'Your thoughts are of little else. You try to control them, but the warp around you tastes of your hate for us.'

Hemellion felt as though he had been struck, as though all his sensations were not his own, as though he was falling without moving.

He knows. They know. This is a trap. He thought of standing, but it was as though the connections between his mind and limbs had been severed. *Witch-touched*, said a voice within. *They see through thoughts, through stone, through flesh.*

+No,+ said Sanakht, and his voice was within Hemellion's skull, echoing through his thoughts. +This is no trap. I tell you this because I will need you. Because everyone must speak the truth to someone. You will have your vengeance. It will have a cost, but it will be yours in time – you have my word.+

The chamber was fading from Hemellion's sight. The world was a white swirl of dust, and the cries of his murdered home.

But if one witch can see my thoughts then others can too.

+I am sorry,+ said Sanakht's voice from beyond the turning cloud. Pain filled Hemellion, blanking out his thoughts, crackling through him like a storm of lightning. He felt parts of himself vanish, crumbling even as he tried to cling onto them. +I trust you,+ spoke Sanakht, +but ignorance is the only thing that will protect us.+ As Hemellion's mind was reshaped, he remembered one thing, one line that now seemed a lie shrieked at the universe.

He… He said he was weak… a child…

+Weakness,+ came the voice from the storm, +is a matter of degree.+

Hemellion blinked. He felt as though he had just stepped from darkness into bright light. Sanakht stood at the centre of the chamber, a dry leaf of parchment in his hand. Hemellion frowned. He could not remember why his master had summoned him, but it was not the first time he had come to Sanakht's chamber for a reason he could not remember. A silver cup lay on the floor, dark liquid spreading from it in a thick pool towards the scrolls scattered across the floor. He bent down and picked up the cup. Sanakht looked at him, and Hemellion had to suppress a mixture of hate and fear as the mismatched eyes fastened on him.

'How may I serve you, lord?' he asked.

VIII
MINDSCAPE

'No one enters.' Ahriman turned and looked at Kadin as the door to the chamber opened. The hiss and clunk of the door mechanisms sounded loud in the empty corridor. Behind him Maroth had crouched against the corridor wall, his hound helm swaying from side to side as though listening to a sound that was not there. The Cyrabor had cleared the deck levels for a kilometre in every direction around this spot.

The chamber beyond the door was not what Kadin had expected. Buried in the *Sycorax*'s machine decks, it might once have been a magazine or store for volatile chemicals. Small, and accessed by a single blast door, its walls were slab panels of plasteel. Dry rust ran round the chamber's edges, and the only illumination came from a yellow light held behind a cage of brass in the ceiling. It had the feeling of a place that had fallen between needs again and again until it was forgotten.

A sarcophagus of black stone sat at the room's centre. Its upper surface was carved in the vague likeness of a human. Kadin could see the impressions of a serene face, and arms folded across its chest. Sigils ran over the surface of the sarcophagus, incised into the stone. Kadin heard voices whisper at the edge of his awareness as he looked at them. He could understand the symbols, but was not sure how; they were demands to the warp to hold the one who lay within the casket quiet.

'That is her?' he asked. 'Iobel?'

'The princess of the blind,' hissed Maroth from the corridor behind.

Ahriman nodded, not moving from the door, his eyes flicking over the chamber. He was armoured but bareheaded. In the space before the casket the deck was marked with lines burned into the metal. The lines and spirals made Kadin blink as he looked at them.

'Why not simply rip it from her mind? If she has what you want, why not just take it?'

Ahriman's eyes darted over the design on the floor, and then to the sarcophagus. Kadin thought he heard Ahriman muttering even though the sorcerer's lips did not move.

'Understanding,' said Ahriman eventually, still not looking at Kadin. 'Knowledge without context is useless. The facts are not enough. I must have everything that gives those facts meaning. Besides, who knows what else her mind might contain?' Kadin saw something that might have been a grim smile flicker across Ahriman's face, and then vanish. 'And to take all of that requires… delicacy.'

Ahriman let out a long, measured breath, and his eyes closed briefly. Kadin felt the air become cold. His machine limbs twitched as pistons and servos spasmed. Maroth gave a low whimper from the shadows.

'No one enters,' repeated Ahriman, the breath of the words white as it came from his lips. 'Sanakht and Ignis have primacy over the fleet while I am here.' Kadin nodded, and unclamped the two-handed chainsword from his back. His machine fingers flexed against the worn grip.

Ahriman stepped through the door.

'You think someone will try to interfere?' Kadin asked. Ahriman shrugged, his face darkening with an expression that Kadin knew must be a frown.

'I am not sure,' said Ahriman. He walked to the centre of the design burned into the floor. Kadin thought he saw the lines and markings bend away from Ahriman's footsteps. 'Perhaps.'

'He sees everything, yet sees nothing,' cackled Maroth.

'You don't trust them,' said Kadin. It was a flat statement. 'Your brothers, you don't trust them.'

'I trust *you* to be what you are.'

'And what is that?'

Ahriman said nothing, but looked at the deck, shifting his position minutely, his eyes flickering across the lines spiralling away from him.

'And him?' Kadin jerked his neck at Maroth. Ahriman glanced up, his eyes fastening on the broken and blind sorcerer. Maroth came with Kadin wherever he went now, attached to him like a second shadow. When Ahriman had summoned Kadin to his side Maroth had come too, hissing and muttering in his ruined armour. Ahriman had not objected, had not even remarked on the broken sorcerer's presence. It was as though Ahriman did not even see Maroth.

'He is nothing,' said Ahriman.

'Is that what Astraeos died knowing?' said Kadin, his voice flat.

Ahriman's eyes snapped up to his. Kadin could feel the fingers of Ahriman's mind in his thoughts, trying to tease through the mangled web of his soul, searching for anger and treachery. He almost smiled. There had been the barest twinge of regret when he had heard that his brother had fallen, but then the fact had simply become one amongst many, as dead and cold as a fire's ashes. He had thought about what that lack of a response meant, but had reached no conclusion.

'I am sorry, Kadin,' said Ahriman, after a moment.

Kadin did not bother to nod, but simply turned to face the corridor. He rested the tip of his chainsword between his feet, and gripped the hilt with both hands. Behind him the door sealed with a hiss of pistons.

'Quietness,' whispered Maroth to himself. Kadin did not reply.

* * *

Ahriman looked at the sarcophagus for a long moment. Around him he felt the warp waiting, its tides shaped by the patterns cut into the floor. In his mind's eye golden planes of light rose from the design. Sigils hung as small suns of meaning and potential, some still, others orbiting one another in clusters. Within the web lay the casket, the slumbering mind within glowing with dreams. He had spent days constructing this ritual. Each part of it was like a vast and delicate machine of thought, symbolism, and aetheric power. It only waited for his mind to set it in motion.

He took a breath, feeling every molecule of air spin slowly into his lungs. He felt the rhythm of his hearts slow until his awareness was suspended between two beats. Everything was still before his unblinking inner eye. He waited, floating in the emptiness. He formed a thought, and sent it rotating through his mind. He formed a string of thoughts, and felt them take life as they fed off memory and imagination. He split his will, breaking apart thought after thought until his mind was filled with whirling and spinning consciousness. The warp tugged at his will, trying to pull the delicate construct apart. Slowly, carefully he let one of his hearts beat. His mind was no longer within his skull; it was floating free, unbound. The ritual designs etched into the chamber met his mind and the two joined. His awareness flowed into the casket, and into Iobel's mind.

* * *

'Is that what he asked you?' said Ignis. Sanakht kept his gaze steady. Ignis was watching him, his face impassive.

The crucible chamber sat at the heart of the *Word of Hermes*, a bowl of raw iron wide enough to swallow a Titan. A ball of molten metal revolved in midair at the crucible's centre, fuming heat and ruddy light. There were no doors, just the lip of the crucible a dozen metres up the curved iron walls. Deep channels ran across the inside of the bowl, straight lines intersecting with circular depressions scooped into the walls. Sanakht recognised geometry that might have made the sign of Thothmes, or the Idris Progression, or the Sigil of the Carrion, but each seemed to blur and merge together with other designs he did not recognise. The whole structure pressed around Sanakht's mind like a metal clamp. He did not like it, but the ways of the Order of Ruin had always been strange.

Ignis waited for a long heartbeat then shrugged. 'When he asked you to betray Magnus, was that how he asked?'

'No,' said Sanakht carefully. 'He never called it treachery.'

Ignis tilted his head but did not look away or blink. The electoos on his face contracted, expanded and multiplied their geometry.

He has not denied me yet, thought Sanakht. *Nor has he tried to kill me.* He felt hope tug at him, and fought it down. He could read nothing in Ignis's expressionless face, and he knew that even if he could have looked into Ignis's thoughts, he would have seen only numbers and symbols, each turning in intricate mental calculations like the cogs of a vast machine. *Perhaps he is simply waiting for his calculation to reach a clear conclusion before acting.* The Order of Ruin was many things, but haste had never been one of its flaws.

'You agreed to join Ahriman, to become part of his cabal.' Ignis paused again, tilting his head the other way. 'Why?'

Sanakht saw it again then: the dust of the Planet of the Sorcerers, the shambling figures whose flesh and armour could not be told apart. He saw the yellow eyes blinking in blind clusters across the faces of those he had called friends. He looked down at his hand and saw it again as it had been, a thing of living metal and crystal scales. He closed his fingers slowly, one at a time.

'We were dying, Ignis. Ahriman was not wrong in that.'

'But wrong to do what he did?' Ignis paused and blinked once, slowly. 'Yes?'

'No,' said Sanakht, and gave a sad smile. 'He was wrong to believe that we were worth saving.'

'So you offer us the obliteration we deserved? Is that not what Amon believed?'

Sanakht shook his head. Like the rest of the Circle he had chosen to answer Amon and serve him. Ignis had not been a part of Amon's Brotherhood of Dust, just as he had not been a part of the cabal who had cast the Rubric.

'It ends with Ahriman. I do not seek to remake our Legion, or to bring us all redemption.' He paused, thinking of Amon; in many ways he had been right, but in others he was the mirror of Ahriman, but a mirror with a different focus. 'I know my limits,' said Sanakht at last.

'And Ahriman?' Ignis asked, his voice level, but the black electoos twitched above his eyes.

'He believes there is a way to save us all. A little more understanding, a little more perfection of knowledge, and he can correct his errors. There is a light dancing on the horizon for him, and what he has done already is only the beginning of the price he will pay to get a step closer to that end. He will drag us all with him. Salvation does not wait for us – only the darkness of damnation closing around us until we can no longer see where we began.'

Ignis did not move or speak for a long moment. The patterns on his face were still. Sanakht watched him, waiting. The clank of distant machines and the hiss of gas from a vent high above trickled into the silence.

'How do you think to do such a thing?' said Ignis at last, his expression as unreadable as ever. 'Do you ask me to fire on the *Sycorax*? Do you hope to break the Rubricae from his will? Do you wish to try and persuade the entire Circle to face him?' Ignis blinked again, but kept on speaking before Sanakht could answer. 'All such methods will fail. The others will not join you. The *Sycorax* could face half the fleet and survive, and he...' Ignis paused, and Sanakht saw something flicker in the black eyes. 'He is a power like I have never seen. More even than before.'

Sanakht shook his head.

'The others will stand against me. Ahriman has them all. They are starting to believe him again, they are starting to hope, just as they did before. I am alone, for now.'

'So what do you intend?'

He still has not refused, thought Sanakht, *but if this does not end as I hope then I will have to kill him.* He had no doubt that he could – his powers were weak, but Ignis's powers were channelled in other ways, and even then a blade would silence him as easily as a thought.

'I will wait until he has no strength, and I have strength he does not expect.'

'You know that such a moment will come?'

'Such a moment always comes.'

Ignis inclined his head as though acknowledging the point.

'Why come to me? We are not... *friends*, Sanakht, we never were.'

'Failure,' said Sanakht, and let the word hang in the air with his breath. 'That is what you called Vohal. We lost three of our brothers, and you said it was failure.'

'A calculation. If we do this to remake ourselves, then to sacrifice ourselves to that end undoes the logic of victory.'

Sanakht nodded, and gave a tired smile.

'So what is the calculation now, brother? Are you with me?'

Ignis stared at him, eyes still, the patterns of his face growing more complex. Sanakht just waited. At last the patterns settled and Ignis opened his mouth.

'Yes,' he said.

* * *

Iobel heard the hab-block detonate behind her. She took a pace, a curse forming in her mouth. The blast wave hit her. The ground vanished beneath her feet. She spun through the dust-filled air. Her armour cracked as she hit the ground and pain stabbed through her torso.

Her ears were ringing. Billowing grey clouds surrounded her. She sucked in a breath of air. Rockcrete dust and ash filled her lungs. She coughed, and felt something sharp shift in her chest. She could hear the mutant creatures crying out in pain. Some of them must have been caught by the blast; that at least was a small comfort.

'Horeg!' she shouted into the vox. She rolled over and came to her feet. The ground swayed under her. 'Horeg? Linisa? Cavor? Any of you?' Whoops of distortion answered her. 'Answer, you useless bastards,' she called again, and pulled the meltagun from her back harness. It lit with a whine. Powdered grey dusted the weapon's silver and black iron casing.

'If any of you can hear this, I think that I got the last of the Prophets, but their family are still everywhere.' She turned, and took a step forwards as she spoke. Her foot crunched on broken rockcrete.

The creature came out of the mist in a single bound. She had an impression of pale skin, and reaching claws. She fired. A line of energy flicked into existence in front of the gun's muzzle. The air shrieked with heat. The creature exploded into black steam. She spat, and wiped cooked blood from her eyes.

It was going to take a while to clear the city, even if she pulled in half the planet's defence forces and the rest of the Arbitrators. It had been luck that she had found the Prophets, random chance playing her a strong hand, and her enemies a very bad one. She had been tracking a recidivist who had been dabbling in some very dangerous alien artefacts. That particular piece of heretic scum was still out there somewhere, but his trail had led her to Carsona and to dig into its under-culture, and there she had found the Prophets.

The Prophets were rogue psykers. They offered glimpses of the future to Carsona's burgeoning underclass. In a sense she supposed they offered hope, a chance to make better choices, and the desperate had paid in coins, in favours, or in whatever they had. The Prophets were slaves themselves. Others held the rogue psykers' chains, and took payment. Those hidden masters were the true criminals, reckless and greedy. A rogue psyker, even one who could just mewl out a few warp-addled prophecies, was a bomb just waiting to explode. And there had been a lot of Prophets in the city, all ticking down to doomsday, and all for wealth.

It was the pettiness that made her most angry.

She had found them though, and even though the city might have to be put to the flame, the other possibilities could have been far, far worse. The only question remaining was the big one – who had begun the whole thing? Somewhere behind the coin-takers and the mutant families, there had been a first mover in this heresy. Now that the Prophets themselves were done with, she would find out where this had begun.

Something hit her on the back and fell to the ground. She looked down. A fragment of rockcrete the size of a finger lay at her feet.

'Oh, Throne of Terra,' she muttered.

She felt another impact, harder this time. Then another and another, and suddenly she was covering her head, her cracked armour ringing as debris streamed past her as though drawn into the centre of a cyclone. A hooting bellow echoed through the fog. Her head snapped up as the sound rolled around her. Worms of mauve light were forming in the air. Screams were coming from the dust cloud. In her mind she could taste desperation and panic. The flavour of metal and rotting fruit itched at her teeth. She had misjudged, and misjudged badly – this was all about to become something much worse. Somewhere close by another uncontrolled psyker was awakening.

A chunk of girder whipped her legs from beneath her, and suddenly she was falling. She never hit the ground. Invisible ropes lashed around her, pulling her up and through the air. She could smell burning silk, and hear the rattle of insects in the rising wind. Ghost voices called to her, promising her infinity. She hardened her will, focusing in the way that had kept her alive on the Black Ships. She was stronger than the voices on the wind, stronger than the whispers which were telling her to submit, to leave her own mind open to the storm of possibility that was just a wish away.

A pillar of shattered stone came out of the mist and slammed into her. She heard a crack of breaking bone, and her left leg filled with fire. She did not scream. The invisible ropes vanished. She hit the ground, and tumbled across it. Black spots bloomed at the edge of her sight. She lay still. The pain was her world now, its edges defined by the walls of her will. Dust and debris streamed past her.

She was in the remains of a hab-block. Its broken structural pillars rose around her like snapped fingers. She flexed her left hand and found it still held the meltagun. She spat, and watched the blood-thickened phlegm whirl away on the wind. The psyker was close. She could feel its presence fizzing in her awareness like a fire made of munitions. She looked up, and saw the entrance to the broken hab's basement. Debris flew through the low door, and she could see light crackling in the darkness beyond.

She tried to move, and felt the pain shiver up her side as she shifted her left leg. She closed her eyes and found the threads of pain pulling through her mind, red and jagged. She began to ravel them together into a place which was separate from her, a place where she could ignore them. It was not a psychic ability, just a consequence of training and willpower.

It took her almost a minute before she could stand. Her bones crunched and ground in the sheath of her muscle as she limped towards the doorway down into the basement.

There were more mutants here, but most were already dead or dying. Splinters of rockcrete and metal riddled most of them. Those that still lived croaked at her as she passed. Quills had sprouted from their skin, and milk-white eyes had opened across their flesh. Tatters of overalls hung from them like the half-shed skins of snakes.

It was quiet in the basement. Above, the aetheric wind roared and the city pulled itself apart, but here everything was still. A man sat in the centre of the space. Detritus had gathered around him, small drifts of scorched paper, and ashes forming a spiral that covered the floor. Blue flames clung to the ceiling, silently rolling across the rockcrete without sound or smoke. The man looked up as Iobel entered. He was not old, but Iobel could tell that toil had stolen the best of his years. The flesh of his face sagged beneath the chequered pattern of his labour-glyph. Blood-shot eyes met Iobel's, and the pupils contracted to dots. Something rippled under his skin.

'What…' he rasped, his jaw chewing the air. 'What do I do?' Iobel took a step closer. 'I don't know what to do.' The man trembled. He was crying, she saw. 'I just want it to stop. Please. Is this a dream? I think it might be a dream. I just want it to stop.' He was shaking now. His cheeks were bright with tears. Iobel's finger tightened on the meltagun's trigger. The gun armed with a low whine.

He looked up sharply, his skin rippling. 'The Sons of Prospero,' he said, and his voice was a hollow rasp. 'I see Prospero's cities now cast down. Its sons call to me. As they are its sons we are theirs. We are their vengeance.' The last word echoed through the basement, rolling louder and louder. Dust and rock fragments rose from the floor. His face bulged. Iobel had an impression of fingers pressing against the taut skin.

She pulled the meltagun's trigger. The ray of heat hit the man in the centre of his chest. The fat and meat of his body vaporised an instant before his distorting skeleton exploded. A chattering scream split the air, rising like a flock of carrion. The blue fire surged across the ceiling, flames reaching like hands. Then it vanished, and Iobel was left in half darkness. A second later the debris began to hit the ground outside. It sounded like hail.

Iobel let out a breath, then collapsed to the floor.

Prospero. The word muttered through her thoughts, while a headache screamed behind her eyes. What had that meant? She had heard the ranting of madmen and demagogues, had taken the truth from thousands of heretics, and in all that time, she had learnt that there was rarely real truth in their words, and if there was it was best forgotten. But the dead psyker's last words rang in her thoughts, like a sound caught in an echo chamber. *The Sons of Prospero…*

'So that is how it began.' The voice came out of the dark. She twisted and brought the meltagun up. Darkness flashed to daylight as she fired. There was nothing there. Just the rockcrete support pillars, and the briefly distorted shadows. She twisted where she lay on the floor, extending her mind again, smelling the warp, feeling its wounded flesh as though it were her own skin. She stopped.

It was not there. The warp was gone. Beyond the skin of

sensations inside her mind there was just a void.

'This is not real. At least not in the sense most would consider it.' The voice was rich, measured. 'I thought it would take you longer to realise.'

A man stepped from behind one of the pillars, and her finger tightened on the trigger, but did not fire. Muscles bunched and flowed across his bared chest and shoulders. Silver and gold rings glinted from his scalp. Huge relaxed hands hung beside the handles of sheathed glaives. Half of his face looked like knotted leather, the scars shaped and folded into a tangle of dragons and serpents. He smiled at her with the other half. The sharpened points of his teeth showed in the twisted corner of his mouth.

It was Horeg, her retainer and bodyguard, or at least it looked just like him. But Horeg had no tongue and could not speak. 'I thought it would take us longer to reach this point,' said the man who was not Horeg.

Iobel squeezed the trigger of the meltagun. Nothing. She pulled it again, and still nothing. She felt a shiver whip through her. The man who was not Horeg stepped closer. He had blue eyes, bright blue eyes, the colour of a sea under sunlight. She tried to rise, but the pain in her leg suddenly grew. She could feel bone cutting into flesh. She gasped.

'As I said, this is not real.' He squatted down opposite her, muscles bunching in his haunches. 'But there are ways of making it feel that way.'

'Daemon,' she hissed, but even as she said it she was not

sure. This felt different, like something that had already happened.

'No, and besides you, I alone am real.'

She felt suddenly very cold.

'What is your name?' she said carefully.

'A good question – names have power, do they not? You want to see if I will answer, and if I do, and if I tell true, then you have the beginning of a weapon to cut your way out.' He smiled Horeg's twisted smile again. 'That is what you were intending, was it not? Resourceful, never yielding, always looking for a path to victory even when all is uncertain – you are a remarkable person, Selandra Iobel. Your mind is very strong, stronger than I would have thought possible for one still mortal.'

'Your name?' she growled, fighting down the pain, shutting out the panic and questions. This was a trick, one of the greater illusions of the daemons that infested the warp. It might not be real, but that did not mean that she had to submit to its lie.

He just smiled again, and shook his head. A line of silver rings rattled in the pierced flesh of Horeg's eyebrows.

'My name is Ahzek Ahriman,' he said. She froze, hair prickling across her arms as though touched by an icy wind. Her tongue was still in her mouth. Her eyes fixed on the bright blue points of his eyes, and suddenly she knew that she was not the Inquisitor Iobel who had purged the Prophets of Carsona, or at least she was not any more. Carsona had been a century and a half ago. She had not known the name Prospero then, had never heard of the Legion it had birthed, and had not known the name Ahzek Ahriman. He was right, this was the start. This moment, in the basement of a broken hab, had been the beginning of her journey from ignorance to enlightenment: the journey that would lead to Apollonia…

She shut the thought down as it formed, thrusting it away from her consciousness and burying it deep within her. That was what he was after, why he had come for her, why he was standing in the ruin of her past wearing the face of a loyal friend.

Ahriman nodded, and stood.

'This memory is close to the surface of your mind. The last things you would have remembered before this would have been the conclave, and the examination of my lieutenant. Your mind would have been fixated on me, and what I intended, but this memory is the first your mind comes to now. Why?' Ahriman looked at her. His gaze hit her like a physical blow. 'Because this is the start of the path that would bring you to me.'

Iobel suddenly felt as though a sliver of cold iron had slipped into her chest. Her mind flicked back through what Ahriman had said, through what seemed to be happening. This was happening in her mind, in her memories. There was a reason she was here, in this exact memory. This was not an interrogation, it was a breach into her memories, a hole bored into the outer layer of her mind. She closed her mouth, pulling her thoughts back, hardening her will.

Apollonia, he has come because of Apollonia…

She forced the thought deeper, burying it down, clamping layers of trained will over it. Numbness spread through portions of her consciousness, sections of her past suddenly becoming cold and dead. Names and facts she had carried for decades vanished from sight, swallowed down within her core.

It will not be enough, she thought, even as the walls grew and the memory blocks formed in her mind. *Not against the likes of him. Escape or death are the only ways to keep it from him. I must find a way to escape, or a way to die.*

'You can hide what I seek, inquisitor, but I will reach it.'

She opened her mouth to speak, but no sound came. The image of the hab basement was coming apart, bleeding into blackness like wet paint dribbling from a canvas. Only the blue eyes remained fixed, glittering as they pierced into her, glowing like cruel stars.

'Is that enough? Can he hear us?'

The voice came from above him. There was light too, sunlight perhaps, falling through a grey fog. He was not sure how far away the light was, though. The voice had sounded familiar, but he was not sure where he had heard it before.

'Probability of normal cognition and sensory awareness is high.' The second voice was a clatter of machinery. 'Adeptus Astartes physiology yields uncertainty quotient of–'

'He can hear us,' cut in the first voice. He heard the speaker lick his lips. 'Can't you?'

He did not reply. No, in fact he did not know how to reply. Could he make words like those he heard? He listened instead. He could hear a low hiss and wheeze, and a buzzing pulse almost below the level of hearing.

Active augmetics, said a voice within his head. He knew it was right but he did not know why. Yes, active augmetics, and… weaponry… no… yes, but something else as well… something low like the purr of power armour. And then the smells came. The thick reek of machine oil, and contraseptic, and wires running hot close to dead flesh. Breath, heavy and wet with the smells of polluted lungs, and spiced food, and burned caffeine, and–

'Can you get him to see?' asked another voice, a different voice. Female, further back from the other two. He could hear her withered chest in the bite of her words. He had heard that voice as well, but he could not remember where. Did it matter that he could not remember?

The fog and hazed sun vanished. The world that replaced them was pale blue. He could see a group of figures in a pool of light. Beyond the light everything was shadow, blurring to darkness that extended to an undefined distance. At the centre of the pool of light sat an object. At first he thought it was a machine, but then he saw the flesh under the mass of tubes. It was a body, clamped to a metal table, its skin and meat punctured by needle-tipped tubes, its breath the slow sucking of fluid through glass flasks. Its head was an eyeless mask of metal, haloed by cables, and with a black slot for a mouth. Two figures stood close by;

the nearest had no legs, but floated a metre from the floor. Two sets of glittering limbs hung from within the shadow of its robe, and three green eyes rotated slowly beneath its hood. The second figure was a human with a thin hard face and plain black robes. Further away a shrunken old woman in a gleaming exoskeleton stood beside a man with shining crystal eyes. Three hooded attendants stood behind the crystal-eyed man, linked to his spine and skull by thick cables. They were all looking at the figure bound into the machines at the room's centre.

He recognised them all, but was not sure why. None of them seemed to have reacted to him suddenly appearing on the opposite side of the chamber to them. He looked at each of them again, tried to blink but without success.

The floating four-armed figure turned to look at him. Its tri-lens eye rotated faster, then clicked to stillness.

'Subject can see us now.' The voice was the same machine clatter as before. They all turned to look at him then. The man with the thin face frowned, and raised a crooked finger.

'Closer.'

He floated forwards, passing over the figure buried under the snake swarm of sucking tubes. As he did so he saw a reflection glide across the glass of one of the fluid-filled vials: a polished skull without a lower jaw, a cluster of lenses filling its left eye socket. He kept on moving forwards, his mind suddenly tumbling. A servo-skull: he recognised it, and felt the shock roll through his narrow awareness.

The thin man's face was now level with his vision.

'Tell me, can you speak?'

No, of course he could not speak. The word echoed through him in mute frustration. He could not...

A sound gurgled up from the figure on the table.

'N... No.'

'Good,' said the thin-faced man, then gave a narrow smile that was not a smile.

He understood then, and knew why he was seeing through a servo-skull, knew why no one had looked at him when he first saw the chamber. He was the figure on the table. The injured flesh was his. The mouth speaking through the slot in the metal mask was his. And he had no eyes.

'Who are you?' he said.

'I,' said the thin-faced man carefully, 'am of no concern. You however, you are very much the focus of things.' He glanced at the hovering tech-priest. 'Though I understand your cognition is impeded at present, we will help you recover it.' He nodded carefully. 'We will help you remember.'

'Remember?'

'Yes, and let me start by giving you something. We will need more of you, much more, but you will need to lead us there, and for that we need somewhere for you to start. Your name.' The thin-faced man paused. 'Your name is Astraeos.'

Astraeos. The name rolled through him, like an echo of a shout carrying through fog. *Yes... Yes. That was... that is my name.*

'Why am I here?' asked Astraeos.

The thin-faced man folded his arms, a long finger resting on his jaw.

'A very good question,' he said.

IX
STORM CALM

The fleet waited in unquiet calm. Two dozen ships lay in the dark, their engines silent. Distant starlight lapped against their hulls, sketching their shapes in silver. Time ticked on and the millions who lived in the ships waited. On the bridges of the warships, in close cramped sub-decks, and in lightless bilges they waited. Most did not know why, but they felt it all the same, a tautness that stretched between heartbeats like a drum skin waiting for the first strike to fall.

In the steam-filled gorges between the *Sycorax*'s shield stacks, the mech-scavengers folded their brass wings over their bodies and hooted into the quiet. The Cyrabor gathered in their forge-fanes, clicking at each other in their half-machine tongue. In the domed library of the cruiser *Metatron* Gilgamos watched the stars beyond the viewports.

At his side three Rubricae stood, statue still, the light in their eyes dim.

In his quarters Hemellion sat, his legs curled under him, staring at the wick of a candle burning lower. He thought of the faces of those he had known, of the sun falling through mist on a cold morning. He thought of the son he had sent away from the capital so that he would learn of the world he would one day rule. For an instant he wondered where his son would be now, then he remembered that he knew. Tears rolled down his cheeks in silence, and he stared at the candle flame and waited.

Silvanus could not sleep. The drugs had stopped working, and would not work again, no matter how many he took. He sat on the hard floor of his oculary, looking at the circle of mirrored glass in his hands. He did not want to look into the reflection; he did not want the answer it would give. But even the hands that held the mirror gave an answer – they were changing. The bones were longer, the skin thinner, the nails finer and sharper. He raised the mirror, and looked at his face. The flesh was sagging under his eyes, and the pupil in his left eye had swollen to swallow the iris. The features of his face were disappearing, melting back into smooth flat skin. Slowly he lowered the glass.

How long? he wondered. *How long do I have before I cannot recognise myself?*

Carmenta drifted between wakefulness and the slumbering dreams of the *Sycorax*. Every now and then she could hear the Cyrabor talking as they stood around her throne.

They were talking about her, their half-machine voices clicking and purring like oiled cogs. They thought she could not understand them. They were saying that she would not last much longer, that the ship would take her soon, that the portents all said that her end was coming.

But I am the mistress. The slow, cold embrace of her ship folded over her. *I am* Titan Child. *I am* Sycorax. *I am a goddess of the void. How can I die?*

No answer came, just the whispers of the Cyrabor fading into the restless quiet.

And on and on through the fleet time drew taut, and the whispers passed between lips both high and low: What now? When would the waiting end? Where would the answer lead them?

The chainblade roared to life in Kadin's hands. Sparks rose from where the teeth caught the decking at his feet. After a second he stopped the blade's motor, and listened to the teeth slow to stillness. The corridor was quiet again.

Kadin watched the stillness of the corridor. The cracked glow-globes cast ragged pools of light over the metal gratings of the floor. At his back the door of the chamber through which Ahriman had passed days before remained shut. Kadin had heard sounds, sand blowing across metal, calls like the cries of birds, laughter even. Frost had leaked from the door seals and spiralled down the walls of the corridor. The door had glowed deep red then cooled with a tinkle of contracting metal. But even those moments had not broken the feeling that the whole ship and fleet had settled into a dreamless night.

Kadin turned his head and looked into the blackness at the other end of the corridor. He kept watching until it melted away from his eyes, and he could see the dot of the distant bulkhead in grey monochrome. He looked back down. He would have closed his eyes, but his eyelids would not stay shut any more, and his eyes saw regardless of how deep the darkness. He had grown in the dark, learned to fight in the dark, killed his first man in the dark. So many memories were gone, but he could still remember the warmth of the blood as it washed over his knife arm. The dark had been mother and father; the dark had been fear and the racing heart of the hunt.

What remains?

He triggered the resting chainblade. It rattled to life and noise filled the corridor, tumbling down the long space. He gunned it louder, felt it shake the metal of his grasp. He cut the motor, listening to the sound drain back to nothing.

A few memories of a child in the dark, afraid and hungry – that is what remains.

He gunned the chainblade again, and listened to the silence vanish as the metal teeth sang.

Maroth knelt. Above him, the daemon stirred, and its silver chains clinked. He raised the blind eyes of his helm. The daemon looked back, its own eyes like pools of mirror-black water. The host body had changed again. Maroth could see the red muscles beneath the stretched skin. Horns grew from beneath the temples of its head, reaching up like bare, twisted branches. Its lips had pulled back from its teeth, and it grinned with a cage of translucent needles. He could hear it breathing, the air sucking wetly, even though its chest was still.

Nothing here is as it seems, thought Maroth. *The silence is not silence, and the quiet is a storm waiting to break. I am not the broken husk of a sorcerer, and Ahriman is not my master.*

'Sire,' said Maroth, his voice strong and clear in the blue light of the burning lamps.

'Now,' said the daemon, its voice crackling like fire spreading through a forest. 'It begins now.'

'Yes, sire,' said Maroth.

Ignis watched the warlords arrive. He had chosen one of the main hangar decks for the meeting, partly because it was as far as he was willing to let the warlords onto his ship, and partly because he had every intention of just opening the blast doors to the void if all went as wrong as it might. Night filled the vast chamber, broken only by the pilot lights guiding the gunships to their stands on the deck. Credence stood just behind him. The automaton buzzed at him every few seconds.

'No,' Ignis muttered in reply. 'That course of action is unnecessary at this point.'

Credence gave a short clatter of binaric.

'In this case your threat assessment is in error,' said Ignis.

Another pause, another blurt.

Ignis glanced up at the automaton's sensor sockets. 'Yes, I am sure.'

He turned back to watching the warlords and their entourages cross the deck. They walked with the blunt arrogance of those trying not to show that they were unsure of why they were there. It almost made Ignis smile. All of them commanded ships and warbands in Ahriman's fleet. Most of them had been part of one Legion or another during the Great Crusade and subsequent rebellion against the Emperor. All of them had fought in the wars in and around the Eye of Terror, some for hundreds of years, some for much longer. And all of them held to no higher ideal than their own thirst for power. They came one by one, each flanked by a clutch of warriors that fumed violence like smoke from a fresh fire.

First came Hzakatris, so called Master of the Hellforged, clad in armour which looked like cancerous bone. He brought three of his blooded warriors with him, each one of them clad in Terminator plate looted from battlefields across the Eye. They clanked with poor repair as they moved. Behind him was Mavahedron, alone apart from his thrall-hounds, the beasts snarling at the ends of taut bronze chains. Sulipicis was last, face shrouded, his black and gold armour half hidden by tattered grey robes. A crescent of blank-helmed and black-armoured warriors flanked him. Each bore a two-handed sword before them. Ignis thought they looked like a mourning guard marching beside a corpse.

Ignis felt the muscles in his jaw tense as the three war-lords halted in a ragged arc before him. His eyes lingered on each of them, his second sight picking up their shifting auras: anticipation, caution, distrust, spite, and hunger. He had a sudden urge to tell Credence to open fire. This was the third of these parlays he had arranged, and by now he was feeling a sense of inevitability about the outcome of each.

It was Hzakatris who spoke first.

'What have you brought us here for?' His voice hissed and buzzed from the vox-grilles of his Terminator armour. He raised a clawed fist, and delicately ran a bladed finger across the horns which curled from the temples and jaw of his helm. 'Does Lord Ahriman still not deign to give us commands himself?'

'Ahriman,' said Ignis, and noticed Hzakatris's aura flicker at the absence of title, 'is locked in a room picking through the dirt of a witch's mind. He does not know you are here, and if he did he would not care. If he knows who you are it is only as a convenient resource for him to expend before those he values more.' Ignis allowed his lip to curl. 'You are less than dogs to him.'

Silence filled the gloom. Ignis waited, counting micro-seconds in his head. Chainblades spun alive, bolters clattered active and began to rise. Mavahedron let a length of chain rattle through his grasp, and the thrall-hounds bounded forwards with a wet howl.

+Hold!+ The thought flashed from Ignis. Frost formed in

the air around him, blanching Credence's carapace from a pace away. Everything in the chamber stopped moving. Arms halted as they aimed or drew weapons. Fingers froze on triggers. Ignis had to fight down the sudden wash of fatigue at the sending. He had never been more than an aspirant in the disciplines of telepathy, and even after the Rubric had remoulded his powers, such an exertion of will cost him. That, and the temptation to allow it to become more than just will was always there, waiting for him to succumb.

'I speak only truth to you,' he lied, forcing any trace of fatigue from his voice. 'And I speak it to you three alone.' They were all watching him now, weapons not lowered but rising no further. 'Ahriman thinks nothing of you, if he thinks of you at all. You are useful to him only because you compensate for his weakness with your strength. Without you, he would be nothing. When we attacked Vohal it was you three who were at the bloody edge of the void fighting, you who spent the strength of your warriors. And before that, on Guncua and the Exodus from Samatis, it was you in the vanguard, was it not?' He watched their auras flicker, some with rage at the insult of his words, some with pride, all with resentment. They wanted to believe what he was saying because it was what they already believed.

Mavahedron nodded once, slowly.

'You speak truth,' he said, voice creaking like an old tree in the wind. 'But why do you speak it?'

'Because I wish your aid,' said Ignis. 'Because I wish you to help me destroy Ahriman.'

The laughter began as a dry rustle, and then rose to a pulsing croak. Everyone in the room looked towards Sulipicis. The hooded figure continued to laugh, then drew a breath and spoke.

'The jester believes himself the king,' said Sulipicis, his voice still edged with laughter. 'Your breed cannot help it, can you? You are like fish that can only swim in a sea of treachery.'

Ignis turned his head to stare at Sulipicis. Behind him Credence mirrored the gesture with a whir of gears. Sulipicis gave another snort of laughter.

'I did not say that I refused to listen to what you say. And as for the rest – I meant it only as a compliment.'

'Why should we help you?' said Hzakatris. Ignis turned to look at him. Rage still flickered around Hzakatris. Ignis saw it form eddies in the warp as it bled from the Terminator's mind.

'Because I will divide the surviving fleet between you three when it is done.'

None of them moved or spoke.

'And,' said Ignis. 'I will gift a sorcerer of my Legion to each, blood bound to serve you alone.'

'You would betray your brothers so?'

Ignis made himself smile. He was not sure if the gesture was right, but he had practised it, and it had worked each of the other times; that it was needed a third time pleased him.

'My Legion is dead,' he said. 'I have no brothers.'

He had them then, he was sure. Now all that remained was to explain what he needed of them. How they would make no move until they had an advantage. How they had to follow his orders alone. And then he would have to reassure them that he would deal with the *Sycorax*...

The pattern of thoughts snagged in his mind.

Hzakatris was shaking his head, the horns of his helm scraping the collar of his armour.

'No,' Hzakatris's voice grated through the gloom. 'Ahriman is a deceiver, and an arrogant bastard, but I would sooner trust him than you. I will not join you in this folly.'

It took two seconds for everyone else in the room to realise that Hzakatris had just ensured that either he or all of them had to die. And two seconds was too slow. Hzakatris's bolters came up. Mavahedron and Sulipicis seemed frozen by surprise. Hzakatris squeezed the trigger.

'Kill protocol!' shouted Ignis.

Fire spat from Hzakatris's bolters. Credence slammed forwards. Rounds exploded off the automaton's carapace. Hzakatris's Terminators were moving now, guns clacking as they armed. Credence fired, the cannon on its back shrouding the Terminators in explosions. Hzakatris burst from the fire, fist raised and writhing with lightning. Credence smashed its hand into the warlord's helm. Its fingers closed with a cough of pistons, and it yanked the warlord up as the cannon on its back rotated down. It fired.

Hzakatris's head and helm vanished in a spray of explosive rounds. Credence threw the armoured corpse aside in time to meet the first of Hzakatris's bodyguards with a kick. The Terminator reeled back, and Credence kicked again, very hard on the exposed flesh of its face. The other two came on, chainfists and powerblades hissing and buzzing. Credence spread its arms wide. Power fields snapped into existence around its fists. The Terminators' charge faltered as, too late, they realised what the automaton intended.

Credence brought its fists together. The Terminator caught in the double blow lived for long enough to feel his armour fracture, and hear the roar as Credence triggered the flamer units bound to its wrists. Fire poured inside the cracked armour, and the Space Marine within became a soup of cooked flesh and bone. The automaton pivoted, holding the dead Terminator like a club, and used him to smash his comrade to the ground. Credence came forwards before the Terminator could rise, and punched down again, and again with perfect machine rhythm.

Ignis let the automaton mash the Terminator for nine seconds.

'Enough,' he said. 'Kill protocol revoked.' Credence straightened, and walked slowly back to stand behind Ignis. Once stationary it gave a lower series of clicks. Ignis looked up at it, eyebrow raised. The automaton's armour was chewed by bolt fire and steaming with blood.

Ignis looked back to the heap of broken armour and pulped meat that had been Hzakatris. It was a shame. He had been sure Hzakatris would turn against Ahriman. A frown formed on his forehead as he considered the imperfection in the pattern of events. It was an unfortunate, but luckily minor flaw.

Ignis shook his head, and looked at the other two warlords. Neither had moved. 'So, do we have an agreement?'

Grimur watched the fire and tried to remember the cold of Fenris. The hall at the heart of *Hel's Daughter* rumbled around him with the voices muttering around a dozen different fires. Once there had been many more fires, and the circles around each had been five deep, and the hall had rolled with voices. But that had been long ago, on a ship now lost to the storms. The hunt for Ahriman and his kin had claimed both ship and comrades. Those who clustered around the fires now spoke in the silences between words. They all wore their armour since the hunt had begun, only shedding it for repair. They were fewer, and older in years and scars. Firelight touched grey hairs, and glinted on teeth grown long through time.

The chamber itself was black from the smoke of the fires. Pillars of raw iron reached up from the floor, their surfaces reshaped into dragons which bit and clawed the distant ceiling. Runes marked the walls, cut into the bare metal by axe blows. The names of those who had fallen on the hunt spoke to Grimur from those marks.

They rarely gathered like this now, and when they did they all knew that they were facing a turning in the hunt. The people of Fenris called such a moment 'the laughter of the wind', when the wind carrying the scent of the prey changed direction, and all might be lost by a single wrong decision. That was why they had gathered beside the fires, both here and on the other ships. The wind was laughing and leading them into a storm, so they looked into the fires and spoke, and remembered sagas no longer told.

Sycld stirred at Grimur's side, tilting his thin face towards his lord.

'You must tell them soon, jarl,' said the Rune Priest in a wet hiss.

'Be silent,' growled Grimur, without looking around. Sycld pulled away, but Grimur could feel the priest's eyes still on him.

We are the wights of the Underverse, thought Grimur. He gulped the bitter liquid from his drinking bowl. The fire danced in his eyes. *We are the night walkers. There is no saga waiting for us, just death at the end of the chase, and the silence of snow falling to cover our skulls.*

Carefully he put the bowl down on the floor. The murmur of voices faded to silence. Grimur began to rise. Faces turned to look at him, amber irises reflecting gold in the dim light. His hand tapped his throat, and the vox pickup activated in the collar of his armour. Across each of his ships, the Wolves of his pack would hear him, and would see him stand in their halls as a hologhost. His axe came up with him. Its edge was a crescent of reflected firelight.

He looked around, meeting the fire-touched eyes, feeling the twisted muscles of his back creak as he moved. He paused, tasting the tang of the smoke, and the scent of the blood mixed with the liquor in the drinking bowls. Fat hissed as it fell into the fires from charring meat. He opened his mouth, and felt his teeth unmesh.

'We remain,' he said into the silence. 'No others stand with us. Others fall, their blood soaks into the snow, their cries fade behind us, but we remain. The years turn, the winters pass, and come again, and still we run on. Others forget the crimes of the past, others forget what was, but we remember.' Grimur brought his axe up in front of him, and let his eyes touch the knotted serpents behind its cutting edge. 'We remember. We run and we do not tire, not if a thousand winters pass.' He looked up again, feeling the stillness amongst his warriors, the breaths paused to hear again the words they had heard so many times before. 'We are vengeance,' he said.

The growls come then, rising through sharp teeth to shake the air. For a second Grimur felt as though he was back at his father's side standing in the halls of the Fang, hearing the mountain ring to the sound of his brothers' voices. He had been young then and was old now, and the growls that shook the air were fewer and heavy with time. This was not the cry of the young wishing for blood; it was the cry of old wolves reminding each other of what they had been and what they still were. He let his axe fall to his side and the cries faded.

He looked up and nodded. Somewhere in the shadows one of the last Iron Priests saw the gesture and called on the spirits of the ship. A sphere of green light appeared in the dark, hanging above the fires. All eyes turned to it. Grimur's ships had been hanging in the dead space between stars for weeks, waiting to hear where the hunt would carry them next. Grimur had kept his plans to himself. It was better that the rest of the pack were told when there was little time to brood on it.

'The Cadian Gate,' he said. 'Our seers have walked the paths of dreams and seen that the prey has passed out of the Eye. He and his slave-kin are within the Imperium, and where they have gone we must follow.' He paused. There was no shock, no ripple of surprise or unease, but he could feel the change in the hall, the shift in the pack's mood. The skin of his back prickled, and the ice at his core hardened. 'They have taken a serpent's way through the storms. Such ways are closed to us, so we must pass through the Gate.'

'If it is guarded, we will not pass.' It was Halvar. The pack leader brought his armoured hand up to his face, and ran his thumb slowly over the scar tissue where his nose had once been. His eyes stayed fixed on the projection. After a long moment he turned to look at Grimur. Lifetimes of war on the borderlands of the Underverse lived in that look.

'We will pass. A scattered fleet flees from the deep Eye, running on the clear tides towards Cadia. They are desperate, wild and panicked and will make Cadia in two weeks. That is when we will also reach the Gate, and slip through while the beasts occupy the blades of any who guard it.'

'And if we do not pass unseen?' said Halvar, and Grimur knew that he was just speaking what all would be thinking.

'What if the guardians of the Gate see us, and bar our path?'

Grimur shivered, and heard his axe clink against the thigh plate of his armour. It was the question that he had come here to answer. The question he knew he would have to answer as soon as Sycld had told him that Ahriman had left the Eye. *What if we must face those who serve the Emperor, and what if they see us as enemies not friends?*

'Then we cut them down,' he said.

X
RECALL

The sky was the grey of beaten iron. Iobel looked up and watched lightning writhe at the base of the anvil-headed clouds. The air was clammy against the exposed skin of her face. It tasted of storm charge and rust. She let out the breath she had held, and looked down. The dead world sank away from her in grey drifts of ash. The jagged teeth of mountains rose in the distance, while sharp daggers of grime-coated crystal covered the distance between like shards from the broken blade of a god.

'Rain's coming,' said Linisa, her lilting voice crackling across the vox. Iobel glanced at her acolyte. Linisa's armour was red and massive, like corded muscle cast in ceramite and exotic metal. The idea of the wisp-thin girl within the hulking suit was almost comical. Almost. The gun tubes ringing Linisa's wrists only added to the effect. 'You will

want to get your helmet on,' said Linisa. 'The scans say
these storms are acidic, bad enough to burn to the bone.'

As though on cue the rain started. A single fat drop
exploded on the ash and left a crater of grey mud. Iobel
clamped her helmet over her head. The rain started to pour
from the sky. The ground around her was a dancing sheet
of liquid. She looked down at her gauntleted hands. The
white lacquer was already blistered, and the grey ceramite
beneath was fuming as the rain poured between her fingers. A bolt of lightning fell amongst the forest of crystal
shards, and the grey world became white.

'You say we have to cross that?' said Linisa.

'Yes,' said Iobel.

'Could the gun-cutter not have dropped us closer?'

Iobel shook her head.

'Atmospherics are too unstable.'

'But walking is safer?' Linisa raised her hands before Iobel
could reply. 'Just saying.'

Iobel turned her gaze back to the broken land. In truth
she was far from sure this was wise, but it had taken four
years to find that this place still existed, and three times
that time to reach it.

Prospero, the world that had sired an order of traitors and
sorcerers. She had been searching for it ever since Carsona,
and here it was, beneath her feet. It had been a long journey, and she had learned things that she would have killed
others for knowing. The Thousand Sons, the breaking of
the Edict of Nikaea, Magnus the Red – all now loomed in

her dreams, and with them the rasped words of a dying psyker linking them like a chain binding the present to the past.

She felt the psychic thread tug at her mind, pulling her out there into the desolation which had once been a great city. It had latched onto her mind as soon as she had set foot on the planet. It was not a voice, more like a path left by the passing of others, a path that had been left for her, or those like her, to find.

'You are sure there is something here?' asked Linisa.

Iobel said nothing, and Linisa had been with her for more than long enough to know what that meant. 'All right,' she sighed. 'Best get moving.'

It took them an hour to cross two miles. The rain had turned the ash into a grey mire. Even with the augmented strength of their armour each step was a fight against the sucking tug of the mud. A white fog had risen soon after the rain had stopped. The readings on Iobel's helmet display said it was both toxic and corrosive. She did not need the readings to tell her the last part, one glance at Linisa was enough. Her acolyte's armour was grey, the red lacquer stripped clean from curved plates.

Linisa swore every step of the way, moving through colourful and creative phrases in High and Low Gothic and the spire tongue of her birth hive. Iobel said nothing to stop the stream of invective; it gave her something else to focus on besides the voices of the dead.

The ghost voices had begun as soon as they entered the

fields of broken crystal. They rose in Iobel's mind, roaring with rage, crying out in pain, babbling, pleading. She closed them out, but they always found a way back in, and each time they were stronger. Several times they almost drowned out her awareness of the psychic trail. She was starting to wonder if she had made a serious mistake. The whole landscape, from grey sky to grey ground, seemed to press on her mind. She was not even sure what she was expecting to find; nothing remained here now, just the shards of crystal cities, and the ashes of its past.

'What was that?' Linisa's voice cracked across the vox, sharp and sudden. Iobel reached for the boltgun clamped to her back. She twisted, trying to see what Linisa had seen. The acolyte had moved close to her, arms raised, weapon tubes focused on the fog. Iobel instinctively extended her senses beyond her mind, and then recoiled.

'Turn back now. You must turn back.'

The voice was so clear that it sounded like her own. She shook her head to clear it. The fog was thick around them. Linisa was braced, legs sunk to the knee in the ash mud. Iobel could hear her own breathing fill her helm. She shifted her grip on the boltgun in her hands.

The figure reared from the grey sludge. Its body was a ragged sculpture of torn armour and heaped bones. It had no head, and only the vaguest similarity to a human shape. Black liquid poured from it. White ice crackled across its growing limbs. A roar of countless anguished voices filled Iobel's mind. She reeled, blood spattering the inside of her helm. The sludge around the creature froze hard. It lunged forwards with a limb made of cracked armour plates and broken blades. Linisa fired from behind Iobel. A deluge of bolts hammered into the creature, ripping it into chunks with explosions. Its arm tore away. Rounds exploded within its torso, and for a second it seemed to shiver. Linisa shook as her armour absorbed the recoil. The creature staggered, its roar now a shriek.

Linisa moved forwards, firing without pause, frozen ground splintering before her. The creature lunged again with its remaining arm. The acolyte ducked, but not fast enough. The creature's fist lifted her from the ground and tossed her into the fog.

The creature turned to Iobel, its chewed body glowing with pale light. She caught herself as she stumbled backwards, and aimed her boltgun. The creature raised an arm of debris. Iobel squeezed the trigger. The boltgun roared until the firing pin clicked on an empty chamber.

It took several deep breaths before she remembered to release the trigger. The creature lay in the mud, a heap of bones and armour. Steam rose from it as the witch ice melted. Iobel moved closer. Her mental senses were silent. The creature was dead, as much as something which had not truly lived could die. Looking down at the remains she recognised the shape of broken power armour within them. Specks of red lacquer clung to the deep recesses of some, ice grey to others.

'So walking was still a good idea,' said Linisa. Her battle

rig was dented, but still seemed to be in one piece. If anything the damage just enhanced the armour's air of blunt brutality. She stopped beside Iobel, and looked down at the remains of the creature. 'Please tell me this is not what we came here for.'

'No,' said Iobel.

'Hmmm. What is it, anyway?'

'An echo of the past,' said Iobel. 'A cluster of shredded souls trapped at the moment of death, like flotsam caught in an eddy. So much was done here – it is no longer just a planet, it is a scar in the warp.' She straightened up and looked back into the fog, reached for and found the tug on her psychic senses. 'We keep going.'

It took them another hour to find it. When they did Linisa just stared, and muttered a sequence of swear words in a dozen dialects. It had been buried in a small adamantine box at the base of a toppled obelisk. A faint psychic aura pulsed from within the box. Iobel had hesitated before opening it, but when she did, she almost laughed. She lifted out what she found, and held it up to the faint light. It was an 'I' crossed by three horizontal bars moulded in polished adamantine; the symbol of the Inquisition. A brilliant blue carbuncle sat at the symbol's centre, winking in the weak light like a single, watching eye.

'What–' began Linisa.

'It is an answer, of sorts,' said Iobel, watching fire kindle at the heart of the blue gem. 'It says that others have followed the same path I have, and that there are more answers for those who have come this far. If they can find them.'

'That's it?'

'It's enough,' said Iobel.

The fog froze. Everything stopped moving. The low sounds of distant rain and thunder cut out.

Iobel lowered the Inquisitorial symbol. She reached for her boltgun.

'Enough,' said a low, deep voice which came from Linisa, but did not belong to her.

Linisa paced forwards slowly, her movements feline smooth despite the bulk of her armour. Cold light burned in the eyes of her helm. Iobel had her bolter in her hand, but she already knew that nothing would happen if she pulled the trigger.

Linisa crouched down, and scooped up a handful of grey ash from the ground. Iobel blinked. Something was screaming inside her, the voice which told her to turn back – a voice which sounded like her own.

Linisa let the dust fall from her fingers.

'The bones of a Legion buried beneath the ashes of all they had built.'

'Ahriman,' breathed Iobel.

'It was enough, wasn't it, to come here, to touch the first grave of my Legion? In this moment you knew that everything you had discovered of us was true.' Ahriman pointed at the Inquisitorial symbol still clutched in Iobel's hand. 'And that bauble was enough to lead you further, and to continue your hunt for the *truth*.' Ahriman stood, the form of Linisa blurring as it moved, spiralling into a rising cyclone of dust. 'And here and now, it is enough for me to do the same.'

Iobel was shaking where she stood. The fog and ground were gone. She stood in emptiness. The shape of Linisa had vanished. Two cold points of lights shone in the spinning cloud of dust before her. She felt her will try to hold her where she was.

'No!' she managed to shout, before the storm of dust enveloped her.

'Why am I here?'

Astraeos watched as the man with the thin face stepped closer.

'You are here because you are a traitor,' said the man in a flat voice. 'You are here because your master deserted you. You are here to give us everything you know.'

'A traitor... I am no traitor.'

The man shook his head. Behind him the crone and the glass-eyed man exchanged glances.

'I am sorry, perhaps you believe that now. Perhaps you believed it before, but what you believe does not alter the truth. You have broken oaths, you have embraced powers that wish only mankind's slavery, and you have drawn arms against those who fight to preserve humanity. You are a servant of ruin, Astraeos.'

'I...' The word caught in Astraeos's throat. '...cannot remember.'

'No, your mind was damaged. Though if you can remember, you will.'

Astraeos did not reply. His head was rolling with fog. Who was he? He recognised the name that the man had given him, but was that really his name? Other images and half recollections drifted close to his awareness, then dissolved back into vapour. Memories were there. He could sense them waiting just beyond his perception, like the buildings of a broken city looming out of the fog. He wanted to know who he was, and why he was here, bound to a metal slab. He had been here for some time, but he was not sure how long. He remembered that there had been questions before, that there had been pain, but he could not remember the details or how long that cycle of pain and questions had lasted. There was just a dull aching feeling that he had been asked these questions before, and asked the same questions in return.

The thin-faced man had not moved; Astraeos had the impression that he was waiting.

'What is your name?' said Astraeos.

'My name is not the question at hand,' said the man, and glanced behind him towards the crone and the crystal-eyed man. 'I am an inquisitor. Think of me as that if you must.'

'Inquisitor,' said Astraeos carefully. Somewhere in the fog of his memory something moved and creaked. The word meant something to him, something more than its obvious meaning. 'You call me a traitor, and think that I will tell you whatever you ask?'

'Do you believe that you are a traitor?'

'No,' said Astraeos without a pause.

'Then you have your answer.'

'I cannot remember who I am, or why I might be here.' Astraeos gave a tired laugh. 'What do you wish to know?'

'Everything,' said the inquisitor. He ran his hand over his forehead, and let out a carefully controlled breath. 'Let's begin with what you can remember – your name is Astraeos.'

'No,' said Astraeos. In his mind he felt a pocket of recollection open before him. It felt good to speak, as though by talking his memory became clear. 'It *is* my name, but it was not my first name.' He stopped, licked his dry lips. Images and sensations filled him. He could see faces, and smell a swirl of scent that had not been real to him for a long time, but was real for him now, more real than the face of the inquisitor, or the ache in his head. He began to speak, and his voice seemed to be coming from someone and somewhere else.

'When I was born they called me Mellik. There was a lot of smoke when I was small, and the sky was always the colour of copper. I remember towers going up to the clouds. They were covered with lights, and bled fire. I think I had sisters. I don't remember what home was called, or what anyone else was called. I just remember that I was called Mellik. I can still hear someone calling that name. I used to hide, find a corner on the roofs, or crawl into passages, and just wait for it to be quiet. I didn't like people, and they didn't like me either. I was different, everyone knew it, even though I never told them. I could hear them, though. I could feel their fear and hate touch my skin when they looked at me.'

He paused. Around him the fragments of memory turned, showing him glimpses of faces, of voices. He watched them, knowing they had all meant something to him, but unable to grasp what.

'Most of your kind cannot remember such things,' said the inquisitor. The images of the past dimmed.

'My kind?' asked Astraeos. The inquisitor nodded.

'A psyker of the Adeptus Astartes.'

'Is that what I am?'

The inquisitor raised an eyebrow.

'You remember how to speak, you remember that this is a servo-skull, but you do not remember what you are.' He smiled, showing silver teeth. 'What else do you remember, Astraeos?'

Astraeos compulsively tried to close his eyes. Shutters closed over the servo-skull's eye-lenses in response. Static-laced blackness replaced the sight of the chamber.

'I remember the day the ships came. They came through the grey sky, bigger than the towers, bigger than anything. They took the light away. I knew they were coming for me, even before the hailers started calling, I knew. I hid, but they found me. People I knew helped them, told them where the strange child liked to hide. When I woke I was in a different place. There was screaming and pain, and darkness and more light than I had ever seen. It stayed that way for a long time. Then I remember being taken to another place where there was more pain. There were questions. There were tests...'

His voice ran out. In his mind he saw men and women in tight buckled masks pulling him on a chain. There had been machines, and screams that went through the walls and into his dreams. It went on and on, but never the same twice. Only the memory of fear and pain was the same.

'Can you remember more?'

'Yes,' he said, slowly. The memories were coming faster now, the mist shredding as he ran through his past. 'I remember another ship, and this time I was alone. The room was silver. It was cold. Then the next thing I remember was a giant made of black armour. He had a skull for a face and red eyes. There was a second giant, but he wore blue, and his... his eyes. I felt them on the inside of my skull. They said...'

'His brain output is fluctuating,' said the tech-priest from close by, voice rising in volume over the sudden chiming of machines.

The memory stopped. The images snagged and juddered. Astraeos wanted to scream and did not know why. He just knew that something in this memory, something which had been with him there all along in the dark, and light, and pain, was trying to live again. He recognised it then. It was terror, it was the memory of a child's terror trying to manifest in a mind that could no longer understand it, that was no longer human.

In his mind's eye, the Space Marine in blue was staring at him with eyes like polished ice. The one in the skull helm was reaching down, raising Astraeos's face to look into the skull's stare. The fingers of the gauntlet were worn, their touch cold.

'They said…' He heard the words come from his lips again. Everything was becoming slow, and soft, and dark.

'Yes? What did they say, Astraeos?'

'Excessive brain activity. Secondary bleeding inside skull. Subject losing consciousness.'

The darkness grew around him and the image of the two Space Marines pulled away, becoming an image seen through a pinprick in a sheet of oblivion.

He felt his mouth open, and his tongue form halting words.

'They said I would become an angel.'

The fortress was grown of ice. Its walls rose in a ring of turquoise and white blade edges. At its centre a lone landing pad sat like a coin dropped onto a frozen lake. Gun turrets surrounded the pad, their barrels swathed in white fabric and their shapes hidden by pale nets. Looking down at the fortress from the lighter's windows, Iobel had thought the surface structure looked like a crown of clouded crystal. Now, shivering despite her fur-lined cloak and thermal bodyglove, she thought it looked nothing like a crown, and more like one of the most desolate places she had ever seen.

'Beautiful,' muttered Cavor, through chattering teeth. The

nihilator's shoulders were hunched beneath his thick crimson coat, his head sunk so deep into the black fur collar that he looked like a troglodyte. Beside them the lighter's engines began to rise in pitch as it prepared to lift off again. It would return when they were done; nothing lingered on the polar ice longer than it had to. Iobel found herself thinking fondly of the lighter's machine-scented warmth.

The planet that they stood on was called AV-213. Tucked away on the frayed edges of the Halo Margins, its equatorial belt was a strip of foetid jungle bound by dry deserts which stretched to the planet's bloated polar caps. People could have lived there, could have scraped some form of life out of the dirt and clung onto it, but they did not. Only a few members of the Inquisition knew of the planet, and a small circle within the Ordo Malleus kept it that way. AV-213 was one of the quiet and forgotten places used by those who fought the enemies that humanity could not know existed. Iobel knew that much, but what waited for her here she did not know.

Two decades had passed since she had set foot on Prospero, and in that time she had seemed to come no closer to real answers. She had tried, of course. She had bent all of her subtle arts to trying to find out the source of the Inquisitorial emblem left on the dead world. She had found only a suspicious absence of information. That had only convinced her to dig deeper; an absence of information was, after all, sometimes as significant as information itself. But two decades of investigation had yielded nothing, until, when she was almost at the point of turning back, a message had come. A mind-blanked courier had brought her a slip of parchment in a puzzle tube covered in Prosperine runes. Inside was a slip of parchment, and a wafer of explosive designed to detonate if anyone had forced the tube open. On the parchment had been the location of AV-213, a clearance code, and a single line of handwritten script: 'the door to the truth stands open'.

The lighter's ramp began to close, and its engines kicked ice dust into the air. The servitor pilot burbled a stream of machine code over the vox, and then it was lifting away. When it was ten metres above the pad, its thrusters fired. Iobel felt the blast of heat wash across her face, and was briefly grateful for the warmth. Then the lighter was gone, a pale speck rising into the cold blue sky. She looked down. They were alone, the expanse of the sky and ice pressing close around them. The wind gusted across the landing pad.

'I don't like this,' said Cavor, turning to look around them. She heard a low click and knew that he had eased a set of pistols from the holsters beneath his coat. She said nothing, but clicked through channels on her vox-bead: a low hiss answered her from each channel. She stopped after a while and waited. If it had not been for the metal of the landing pad, and the covered gun emplacements, she would have thought they were in the wrong place.

'Selandra Iobel.' The voice came from so close that she felt her muscles tense. Cavor spun, guns rising. 'Peace, Cavor,' said the voice, strong but calm.

She turned more slowly than Cavor, careful not to seem hurried or surprised. A tall, thin man stood a few metres from them. He wore a quilted black bodyglove without mark or symbol. There was a square hole in the ice-covered ground just behind his feet. She nodded slowly, but did not smile. She was pleased to notice that Cavor had not lowered his guns.

'Yes, and who are you?' she replied. The thin man smiled.

'I am glad you came,' he said smoothly, and turned to Cavor. 'You are as fast as your reputation, Cavor. What is your kill count now?'

'Three hundred and thirty-three,' said Cavor, keeping his guns steady. The thin man kept his expression fixed, the pleasant smile in place.

'Another eighty-nine and you will be the apex of your clan, will you not?' The man gave a cough of mirthless laughter. 'At least you would be if you had not broken their first and second edicts.'

Cavor nodded, but Iobel could see the muscle twitch in his jaw. He never talked about why he had left his gun-clan, and she had thought that she alone knew the reasons. That this man knew as much as she about her own acolytes made her more than tempted to give the command word and see Cavor shoot the patronising bastard's eyes out.

'To answer your question, Iobel – I am Inquisitor Castus Izdubar, and it is very good to finally meet you.'

Iobel kept her face still, and her eyes cold, but felt the pulse of her blood rise in her veins. Izdubar, that was a name she knew, a name that was spoken in the circles of the Ordo Malleus with respect; and when it was spoken it was not as Inquisitor Izdubar, but Lord Inquisitor Izdubar, Convenor of the Ephisian Conclave, Watcher of the Cadian Marches.

Izdubar nodded slowly, as though in acknowledgement of her thoughts.

'I think you have something of mine, do you not?' he said and reached out with a gloved hand. Iobel nodded stiffly, and fumbled the Inquisitorial symbol she had found on Prospero from around her neck. She felt Cavor's thoughts tense with readiness as she placed the symbol in Izdubar's hand. Izdubar looked at the symbol, tilting it slowly so that the blue gem at its centre caught the light.

'We should get inside,' he said. 'Once the sun sets it gets even colder.' He turned and moved towards the open hatch in the ground.

'Why am I here?' she asked before he had taken a step. He turned back, glanced at Cavor's still levelled pistols, and then back to Iobel.

'For answers, Iobel. Isn't that why you went to Prospero, why you have searched out all you can find about the Thousand Sons, and why you have been looking for us for the last two decades? Well, now we are here, and so are the beginnings of answers.'

'Who are *we*?' she said, without moving.

'A circle of a few who have seen what you have, and who have walked down the same paths in search of the only weapon which can cut our enemies – knowledge.'

'And what is here?' she said, flicking her eyes across the ice-bound landing pad.

'You will have to see.' Izdubar turned and began to descend the steps into the ground. Iobel glanced at Cavor. The nihilator was watching Izdubar's retreating back, his face utterly still, his augmetic eyes glowing with cold light. She paused, blinked and shook her head. She had the sudden sense that she had been here before. She opened her mouth to speak.

'We follow?' asked Cavor. She nodded slowly, still uncertain. Cavor watched her, still not moving.

'Yes,' she said at last. 'We follow.'

She shook herself and stepped through the hatch. Behind her Cavor lowered his pistols, the light in his eyes shifting from green to blue, then he followed the inquisitors beneath the ice.

XI
LAND OF LIES

'He is lying,' said a voice. It was a dull voice, washed of emotion, as though the speaker thought greater expression wasteful.

Astraeos tried to open his eyes, and then remembered that he had no true eyes any more. His head still ached, just as it had since he had first woken, but his thoughts felt clear. Memories of before he had fallen unconscious snapped into focus. He knew other things now, though he was not sure why. He knew from the sound of the voices that the chamber extended far beyond the pool of light around him. He knew that besides damage to his skull, his body was trying to heal deep burns to his back and legs. He knew that there were charged and readied power weapons within twenty paces of where he lay. He knew all this and he knew that he was here because the Inquisition said he was a traitor. It could not be true, he knew that, but then why would they have taken him? Why would they have questions?

'No, no I don't think he is,' said another voice. It was the voice of the inquisitor, Astraeos realised. 'Damage often leaves part of the structure of the mind standing while the rest is buried or swept away. And before you say it, Erionas, I am not going to ask Cendrion to go into his mind. I want what might remain inside, and I want it without further damage.'

'This costs time.' Another voice, female this time, the words rattling in an old and damaged throat.

'I am aware of what it costs,' said the inquisitor. 'Cendrion looked into his mind once, and said that it was like a half-collapsed building. We can reach the deepest layer, but we must be careful or it will collapse again. If this fails there are other methods, but with each of them we diminish the chances of success. That is what we want here, isn't it, to find what Ahriman intends?'

'He is awake,' said the machine voice of the tech-priest. Astraeos heard the crinkle of fabric as people turned, then the sound of steps as they came closer.

'Let him see,' said the inquisitor.

Light suddenly filled his sight, and he saw the inquisitor standing beside his body.

'I am no traitor,' said Astraeos, and then coughed. His body jerked against the restraints, and he tasted wet iron in his throat.

The inquisitor's face showed no response.

'What do you remember?'

Astraeos paused. He could see more now, things opening up in front of his mind's eye like the features of a dark room before a lamp beam. He paused. He did not know how he came to be here, but he knew that he was not a traitor. He was an angel of death; he had been forged to serve the Imperium mind, body and soul. What could he remember that could undo that purpose?

'Tell us,' said the inquisitor.

I must answer. Only the heretic refuses to speak the truth. They will see that I am true, they must see.

He told them what he could. He told them of the world that had remade him. Much of it was a fog of confusion at first. Details emerged, and then sank back into the murk of his mind when they were on the tip of his tongue. He talked until he could not remember why he was talking. He told them of the land beneath the mountains, of the echoing dark, and the sound of his heart beating to itself. His brothers came from that underworld, children taken from the people who lived out of the light of the sun. He told them of the towers of the fortress rising towards the sun which burned without end in the cobalt sky.

As he spoke more came to him, images and truths coming to his mind and lips with sudden clarity. It was as though his mind was a ball of unravelling thread. He remembered the Three Towers of Truth, at the summit of which each aspirant swore their great oaths. He remembered the feeling of his bolt pistol in his hand, the names of all its other bearers carved into its grip. He remembered the first time he killed, and the first time he smelled the red offal stink of a battlefield. He remembered the feeling of armour. He remembered that he had become a Space Marine.

Astraeos had fallen quiet. He could taste metal in his mouth, and his skull ached to the core. The servo-skull that had become his eyes twitched to look at the figures that stood behind the thin man. There were three of them, bent under ragged robes covered in symbols stitched in golden thread. They had always been there, but now they were closer, as though they shuffled a step nearer each time he remembered a new detail. Astraeos did not like them. Something about them made him wish he could shoot them.

'Yes?' said the thin-faced man.

'What is your name?' asked Astraeos. The ache in his head was getting worse. He wanted to blink, but had no eyes. Something was rising into his thoughts; he could feel it spilling into the edge of awareness like the first light of dawn.

The inquisitor stood back.

'I am judgement, Astraeos.'

'You say I am a traitor, but I can only remember service and sacrifice. There are battlefields on Carnius Seven, on Keed, on Maltrix that were watered with the blood of my brothers, blood that we shed for our oaths to the Imperium. How can that be if I am a traitor?'

'What do you remember?'

The light of fresh memory came in a rush, pushing through the darkness, pressing against his mind's eye.

'I remember…'

He remembered ships. Ships sliding across the sky like stars set free. *Silver.* Their hulls had been silver grey, and they had arrived like ghosts. None had seen or sensed their coming, not the astropaths, not the other Librarians, not the system monitors. He had…

He looked up. Around him the fortress-monastery screamed. Sirens echoed through the halls and across the high parapets. The ground shook as blast doors slammed shut from the highest towers to the fortress depths. Void shields crackled into life, daubing the sky with static. The silver ships dropped lower. There were three of them, three jagged shapes glinting in the sun. The defence lasers began to fire. Columns of light burned into the heavens. The air was crackling with lightning. False winds spilled around Astraeos as the unleashed energy cooked the air.

Behind him a door peeled open. Astraeos turned, saw who walked onto the tower summit, and fell to one knee.

'Rise,' said Thidias. The Chapter Master's face was unreadable. The burning light gleamed on his armour, and the ozone-laden winds spilled his red cloak behind him. Kadin stood at the front of Thidias's honour guard, the banner in his hand stirring as he looked at Astraeos with hard eyes.

'My lord,' began Astraeos. 'What–'

The ships above them fired. Lines of flame spread across

the sky. The fortress roared back, pouring stuttering lines at the heavens, even as the fire from the ships reached towards the ground.

'What is this?' he shouted above the roar.

Thidias turned to him. His eyes were empty, as though what they had seen had burned away the soul behind them.

'This is the Imperium we serve coming to destroy us,' he said.

The memory flashed to nothing. Astraeos was shaking, his muscles bunching. Somewhere nearby something was shouting about neural overload. All Astraeos could see through the servo-skull's eyes was the inquisitor looking at him, his face as calm and uncaring as an executioner's blade.

'Subdue him,' said the inquisitor.

Cold spread from Astraeos's chest. He could not feel his limbs. He forced his mouth open, feeling the muscles in his jaw begin to numb. The inquisitor was watching him, his head tilted slightly to one side as though considering a thought.

'We were loyal!' Astraeos screamed at the thin face.

And then there was just the numb cold, and the remembered light of fire spreading across a blue sky.

The armour lay at the centre of an adamantium slab. Thick loops of the metal circled its arms, chest, and legs. Layers of energy fields shimmered in the air around it. Iobel could feel the headache purr of active null generators. It was surprisingly warm in the underground fortress, and the crystal floor of the viewing chamber buzzed with heat and static.

Iobel shivered as she looked down through the crystal floor. The armour was black, as though it had been carved from coal. She would have thought that it had been burned if it had not been for the polished bronze that edged its plates and snaked across its shoulders and greaves. A high crest extended above the crown of its helm. The symbol of a baleful eye worked in beaten copper stared out from its chest. It had been the armour of a Space Marine, without a doubt, but this could only be a relic of those who had turned on the Emperor in ages past.

Iobel looked up from the view beneath her feet. She could hardly believe what she was seeing. Izdubar was still looking down, hands clasped behind his back, face almost serene.

'Is this…?' she began.

'You have never seen one of them before, have you?' said Izdubar softly. 'Yes, this is one of the Thousand Sons of Magnus the Red. Or at least what remains of one. It is an abomination. Alive, after a fashion – animated by the energies of the warp, at once a body and a prison for the spirit within. Some call them the Rubricae. This one was taken during the incursion onto Vess. A dozen primaris-grade battle psykers died capturing it.'

'The colours and emblems…' began Iobel.

'Marks of fealty to the one they call the Despoiler.'

Izdubar looked up from the crystal floor, and ran a hand over his scalp. Brief pain stabbed through Iobel's head. Her eyes squeezed shut, and she gasped. The chamber jumped out of focus, then snapped back into clarity. Iobel blinked and breathed hard as she tried to focus on where she was. Izdubar didn't seem to notice, but just carried on talking. 'That is not why it is important. It is important because of what it means.'

Iobel's head cleared as suddenly as it had clouded. She looked at Izdubar. He was looking at her as though he had just asked a question which required a reply. She felt as though she had just come back into a conversation that had continued without her realising. She hesitated, and then knew what she needed to say next.

'On a world, long ago, a dying psyker spoke to me of Prospero. He said that he was the vengeance of the Sons of Prospero.'

'Yes,' said Izdubar. 'On Carsona, was it not?'

Iobel felt surprise fill her face. Izdubar glanced at her, then back to the bound Rubricae.

'I have been following your progress towards us since soon after your search began. We must be sure, you see.' Iobel opened her mouth to speak, but Izdubar continued smoothly on. 'The psyker who spoke those words to you was right. The will of one of the Thousand Sons had touched him. He and many more like him, in thousands of cults and psyker cells spread through the body of the Imperium, growing in its flesh like cancers. Fed by dreams, and manipulated from beyond by the sorcerers who are all that remain of the Thousand Sons.'

Iobel let out a snort of breath. Behind her Cavor stirred as though waiting for a command.

'I have found the records, and seen the insides of heretics' minds. What you have said is nothing that I have not learnt myself.' She pointed down at the Rubricae beneath their feet. 'This is just confirmation, not revelation.'

Izdubar laughed, the sound as sudden as it was brief.

'*Revelation.*' He rolled the word over his tongue. 'I went searching for answers, just like you. For a long time I sifted through rumours, through myths left half forgotten, and lies still whispered in lost places. I learned much, but I always knew there was more. I could feel it, as though it waited around the next corner – a secret so large that its existence drew other secrets into its darkness. I found it at last, and I found that I was not the first. There were others of our kind watching me to see how far I would come on my own, to see if I was ready. I asked just as you asked, and as answer, or perhaps as punishment, they gave me knowledge.' He reached into a pocket in his bodyglove and pulled out the Inquisitorial symbol with the blue gem at its centre. 'Do you wish for answers, Iobel? The door to truth stands open. Walk through, or turn back now.' He held out the symbol to Iobel.

Turn back! The thought cut into her awareness, and the room swam in her eyes. *Turn back now!* Grey dust swirled across the edge of her sight. The sensation vanished.

The symbol sat on Izdubar's hand, waiting.

She paused, and then reached out and picked it up. It felt warm in her hand.

Izdubar smiled sadly. The expression surprised her.

'There is a room on a moon which orbits a far world around a nameless sun,' he said. 'It holds a record made by a man who was called Kalimakus. We call it his Athenaeum. It speaks of many things: of the past, of the future, of things that cannot be and the ways to find them. Besides those that keep it, only a few others have seen it.' He let out a breath, and rubbed a hand over his left eye. 'Only we of the Ordo Cyclopes have seen it.'

'What is the Athenaeum?' she said. At the back of her thoughts she wondered why it felt as though she had said those words before.

'It is the thoughts of Magnus the Red,' he said. Iobel stared at him. She could feel the shiver rise as bumps on her skin. 'It is not just a record, it is a window. Kalimakus died long ago, but still his remembrance is being written, its lore dividing and multiplying without end. With every day that passes more words are added to it. Words that have told us what became of the Thousand Sons within the Eye of Terror, and given us glimpses of what they may yet become.'

'How can you know it is true?' Iobel's voice sounded distant to her, the shock still rolling through her in waves.

Izdubar stepped back, and looked down through the crystal floor at the Rubricae beneath.

'There is the proof, lying beneath our feet. The Athenaeum

told us of how the Rubricae were born from the power and delusion of one called Ahriman.'

Ahriman... The word echoed in Iobel's mind.

Ahriman...

Ahriman...

'But for centuries we were not sure, until we took this one and others. Until we could hold the proof of truth in our hands. Once that proof was found, then the rest of what the Athenaeum told us had the possibility of truth. That was when our war to prevent what it foretells truly began.'

'What does it foretell?'

'A storm,' said Izdubar. 'A storm rising in the future.' Izdubar closed his eyes. A muscle twitched on his jaw line. In that instant she saw that he was not as young as he seemed; he was old, and very tired. 'Sometimes when I think of it I can smell the pyre of that future.' She saw a shiver pass through him. 'That is what we fight against, Iobel. That is the war demanded by the truth you have sought for half your life.' He pointed to the symbol she still held in her hand. 'Will you join us in it?'

You must not go further... the voice whispered from behind her, and Iobel turned, but there was only Cavor looking down through the crystal at the Thousand Sons legionary. His hands were thrust into his coat pockets, his augmetic eyes glowing bright as he stared at the black suit of armour. She frowned; the light of his eyes was blue. She was sure that...

She felt her mouth opening and words rising to the

surface of her mind, pushing towards her tongue. She tried to bite them back, to scream. A clinging feeling of nausea slid through her. She swayed. The chamber was rolling and spinning around her.

What is happening? What is–?

The room blinked. Blackness surrounded her. She was so cold. A wind scraped dust over her skin, but there was no wind and her skin was buried beneath layers of fabric.

The crystal-floored chamber snapped back into place around her.

Iobel was standing looking at Izdubar who was looking back at her, his face grave.

Something had just happened, hadn't it? She blinked, but the feeling was fading. Izdubar was still looking at her.

'Will you join us, Iobel? Will you see the Athenaeum of Kalimakus?'

'Yes,' she said. 'I will.'

Everything in the room stopped moving. Izdubar stood still, his face frozen between expressions.

Footsteps rang on the crystal as Cavor came to stand in front of her. He crouched, looking down at the Rubricae with his bright, blue augmetic eyes.

'His name was Kyloris,' said Ahriman with Cavor's mouth. 'He was born on Prospero, on the ninth day of the first transit. Clever, but never gifted. He was a good warrior. Now he is just a memory within a memory.' He looked at Iobel. 'You know why we are here, don't you? I could see part of you struggling to keep me from the end of this memory.' He smiled. 'Strong Selandra Iobel, so strong for a human.' The chamber began to fade. 'But not strong enough.'

The shadows in the walls began to grow. A wall of pressure clamped around her, bearing down on her thoughts. Heat blazed through her mind. She felt the shell of her defences buckle. The room had almost vanished in a grey blur of swirling dust. This was the end, she knew. One more step through her memories, and Ahriman would have what he wanted: Apollonia, the secrets of the Ordo Cyclopes, the Athenaeum of Kalimakus. Her will had proved to be weak, and now it would not only betray her, but mankind.

Ahriman stepped towards her, growing taller, the details of Cavor's stolen face falling into darkness. His hand was reaching for her, its fingers growing like spreading shadows.

No, she thought. *No.* And the thought became iron. There was another way. A way of seeing what was happening that she had not realised before.

This is a memory. And it is mine.

She was not a powerful psyker, but here she did not need to be.

Beneath them the shields and manacles holding the Rubricae boiled away in a flash of light.

'Tell me,' she said slowly. 'If this is a memory, what if I choose to remember it differently?'

The Rubricae exploded through the crystal floor. Ahriman fell, his imagined body flickering between substance and shadow. Iobel was already across the room, running towards the door and whatever was beyond. The Rubricae landed in a crouch on the cracked floor, eyes burning bright. Ahriman rose into the air, shedding Cavor's shape like a cloak. He reached for Iobel.

The Rubricae came up from its crouch in a single bound. Ahriman twisted in the air as the Rubricae slammed into him. Flames and lightning exploded from them as they hit the wall.

The door was in front of Iobel. She reached out, and she turned her memory over like a key in a lock. The door vanished in a burst of debris. Iobel ran through the cloud of dust. She could feel her pulse hammering through her. Splinters of metal and rock raked her face, drawing blood.

It is not real, she screamed at herself. *It is not real.*

Her feet skidded out from beneath her and she was tumbling across a floor of white marble. She rolled, and came to her feet. A long corridor stretched in front of her. Closed doors led off it on both sides, and sunlight was streaming through windows open to a blue sky.

Where is this? Where am I?

Locked together, wreathed in flames. Ahriman and the Rubricae came through the remains of the door behind her.

XII
BROKEN

The inquisitor was there when Astraeos woke again.

'Tell me what you remember,' said the inquisitor.

Astraeos did not speak. In his mind he saw his brothers firing from parapets, the light of their burning home staining their armour. Silver-grey warriors walked through burning halls, haloed by warp light, cutting down all they found without a word. The towering form of a Dreadnought walked before the grey warriors, shaking the tiled floor with its tread. He saw Chapter Master Thidias take his cloak of office from his back as the pyre leaped higher.

'What is a king when there is nothing left to rule?' Thidias had asked.

'Silence,' said the inquisitor. 'Do I take it that the memories of your treachery have returned to you?'

Astraeos felt the muscles of his jaw clench.

'We broke no oaths,' he said.

The inquisitor raised an eyebrow.

'We? So you are a son of greater treachery, rather than a lone creature of heresy? Or perhaps you mean Ahriman, and the rest of his enslaved kind.' The inquisitor waited. The tubes puncturing Astraeos's flesh sucked and clicked in the silence. 'You are not like him, are you? You are not one of the Thousand Sons, even though you serve one. Even amongst my fellow inquisitors there are few who could tell you this, but the Thousand Sons did break their oaths. They broke one after another until there was nothing to hold them back from the abyss. That is the truth.' He watched Astraeos, the ghost of a frown on his face. 'Do you remember your master? Do you remember Ahriman?'

Do you remember Ahriman…? The words echoed in his head. Pieces of things he did not understand, or had not realised were there, clustered around the words.

Remember Ahriman…

He saw Ahriman in battered armour the colour of rust and dried blood. He saw the sword glow as it severed his chains. He saw a million candles burning in the darkness of his mind. He saw his brothers: Cadar the instant before the chainblade opened his chest, Thidias standing in the airless dark of a dead void station, Kadin with his face a mass of blood-slicked scar tissue.

Ahriman…

'He is not coming for you,' said the inquisitor. 'Not

now, no matter what oath he swore. You are abandoned, Astraeos.'

I am a traitor, thought Astraeos. *No matter what the cause, I have made the fallen my brothers.*

'What did he promise you? Power? Revenge?'

'If there is a way to undo what has been done I will find it,' Ahriman said in the stillness of his mind. *'You have my oath.'*

'Hope,' said Astraeos. He felt cold, as though something of the memory of the lonely human boy he had been bled into the present.

He has abandoned you… He is not coming… no matter what oaths he made.

'Hope?' The inquisitor shook his head slowly, and rubbed a hand over his eyes. 'We make your breed so different, don't we? Take a boy, cut away his future, his fear. Fill him with secrets that only the Emperor can truly understand, clad him in muscle and armour and surround him by war. What are we left with? Machines? No, machines cannot feel loyalty, cannot reason, cannot strive to reach the impossible. They can break, but they cannot fall. What hope did he offer you, Astraeos?'

Silence hung in the seconds after the question.

The inquisitor let out a slow breath, and shook his head.

'I do not wish to do what must be done, but I will. You are a traitor, Astraeos, but you could still serve the Imperium if you choose. Tell me what else you remember, tell us of Ahriman and what he intends.'

Astraeos felt anger rise in him. They had killed his

Chapter, they had made him an outcast, stripped him of everything which had made him loyal.

'An oath binds us above all else, but for loyalty there must be an oath from kings to those they serve.' They had been Thidias's words. *Thidias.* Now dead and left in the dark.

'No,' said Astraeos.

The inquisitor nodded. There was no sorrow in the gesture, just acknowledgment that there was no other way.

'Cendrion,' said the inquisitor. A Space Marine in hulking silver armour stepped forwards. Astraeos wondered that he had not noticed him in the shadows. His false eyes skated over the warrior, taking in the script marching over the pauldrons, the vials and rolled scrolls which hung from golden wire across his chest and shoulders. Silver tattoos spiralled over the warrior's night-black skin, as though his armour was growing over him. A sword as tall as a man rested in his hand. He looked at Astraeos with steel-grey eyes.

It is one of them, one of the kind that killed our Chapter. One of the kind who made me a traitor. Shock spilled through Astraeos, and then the rage returned, brighter, burning deeper and clearer than before.

'You do not wish to do this?' said Astraeos, and felt the ice pour into the words as he spoke. 'One day, inquisitor, you will be judged, and in that moment you will look up into your own face and know the truth. Your soul will shriek when it passes into the fire.'

The inquisitor's expression did not flicker.

'Withdraw the Seraphs,' he said. 'Let the warp in.'

'Are you sure?' said Cendrion without looking away from Astraeos. The inquisitor's lips twisted into a weak smile.

'You are here, are you not, my friend?' The inquisitor glanced to the other figures standing half in shadow. Beside the crone and the glass-eyed man, the three hunched figures stirred under their black shrouds. 'Withdraw,' said the inquisitor, and the bent figures shuffled backwards as though melting into the gloom.

The warp touched Astraeos's mind, and he was aware of it curling and flowing a shadow's width away. He was also aware of Cendrion. The warrior's presence battered into his mind like the heat of a young sun. Astraeos's own mind was sluggish, and even as he tried to reach for the warp he knew something was wrong. Pain lanced through him. He tasted blood again, and felt his sight blur with nausea. He pulled his mind back. A smell of metal and cooking meat came from the machines clamped over his head.

The inquisitor looked up at Cendrion.

'Open his mind,' he said.

Iobel ran. Behind her Ahriman and the Rubricae rammed into a pillar of white marble. Splinters and flames exploded from the impact. The Rubricae's hands locked tight around Ahriman. Iobel glanced back as her feet pounded down the corridor. Her eyes met Ahriman's for a split second. Dazed confusion flared in her. She did not know what was happening, or how it had happened. She had made a terrible,

terrible misjudgement. Their gazes broke, and the feelings vanished from Iobel's mind. She stumbled, half falling.

Ahriman broke the Rubricae's grip. It reeled back a pace, found its balance and launched forwards again. Ahriman rammed his palm towards it. Iobel screamed as the Rubricae's chestplate shattered. Pain exploded across her torso. Confusion came fast after the pain. The Rubricae took a shaking step towards Ahriman, its hands rising weakly. Cracks spread across its shape, radiating from its chest. It came apart, pieces of its empty shell falling to the floor like wind-blown leaves.

Iobel did not move. Ahriman turned towards her. He looked as he had when she had seen him in the moment he had come for her on Vohal: armoured in blue and silver and robed in turquoise, his head covered by a six-horned helm. He took a step forwards and the helm dissolved into a face with smooth lines and bright eyes. The armour rippled and became a plain robe of white, tied at the waist with a knotted red cord. He moved slowly, as though wary of provoking her.

She was breathing hard, muscles held between stillness and flight. But of course she was doing no such thing, she realised. Wherever her body was, this was just a creation of imagination, a landscape of the mind. From the need to breathe to the fatigue in her limbs, all of it was a fiction.

Ahriman took a step closer, carefully, eyes not moving from her. Then she realised why, and where she must be. This was not her mind; it was his.

She met his eyes and knew at that moment he saw the revelation in her. She felt a cold smile form on her lips. 'You have made a mistake, Ahriman. There is no sorcery here, only strength of will. Here I am as strong as you.'

He began to move. Iobel closed her thoughts like a fist and slammed them outwards. Ahriman froze. His face was as unreadable as carved stone, but Iobel knew that something that might come close to fear moved beyond the mask.

'You cannot run,' he said. His voice was measured and calm. 'There is no way out of here, inquisitor.'

'True, but what will it cost you to bring me down? How much damage could I do here, inside your mind?'

'You are here until I have what I need.'

'The location and secrets of the Athenaeum.'

'You will give it to me one way or another. All I have to do is reach into you and take it. You buried it deep, but it is there.' He raised a slim finger and placed its tip against his temple. 'I can feel it.'

Iobel kept her thoughts steady, her will poised to break or remake more of this mindscape if he moved. She needed time. Time to find a way out, time to destroy her memories of the Athenaeum.

'Why seek it?' she said. 'You must know what it says already. You were there, weren't you?'

He shook his head slowly.

'Mistakes, inquisitor. Mistakes made in the past that I did not understand at the time, and that I will set right in the future. That is what the Atheneaum will help me do.'

She did laugh then, and the sound made the cracked walls shake.

'You wish for atonement?'

'Not the atonement your kind can grant, inquisitor.'

His eyes were bright in his unmoving face. The laughter died in her throat.

'Oh, great Throne on Terra, it is true.'

Ahriman seemed to let out a breath.

'I have broken everything I sought to save. That is my burden, but one that I will see undone.'

'Your burden? You are damned, Ahriman. There is no salvation in hell for your kind.'

'How can I have betrayed something that no longer exists? The Imperium you serve is not the Imperium I helped create.'

'Then what salvation do you seek?'

His eyes widened, then hardened.

'The only kind that matters,' he said softly, and seemed to shiver. When he looked back at her his shape seemed to have blurred and stretched. Behind him, the light dimmed to shadow. 'You speak of the Imperium and our kind, but what of your kind, inquisitor? I have seen what your kind do through your own eyes. I have seen worlds burned to take one life. I have heard the arguments for what must be done for the good of all. I have touched the ashes that form in your steps. You ask me what salvation can be mine. I ask you, what can be yours?'

She could sense the palace shifting around her, corridors reconfiguring to trap her, walls forming to close off doors into other parts of Ahriman's mind.

'There are no innocents,' said Iobel. 'If we do not act then who will? Being right does not make me inhuman, it just makes us see that the inhumane is necessary. But what you do, it is beyond that, it is a pyre made of reason for the sake of false ideals.'

Her mind was ghosting through every detail she could sense, searching, probing. But as she opened her mouth to speak again she knew that she had bought what time she could. There was only one option left to her.

'Fine words. I might say the same of you, Selandra Iobel.' Ahriman nodded, with a sad smile.

'You might, but there is a difference.'

Ahriman raised an eyebrow.

'I *am* right,' she said, and swung the full strength of her mind at the imagined world like a wrecking ball.

The walls and ceiling around her blew apart. Splinters of stone, wood and glass spun into the air beyond, falling against gravity. Iobel soared through the destruction, and out into the air and sunlight beyond. Wings snapped free of her shoulders, armour sheathed her skin in silver. She swooped, struck a white tower, and felt it break apart at her touch. Half-formed memory images spilled into the sunlit air, flapping like silk pennants. She spiralled back into the palace, trailing a shock wave of destruction. A cyclone of shattered stone, glass, and wood spiralled around her as her flight corkscrewed through the palace. She burst back into daylight. The light in the sky flickered between neon white and yellow. She did not know where Ahriman's manifestation was, it did not matter. Every part of this place was Ahriman, every stone a fragment of his mind to break, every tower a pillar of his thoughts. She would not survive this, of that she was sure, but she would break him before he could take her knowledge.

She landed on a tower top. The white stones shook beneath her as she gripped them. The world was juddering around her, the sky swimming. It was trying to shake her free, trying to spit her out. High above her, a black stain was spreading across the face of the sun, spilling across its burning circle. She had to keep moving. She gripped the parapet, pulled herself up, and leapt again before the tower toppled.

The cries of crows cackled through the air, louder than the roar of falling rubble and shattering stone. Far below her she heard thousands of wings beating against the air.

She landed on a higher tower. Cracks spread across the stones. A roar of fracturing marble rose around her. She took another step as half the tower top broke away just behind her. She jumped. Her wings beat. She looked down. The tower fell away beneath her gaze, crumbling downwards in a fountain of dust and stone. Around it more and more towers began to topple, blocks and fragments of glass flowing down as a void opened beneath. She beat her wings and rose towards the sun even as it became a black disc.

'Iobel!' The roar shook the sky. She looked down, and saw Ahriman rise from the collapsing palace. He came as a murder of crows, a storm of black wings and jagged shrieks. They poured up to her, moving faster and faster even as the ground dropped away below and the palace fell into the abyss. Iobel could feel her wings becoming heavier. She tried to focus, to hold onto the possibility of the idea of flight, but it was draining away from her even as she tried to grasp it. The crows surrounded her. Black feathers hid the blue sky. Carrion cries rose higher and higher. She realised she was screaming as the crows swallowed her.

'I have you now,' said Ahriman in the chorus voice of the crows.

Iobel lashed out with her will, but hundreds of claws and beaks were tearing into her flesh, ripping her consciousness apart as she fell and fell without end.

'It will not bring you salvation,' she shouted with all that was left of her strength, as Ahriman tore the last of her memories apart, and then there was nothing but the cry of crows and the caress of claws.

Pain exploded inside Astraeos. It was everywhere, stabbing through him from the depths of his soul to the ends of his fingers. He was burning, and becoming ice, and bleeding and crumbling to dust. He pushed back, tried to form his mind into a weapon, tried to call the warp to him. The pain grew and grew. He felt its fingers pulling at the iron he had trained into his mind. He could remember everything now, every moment from the towers of his birth world to the moment that Ahriman had left him as a corpse on the floor of the tiered chamber. It was all there, laid out as sudden and clear as a spray of blood in sunlight.

'He left you here, Astraeos,' said Izdubar, his voice reaching through the pain. 'Hate us if you wish, but see *him* for what he is. He is a son of betrayal. He has led you to this fate and left you. And you will end here, loyal to a master who has spent you and cast you aside.'

He could feel the psychic fire burning deeper into his mind, lapping against his will, pressing into every weakness. Sensations and emotions sputtered through him: elation, hate, joy, rage, disbelief.

And over it all was a visage which spoke in a voice that sounded like Thidias. *Ahriman did it all for his Legion, but even then he killed Amon. And what are you?*

'You are less than nothing to him,' said Izdubar. 'A tool, a weapon left broken on the battlefield.'

The pain was all of him now. His body was thrashing against the restraints, masked head wrenching from side to side. One of his hearts exploded in his chest. His ribs and spine cracked as his muscles spasmed. His lungs began to crumple. There was a smell of cooking fat, and ozone. He thought of the Rubric, of the moment when Ahriman had changed his Legion, and wondered if it had been like this, if there had been pain in that moment of transformation.

I was never part of them, shouted a voice from the edge of the pain. *I can never be a part of them.*

'The Athenaeum.' The word cut through the pain and rang through the darkness. The pain receded, became a fire-edged blade held against his awareness. 'The Athenaeum,' Astraeos gasped. Sweat was rolling from his skin, his chest heaving as breath wheezed from his remaining lung. 'He seeks the Athenaeum of Kalimakus. That is why he came for the one called Iobel. He saw it in her mind. Chance, it was just chance, but he followed her. He wants to know where the Athenaeum is, and how it is defended.'

His sucking breaths filled the moment. Izdubar was watching him, his eyes still. Cendrion stood immobile, hands crossed on the guard of his sword, silver armour fuming aetheric mist and melting frost.

'And once he has that information, he will go there?'

'With strength enough to break any defences.'

'Tell me everything.'

And he did. He told it all as though a dam in his soul had opened, and the last of him was pouring out of a reservoir of doubt and hate. He told them of Cadar, of the creature that now wore his skin. He told them how Thidias had died. He told them of Kadin, and what remained of his last brother. He told them of the Circle Ahriman had drawn around him, of the renegades and the sorcerers, and the ships whose hulls crawled as though alive. He told them everything he could remember.

At the end he lay, tasting the blood on his breath.

I am dying. He tried to think of what he had just done, but there was only a numb emptiness in his mind now.

Around him the warp shifted, its currents tugging at his ragged thoughts, chuckling as it passed.

'Thank you,' said Izdubar. 'I cannot forgive what you are, but I thank you. Ahriman will fall. We will be waiting for him.'

'If it is not too late,' said the crone from the shadows.

Izdubar remained silent, watching Astraeos, and then turned away. Cendrion did not move, but looked at Izdubar, a question flickering in his grey eyes.

'No,' said Izdubar. 'Not yet.'

Cendrion turned away, his armour purring and clicking. The last thing Astraeos saw before the tech-priests shut down the servo-skull were the three black-swathed Seraphs shambling forwards. The warp's touch drained away, and in the last moment before it fled, he thought he heard a chattering laugh, like a cloud of crows calling over the dead.

Sparks and shadows filled the cave. Iobel sat watching the fire dance over the pile of logs. She shivered despite the heat, and pulled the frayed blanket closer around her. Ahriman sat on the other side of the yellow tongues. At least she thought it was Ahriman, who else could it be? He wore a tattered red robe, his head covered by a cowl. The hands which stirred the fire with a stick were scarred, the flesh puckered and shiny. He said nothing, but just watched the wood split and crackle as it burned.

'I can remember,' she said, and heard the defiance and anger in her own voice. 'I can remember each step that we have taken to get here. Is that not a mistake? Shouldn't I be thinking this is real, like I did before? Where is the trick?'

'Trick?' said a voice from behind her. She twisted around. Ahriman stood behind her, his face bare, the smooth skin blurred by the sway of shadow and light. He wore the white robe, and his hand held a staff of worn wood. 'Why would I trick you now, Iobel?'

She glanced back at the figure in the tattered red cowl.

'He can't see me,' said the figure, in a voice as dry as thirst. 'And he can't hear me.' A single point of blue light looked back at her from the blackness beneath the cowl. 'I am here for you, and you alone.'

'What is this, then?' She gestured at the hooded figure. 'If not another trick.'

'The cave is many things, but at this moment it might be best thought of as a shelter,' said Ahriman, as he walked around her and looked down into the fire. 'You did me a lot of damage, mistress.'

'He admires you,' said the cowled figure. 'Do you know how long it has been since he admired a human?' She glanced between them. What was this? She had to think. She had to understand what Ahriman was trying to do. She had broken free before; should she just do it again? She tried, but nothing changed.

'We have been walking in memories and in the lands of the mind,' said Ahriman. 'But there is only debris and chaos now: memories and imaginings jumbled together in my head.' Ahriman sat down beside the fire, his staff across his knees. Slowly he extended his hands towards the warmth. 'You did that. For the first time in a long time I am a stranger in my own thoughts.'

'You see?' said the cowled figure.

Iobel shook her head.

'What are you?' she said.

'What am I?' said both Ahriman and the cowled figure at once.

Ahriman frowned briefly.

'I am someone who sees and knows more than others, and does what he must.'

'He is a liar,' said the cowled figure, and Iobel thought she heard a chuckle at the edge of the words.

Iobel suddenly felt very tired. She had run and fought, and fought again, and relived her life in glimpses. Even if she did escape there would only be more. She would run to the end of her days and beyond. Better that she die here, that she let this lost dream of herself fade.

'No,' she said, and the sound of her voice surprised her. She sounded old, wrung out and too tired to hide it. *You sound like Malkira*, she thought, and the idea of the old woman, scowling in the exoskeleton, made her want to smile, though she did not know why. 'No, Ahriman, you are a monster.'

'I have seen the Inquisition through your eyes. I know what you do. Tell me, if I am a monster, then what are you?'

'I am a servant. I serve humanity. I fight for the survival of our species. I am survival, Ahriman.'

'Very good,' chuckled the cowled figure.

'I–' began Ahriman.

'No, I can guess what you want. I have seen the inside of your soul, Ahriman. I do not need you to tell me what you believe. I understand you.'

'He always was blind to himself. It is his weakness – all our weakness, in fact.'

'You think that you are on a quest to set things right, but the path you walk is a path of corpses.'

'I have a debt to my brothers. I will repay it.'

'Your brothers are like you – drowning in lies, sucked down so deeply into the ocean of Chaos that you cannot see the surface. They, like you, should not be.'

'Tell me, then, inquisitor. When you killed your first man for the Emperor, when you ordered your first purge, when you ordered a world to die for the failings of a few, what did you tell yourself then?'

'That the price had to be paid, or all would fall,' she said, feeling anger come at last. Ahriman's mouth opened, but she carried on. 'Do not try to say that you do the same. I do what I must, and if that includes my death, or the death of all I care for, then so be it. That is what I am. I am what you can never be, because you meet the cost but never pay it yourself.'

Ahriman just looked at her. She stared back. Between them the fire crackled.

'So human,' said the cowled figure. 'I might have said the same once.' It shrugged. 'Perhaps I did.'

'We,' said Ahriman slowly, 'see things differently.'

'If you were like me you would be loyal to more than yourself. If you were like me you would have killed your Legion, not tried to save it.'

Iobel stood, the blanket still wrapped around her, and turned to look at the cave mouth and jagged sliver of night beyond. She stepped closer.

'He believes you,' said the cracked-paper voice from beside the fire. 'Part of him, deep down, believes you.'

'You won't get far,' said Ahriman softly. 'Not here, not now. It is over, Iobel.'

She stepped to the lip of the cave and looked down. The cliff face dropped away, its base hidden in darkness. The wind lifted against her skin. She raised her head, and far off she thought she heard wolves howling. She looked down again, and wondered if the idea of a fall could kill you.

'I will not let you have it,' she said and looked back at the fire, at the two figures sat beside it. 'Even if I must die, I will not let you have what you seek.'

Ahriman shook his head slowly.

'I said it is over. I already have your knowledge of the Athenaeum. I know every detail of your life, every moment you have forgotten, everything you kept secret, everything you wanted and never achieved.'

Iobel's mind was empty, as though she was floating in a still sea, feeling nothing, thinking nothing. Then the blackness opened in her, spreading wide like a scream.

'Everything,' she said. Ahriman nodded, though it was

not a question. 'Then you knew what I would say, here, you knew that I would die if I could to keep the Athenaeum from you.'

'Yes.' He nodded.

'And what I saw in the Eye, the worlds broken, the scars on the warp itself – you saw that too.'

He nodded, and for the first time looked away from her, back down to the fire. Beside him the cowled figure stirred, and turned his hidden head to look at Ahriman.

'None of that has happened yet, has it?' she said. 'It is your future, isn't it? Stars dying, hell screaming your name as though calling for mercy – that is what waits for you.'

Ahriman said nothing.

'Fate can be changed,' said the cowled figure.

'Fate can be changed,' said Ahriman.

'But you won't, will you? You see what you will do and now you know that you will choose that path, that you have already chosen.' She let out a tired breath that was almost a laugh, and turned towards the night beyond the cave entrance. She took a step forwards.

'There is no point in jumping,' said Ahriman, quietly. Iobel turned back to look at him. 'You are already dead. You began to die as soon as you began to fight. The palace was the last of you.'

Iobel just stared at him. He looked back.

'But I am here.'

'No, you are not. You are a memory – all your memories and thoughts living in my mind, dreamed to reality, thinking with part of my mind, a ghost.'

Iobel turned her head slowly. The cowled figure was looking up at her.

'He is right,' it said, but she thought she could hear a smile in the words. 'But nothing is ever as it seems.'

Iobel shivered. Behind her the wind rose and she heard wolves again. She turned and jumped. As she fell she saw the cave become smaller above her, dwindling until it was just one light in the night sky.

XIII
BLADES

Kadin did not turn as the door opened behind him. The corridor outside the sealed room was as still and silent as when Ahriman had set him to guard... how long ago? He heard a cough and a slow suck of breath, but still did not turn.

How long had it been since he had last heard a noise, or moved more than to breathe? He did not know. It did not matter.

'Help me, Kadin,' said Ahriman. Kadin looked and saw Ahriman in the open door, the metal of the doorframe bearing his weight. His armour had a glazed sheen, as though flame had polished it to an oily finish. Ice clung to its recesses. Through the open door Kadin could see scorch marks spreading across the floor and up the walls. A single circle of unmarked metal remained just in front of the black stone coffin. Water dripped from the ceiling as frost began to thaw. Kadin thought that the burn marks looked as though vast wings of heat had spread to the walls.

Ahriman looked at Kadin; his eyes seemed to have sunk into his skull, the skin grown taut over the bones of his face. As Kadin watched, a drop of blood formed on Ahriman's lip, grew and ran down his chin.

Ahriman took a slow breath, and Kadin heard the rattle and wet gurgle in it.

'Kadin,' said Ahriman again, and began to slide slowly down the doorframe. Kadin caught him and gripped an arm with a piston-driven hand. His machine limb tingled where it touched the sorcerer; the sensation puzzled him, but he said nothing. Slowly he pulled Ahriman to his feet.

I could kill him, he thought as he steadied the sorcerer. Blood was dribbling from Ahriman's lips now, and his eyes had closed. *I could kill him now, and there would be nothing he could do to stop me.*

'Thinking of killing me again, Kadin?'

'You once said that you would leave me my thoughts.'

'I did. It was just a guess.' Ahriman's bloody lips twitched. 'Besides, I need strength for more than reading your thoughts.' He spasmed and his eyes opened, pupils wide in blood-streaked sclera. He went very still. Kadin smelt hot metal, and looked down. The fingers of his hand were glowing with heat where they held Ahriman's arm.

Ahriman exhaled slowly, his breath white in the warm air. His pupils shrank, the blood crazing his eyes draining away to leave their usual cold blue. He straightened, strength seeming to return to him, though his face still seemed drained and hollow. He brought up a gauntlet-covered hand and wiped the blood from his chin.

'Thank you,' said Ahriman. Kadin took his hand away. Ahriman took a step, stumbled and caught himself against the wall. 'Cursed silver,' he said and spat. The bloody saliva hissed on the floor. Ahriman took another step, which seemed surer, though Kadin could tell that the movement was an act of will. Ahriman looked up at the long corridor, then back at the scorched room beyond the open door. 'Seal it,' he said.

Kadin nodded, but Ahriman was already turning away. Kadin felt something he could not place. He had been numb for so long that it took him by surprise. Somehow he had expected Ahriman to say something else, to be different, and as the silence folded back around him he knew what the stray feeling was. He felt suddenly and completely alone.

'What shall I do then?' Kadin called. Ahriman turned, his mouth slightly open as though to help him breathe, his shoulders and back stooped.

'Wait, however you wish.' Ahriman blinked slowly. 'I will call for you, Kadin. When it is time.'

'Did it work?' Kadin asked the question before Ahriman could turn. 'Did you get what we needed?' What *we* needed… the words sounded strange even to Kadin. Ahriman turned to look at him, surprise blending with pain on his face.

'Yes,' he said, 'we have what we need.'

'And Astraeos – do you know if he lives?'

Ahriman remained still, his eyes holding on Kadin's.

'There was no choice,' said Ahriman. After a second Kadin nodded, still feeling the strange emotion flowing through him. He nodded, dropping his gaze.

'I…' he began to say as he looked up, but Ahriman had gone, vanished beyond sight, as though he had never been. Kadin took a final glance at the open chamber door, and then followed Ahriman. There was nothing left in the scorched room that needed guarding, not now, not any more.

Once both were gone the quiet began to settle. Slowly, so slowly that he seemed to be made of stillness, Maroth came from the shadows. He paused at the door of the scorched chamber, his blind eyes fixed on the way Kadin had gone. Then he turned his head, until he was facing the open door and the room beyond.

+Do you understand?+

Ahriman's thought sank into the waiting silence.

Sanakht said nothing, and beside him the rest of the Circle kept their eyes on the great crystal sphere, in which muted colours swirled, echoing the doubt of some. In its depths the image of the Apollonia system turned, its four planets and bloated sun sketched in cold light. The outermost planet glowed, haloed by Prosperine runes and lines which extended out into the space beyond. It was a gas giant, its blue and ochre surface swirled with titanic storm systems. Sanakht watched the cloud patterns change under his gaze. For a mental projection it was very precise, almost as though it was taken directly from first-hand memory. Normally Ahriman would have joined his mind to that of his brothers to share such information, but for this he had called them to the bridge of the *Sycorax*, so that they could look at it with their true eyes. Sanakht wondered why.

He glanced to where Ahriman stood in front of Carmenta's command throne. Ahriman wore full battleplate, and his head was hidden by his helm. Power arced in the air around him, rustling the silk of his robes and the parchment hanging from his armour. That was new, and there was something else, something raw and feverish about the way Ahriman's mind spoke. The hunched shape of Kadin stood a pace further back, the pistons of his arms and legs hissing and clacking like twitching muscles. Sanakht noticed that the augmetics had taken on a wet rainbow sheen, as though they were sweating oil. He looked up, and met two green slit eyes looking back at him. Kadin blinked, the eyelids sliding in from the sides of his eyes. Sanakht kept the sneer of disgust from his face.

+The objective?+ asked Ignis, his thought voice cold.

+The Athenaeum lies at the centre of a labyrinth beneath the surface of this moon. The moon alone in the system has a name – it is called Apollonia.+ Fresh light kindled within the crystal sphere, haloing a grey orb close to the system's outer planet. +The moon and its parent planet are locked into an orbital arrangement which creates a permanent eclipse. No sun reaches Apollonia.+

+Kept always in darkness,+ sent Sanakht.

Ahriman turned his head to look at Sanakht, but said nothing. The look made Sanakht's skin prickle.

+Defences?+ asked Ignis.

+Orbital, and ground-based batteries.+

+Nothing else?+ sent Sanakht. +No standing garrison? No Titans? None of our mongrel cousins living out their lives in a fortress?+

Ahriman shook his head.

+Not that the inquisitor knew of, but we should prepare for the possibility that there might be. Ignis, this task is yours. Break the moon open, and get me into the labyrinth.+

Ignis nodded, his eyes still on the sphere.

+What are the other known factors?+

Ahriman paused, the slightest of shrugs moving his shoulders.

+There is an order of humans that keeps the Athenaeum – its curators. That was what the inquisitor called them.+

+Humans?+ sent Ignis, the flatness of his thoughts struggling against disbelief.

+Yes. A dozen at most.+

+A dozen?+

+That is what was in the inquisitor's mind,+ sent Ahriman.

At the edge of the circle Gilgamos shifted, lips pursing on his wide face. Sanakht caught the taste of doubt from his brother as it rippled from his open mind. He looked at the former Corvidae prophet, but Gilgamos was looking at Ahriman.

+If this is truly the place we seek, then the Imperium will make us pay a blood price to break it.+ Gilgamos's thought voice rumbled like stone grating on stone. +A door is rarely left open in a fortress. I have looked down the paths, turned the courses of fate over one by one, but I cannot see how this ends. Uncertainty clouds it. I do not like it.+

+And you are right not to,+ sent Ahriman. Slowly he reached up, and released the catches of his helm. The face beneath was a mask of fatigue. Sanakht felt the wave of surprise run through the Circle. Ahriman looked around each of them, a wan smile on his lips but not in his eyes. +It has cost us much to get this far, and it may cost us more. Nothing is certain. Nothing can be certain. Not with what we intend, not in the war we fight. We are fighting fate, not being guided by it. There is always a chance that we may fail, that we may fall.+ He paused, closing his eyes briefly. +But that is as it must be. We are not on a path of certainty, but a path to break what is fated.+ Silence filled the warp, trembling like a taut string. Then Ahriman turned from the Circle. The image in the crystal sphere vanished.

'Ignis,' said Ahriman, his true voice thin as it came from his mouth. 'Coordinate the rest of the fleet. We will make warp passage within a cycle. The rest of you, order your forces.'

'Do we accompany you again in the assault, lord?' asked Gilgamos.

'No. Sanakht, Kadin and a cadre of Rubricae will go with me.'

'By your will,' said Gilgamos.

Ahriman turned away from them, not even making the sign of passing. Sanakht thought he saw Ahriman's image flicker at the edges, as though it briefly had cast shadows from a light that was not there.

And so, we will have our chance, Sanakht thought within the hidden reaches of his mind. Around him the rest of the Circle moved away, their unsettled thoughts flavouring the warp. The Cyrabor slunk back from the edges of the bridge, cooing over the space the Circle had left. Ignis was the last to go. He caught Sanakht's eye, and gave the smallest of nods.

'You are injured,' said Carmenta. The lenses of her eyes refocused, and Ahriman's face was overlaid by the rainbow colours of infra-sight. His face was red with warmth, cooler than the white-yellow of the Cyrabor priests in the background, hotter than the cool green and blue of his armour. He did not say anything. She watched a muscle in his jaw twitch. He closed his eyes. 'You are, aren't you.' It was a flat statement. 'Worse than before.'

'Is that you speaking?' he asked, his voice low, heavy with tiredness. 'Or the ship?'

Something connected to her thoughts clicked through the question and formed an answer.

'Yes,' she said.

Ahriman laughed softly, then nodded, and let out a breath.

'The information extraction did not proceed as intended?' she asked.

'No,' said Ahriman, then shook his head and said no more. He leant on the arm of the command throne, head bent. She could hear a wet click in his breathing.

'There are cracks in you,' she said. 'And they are widening.'

He gave her a long look, then shook his head with a low humourless laugh. She wondered why.

'Keep Kadin close,' she said. 'The others… they are unsure, Ahriman. Remember that they followed Amon once, and that they tried to destroy you. They serve you now, but they do not trust you.'

Ahriman stood slowly, his armour purring.

'And I should trust Kadin?' he said.

'Yes,' she said.

The muscles in his jaw hardened as he turned away.

'Sleep, mistress. We are almost there.'

'The end,' she said, but the word stuck in her throat, and became a hiss of cogs and code. Ahriman walked from her. On her throne, Carmenta's head drooped and she went back to listening to the machine within.

'We must have an advantage,' said Ignis.

'This is our advantage,' said Sanakht. They had walked far from the bridge of the *Sycorax*, down through the High Citadel into the layers beneath. The space they walked now was a narrow gully between dust-covered machines. High above them, sparks discharged between the metal cliffs.

False thunder broke the humming quiet as blue flashes of light stole the gloom. They spoke with their true voices, their minds shut away from the warp by the brass discs that floated beside them. Acid-etched lines and circles covered their surfaces, and each floated and turned in time with each other as though invisible cogs and threads connected them. Inside their orbit they could talk and no other mind could hear them. The discs, like the tongue they spoke, were old and had been made on Prospero before it became ashes. Credence walked three paces behind them, clicking to itself.

'I will have him alone, separated from the rest of the Circle while you command the fleet in space. How many of the mongrel warbands now will answer to you alone? What would you call that if not an opportunity?'

Ignis stopped and the orbiting discs slid to a halt around them.

'He is going into the labyrinth alone apart from you and Kadin. Why?'

'Trust, brother. He does not trust any of you.'

'But he still trusts you.'

'I almost died for him once,' said Sanakht quietly.

Ignis shook his head.

'There are too many unknowns, too many values that are not set. This may be an opportunity, but we need more than opportunity, we need an advantage,' said Ignis carefully. 'You will be alone with Ahriman beneath the surface of Apollonia, but so will a guard of Rubricae bound to

Ahriman's will. And can't be ignored that abomination Kadin – he might take some killing, even for you. That and we are still talking of Ahriman, no matter how isolated. And all the while here in orbit is a fleet's worth of firepower and troops. Carmenta is loyal to Ahriman alone, and the *Sycorax* is strong enough to break us if we move against him.'

Ignis stopped, and frowned. Sanakht wondered if the Master of Ruin had ever spoken so much before.

'We have an advantage. Several in fact,' said Sanakht.

Ignis simply stared at him and waited.

'There is something that Ahriman does not know about Apollonia and the Athenaeum.'

Ignis raised an eyebrow.

'But you know this fact that has escaped him?'

'Yes.' It was Sanakht's turn to wait in silence.

'What is it?' asked Ignis, eventually.

'That,' said Sanakht carefully, 'is something I will keep to myself.'

Ignis shook his head very slightly.

'How does he not know?'

'Because the witch inquisitor he captured kept it from him before she died,' said a voice from above them.

Ignis whirled, his bolter arming with a metallic ring. His eyes went to the dark above, found his target, and pulled the trigger.

Sanakht's blow sheared the muzzle off Ignis's bolter an instant before the trigger clicked back. The bolt in the gun's chamber exploded. Credence surged forwards with a hiss of pistons, fist rising.

'No!' shouted Ignis. The automaton halted.

Sanakht held the tip of his sword steady in front of Ignis's eye, its power field throwing electric blue shadows over his face. Credence stopped.

'Peace, brother,' said Sanakht, carefully. Ignis's blank eyes looked back at him. For a second Sanakht wished he could read the play of the Master of Ruin's thoughts. Then Ignis nodded, and glanced at Credence.

'It's all right.'

The machine burbled back at him in machine code.

'Yes,' said Ignis. 'All right in all senses.'

Credence lowered its fist, and took a slow step back. Sanakht let out a sigh and turned to look up to the shadows from which the voice had come.

'I did not summon you,' he said.

'Summon? No but you called, oh yes you did. I heard, you see. I heard and came.'

Behind him he heard a heavy *clang* as Maroth dropped from the machines above. Out of the corner of his eye, Sanakht saw Maroth half rise then fold into a crouch on the floor.

Ignis's eyes flicked to the figure. He stared, and then looked up and nodded once. Sanakht moved the sword away, and felt the blade shiver as the power field shut down.

Ignis stood, looking between the crouched figure and Sanakht.

'So, another traitor,' he said.

Maroth laughed, the noise cracking down the machine gorge. High above, a false peal of thunder rolled. Sanakht could smell ozone and lightning charge. 'This knowledge that Ahriman does not have, it came from…' Ignis paused, his tongue twitching against his teeth. 'From *it*.'

'The other secret, yes,' said Maroth. 'The one that the witch held back before she died. Ahriman thought he had it all but she held one thing back. Clever, strong. Very strong.'

'But you took it from her after she died?' asked Ignis.

Maroth nodded, fingers tapping the snout of his hound helm.

'How?'

'I ate her corpse.'

Sanakht felt his hands twitch on the jet and alabaster handles of his swords.

'And what did you learn?' asked Ignis.

'Oh no. No. I have told once, and that is too many times to tell it, perhaps.'

Ignis looked at Sanakht.

'A secret is best kept by ignorance,' said Sanakht.

Ignis inclined his head.

'So you have an advantage, but the matter of Kadin and the *Sycorax* remains.'

'The iron crone and the beast,' gurgled Maroth. Sanakht felt his skin itch as he heard the words.

'The ship is a matter that can be dealt with.'

'And Kadin?'

'Will fall before he ever reaches battle.'

'Treachery is an answer to many questions,' said Ignis, then smiled, lips pulling back to show teeth etched with black digits. It was one of the most unsettling expressions Sanakht had ever seen on the face of another living thing.

They don't even see me. Hemellion watched the figures move around him as he crossed the upper platform of the bridge. *At least,* he thought, *they do see me, but none ask why I am here.*

A tall spindly figure in billowing ochre moved past him, its long beaked mask not turning to notice him. He shivered, though the air was as warm as blood. *I am part of this place. I am marked by one of their masters, and any who see me just see one of themselves.*

This part of the bridge was broader than the widest town square he had ever seen, and its roof hung higher than the tallest temple he had ever stepped into. Beyond its distant edge the next level of the bridge extended on, its vast space cleaved by gullies filled with machines, and crowded with cable-hung stacks of metal. He turned his head, blinking, allowing his eyes to adjust to the dappled half gloom. Thirty or more paces away a vast sphere of crystal hung above a plinth of black stone. The air around it shimmered, and its surface seemed to flow like oil poured onto water. A sharp pain brightened just behind his eyes. He coughed, and tasted blood in his spit.

The throne sat before the crystal. Carvings of beasts with claws, feathers and crooked wings covered its back and arms. Polished stones winked from the eyes of the metal beasts. Cables snaked away from its base to vanish into the floor. He could see a figure on the throne, wrapped in red, its small shape shrunken by the seat's bulk.

He took a step towards the figure and then stopped. He looked around, suddenly uncertain.

Why am I here? There is no need for me to be here. He looked around him, eyes flicking between twisted figures and hissing machines.

This impossible city will burn one day. This throne room will be a coffer of ashes. It will happen. It is certain.

He frowned, pausing, his steps halting on the azurite-inlaid floor. It felt like someone else had spoken those last thoughts. He shook himself, and the questions and doubt vanished. He looked back to the throne. *Is this the king of this star city? Ahriman rules here, but is this a monarch of a different kind?*

He moved closer, waiting for someone to stop him, for a bone and metal hand to close on his shoulder, or a challenge to ring out. A bloated figure with a mask like a mutilated bear glanced at him from the base of the throne's dais. Hemellion stopped, wondering if he should run or speak. The figure looked away again. Hemellion waited a second, breathed once, and waited for his heart to slow. He stepped onto the throne's dais, and felt the stone and metal vibrating beneath his feet. The smell of hot metal and cinnamon that filled the bridge was much stronger here.

Now he was closer he could see that the figure on the

throne was slumped in its embrace. If it had a body or shape, it was lost beneath a ragged robe. Cables connected to the throne vanished within the folds of fabric.

'Who are you?' said the figure on the throne.

The voice was a half croak.

Hemellion staggered back, and almost fell from the dais. The robe was moving, a head beneath a deep hood rising slowly to look at him. The face within the hood was a mask of cracked red lacquer. Its eyes were lenses of glass lit by green light. He stared back. The mask made him think of someone beautiful, and the voice sounded very human, female, young even, though worn and brittle.

'I… I am Hemellion,' he said at last.

'Yes. The One Time King. That is what they called you when they told me of you.' She paused. Hemellion heard something click and whir inside the hood. 'I am Carmenta. I am mistress of the *Sycorax*.' Hemellion stared at her. 'And why are you here?'

Mistress. So this ship, this city of the stars, had a mistress, a queen who ruled it for its master. He glanced at the cables running over the throne to the floor, and then out across the bridge at all its movement and thrumming metal, and out beyond that at the mindbreaking bulk of the *Sycorax* beyond the viewports. All of it extended from this point. This throne was the centre, and this hooded creature, with the voice of a weary girl, ruled from here.

'You wander much. Is there no purpose to it?' she asked.

Hemellion looked down again. There was genuine curiosity in the words.

What are you? he wondered, as his gaze flicked over her false face and eyes.

'I watch and I see,' she said as though his silence had been a question.

Still he did not reply. She did not look like the Cyrabor, with their yellow robes and beast masks, and hands which could be metal or could be flesh. She sounded different too, like a voice speaking from the sanity of his lost life. Yet here she was.

'You have a question,' she said.

'No,' he said, and shook his head.

She laughed. Far off across the bridge, machines crackled with blue sparks.

'Everyone has a question.'

He felt odd, as though, in all the months of hate and strangeness, this moment was a window into something he had lost.

'Why did they keep me alive?' he asked. She let out a breath. He found the gesture strangely disconcerting.

'Forgiveness.'

'Forgiveness?' He felt his face twist in puzzlement and disbelief.

Carmenta nodded carefully.

'And perhaps hope. What else can creatures like them want? What can any of us want?'

Hemellion found his gloved hands had knotted together, his skin prickling. He opened his mouth.

The light in Carmenta's eyes fizzed. Her head rocked from side to side. Her robed body jerked in the throne, sending the mass of cables thrashing. Jagged sounds spilled from her. He took a step back. Discordant noise filled the vast chamber: clanking, crackling, hooting. Cyrabor froze where they stood, their masked faces turning towards the throne. Hemellion stepped back. A brass hand whipped out from beneath Carmenta's robe and fastened on his wrist. The hand clamped tight. Hemellion cried out as he felt joints begin to pop under the pressure. Carmenta's head was twisting, eyes scanning the room.

'Who are you?' Desperation and panic bubbled in her voice. Behind him Hemellion heard running feet, and raised voices. 'Why are you here? What is your name?' He tried to pull his hand free but the brass fingers just squeezed tighter. She yanked him closer, so that his face was inches from hers. He could smell machine oil and human sweat and burning. 'Please, what is your name?' she pleaded, and her voice was no longer that of a woman or a machine, but a child. 'Please tell me why I am here? Where is father? Is he coming back? Help me. Plea–'

The light in Carmenta's eyes cut out. Her body slumped back into the throne, her head lolling on her neck. The light from glow-globes and terminals dimmed across the bridge. The vast space was suddenly quiet, as though every breath was being held, every machine waiting for a delayed command. Hemellion stood staring, unable to move. Hands and metal pincers and bronze-cased tentacles pulled at him. His arm was pried out of Carmenta's grasp. Voices were whispering angrily in his ear. He shook his head, still looking at the collapsed figure beneath the red robes. A moan trickled into the silence.

The lights flickered back on. The air clicked and buzzed as thousands of machines woke to life again. Carmenta's head rose slowly. Hemellion could see the smallest tremble in the movement.

'Let him go,' she croaked. Only then was Hemellion aware of the Cyrabor clustered around him, holding him. Their touch was warm, and their cinnamon stink made him want to gag. They hooted and clicked in reply. Carmenta shook her head. 'No, it was not his doing. Besides he bears Sanakht's bond, so I would not consider that course of action wise.'

The Cyrabor glanced at each other, muttered in low machine noises, and let Hemellion go. He shivered, and pulled his robe closer about him. He had no idea what had just happened. He could not remember why he had thought to come here in the first place, but he was very sure that he did not want to be here now. He turned and began to hurry away.

'Thank you, Hemellion,' came Carmenta's voice from behind him. But he did not turn back.

Kadin stopped. Something itched inside his thoughts.

Steam hissed in the air around him, venting from breaks in the pipes which formed passages along the walls and ceilings.

He turned to look behind him, feeling the pistons in his leg twinge with pain. There was nothing there, just the clouds of white vapour and the smudged glow of the lights beneath the floor grilles. All that lay behind him was half a kilometre of passage. In front of him there was another kilometre before the arterial hub. No one else came down here. Even the Cyrabor rarely walked here, and when they did it was mostly the most machine-made of their kind who came clanking and clicking over the metal grates. It was about exposure to something, though Kadin had never tried to understand what.

He knew these parts of the ship inside out. For years now he had walked them while the mockery of night fell on the *Sycorax*. The ship was a city without days, just the rhythms of the ship's systems dimming lights and thickening air. Some amongst the slave crew clung to that slow rhythm, calling the down cycles night, the return of brightness dawn. Kadin had wondered why, when Silvanus had told him of this custom, but then he had realised that it was always 'night' when he chose to walk the lowest decks. Ever since then he had not been able to think of the gloom-tarnished hours as anything else. After a while he had given up trying.

He turned and took another step. The feeling of unease came again, stronger, like a spider running on the inside of his skull. He kept moving. The grilles clanked under his steps.

+Kadin.+ The word came from just behind him. He

turned, shrugging the chainsword loose from his shoulders as its teeth began to turn.

There was nothing there. Part of him just wanted to laugh. He let the teeth of the chainsword slow to quiet, and turned back towards the way he had been walking.

Sanakht stood amidst the clouds of steam. He wore his high-crested helm, its faceplate polished silver and its eyes amber. His hands rested on the pommels of his sheathed swords.

Kadin felt a twinge of pain in his head. He could taste burned meat. He grinned, showing his teeth in their black gums.

'Get out of my head, witch,' he growled.

'You are resistant, aren't you,' said Sanakht. 'Your soul is like an unhealed wound, still slippery with blood.'

It was Kadin's turn to shrug. He reached over his shoulder and relocked the chainsword to his back. Sanakht watched the movement in silence.

'Why does Ahriman summon me now? We have not even gone into the warp.'

'He has not summoned you,' said Sanakht softly. Kadin went still, the feeling of unease still in his head, growing stronger now, pushing into his awareness. The pistons in his arms hissed, and his slab fingers twitched shut. Sanakht was speaking again, his voice still low, as though he was confiding, or confessing. 'We were once alike, you and I, at least in one respect. The warp once wanted me too. It had its fingers in the dreams of my mind, and in the shape of my flesh. My eyes changed first. They became like stars, and where I looked I could see the truth of things, all laid out in front of me. It was beautiful for a time. I stopped thinking about why I could not take off my armour. I stopped wondering why I didn't breathe.'

Kadin felt his machine hands twitch again. The feeling in his head was a building pressure now. His eyes flicked to the pommels of Sanakht's swords: the alabaster hawk head and jet jackal rested under the blue fingertips. He thought of the weapon on his back, the distance to Sanakht. He shook his head, and made as though to turn away.

'We share nothing, cripple,' he spat.

Sanakht seemed to tense, and then shook his head, relaxing again.

'No, no,' he said, carefully turning and taking his hands from the pommels of his swords. 'You are right. We are nothing alike and any similarities we might share, are skin deep.' Kadin was sure the swordsman was smiling with the last words. 'But even so I wanted to talk to you.'

'Why?' managed Kadin. The sensation in his skull made him feel as though it was about to explode.

'We once called it honour.'

Move! The thought exploded inside Kadin's head. He twisted.

Sanakht's sword cut and activated in a single movement. Kadin had not even seen it leave the sheath. The edge scored across Kadin's chest. Pain and fire spread from the wound. He smelt the ozone as the blade's field met the air. The second sword was already in Sanakht's left hand, slicing out from the scabbard, edge crawling with green flames. Kadin punched out. The force sword was burning a line across his vision. His fist slammed home. Sanakht hit the passage wall with a crack of shattering ceramite. Kadin stepped forwards, his hand pulling the chainsword free from his back in a snarl of spinning teeth. He cut down.

Sanakht's swords came up together, force and power-blades shrieking as their energies clashed. Kadin's blow hit the crossed swords in an explosion of light and spinning metal. The chainsword's motor kept churning teeth into the air. Kadin tried to pull back, but Sanakht was already moving, turning as he scissored the chainsword in two. Light flashed through the steam-thickened air. Half-molten chain teeth smacked into the flesh of Kadin's face. He stumbled, half falling, blood streaming into his eyes, hand still gripping the squealing stump of his chainsword.

The fall saved his life. A blade hissed above his head, trailing golden sparks. His shoulder crashed into the wall, and he rebounded with a shout rising from his throat, metal fist lashing out.

He could feel something scrabbling at his mind, clawing to get in, mewling as it slid off the tatters of his psyche. The world slowed, the edges blurred, the uncoiling momentum of his body a paused instant.

You are going to die here, said a voice at the back of his thoughts.

His lead foot hit the decking. Sanakht was sliding back,

both swords low, green eyes glittering in his silver helm.

He is faster than you are, faster than you ever can be. For an instant he did not place the voice, then he recognised the low tones of Thidias: his lord, his Chapter Master, his comrade in exile. Thidias, long dead in the cold dark.

You die here, brother.

Kadin's hand descended towards Sanakht's face, metal fingers wide.

'No,' hissed Kadin. 'Not yet.'

Sanakht whipped his power sword up. The lightning-wrapped edge met the palm of Kadin's hand. The power field buzzed as it kissed the metal. The fingers snapped shut. Light exploded through the corridor. Steam flashed to white sheets. Kadin's hand and arm vanished, molecules tearing apart as the power field splintered. Sword fragments rang against his armour and he staggered, the stump of his arm drooling black blood and piston oil.

Sanakht was spinning back, his shattered sword still held in his right hand.

Pain, thought Kadin, the revelation as sudden and shocking as the sensation itself. *I feel pain.* And something within him, a memory, a last seed of what he had been, broke open. Rage hammered through him, clear and bright. It felt like cold water and ice. It felt like fire, like waking to the sun's light.

Sanakht spun back, his sword a spike of rainbow flame. Kadin stood tall, pistons hissing. Sanakht lunged. Kadin's kick snapped out. Clawed toes hit the join between chest and torso plates and punched through. The sound of shattering ceramite cracked through the damp air like a bell breaking as it tolled.

Sanakht fell, blood spraying in his wake, the fire of his sword guttering. Kadin watched him hit the wall, and tumble to the deck. Kadin smiled, feeling the sensation spread across his twisted face. The world was suddenly bright again, living. Part of him wondered why now, but he pushed the thought away.

Sanakht was trying to rise, wet breath hissing from his speaker grille as he scrabbled at the wall. Blood was pumping from the crack in his armour. Kadin listened to the sound for a heartbeat, and watched as the swordsman pulled himself up a few centimetres.

The stump of Kadin's right arm was still bleeding, but more slowly now, as though machine and flesh were closing off the wound. He raised his foot and placed it on Sanakht's chest just above the cracked torso plate. He pressed down, slowly, feeling his pistons moving in the place of muscle.

'Do you wish me to talk to you before you die?' said Kadin. 'Or does honour not demand that now?'

Edges of broken ceramite ground over each other as he pressed harder. Sanakht looked up. Kadin saw something move in the swordsman's eye-lenses, a reflection of something behind him. He began to turn.

The power blade activated the instant before it punched through the right side of Kadin's chest. Inside his ribs he felt his lung and left heart explode. The blade sawed out of the front of his chest with a hiss of atomising flesh and bone. The world was suddenly slow again, slow and grey-edged and tasting of blood. He tried to bring his arm up, but it was just a stump now. Sanakht was rising, steadying himself on the wall with one bloody hand, force sword gripped in the other. Kadin tried to take a step, but his legs would not move. The power blade stabbed in from behind again, up and through the backplates on his right, and into his remaining heart. He turned his head, feeling the muscles in his neck losing strength even as he moved.

Maroth tilted his blind hound helm as he pulled the power blade free.

'Trusted…' rasped Kadin. His lungs were bags of blood. The beat of his pulse in his ears went silent. He no longer had hearts to beat.

'Exactly,' hissed Maroth.

Kadin felt Sanakht's force sword punch through his chest.

It felt like being cut by ice. He had time to think of his brothers, to think of Thidias, of Cadar, and Astraeos, all dead, all grinning at him out of faded memory. Their faces were skulls, and then they were laughing, and then the laughter was all there was.

XIV
CLAWS

Hel's Daughter was the first to kindle her engines. Behind her the *Storm Wyrm* and *Crone Hammer* followed, sliding into position behind the lead ship. *Death's Laughter* and *Blood Howl* came with them, holding station between the larger vessels. All of the ships were scarred black, their colours lost beneath the touch of flames and storms. Damage marked their hulls: jagged gorges ran like smiles across their bellies and backs, rippled craters pocked their prows, and the mouths of their guns shimmered with heat scarring. There were other marks too, twists in the metal and stone of their hulls, as though their substance had run like molten wax and then hardened. Around them, howling storms of light rose against the star field. The faces of beasts seemed to shimmer there briefly. Drifts of vapour the size of continents reached to brush the five warships. This was the edge of the Eye of Terror, but even here the warp storms spilled into the real, lapping against the channel of calm which led to Cadia. Beyond that the Imperium waited.

The Wolves' ships had sat in the folds of the storm, the clouds of ethereal energy gusting against their shields, thrusters holding them steady beside their sisters. They had sat, waiting, as patient as the turning of seasons, watching for what they needed. It had come at last: a scattering of ships, tumbling towards the light of Cadia's star. First there had been just one, its engines spluttering red, its hull bleeding gas and energy, rolling on its course like a drunkard. Then another had followed, its weapons firing at nothing, scattering fury and light in every direction. Then another, bloated and black, its hull weeping ectoplasm. Then ten, then ten more, then a hundred: all of them tumbling towards Cadia like a herd driven into a stampede. It was not a true fleet, it had no central command and little drove it towards Cadia besides the blind instinct of a starving predator drawn to light. The storms howled in its wake, and the Wolves waited. Only once the fleet had passed did Grimur give the order to follow.

The ships accelerated forwards, firetrails lingering in the warp's tainted void. On the bridge of the *Hel's Daughter* Grimur listened to the burble of the servitors in the red-stained light. The ship was shaking, the scream of its spirit rising as the reactors poured fury into the engines. An Iron Priest in a plough-fronted helm glanced up at him. Grimur nodded. The ship began to sing in pain as its engines strained.

Beyond the hull the five ships of Grimur's pack were streaking towards a distant point of light. If the calculations of the Iron Priests, and the augurs of the runes had told true, they would reach Cadia just after the ragged fleet they followed. By that point they would have been accelerating for days, their reactors close to rupturing, engines on the edge of failing, and going fast enough that they would hit the Cadian Gate like an arrow shot from the nether world.

Fire ringed the light of Cadia. Ribbons of explosions lit the void as mines and deadfall torpedoes detonated amongst the first wave of ships emerging from the Eye. Warp-twisted hulls became burning shards and scatters of melting slag.

Within the outer ring of mines the Imperial fleet waited. Hundreds of Imperial cruisers, destroyers and frigates marshalled beside battleships like knights holding station beside their kings. All were commanded by men and women who had earned the right with blood and victory; and as the Eye-ward hemisphere of Cadia filled with fire, they waited.

The rest of the incursion fleet came on, accelerating through the death fires of their kin. Cadia's defence platforms began to fire, tracing nets of light across millions of kilometres. Chaos-wrought ships burned, exploded, twisted, died and screamed into the silence as they bled. And still they came on.

The Cadian fleet began to move. Battle groups spread into position, squadrons folding out into webs of overlapping fire arcs. Eyes and minds across the fleet had seen the pattern of the threat and measured the response. This was not an attack, at least not one that was likely to succeed despite its size; it was an outpouring, the Eye vomiting out some of the damned held in its guts. It was violent yet predictable, a charge of unfocused fury. It would cost blood but the line would hold and cut the incursion down before it began.

Clouds of bombers dropped from launch bays and began to spiral outwards from their carriers. Wave after wave of torpedoes struck the warp-touched ships in an unforgiving drumbeat of explosions. Hulls became kilometre long shards, fuming flames and metal as they spun. The Imperial bombers fell on the remains, melta rockets and seismic bombs reducing wreckage to crumbs and molten spray.

Dozens of warp-touched ships died in the first rolling firestorm of the engagement, but not all. Some had changed in the Eye, the substance of their hulls bloating, becoming like a living thing, becoming like cancer grown from nightmare. These behemoths came on, heedless as parts of their hulls sheared away and burned, screaming with the voices of the dead. Across the system vox-relays blew out, and people woke from dreams with voices still wailing at the edge of hearing. Behind the sheet of flame formed by the ballet of destruction the warp storms coiled, reaching deeper into reality to caress the bloodshed.

The Cadian fleet met the surviving invaders with sheets of intersecting fire. Battle groups already in place fired on the enemy vessels' engines as their momentum drove them past. Fast frigates and gunboats cut closer, firing into already open wounds. The first of the great ships died under the guns of the battleship *Imperatrix*; already bleeding and wailing its pain into the warp, it exploded, the fire and gas of its death shimmering to blood and tatters of oily matter. But the rest of the corrupted vessels were not without teeth, and they did not die easily. Some fired back, roaring tainted plasma at their attackers, swallowing squadrons with sweeps of macro cannon fire. The invaders and defenders locked together, raking and cutting at each other even as they died. And all around them the blackness became an inferno.

Grimur's ships hit the sphere of Cadia as the battle reached its zenith. Their course had been calculated long before, washed through the half-machine brains of slaved lexmechanics until it was like a line cut by a razor through skin. The ships of the damned had struck the Cadian system in a wild rush, but they were still predictable. In the long weeks of waiting the Space Wolves had guessed how the defenders of Cadia would respond to such an attack. They might not know the precise shape of the forces defending Cadia, but how they would respond to a predictable enemy was itself predictable. The Wolves had picked a path that would slide past the defenders like a stone skimming over water. They had waited for the Eye to lash out at Cadia, lit their engines and begun to accelerate down their chosen path towards the cool darkness waiting on the other side of the system. Now, as defenders and invaders met, and burned together, the Wolves sliced through the edge of the battle sphere.

On the bridge of *Hel's Daughter* Grimur listened to his ship sing as the warp storms clawed at it and the fires of battle kissed its prow. He swayed as the ship creaked, his eyes closed, feeling the seconds flick past and finding that they were all still breathing. In his mind he was remembering ships cutting waves like long knives, the wind hissing as it cracked the sails taut, the spray flicking across the bow as the waves met its cutting edge. 'Running the claws of the storm', they had called it, dancing across a sea of white-crested mountains with thunderheads spread from horizon to horizon at their backs. And in that moment, his mind living in the past while the present trembled all around him, he knew joy for the first time in a thousand years. It was the joy of skill tested against chance, of running at a shieldwall and knowing that you were rolling the bones of fate and hoping for favour.

'Entering outer system sphere,' called a servitor in a dull monotone.

Well now. He felt his lips split over his teeth. *Let's run the storm's claws, and see if we are still sons of Fenris.*

The hull shook, and shook. Alerts and sirens began to ring through the cavern of the bridge. Servitors were calling out in their iron voices. Beside him his brothers stood, weapons held loose in their hands, red warning lights glittering in the coldness of their eyes. The ship shook again. The note of the engines rose and rose. Grimur tilted his head back, his grin splitting wide.

The song of the ship and the scream of the storm were one note, rising up to the sky like the call of the hunt.

Grimur howled. Death's blade was resting on the threads of fate. Beside him the other Wolves joined their cries to his.

Out in the void the arrowhead of ships cut through the system edge. Weapon fire reached after them. The Wolves' ships danced and spiralled, kissing the edge of explosions. The pursuing ships began to fall behind, their engines already burning to their white-hot limit. But two did not.

'They are still coming.' Halvar's voice reached through the howls. Grimur went silent, the joy draining from him as he looked at Halvar bent over an auspex readout. One by one the howls of the other Wolves faded. Just the snarl of the ship remained, rolling about them like thunder. Grimur looked at Halvar, his expression question enough.

'Two ships,' said Halvar. 'Very fast. They have stopped firing weapons.'

Grimur nodded. Fire power traded for speed: that was why the two ships were not firing. They had guessed that Grimur's ships had made the same trade-off, and so would be unlikely to fire back as the distance closed. They were racing to get close, and that meant they intended to use weapons that needed no power; they intended to board the Wolves' ships.

'What are they?' he asked, although he thought he knew the answer already.

'The mark of Ultramar is in their lines,' said Halvar, nodding grimly. 'They are Legion kin, jarl. They are Space Marines.'

Grimur took a breath, let it out, and shifted his grip on his axe, feeling the familiar sensation of its weight in his fingers.

'Make ready for battle,' he said.

The Space Wolves ships ran and their hunters came after them. There were two, their engines gouging wounds of flame across the void towards *Hel's Daughter* and her sisters. The *Lament of Calth* was a notched spear blade, the *Rubicon* a blunt hammer head. Both had once served the Ultramarines, but for two millennia they had borne new colours and oaths. The White Consuls aboard the two ships had served in the shadow of the Eye for a decade and blood had often hidden the white of their armour. They knew their trade, had been bred for it and honed by genetic mysteries.

As the distance to the target ships closed Lepidus, sergeant of the Fifth Squad of the Fourth Company, waited in the boarding torpedo's dark insides. Around him his brothers sat still, the white of their armour lost in the dark. They waited as the silence stretched, and the torpedoes shook around them. Phrases rolled through his thoughts, canticles and teachings worn smooth by repetition. Under the words his mind worked, flicking through dozens of conditioned possibilities and responses with every double beat of his hearts. Calm, total and complete, filled him. He had seen human warriors tremble before battle, their fear ooz-ing out of them in nervous laughter and hands shaking on weapons. He had heard that Space Marines of other breeds relished the moments before battle, as adrenaline surged in their blood. Both were unfathomable to him. Battle was focus, uncluttered by feelings or thoughts that did not serve the moment. There was a time for fury, a time to take lives like a reaper wading through corn, but they were moments to be chosen and put aside like any other tool of war. That was what the Codex taught.

He blinked, and an image of the space outside the ship opened in his helmet display. The engines of the *Lament of Calth* and *Rubicon* burned brighter. Each of them would need weeks to recover from the damage they were doing to themselves by pushing their engines, but they had no choice. Their quarry was almost at the system edge, almost free and clear into the waiting black beyond.

The boarding torpedo rang as mag clamps disengaged. Lepidus felt the vibration through his armour. He kept his eye on the image of the fleeing ships. He wondered what manner of corrupted creatures they held. He dismissed the thought. It was irrelevant. He would see the enemy soon enough, and speculation could cloud judgement.

Red light pulsed through the torpedo. A siren sang in Lepidus's ear and alerts pulsed at the edge of his sight. The torpedo felt tense, an arrow held nocked and drawn, wait-ing for flight.

The White Consuls ships waited until their reactors were

screaming, until they could go no faster or further, until the quarry were as close as possible.

Lepidus felt the launch as a blow. Amber alerts washed his eyes. His flesh pressed against the skin of his armour.

The torpedoes hit the void and ran clean to their targets.

Grimur felt his fingers twitch on his axe haft as he ran through the *Hel's Daughter*. At his back his brothers followed, boots ringing on the floor, strings of claws and teeth rattling against their armour.

'Mid section, lower arterial corridor. Incursion confirmed.' The dull drone of the bridge servitor filled his ear.

'Number of impacts?' he growled.

'Uncertain. Two probable. *Storm Wyrm* and *Blood Howl* report incursions in progress.' Grimur gave a silent curse. The boarding torpedoes had struck true and now most of his ships were compromised.

'Lower arterial corridor. Internal bulkheads breached, sections one hundred and five through thirty. Moving aft.'

Blood of Fenris, they are quick, Grimur thought. Whoever the Space Marines who had boarded the *Hel's Daughter* were, they were cutting their way through the ship with ruthless directness. They would be making for the reactors and engines. If they could damage them, the *Hel's Daughter* would drift on powerless, easy prey for the rest of the defenders to destroy once they caught up. It was an old tactic, as old as the first time a man had cut the ties of a sail to leave a ship as prey for the waves.

Grimur began to run faster, his twisted frame lumbering through stuttering strides. At his back a pack of Wolves who had once been men quickened their pace. The decks rang like thunder.

Lepidus pivoted from behind the corner, and fired four rounds – two high, two low. He was already running forwards as the gun-servitor's head and track unit exploded. Behind him his brothers advanced in a staggered line, hugging the walls of the passage.

They were thirty paces from the next bulkhead. One narrower passage opened to the right after ten paces. His eyes had marked it as soon as he had spun from the last corner. This close to the ship's engines the air itself shook and hummed with power, which meant he heard the servitor only an instant before it came around the corner. He dived towards the opposite wall as heavy bolter shells chewed the air and decking where he had been.

He came up and kept running forwards. The drum roll cough of a bolter echoed behind him, and the gun-servitor went silent. His brother behind him in the line had aimed and taken the shot the instant Lepidus had moved. They had not even slowed down. That was what brotherhood and the Codex meant – thinking as one, moving as one, synchronising without consideration and without pause.

Five strides from the bulkhead he shook the melta bomb free from his belt. He reached the door and swung the charge up, felt it mag-lock, and let go as he ducked to the right of the slab door.

One second.

He dropped into a crouch, pulled the two-thirds-empty clip from his bolter and slid a full clip home. An ammo counter flashed green in his lens display.

Two seconds.

Blue markers went still in his sight as the rest of the squad dropped into place either side of the door. Lepidus's eyes skimmed the walls, noting the soot of old fires and the rune marks scraped through to the bare metal beneath.

What enemy do we face here? part of his mind wondered. He tensed his leg muscles, and felt his armour mimic him.

Three seconds.

The melta charge detonated with a scream. Liquid metal exploded down the corridor from the centre of the door.

Lepidus was up and running through the glowing wound. Molten orange light fought against the darkness beyond. The passage broadened into a junction. The mouths of three other passages yawned darkness from across a wide floor. Lepidus had taken two strides when he heard the howl.

The sound ripped from Grimur's throat as he broke from the dark. A ragged hole still glowed red in the breached bulkhead. A Space Marine in white armour had just run through it, two more behind him. Grimur could see the raptor head on their shoulders, and the flecks of liquid metal cooling on the armour plates. Blue light danced across his axe as he leapt across the gap. Behind him he heard chainblades and power fields light as the pack broke from the dark at a run. The white-armoured Space Marines were turning, the muzzles of their guns moving with their eyes.

They move as one, thought Grimur as his arms swung up, the head of his axe dragging lightning behind him. *Like a single animal.*

The Space Marines fired.

Lepidus's first round ripped the left side from the howling warrior's helm. The figure dropped to the deck. The second hit square, exploding across its chest in a spray of fragments and light. He ran on and switched fire, hammering rounds low into the mass of warriors swarming from the tunnel mouths. His brothers were already clear of the breach, firing as they moved. Explosions danced across the decking, throwing armoured figures to the floor. Plasma whipped through the air, glowing and shrieking as it turned armour and flesh to vapour.

Strength thirty to forty, Lepidus thought. He reached the corner of another tunnel. Two of his brothers dropped close behind him. Movement and light filled the junction. Threat runes spun in front of his eyes. As one, Lepidus's squad chose the leading threats and fired two rounds each. The first enemy fell, and they were already firing into the next, and the next, hitting each of them with a deluge of bolt fire.

He saw grey armour, blackened and dented, hung with bones and teeth, matted beast furs hanging from hunched shoulders. Yellow eyes flashed above mouths which glinted with sabre teeth. These creatures were not Space Marines, not any more. Their jaws distended as they howled, skin and muscle stretching. No matter what flowed in their veins, they were creatures of the Eye now, and they would not pass into the Emperor's realm. Yet they poured into the fire and blood-daubed junction even as their brothers were cut down.

They were fast, of course they were fast. But they expected to have cut down their foes by now. Lepidus could read it in their movements as though they had screamed it. He pulled a frag grenade free, armed and threw it as he ran to the next tunnel mouth. Three more followed it from the hands of his brothers. A drum roll of detonations thumped into the air.

They just had to keep moving, keep pulling the enemy apart before their numbers and ferocity could prevail.

Lepidus dropped into cover, and raised his bolter. There were too many of them, even in an optimal position there were too many, and this was not an optimal position.

He did not see the blood-masked figure until it broke from the swirl of fire, its axe keening as it cut down.

Grimur felt the blow thump through the axe as it cut armour and bone. Inside, his blood was howling, straining at his skin. The white-armoured Space Marine staggered, crimson streaming from the stumps of his arms. Grimur could almost smell the warrior's shock in the iron-scented air. He cut again, spinning his axe low. The Space Marine tried to jerk back, but he had misread the blow. The axe head slammed into the Space Marine's knee. He fell. Grimur stamped down, felt, and heard, bone and armour break. Deep inside he could hear howls ringing across the moon-silvered night of Fenris.

No. Not now, not at this moment. These are noble warriors who die under our blades.

But the thought died, and he could feel the howling growing louder, echoing out of a dream.

He could feel his mouth opening inside the broken shell of his helm. Cartilage and bone cracked. He sucked a breath, felt his ribs and bones shift as blood-scented air filled his lungs.

Out of the corner of his eye he saw Halvar split another of the white-armoured Space Marines on a broken sword blade. The Space Marine fired, even as Halvar wrenched him from the floor. Bolt-rounds shredded the front of Halvar's armour. He jerked but did not let go, even with his armour ripped from his body. The Space Marine slid down the sword blade. Halvar's hands were wet and black with blood. He snarled, the sound echoing from his broken speaker grille.

The broken sword ripped free. Blood glittered like red pearls as it scattered and the dead warrior fell. Out beyond them the pack was ripping into the remaining warriors. All control had gone. Feet skidded on the offal-streaked floor. Blades rang and screeched across armour plates. There were dead Wolves on the deck, their heads and helms ripped open by bolter rounds shot into their eyes.

It should not be like this, thought Grimur, but his hand was already ripping the remains of his helm free. His eye caught a strip of honour parchment smeared to the warrior's shoulder with blood. The name 'Lepidus' was still clear beneath the gore. Grimur stopped. His limbs were shaking, his whole body was shaking. Around him the fire and clash of weapons was a dim tide that echoed the racing of blood in his veins. He had not felt like this for a long time, not since before the hunt began. He wondered if it was the Eye, its malign presence tugging at their flesh and minds one last time before they broke free.

He forced his muscles to stillness. He looked down. Lepidus was still trying to rise, still trying to fight, but his blood was deep on the decking, and his movements were becoming weaker. Grimur looked into the dying warrior's eye-lenses. A reflection looked back, stained in the red lenses' light: a hunched warrior in chewed power armour, his face bared to show yellow fangs as long as fingers.

'This is not a good death.' The words were heavy on his tongue. 'But you died well, cousin,' Grimur said and swung the axe down in a clean arc.

Four of Grimur's ships shook free of their attackers and clawed into the clear black beyond Cadia's rim. One remained, the *Blood Howl*, tumbling on as its engines cooled and power dimmed. It would die later, its hull broken open by macro salvoes from three system monitors. The Space Wolves on board would die standing, their weapons in their hands, howling as the fire and void took them. As their brothers ran beyond the reach of Cadia's defences, the Wolves of the *Blood Howl* called out a final message shouted into the night.

'To the hunt's end,' they said. Spattered with the blood of a foe he wished he had not had to fight, Grimur Red Iron heard the signal, raised the amulet at his throat and touched it to his lips. It tasted of cold blood.

'To the end,' he whispered. Around him *Hel's Daughter* shivered as power touched its warp drives and Geller fields. He turned, and walked from the blood-painted junction. His pack brothers watched him go, but did not follow.

'Sycld,' said Grimur into the vox.

'Jarl,' replied the Rune Priest's thin voice.

'We are clear of the gate. Go back to the Sea of Souls.' He paused, thinking of the face he had seen reflected in the dead Space Marine's eyes – the face of a beast dragged back from hell. 'Dream us a course. Take us to him.'

XV
CONNECTION

'I don't like it. Leaving my tower, I mean.' Silvanus glanced at Hemellion as they turned a corner.

The red-robed serf said nothing, his face a fixed mask inside his hood. Hemellion looked old. His skin was folded, his mouth a line in a pattern of wrinkles. A slight stoop to his shoulders showed through the thick fabric of his robe. In truth he was no more than four or five decades old, but that time seemed to have cut deep marks in passing. *Apart from the eyes*, thought Silvanus. There was young anger in those eyes, glinting just beneath the surface.

Silvanus licked his lips. They had been walking for three hours, weaving their way through the ship towards its forward decks. Silvanus was already sweating under the layers of his attire. Black velvet and silver gauze covered him head to toe, hanging in heavy swathes. What he had said was true; he did not like leaving his tower. He did not like the other things that walked the *Sycorax*. He also did not like the way they looked at him: like he was no different. He coughed nervously.

'Did they say why I had to come now?' he asked. Hemellion said nothing, but turned through a wide door framed by feathers cast in brass. A platform of worn metal waited beyond, red-lit tunnels extending to a vanishing point at either side. Hemellion and Silvanus stopped in the centre of the floor. The doors closed like biting teeth, and the platform began to clank down the tunnel.

'We are ready, is that it?' said Silvanus, raising his voice above the clatter and clunk of the platform. Hemellion looked down, refolded the sleeves of his robes over his hands. The man was wearing gloves, Silvanus noted, rough black leather, worn at the palm. *Why am I talking?* wondered Silvanus. *He does not want to talk, but I want him to so much that I am babbling like an idiot.* He shook his head. *You are an idiot, that is why,* he said to himself. At the back of that thought, another voice wondered if it was because the man was the closest thing to a normal human being he had seen for a long time. 'But why did Ahriman not come himself?' he wondered out loud. 'Or Sanakht?'

Hemellion turned his head slightly, and looked at Silvanus. The expression on his face was the same as if he had been looking at a plate of spoiled meat. He looked away.

The platform was moving faster now, the clatter of its cogged wheels and chains a single vibrating note. Cracked red lamps and dark openings flitted past. Silvanus thought he saw a cavern through one, a vast half-lit space filled with silent machines. He wondered if he had started the wrong way; he had seen Hemellion only once at a distance since the man had come on board.

'You are Sanakht's bondsman now, aren't you?' Silvanus called the question over the rattle of gears and rush of air. 'Hemellion, yes?'

'Slave.' The word was so soft Silvanus almost did not realise Hemellion had spoken.

'What?'

Hemellion was looking into the tunnel in front of the platform. The wind ruffled the hood of his robe around his head.

'I am a slave, as are you, as is every soul in this… prison.'

Silvanus felt a lurch of elation, then a twinge of fear.

'You should be careful of what you say.'

'Why?' Hemellion snorted. 'They know.'

'I–'

'Witches, with sight to see through souls. That's what they are. How can anything be hidden from them? They know what I think, and they don't care. My thoughts are less than nothing to them.'

Silvanus shook his head. He suddenly wished that he had not nudged the man into speaking.

'Such words are dangerous.'

Hemellion laughed, the sound loud enough to grate against the false wind. It was a nasty sound, cold and bitter.

'Is that why you serve them so meekly? Because you are afraid of dying?'

Silvanus's skin prickled cold. He thought of the voices that scratched in his senses when the warp closed over the ship, the faces he saw in the twisting of its storms, faces he had known, faces he wished he could forget.

'You don't know what you are talking about.'

'Oh no?' Hemellion laughed again, throwing his head back, so that his hood fell away. He stopped laughing, and looked back down. His eyes were polished points of reflection in the stuttered light. Silvanus felt the instinct to run, but there was nowhere to go. Hemellion lunged for him, gripping layers of gauze and velvet. Silvanus flailed, but the veil and hood were ripped from his face. He fell trying to cover his head, braced for the blows he was sure would come.

Hemellion stood above him, the crumpled mass of fabric hanging from his gloved hands, its edges snapping in the air. 'Look at you,' he said.

Silvanus was suddenly aware of the folded skin of his face beneath his fingers, of the space where his nose and ears had been, of the red pupil which had formed when his left eye had become black from edge to edge.

Hemellion let out a slow, controlled breath.

'I see you... and the rest, and I know everything I need to know about what the rewards of this life will be.' He let go of the fabric. It whipped away into the retreating distance. Silvanus felt himself rise and reach as though to

catch it, but it was already a ghost vanishing out of sight.
He slumped back to the floor.

The platform was slowing, the flicker of lights steadying. They stopped before a doorway. It was larger than the one they had entered through, its frame thicker and unadorned, the metal of its surface darkened with a film of grease and dust. As the door opened, Hemellion stepped towards it.

'Why live, then?' Silvanus called, hearing the anger and hurt in his voice. 'Why not put a knife through your throat, and be free?'

Hemellion looked at him. Silvanus thought he saw puzzlement form on the man's face, but then it was gone, as though wiped away. Hemellion turned and walked from the platform.

Somewhere inside he is hiding something, thought Silvanus as he pulled himself to his feet and stepped towards the door. Hemellion stopped, turning his head, face puzzled.

'What was that?' he asked.

'I didn't say anything,' said Silvanus. After a second Hemellion shrugged and walked on.

+You called, mistress.+ Ahriman's voice came to Carmenta out of the buzzing of the ship. Part of her found it reassuring to hear him. Part of her wondered why.

'You are returned from your dreams,' she said, and tried to make her voice sound strong even though she knew that he would sense the truth. She was talking through the ship's

mind interface units, thinking words which were transmitted into the systems of the ship. In a sense she was talking to the ship, or to herself, depending on how one chose to look at things. But she knew that Ahriman was there, his mind brushing the machine's systems, so she was actually talking to him.

+You realised I was back before I could announce myself.+

'You are surprised?' She paused and felt tiredness bleed through her. *'I can feel the ship, every rivet, every straining link of power and force. I can feel every soul breathe the air I exhale. There is a fire a kilometre down in the lower bilge levels. A fuel-flooded chamber was opened by a bilge gang. They lit a torch. Ten are dead. One is still screaming. There is a crypto-shunt linked to the forward sensor arrays that sings a song of pain to me, and always will, because no one can reach it without cutting through three metres of armour. I see all this and feel more. So yes, I noticed you return.'*

+It hurts to see so much, doesn't it?+

'Yes,' she said, and paused *'I am going, Ahriman. I do not know if I will last another battle. The ship is taking more of me. It's better now – when we are out of the warp. But when we cross back, when it wakes for battle… I did not understand why the Mechanicus called me a heretic all those years ago – now I know that they were right. One mind cannot harness a machine this powerful. There are other voices in here with me, all the time. They are getting stronger and I am getting weaker. Soon I will be gone, and they will remain.'*

+You are stronger than that, mistress. You always were.+

She laughed, the thought sound ringing like breaking glass.

'Liar. You always were.'

+You cannot be certain what will happen.+

'For you to say such a thing? I can. I can feel it, Ahriman. I am not like you – I don't need to see the future to know its course. The Sycorax *will take me, or…'* She paused, and Ahriman sensed a focusing of thoughts and will. *'Everything ends, one way or another.'*

+I have never believed in futures I do not make.+

'Of course not.' There was laughter in her thoughts again. *'You trust too much, and too little. You know almost everything but overlook what you do not understand. Your eyes see far but miss the cliff at your feet.'*

+Was that a rebuke?+

'No,' she said, and he felt the shrug without needing to see it. *'No, it was a farewell. That is why I called you, while I could, while I am still able. We are about to pass beyond and then into the crucible of battle, and everything has an end.'*

She thought she felt an echo of uncertainty, as though Ahriman had formed a mental message only to leave it unsent, like a word lost in an open mouth.

'Good luck, my friend,' she said.

'Are you ready, Navigator?' asked Ahriman.

Silvanus looked around and swallowed. Eyes looked at him from every part of the chamber. Some were human eyes, or at least eyes of things that looked like humans, the dull ghost-light glow of the Rubricae's eye-lenses, or the crystal glitter from within the Cyrabor's masks. This was not what he had expected, but he should have realised that they were waiting to go somewhere, and wherever that was they would have to return to the warp. But even if he had been prepared he would not have expected this.

The vaulted chamber had the signs that it might once have been a place of gathering. A single platform wound up the inside of its five walls. Corroded balconies hung from its tiered roof, and its floor was a gentle bowl of worn stone. Cyan and orange rust blooms bulged from the walls, and formed jagged stalactites amongst the slumping balconies. Figures crowded the chamber, standing at the sides, lining the winding platform from floor to ceiling. At a glance many seemed to be the white-robed thralls, but others were hunched and twisted creatures bound in chains and watched over by masked guards. A crystal sphere floated in the centre of the chamber. Silvanus recognised it as a duplicate of that on the *Sycorax*'s bridge. Other small globes hung in the air around it, like stilled planets in a vast orrery. Silvanus dropped his gaze as soon as he looked at the spheres. He had a sudden urge to close his eyes and never open them again.

The air shimmered before his gaze, as though he was looking through a heat haze. A smell of rain, steel and charring wood filled his nose then vanished, then returned again. Beneath the black silk bandanna, Silvanus's third eye was throbbing.

Beneath the floating spheres Ahriman stood. Focus radiated from him. Silvanus had to fight a sense of dizziness when he looked at him. He breathed in. The air tasted sour in his mouth.

Everything was about to get much, much worse. He was certain of it.

'Silvanus?' Ahriman spoke again.

'Lord Ahriman.' He nodded and made himself cross the floor. Behind him Hemellion had dropped away, vanishing to whatever insignificant shadow was his appointed place. Silvanus wished he could have gone with him.

'Once again we have a course to steer,' said Ahriman. Silvanus glanced up at the watching eyes, at the thrall psykers swaying in their robes, or rocking in their chains.

'A simple one?' he said, before he could bite the words off.

Ahriman said nothing, but tilted his horned helm to the side. Silvanus could not tell if Ahriman was looking at him or at the chamber.

'Are you ready?'

Silvanus came to a halt three paces from Ahriman, and bowed his head. Above him the vast crystal sphere seemed to press down on him. He was sweating. His velvet and silk robes clung to his shivering limbs.

I must do this. It is what they keep me for. I cannot refuse. Hemellion's words floated through his mind, heavy with scorn. *Is that why you serve them so meekly? Because you are afraid of dying?*

'I am ready,' he said, and looked up.

The red eyes of Ahriman's helm were like slits cut into a furnace. Behind Ahriman the eyes of hundreds looked down at him. He frowned, then tried to hide it. *Where is Astraeos? Where is Sanakht, and Ignis? Are they not needed for this?*

+No,+ said Ahriman inside Silvanus's skull. +It is I alone who will help you, and weave the path for you to follow.+

Silvanus's eyes twitched to the figures crowding the chamber's wall. *What are they here for, then?* he wondered, and wished he had not.

He looked back to Ahriman and nodded.

The world vanished. He was floating through clouds of light and patches of dark. Patterns were forming, spirals and lines stretching between absences in the light. It was beautiful, like watching creation flower. Silvanus had no idea what he was looking at or what it meant.

Follow the path, Navigator, he thought, then realised that the thought was not his own, and that somewhere he was reaching up and unwinding the silk from his forehead. The chamber was there, outlined in front of his eye in the flaring candle flames of hundreds of minds. As one, every psyker in the chamber screamed as their minds fused, and became a pyre. The crystal orb was a sun. The smaller spheres were spinning, changing colour and size. Silvanus looked into the crystal sphere. The patterns inside his mind spun, reconfigured and became a rushing tangle of threads.

Out beyond the sphere of Silvanus's awareness, the *Sycorax* and its fleet breached the skin of reality and slid behind the stars. Beneath the sphere, his third eye burning white in his skull, Silvanus saw the path and its end.

+Follow,+ he said in Ahriman's voice, and across the fleet sorcerers heard and obeyed.

PART THREE

LABYRINTH OF
A LOST KING

XVI
APOLLONIA

'Help us, Silvanus. Please, my son, help us.'

The voice was real. Silvanus could hear its rasping tones tingle in his ears.

Ropes of green, gold, and red liquid streamed past him, shattered, reformed, changed, swirled and tore. Black voids opened and closed in the kaleidoscope, like winking eyes. Sound screamed in his ears, stuttering like a looped recording, billowing like a storm wind, shrieking like glass shattering over and over again. And all the while he was racing forwards, accelerating, spinning like a seed caught in a gale.

This was not the warp Silvanus knew. Before it had always appeared to him as creases of white and black lines, like an ever redrawn and folded sketch on parchment. This was a different warp, one seen and given shape by another mind.

And there were the voices, which called to him from the edge of his sight.

'Please…'

The worst of them was the voice of his father.

'Help us…'

His father, a decade dead by the time Silvanus went into the Eye.

'Can you hear us, my son?'

The old man had withered away in darkness on Terra. In life Silvanus had met the man who had sired him twenty-one times. They had said that, in the end, Yanved Yeshar had died scrabbling in his own vomit, his bloated body unable to rise, his heart no longer able to beat. Yet here was his voice as clear as though he sat just behind Silvanus's shoulder. Silvanus did not look around. He would not look around.

A sphere of gloss blue and silver stars imploded in front of him. Expanding droplets scattered outwards. Silvanus dived, stretching himself to slide between two spheres which had started to burn with white and black fire. Somewhere, he knew the *Sycorax* had moved with him, its shielded bulk cutting through the squall. His path was the ship's, he was the Navigator.

A giggle bubbled up from somewhere out of sight. It felt soft, velvet and milk made into sound.

'So long watching, but never listening,' purred a slow voice, both deep and sharp. 'Do you not want to listen now?' Stars of silver spun around him. He could taste sweat and smell morning dew.

So soft, so warm, a voice to drown in and never wish for air.

'Do you not want to touch? Yes?'

He felt his gaze waver. The colours changed faster. The floating spheres broke. Dribbles and strings of rainbow colour became vast cubes, which stacked and combined and broke, tessellated and reformed.

What is happening? The thought screamed in his mind, and he wondered if somewhere he was shouting the question from a mouth he could no longer feel. Even in the Eye it had never been like this, it had never been…

'What do you wish?' The voice was the clatter of counting wheels, and the scratching of quills. 'It can be yours.' The voice cackled, now buzzing like a hive of insects. 'It can beeeeee–'

'Please, my son.' His father's voice broke through, louder than before. Silvanus could feel the tears in the old man's words. 'We watch you, son. We watch you as you dream and wake. Please help us…'

Then the other voices were all around him, growing louder, blurring into one.

'Help… Can be… Touch, yes..? Watch… Watch… Watch…'

The way ahead was suddenly a canopy of dark leaves lit by twilight. He could hear howls behind him, chuckling on a wind that made the branches and leaves thrash as he spun towards them. He could feel breath behind him, could smell rank meat caught in sharp teeth.

He wanted to turn to look behind him.

He would turn, he would look.

His gaze began to turn. At the edge of sight he saw yellow eyes glitter through the wind-tossed leaves.

+Follow my voice.+ The words gripped Silvanus and yanked his gaze around. +It is I, Navigator. I am here. I am here beside you.+

Ahriman. Before him the leaves parted to show a gap leading into the dark beyond. Behind him the howls rose, and the voices screamed and pleaded and laughed.

+Follow my voice.+ The words were clear, like the ringing of a bell on a still night.

'If we can just come with you...' said his father.

+Only my voice.+

The twilight jungle was falling past him now, faster and faster, the path twisting but never fading.

'We could be free...' said a voice.

+They are phantoms, Navigator.+

'We could all be free...'

How long have I been in here? Am I still navigating the ship or am I gone? Cold terror rose in him. *Am I just one more voice trapped in the storm?*

+My voice is all that is real.+

'We could help you...'

And then the canopy of leaves fell away beneath him, and emptiness was all around him.

+Now,+ commanded the voice of Ahriman, and Silvanus closed his eye. The warp vanished and he was flying through blessed blackness, the fading screams of his dead father following him into the welcome silence.

The *Sigillite's Oath* trembled as it cut through the warp. Nightmare claws clattered and sparked against its shield, and black currents pulled at its course, but it cut on, straight and true. In its empty strategium Brother-Captain Cendrion watched the image of the moon turn in the cone of cold light. It looked pitiful, a discarded bauble on the edge of greater things. The true planet which it circled was many, many times its size. A vast bloated sphere of gas, its violet surface swirled with white clouds, it owned the right to be called a planet, yet it was its child moon that gave the system its name.

Apollonia. He had read that name on bloodstained pages in the deep archives on Titan. Fragments of prophecy, lore on the nature of the warp and its potential – he had seen all marked with the glyph of the moon whose image now revolved before him. He knew now where those pages of lore had come from he had not known until now.

So many secrets. One layered upon another until it becomes our skin, until it becomes armour.

But that was the point, he realised; there was no absolute armour, nothing which could be buried so deep that it could not be found.

He waved a hand and the projected moon shrank. Apollonia became a speck, pirouetting without a care against the swirled background of her parent planet. The moon's necklace of weapon stations vanished. The silent drifts of torpedoes and mines waiting in cloud banks became a smudge of distortion. There were defences enough around Apollonia to turn back a small fleet, but it was not a small fleet that they would face. If Ahriman had learned what he needed from Inquisitor Iobel then he would come with all his might. The defences would not stand that.

And so we race through the warp, thought Cendrion, *and hope that we are in time.* Around him he felt the creak of the *Sigillite's Oath*'s shields as the warp tried to grip its hull. It was a fast ship, fast beyond what most would believe possible. Far behind her, lost in the shattered swirl of the warp, a greater fleet followed, heavy with warships loaded with fleet-breaking fire power.

But will even that be enough? He was not a pessimist; he was a warrior, and a warrior could allow himself no false hope. *Truth is our weapon, as ignorance is a shield.*

Cendrion shivered. His armour buzzed in sympathy.

'Cold, my friend?'

Cendrion kept every part of his features set, but inside he stiffened. Izdubar stepped up beside him. The inquisitor had donned armour. Black lacquered plates hid his slight body, and a sable cloak hung from his shoulders. A tri-barred 'I' ran down the moulded muscle of his chest, wreathed in silver laurels. A tiny daemon's skull with ruby eyes stared from the symbol's centre.

Izdubar raised his hand in front of him, thumb and forefinger held apart, as though he was sighting through them at the holo display of Apollonia.

Izdubar's thumb and finger snapped shut. The inquisitor held his hand still for a second then dropped it with a sigh of servos.

'If only it were so easy,' breathed Izdubar. 'Take what is at this moment one of the greatest dangers to mankind and make it vanish with a snap of our fingers.'

Cendrion shifted, and his silvered armour sighed as it moved with his muscles. He bore no sword, and though that was right and proper, it made him feel uneasy. Within him a fragment of his subconscious spoke the words of detestation and the names of the fallen in a never-ending litany. He listened to the thoughts rise and fall in rhythm. Far off on the edge of his awareness he heard the minds of his brothers, each an echo of his own. The *Sigillite's Oath* was just one ship, but seventy-three Grey Knights walked its decks, their minds like torches beside the thousands of candle flames spread through the rest of the ship. Comfort was not a concept he easily understood, but in moments like these he came close to understanding what it must mean to humans.

'You think that I had that power already?' said Izdubar, as though in answer to a remark that Cendrion had not made. 'That I should have destroyed the Athenaeum? If it no longer existed, then Ahriman and his kind would not seek it. We would not now be at risk of letting it fall into his hands.' The inquisitor rested his hands on the brass rail which circled the cupola. 'Yes, I could have done that long ago, with a word, with a… a click of my fingers.'

Cendrion turned to look at Izdubar. The man looked young, but was not. Two hundred years, three hundred? Cendrion was not certain, but in all the time he had known Izdubar the inquisitor had never seemed to age, as though he did not have time for it. Direct, deep, ruthless: those were the words which followed Izdubar. Cendrion supposed others found those qualities admirable, but he just found Izdubar unsettling, like a weapon whose balance never felt true but no one could understand why.

'One gesture and it could all have been gone, but what then? What would we lose? The war we fight is a war of knowledge, and we cannot fight what we do not understand. Destroy this and we blind ourselves. And does it not serve a purpose? A light that draws our enemies to us just as fires once drew wolves to our ancestors. We do not act only as protectors here, Cendrion.' Izdubar looked up from the star field, his eyes emotionless but glinting with reflected light. 'We are hunters.'

The Wolves rode on the edge of the storm. It rolled and roared around *Hel's Daughter*, rattling its hull with fury. It had begun soon after they had returned to the warp after clearing the Cadian Gate. The storm had grown even as they had tried to outrun it, as though it was pushing them before it. Grimur did not like that; it was an ill omen, one amongst so many.

'The moon broken at midwinter looks at us,' rasped Sycld

from where he lay on the floor. Ice radiated from the Rune Priest's body and climbed the navigation chamber's walls. Blood marked Sycld's lips, and formed pink crystals on his cheeks. 'Silver are the warriors of blade and book, and they come to the fire.'

Grimur touched the fragment of red iron on its thong about his neck. They had been riding the bow wave of the storm for days now, and all the while Sycld dreamed and Grimur watched over him, axe in hand. The Rune Priest's dream was the thread leading them on towards Ahriman, but it was taking its toll. Sycld's skin was snow white beneath its crust of ice, his face so hollow it seemed a skull. Grimur did not want to know how Sycld was holding onto his dream hunt. Other Rune Priests guided the other ships, but each followed Sycld's lead; he was the master of the pack, the strongest, and the one who saw the path most clearly.

What if he fails now? thought Grimur. *What if the evil that has touched us worms its way into his flesh? What if I have to cut his thread?*

'The king without a land, with a blade like the moon in his hand,' gasped Sycld, and Grimur's fingers twitched on the haft of his axe. Around him the witch ice thickened on the navigation chamber's walls, and the storm beat on their hull.

'Peace, brother,' whispered Grimur, although he did not know why. 'Lead us true. Do not fail us now.'

* * *

A storm was coming. Silvanus lay on the floor of his tower and wept. The tears were pink with blood against his white skin. He could feel the warp itch and tug at the edges of his thoughts. They had ridden a storm to reach Apollonia, and now it seemed to have followed them, circling the moon, its growing fury grating against reality like claws. He could taste it, could see it sometimes out of the corner of his eyes when he opened them. He kept them clamped shut now, but even in the darkness behind his eyelids the storm still laughed at him.

'Go away,' he moaned. 'Please, please leave me alone.'

The chamber door hissed open. Silvanus did not look up. It would be one of the other slaves come to bring him food, or… He did not care who it was. The storm was inching closer with every beat of his heart. The laughter was a raw chuckle of sharpening steel and dry bones now.

The floor rang like a struck gong. Silvanus looked up, eyes wide. Colours blurred and mixed at the edge of his sight, but even through his tears he could see the shape that stood above him. It towered to the ceiling, a brutal approximation to a human form made from pistons and flame-orange plating.

'What are you…' he began, then realised what he was talking to, and swallowed. Above him Credence cycled its shoulder plates. The whir of gears grumbled like a resigned sigh.

'**Navigator.**' The word boomed from its speaker grilles. Silvanus clamped his hands over his ears, but in the ringing echo he recognised the recorded voice of Ignis. The cannon on Credence's back turned from side to side, before arming with a cold metal *clang*. 'You. Come. With. Me.'

The seismic shell rushed into the void on a tongue of flame. Twenty-seven milliseconds later its secondary charge fired. Rockets drove the fifty-metre-long metal dart down into gravity's grasp. Thin atmosphere skidded down its length. Its point began to glow. Thirty-six seconds after it had left the muzzle of its gun, it shed its primary rockets. Curved sheets of ceramite came free, caught the moon's atmosphere and snapped away. Now a finned blade of silver, the warhead fell, spinning, drawing a luminous line across the moon's black sky. Inlaid patterns of golden wire began to melt from the warhead casing. White-yellow drops formed spirals in its wake. The slim silver arrow struck the grey crust and vanished. Dust plumed into the thin air, rising high on the weak gravity. Driving deep, its adamantine casing glowed as it drilled through rock and compacted dust.

The warhead reached its final depth and detonated. It had lived in flight for a hundred and seventy-two seconds. The surface of the moon crazed around the impact site, collapsed and then exploded upwards. The ground rippled like water, dust rising in waves across grey dune seas. Rocks sheared and slumped into chasms. At the centre of the detonation a jagged wound stared up through the spreading clouds of dust like a shattered pupil in a blind eye.

Ignis watched as the breaking of Apollonia's surface

unfolded across his helmet display. His armour was shaking around his flesh, ringing in time with the *Word of Hermes*'s rolling fire. In his right eye the latticework of fire and explosions above the moon multiplied in complexity.

The moon's defences were still active. Slaved weapon platforms, drifts of mines and deadfall torpedoes glittered like chains of jewels hung against the sable of space. The defences were formidable indeed, but not enough, never enough. Grids of turbolaser fire reached out towards the ships of Ahriman's fleet. Energy shields shattered. The fleet replied. Torpedoes slid into weapon platforms to explode in flowers of white light. Broadsides of plasma fire sliced through orbital stations. Globules of burning matter tumbled through a haze of vented gas and liquid. The numbers, the timings, the angles, all were just parts of a growing pattern which he had set in motion and he controlled.

Something stirred at the back of his mind, and he felt a silent chuckle shiver through him. He stood at the pattern's centre, his mind linked to a psyker on each of the vessels, his soul feeling the warp echo as the numbers and angles built and built. The warp spun around the moon, spiralling into it like a whirlpool, pressing close, thinning the skin of all things. The moon itself glowed like a sun in his mind. Space close to it blurred with skeins of colour. Distances seemed to change as he looked at them, and smudges of unlight crackled across its surface. He could see it with his soul, like lightning bleaching storm clouds to white. It had been a long time since he had let the ratios of ruin have full sway, and the possibility was just too tempting, and far, far too dangerous.

Ignis shook his head, and went back to watching his ships strip Apollonia's defences a piece at a time. Another weapons platform fragmented into fire. Thick lines of laslight flickered out from another platform and drew a line across the hull of a ship, slicing off sheets of pale bone and oily blue growth from the hull. The ship rolled, its engines misfiring.

The *Synetica*, thought Ignis, and recalculated the fleet's effectiveness based on this loss. Numbers spun through his awareness. His hearts beat faster, as wild deviations entered into the matrix of destruction. The *Synetica* exploded, its hulls bursting with fire like a corpse bloated with air. Behind the fire cloud the rest of the fleet moved around the moon. Flowers of plasma bloomed amongst the laslight and the stitched lines of turret fire. It was beautiful to Ignis's eyes, a sculpture in calculation etched in fire. The calculations resolved and became a sum which reached into the infinite. All was ready.

+Surface breach open,+ he sent.

Astraeos lay bound to his bed of steel. Consciousness returned to him again, and with it came pain. The empty sockets of his eyes ached with the dull rhythm of his pulse. The bolts securing the metal hood to his scalp were hard points of sharpness. The needles linked to the tangle of injector tubes twitched every now and again, as they sucked blood from his veins and pumped drugs in. Over it all the sickening shadow of his warp-blocking guardians smothered every thought and sensation in a coiling blackness. The shackles were vibrating against his flesh. The edges had rubbed and cut into the meat of his arms. And he could feel dry blood layering his skin.

This time when he awoke he made no sound. He had already emerged from the drug coma several times over the last... in fact he had no idea how long it had been since the inquisitor had left. There had just been dreams in which he would see the home world of his Chapter burn again and again. The dream always ended in the last moments before he fled the inferno. He would look back through the flames and see the silver warriors, and the Dreadnought striding at their head. He would wake, as now, to the bitter sharpness of his imprisonment. He would lie for a few moments in the blackness of his blindness, then the needles would jerk in his flesh, and the drugs cast him back to his dreams of a burning fortress and a dying world.

He kept his breathing low, his pulse controlled. The vibration of the shackles and the slab beneath him was a new sensation to wake to. He thought he knew what it was – battle. The ship he was on was firing its guns and receiving fire, recoil and explosions juddering its metal bones. He tried to judge the severity of the battle from the shudder of the metal; intense was his guess, a big storm of a fight.

Is this the death of Ahriman? he wondered. *Have I woken to the moment when the Inquisition enact their execution?* A hollow space opened within him at the thought. *My last oath broken.*

He felt his pulse rise, fought to slow it, but too late. A machine chimed nearby.

'Biorhythms rising,' said a metallic voice. He heard a rustle of fabric and a click of gears as the tech-priest came close. He opened his mouth, drew breath. The needles in his flesh twitched and he felt the dull hammer of the sedatives fall.

'No–' he managed, and then he was falling back into soft darkness and the rising crackle of memories.

Hemellion sat and listened to the scrape of steel on stone. Every now and again, he stopped and raised the crescent of metal up, so that its edge caught the light of the oil lamp. He turned the blade over, watching its sharpness emerge. A distant *clunk* rang dully through the small room. Beside him the flame from the bowl of burning oil fluttered. He turned his eyes up to the shadow-clung corners of the chamber. The sound faded. He dropped his head and started sharpening again.

The blade had been a piece of metal he had pulled from the edge of a floor. He had been sharpening it for days now. First by the light of the glow-globes, then in the half dark when the globes had failed a few hours before.

He began again. The stone scraped down the edge, and he listened as it became sharper.

He thought of Helana back on Vohal, scraping a stone

down the edge of her sword every morning. She had stopped every now and then, raised the sword, looked at the edge and continued. Ten years. Ten years of keeping her blade sharp to protect him from assassins. She had been one of the last to die. He thought of looking down into the fortress courtyard on so many mornings, of the sparks flying into cold winter air as the grindstone sharpened swords, and scythes, and knives. He thought of the corpses he had seen in the last days before Vohal died. Ragged smiles grinned up at him from necks, and he saw the knives still clasped in the hands of the corpses who lay furthest from the others. Mercy, a gift given at a knife's edge at the end of hope.

He thought, and listened to the whisper of the stone on the blade's edge.

He thought of the dust on the cracked lips of starving mouths.

Dust.

That was all that remained.

Dust scattered on the wind, dropped from an uncaring hand.

Ahriman's eyes had looked down at him, and then Sanakht's.

He thought, and thought, his memories winding around his hate. He did not think of the passing time, or of the shake and shudder of the ship, or why he thought of it now as a ship and not a city. He did not wonder why no other thoughts entered his mind, or what he was going to do. He thought of the blade, of the razor scrape of the stone on its edge, of its sharpness.

+Send us,+ sent Ahriman. Light shot into the air from the serpentine patterns cut into the floor. Sanakht felt the warp twist around them. He fought to keep his head from spinning. He stood beside Ahriman. Beside them sixteen Rubricae stood in two perfect circles. The chamber was a blur beyond a brilliant curtain. Rainbow light shattered from the crystal pyramid above them.

Sanakht's lips peeled back from his teeth as pressure built in his skull. The transposition to the inside of Apollonia was possible only now that its shell was broken. Wild currents of warp energy surrounded the moon like a shifting mesh. Something about the moon itself seemed to cause these distortions, as though to protect it from exactly what Ahriman was doing. Opening up a gate through such a tangle of warp eddies and streams was close to suicide.

The breach blown in the moon's crust by the seismic charge had opened a channel of opportunity. That channel was narrow and dangerous, but Ahriman was still going to take it. They could have dropped into the labyrinth by gunship, but he had wanted to get as close to the core of the moon as possible. That, at least, was what he had said.

The curtains of light surrounding Sanakht and Ahriman turned blinding white. Ahriman's focused power screeched around Sanakht's mind. The chamber vanished around them and he was streaking through oblivion like a burning arrow shot at the night sky.

XVII
PATTERNS

Darkness ahead, darkness behind, thought Sanakht, as he followed Ahriman. The tunnel around them was circular and completely smooth, as though carved from the black rock by water. No light reflected from the walls, floor or ceiling. The Rubricae's eyes shone cold and lifeless in their helms, but did nothing more than sketch the lines of their armoured heads. Even his helmet display could not pierce the gloom. The warp did not help either. He had tried to reach out with his mind, but at once had found his focus ripped away as though caught in a racing river.

The Labyrinth. That was what Ahriman had called it, and Sanakht now understood why. The moon was not solid. Tunnels extended beneath its surface, forming a vast honeycomb of polished black rock. At its core, at the end of a path twisted through the dark, lay the Athenaeum.

The warp was here, running through the walls and the still air of the tunnels, pouring down to some invisible depths. It was not just a labyrinth in the physical realm, it was a labyrinth of the psyche. It felt familiar, though he had no idea why, like walking through the ruin of a long-lost home. How deep they had descended or how far there remained to go, he did not know. Ahriman alone moved with purpose, floating ahead of them, robes rippling as though in an invisible wind.

Sanakht felt the sudden tug of the secret that he had buried within himself beneath layers of thought baffles and masking. It nestled there, warm and tempting with its promise. It would begin soon. No, he would not allow it to come to the surface. Not yet. He was too close and there was still too much risk.

Ahead of him he saw Ahriman twitch, and then stop. The Rubricae froze around him. Sanakht felt his hearts still. Had his mask of surface thoughts slipped? Had Ahriman looked deeper into his mind for some reason? No – he would have known. Weak as he was, he would have known, and besides what cause would Ahriman have not to trust him?

+Is something amiss?+ asked Sanakht, and heard his thoughts echo as real sound.

'Amiss… amiss… amiss…'

+Is this labyrinth different from what the inquisitor told you?+

'Told you… you… you…'

Ahriman turned where he hung, and looked up as though at a sky which was not there.

'It is not a labyrinth,' said Ahriman with his true voice. No echo followed. 'These tunnels and the warp currents which surround them are simply a by-product of how it formed. It is a map, carved out of the moon's cold core by the warp. The whole structure is a stabilised ball of substance and aether.'

'It was made by chance?' said Sanakht.

Ahriman's reply cracked dully through the air.

'No, nothing here is chance. Its passages are a map of trickery and deceit, and the warp vibrates through it.' Ahriman pivoted back to face the darkness ahead. 'It was made by thoughts pouring from beyond into reality. It is an echo of those thoughts, like a footprint left on the soft sand beside an ocean.'

The Rubricae clattered back into motion as Ahriman glided forwards. Sanakht followed, his hand brushing the pommels of his swords.

'Whose thoughts?' asked Sanakht, as he came level with Ahriman. 'You said that this place was shaped by thoughts, but whose?'

'Our father's,' said Ahriman.

Hemellion stepped onto the *Sycorax*'s bridge. He stopped, staring down at the worn brass of the floor, noticing the old marks cut into the head of each rivet.

Why am I here? He knew where he was. He had been

here before, many times. He knew that, knew that this was the... bridge? Yes. That was it. He knew that this was the centre of the ship...

But what is a ship?

A figure moved past him, moving fast, its tattered robe flicking in its wake. He blinked. He was not sure he knew what a ship was or why he knew that he stood on one, but he knew that it did not matter, and neither did why he was here. All that mattered was that he *was* here.

He looked up, his eyes slowly focusing. Something was happening. He could see figures moving about the tiered pits of metal sunk into the bridge's deck. They wore yellow and had masks like animals. He stared at one. Its mask was in the shape of a snake or a lizard with scales of opal.

Cyrabor... Was that their name? It felt like it should be.

More cries filled the air, rising over the metal clatter. There was some kind of panic, he was sure, but it all seemed very distant. He was where he needed to be, and that was good.

He looked down at his hands. They looked old. How had that happened?

No. That was right, he was old. He had grown and lived on a world of stone, and rain. He was not there now, he was here, on a ship...

He began to shuffle forwards. The silver chains around his ankles clinked against the brass floor. No one seemed to look at him. Shouts and clanks of metal echoed up to the high roof above. Black smoke chugged from a cluster of slab-like machines. Strange thick smells filled his mouth and nose. He kept moving, weaving between hurrying Cyrabor. In the distance the command throne rose above the smoke, sound and rushing figures. He could see a red figure on the throne, made small by distance and the vastness of the chamber.

In the folds of his robe the sharpened sickle of metal sat in his hand. It felt cold. He could not remember why he had it, or where it had come from, but that did not matter. All that mattered was that he was here.

He kept moving.

Ignis glanced up as Credence came to stand beside him. He did not need to ask if the Navigator was secure; he could feel the pathetic man's thoughts scratching at the walls of his new prison.

The automaton clattered and buzzed at him.

'All is well,' he said, then nodded to himself. It was true, all was as it should be, every piece was in place, every factor in the pattern calculated, and every progression unfolding on its necessary path. His mind was connected to other minds throughout the fleet. Some of those minds commanded ships, some simply stood beside those that did. That web of coordination had been necessary to get Ahriman into the correct position, but it was not necessary now, at least not in the same configuration. He broke the connection to several minds, and focused on others, bringing them to the surface. They had all been waiting for this moment; all of them stood ready to act.

+Now,+ he sent, and in his mind the pattern bloomed into full life.

Carmenta saw the first shots and thought it was a mistake. Ahriman's fleet was spread in high orbit above Apollonia. Some clustered together, others spread far apart, arranged by Ignis in a pattern that she had not tried to understand. The last of the moon's defences had been stripped and most of the ships had settled into silence.

The *Malicant* was the first ship to move. Shaped like a serrated spearhead of soot-crusted copper, it was the warship of Mavahedron and his slave clans. It pirouetted away from the rest of the fleet on a burst of thrust. Carmenta watched it, her sensors drawn by the movement. The *Malicant* fired its guns. Light raked the void, and exploded around a pair of black-hulled frigates. Carmenta saw the shockwave as their shields collapsed, and suddenly time was crawling as surprise flooded her. The *Malicant* fired again, and the frigates exploded one after another.

Then time snapped forwards, and more ships were breaking formation and firing. Sound exploded from the vox. Cries of shock and rage rang through Carmenta's sensors. Fire slashed the dark. Shields burst. Plasma and laser energy carved into hulls, and atmosphere vented into the void. Where there had been order, there was now a spinning tangle of ships scrambling to bring their guns to bear. Where there had been a single fleet there was now the fire and rage of battle.

Treachery, or terrible error, it did not matter; Ahriman's fleet was tearing itself apart. She had always doubted that the ties of allegiance binding the fractured warbands together would hold, and now they were shattering before her eyes. She would not allow it. Orders flowed from Carmenta into the *Sycorax*. She began to turn, her sensors reaching for firing solutions, tiered batteries of her guns rotating to targets.

She froze. The impulses commanding her weapons teetered on the edge of completion. She had missed something, something obvious yet significant. She gazed at the ships spinning wildly above Apollonia, at the streaks of flame and the fires kindling in wounded hulls. Then she realised what had held her will from firing. None of the ships tearing at each other had fired on her. She sat untouched, while the rest of Ahriman's fleet began to burn.

No, not all of the rest. She saw it then, the ships that floated amongst the unfolding carnage, untouched, serene.

What was this? What was happening?

She thought of her words to Ahriman.

'Remember that they followed Amon once, and that they tried to destroy you.'

She felt numb. Treachery: it was the only answer. Ahriman had gone, and now his enemies moved against him.

Her will surged into her guns, and her sensors reached and locked onto targets.

The silver ship ripped into existence with an exploding pressure wave of aetheric energy.

* * *

The *Sigillite's Oath* punched through the fabric of reality like an arrow through ragged cloth. Its engines burned to nova brightness. Around the fire-ringed moon of Apollonia ships began to turn like vulture heads looking up from a corpse. The strike cruiser accelerated, twisting its course into a corkscrew as the first distant salvoes streaked past it. Its own guns were still out of range, but would not be for long.

Transit from the warp to reality was dangerous. Making that jump within the bounds of a star system was suicidal. The smallest of navigational errors and a ship could exit into the heart of a sun or the core of a planet. Few ships ever attempted such a feat and survived, but that was exactly what the *Sigillite's Oath* had done. Steered by the finest Navigators in the Imperium, it had cut through the warp storm gathering around Apollonia, and emerged almost on top of Ahriman's fleet.

Cendrion felt the backwash from the warp exit spill over him as he marched through the pulsing yellow alert light. His brothers marched beside him. The clank and hiss of armour echoed in time with the ring of their strides. The shriek of torn reality was fading in his mind, but he could taste the rise of the growing storm. It tasted of lightning and blood. Above it the psychic voices of the Eighth Brotherhood rose in communion.

+Mahalalel stands ready.+

+Iofiel stands ready.+

+Gadal stands ready.+

The sendings soared through Cendrion's awareness. He could feel the ghosts of his brothers' thoughts. Barakon's psycannon was a brief weight in his hands. The dark closed over him as the hatch of a Stormraven hissed shut behind Sabaoc. Pain itched up his spine and neck as he was Anak waking in the embrace of his Dreadnought coffin. He listened, allowing the walls between his mind and his brothers' minds to dissolve. They were one, a brotherhood joined in blood and soul.

+Strike force Ishen stands ready. Launch pattern locked. The blade is drawn.+

+ Strike force Sangrian stands ready. The blade is drawn.+

+Strike force Caspian stands ready. Teleportation targets confirmed. The blade is drawn.+

'They have already broken through to the labyrinth fortress?' Izdubar's words pulled at Cendrion's focus. The inquisitor lord strode ahead of him, his oil-black armour gleaming in the pulsing light. The two other inquisitors, Malkira and Erionas, walked beside him. Both were armed and armoured. Malkira was a giant of pistons and chrome, Erionas a spectre in grey robes and layered red plate. Cavor followed them, his body bulked in an armoured envirosuit. Holstered pistols and bandoliers of bullets clinked in time with his steps.

'Apollonia's surface is breached,' said Erionas. He was breathing hard, as though not used to moving so swiftly. 'An assault is likely to be in progress. But...' Erionas stopped in his tracks, crystal eyes dancing with data.

'What?' barked Izdubar.

'The enemy fleet is firing on itself.'

'An unexpected advantage,' nodded Izdubar. 'How long until the rest of the fleet catches up to us?'

'We don't know,' said Erionas. 'The storm is rising up fast. Perhaps they will not arrive at all.'

'Then we stand alone,' said Izdubar.

They turned a corner and a blast door peeled open in front of them. Before them a wide chamber opened and spread into the distance on either side. Machines towered into the space above, crawling with lightning. Incense and ozone hung thick in the air.

+Ship weapons approaching range. We are at the moment of execution.+

Cendrion stopped at the centre of a circular depression in the deck. Behind him the thirty brothers of his strike force followed to stand in clusters around him. The inquisitors stood next to him. He could hear the pulse of their thoughts: Malkira's eagerness bright beside Erionas's cold indifference, Cavor's fear of what they were about to do bleeding out of him even as he tried to control it. Above them the vast machines began to keen. The beat of the yellow alert lights rose. The warp was churning around them now, scraping the skin of reality thin.

He glanced at Izdubar. The inquisitor lord looked back, the red eyes of his lion helm glowing bright.

He nodded once.

Cendrion blinked an amber rune at the edge of his sight.

The yellow light became red. A heat haze blur rose around the machines.

He looked at the red rune. Cendrion could feel the teleporters poised to reach into the warp, gripping it like fists ready to yank them through space and time. In their gunships and boarding torpedoes the rest of the brotherhood waited to be unleashed into the void.

+Strike force Cendrion stands ready.+ He blinked the activation rune. The machines shrieked. +The blade falls.+

Ignis was shaking. Geometry glowed in the air of the crucible. Lines and circles broke, reformed and connected into a different pattern. This was how he saw the battle as Ahriman's fleet consumed itself, not as the projection of machines, but as arcs of warp fire cut into reality. His mind held all the values of strength, and his senses saw the death he wrought as it created geometry in the beyond. The storm rose in answer. The patterns and ratios written in death and fire pulled the billowing fury of the storm on and on, faster and faster. It was coming. It was almost complete. Almost.

The silver ship flickered into his awareness. It streaked across the void, dancing between the fires of the slaughter. It was fast, very fast, and more importantly it should not have been there. For a second his mind just stopped. The plan, so carefully crafted, was about to fall apart.

'No,' he gasped, and the word misted cold white in the heat of the crucible. 'No, no, no! Not now. Not now.'

The growing pattern began to change, slowly at first then

faster and faster. Lines and sacred ratios shifted, values exploded to infinities, and all the while the warp roared in the voice of an oncoming storm.

Too fast. His mind danced with calculations realigning the fleet into a thousand possible configurations, homing in on one that would still fit.

Behind him Credence was clattering in machine cant.

He could still do it, he could still bring the pattern into alignment. The plan could still work...

His mind stopped. The geometry of his battle design began to crumble into shadow and sickly light.

It was not supposed to happen like this.

Alarms began to shriek around him.

The shockwave of teleportation displacement blew him across the crucible.

He rose in time to see the silver-clad Space Marines come at him in a blur of blades and gunfire.

+What was that?'+ Sanakht sent.

The smooth walls of the labyrinth were ringing with the clatter of feet and the thrum of power armour. The pressure of the warp was tight around his mind. His teeth ached, and he could taste burning sugar and stagnant water. Ahriman was gliding beside him, robes rippling as though in a wind. The Rubricae marched behind.

The walls shook again.

+What−+

+Battle,+ said Ahriman, still moving, not even looking

around. +The Inquisition have raced to stop us before we can reach the Athenaeum.+

+You have seen this?+

+No, but who else could it be?+ asked Ahriman.

Sanakht twisted to look. A glow formed in the darkness behind them, growing even as he stared at it. A high keening filled his ears.

+How could they find us in this?+

+It is their fortress,+ replied Ahriman. +They move swiftly, but we are close, very close. I know it.+

Maroth began to run as soon as he was in the passage. The silver doors at the end of the narrow corridor were already glowing, the runes on their surface reacting to his presence. He breathed a curse and they guttered to shadow.

He had nearly left it too late. Things were moving faster than they were supposed to.

He raised a hand and the doors hinged open before him. He bowed his head as he crossed the threshold. The chamber beyond was white with frost. Icicles hung from the chains holding his master's host. The body floating above him had changed again. Skeletal wings hung from its shoulders, the tips of iridescent feathers budding at their edges. Its head was smooth skin broken by a wide grin of teeth. An extra set of joints had appeared in its arms and legs. It looked down at Maroth slowly. Air hissed from between its teeth. Even without eyes Maroth could see his master in his mind as a shadow defined by blue fire.

'Sire,' he began.

+Yes.+ The daemon's voice crackled like burning paper. +He will call me soon. This part of me must be free when that comes to pass. I must be able to go to him.+

'Sire…'

+Rise, Maroth.+

Maroth stood slowly, head still bowed. He was shaking, his dented armour rattling.

+You have served me well.+

'Please,' said Maroth.

+But you are a weak soul.+ The daemon hung in silence and turned its sightless head, looking at Maroth. +You have been part of something greater than you understand.+

'No.' Maroth forced the word out of his mouth. His flesh was trembling as though he was a human child standing lost in a blizzard. He could feel his tongue burning behind his teeth. 'No…'

+Maroth,+ the daemon purred. Pain skewered through Maroth. He tried to cry out but his tongue had gone. He felt hands reach into his muscles, felt fingers that were not his own flex. His hand began to rise. +You will serve me once more, Maroth.+

Maroth's hands were reaching for the daemonhost's pale skin. The fingertips began to burn.

You said I would not die, he screamed inside his skull. *You said I would rise.*

+You will, my broken son. You will.+

* * *

Carmenta saw the silver ship skim the atmosphere of Apollonia and spiral back out into the fire-kissed void. It was a ghost, a blur in her sensors like a moving patch of fog. Around it the ships of Ahriman's broken fleet spun about each other, firing and taking fire. She had to reach the silver ship, had to burn it to nothing. It was the Inquisition, she was sure. But still she did not fire.

She could feel the *Sycorax* waiting for her to unleash it, waiting for her to let it become. She could no longer remember who she was. She tried to remember her name but there was just a growing pressure in her mind like a hand clamping over her skull. Screams of static howled in her sensors. Outside her hull the stars were shimmering as though through a heat haze.

It is coming, my sister, said a voice in her thoughts. *It is coming as it was called. Can't you feel it? You will not live through this. Give yourself to us. Let us be one. Let us rise.*

No, she thought. *No. I will not. I am Carmenta, I am mistress of this ship. It is mine. It is…*

Her thoughts ran out, and she was just aware of the battle, of her guns fuming heat as they hungered to fire, of the warp rising in a storm wave just beyond the veil.

The *Sycorax* reached into her senses and embraced her. Her skin was iron, and her heart was the roiling fire of plasma reactors.

No… I am Carmenta… I am Titan Ch… *I am… I am… I…*

* * *

The blade was cold as Hemellion touched it. The command throne loomed from the polished deck. There seemed to be some form of panic. Lights pulsed on and off across the vast chamber. Metal screeches and rumbles rolled like thunder through air, which smelled like smoke and storm charge. Figures rushed past him, sound beat against his ears, but he moved without seeing or hearing them. His fingers closed around the fabric grip of the blade. He took another step, and another.

Your world died, said a thought in his head. It felt different, softer, deeper, like a command.

My world died.

The anger came then, bright and clear like a sun rising above the dawn horizon.

You were made a slave, said the voice in his mind.

I was made a slave. He had been a king once. He had tried to rule well, to do his duty to the Imperium, to be just, and fair, and without malice.

Ahriman took that from you.

Ahriman took that from me. The sorcerer had made him a king of dust. He should have died there, in the dust of his world. He had failed his people; he had failed them all. What is a king if he rules only the bones of the dead?

You lived for a reason, said the voice, but Hemellion was not listening now. He did not need to listen. His mind was already a narrowing point of fury. He was not feeling the deck beneath his steps. *You lived for vengeance.*

He was at the foot of the throne now.

My world, my land, my people…

He climbed one step higher. Carmenta sat unmoving on her throne, her form hidden beneath robes and cables.

My realm is ashes and dust…

He was beside the throne. Carmenta stirred, but did not raise her head.

As his realm will be…

He pulled the blade from beneath his robes. Carmenta quivered again. He leant closer. Her hood-framed face jerked up. Two glass lens eyes flared with light and recognition.

'Hemellion?' croaked a voice that sounded so human.

XVIII
REVELATION

The *Sycorax* went dark. Her engines spluttered then cut out. Her guns went silent. The arc of her course twisted as thrusters fired at random. Night fell in her hull, flowing down through the kilometres of passages and chambers like a cascade of black water. In the deep engine spaces hundreds of eyes that had never seen the light of stars looked upwards as their world turned black. Gunfire became strobing light in the passages and chambers as gun-servitors and thrall warriors opened up on each other. Lightning ran across every surface, cackling with a madman's glee.

In a deep and forgotten corridor an armoured figure in a hound-shaped helm raised his head as the feeble light cut out. Beyond the open door behind him, the pale, mutated body thrashed in its web of chains. The sigils worked into the silver chains and shackles pulsed with a dull blue light. It was trying to scream, but the only sound to come from its mouth was a rattling hiss. The flesh host held within the chamber had served it as needed, had kept part of its essence anchored in reality close to where it needed to be. But now that flesh was a limitation, and so it had taken Maroth's skin and bone as its own. The wards and spells woven into the chamber, which had been its home but never its prison, needed a soul to hold. So it had exchanged places with Maroth, one soul for another. Maroth's essence and mind now thrashed and hissed from the body held in the web of chains, while his body became a vessel. That would not last; Maroth's body would burn out with change in time, but it did not need it to last for long.

The figure in the hound-shaped helm gazed back. The chained creature thrashed more wildly. Then the figure raised a hand and the silver doors closed. Flames flared from the torches lining the corridor. A trembling ran through the deck. Night filled the *Sycorax*, and beyond it all the pieces moved as they should, unknowing and blind. Things were almost at the point that it required. It just needed to wait now. Once when it had lived it might have indulged in hope at such a point, but hope was only needed when faced with uncertainty, and though matters still had to run their course the mortals involved were nothing if not predictable. What they imagined made them unique simply made their choices certain.

No, everything would proceed as it needed to.

The figure began to walk. The blue flames blinked out in its wake, and the shadows crawled beneath its steps.

The darkness closed over Sanakht and Ahriman when they saw the doors.

The doorway was circular, an open mouth stopped with a plug of copper and silver. Faces circled its centre. Rags of silver covered the sculpted eyes and mouths. Intricate designs spiralled out from that centre. Sanakht recognised them – they were a mirror of those that had once closed a door on dead Prospero. They were the marks that had guarded the sanctum of Magnus the Red. The warp dispersed as the recognition filled his mind.

The blankness began on the edge of his thoughts, and moved inwards like night falling across a sun-drenched land. The sensation of the warp flowing around him vanished. Chill clutched at his skin. He stopped in his tracks.

In front of him Ahriman tumbled from the air to the floor. The Rubricae kept moving, and then one joint after another locked. Juddering, they turned their heads towards Sanakht. The lights in their eyes dimmed, spluttered, and went out. The dead suits of armour looked down at him.

They must be screaming, but I cannot hear them any more.

Silence closed around him. His breath and the beat of his hearts rang inside his helmet. He took a step towards Ahriman, aware of the buzz of his armour. He could hear running feet close by. He wondered how much time he had. He thought of all the years, the slow centuries, the dead and lost heaped in the desolation of his past. He thought of Khayon, of Amon, of all the rest. His hand went to his power sword. The steel whispered free. Ahriman was pulling himself slowly from the floor. The sorcerer seemed shrunken, as though he had withered while staying the same size.

'It's the keepers of this place,' said Sanakht, softly. Ahriman looked around. The vox clicked. Wet laboured breath filled Sanakht's ears as Ahriman fought to speak. 'They wait beyond that door. An order of untouchables to watch over the Athenaeum. We are close enough now that the warp is lost to us.'

Ahriman was reeling where he stood, as though the floor beneath him was a wave-tossed deck.

'Sanakht…' rasped Ahriman. His hand rose towards the swordsman as though trying to reach something to hold onto. Sanakht did not move. Part of him could not believe that it had worked; that the misdirection and plans had brought him to this point. Ahriman drew a rattling breath to speak again. 'San–'

'Does it hurt?' said Sanakht and the words echoed in the stillness. 'To be without the warp again, to be just flesh? Is the silver eating your hearts yet – does it hurt, old friend?' Ahriman shivered and tried to straighten. Effort screamed from every movement. Sanakht paced slowly forwards, his movements careful and controlled. 'This was a secret the inquisitor witch never told you – that you would have to walk through the dark without the warp to reach the

Athenaeum. But I knew.' He stopped three paces from Ahriman. The power sword crackled to life in his hand. Cold, bound lightning made the gloom into dancing shadows. 'You have done so much to get us here, to lead us into the next step of your design, but this moment is mine, not yours.' He took another step closer. Ahriman's breath was a ragged hiss on the vox. 'Even now your fleet is being torn apart, your few allies are dead, or have turned against you.'

In the tunnels behind them the glow of light which had followed them grew brighter.

'Even our enemies are here,' said Sanakht, glancing around at the light and then back to Ahriman. 'This is the end, Ahriman. There is nothing beyond this, no dreams of salvation, no false hope.'

Sanakht raised the power sword, its lightning crackling over the blank plate of Ahriman's helm. With a flick the power field vanished. Sanakht held the deactivated sword for a second, and then tossed it at Ahriman's feet. Slowly he drew his force sword, the lifeless steel remaining cold, its runes unlit. 'I could never face you with the warp open to your call. But here, here on the threshold of our father's secrets, this is just a sword, and you. You are just flesh.'

Ahriman turned his head, and looked at the sword at his feet.

'Why?' he rasped.

'Pick up the sword,' said Sanakht.

'The Legion–'

'Is dead!' roared Sanakht, rage sudden and bright in his

338 • JOHN FRENCH

skull. 'Everything we believed was a lie, every decision was flawed. We are lost. We are damned, Ahriman.'

Ahriman shook his head.

'No, no, we can rise, my friend. We will rise again.'

'Pick up the sword,' said Sanakht, taut control in each word.

Ahriman reached down, and gripped the hilt of Sanakht's power sword. He straightened stiffly to full height.

'Don't do this, Sanakht,' said Ahriman, his voice a dry whisper. 'There can be another way. This is a path you don't have to choose.'

'Light the sword,' snarled Sanakht. Ahriman raised the power sword, and it shook in his grip. The lightning field unfurled down the blade. Sanakht raised his own sword in salute. The vox clicked as though Ahriman was about to say something.

Sanakht unfolded in a blur of cuts. Ahriman moved back, sword rising to meet Sanakht's and finding only air. Sanakht read the sorcerer's movements, fast for a human, but slow for him, so, so slow. The sword was a flicker blur in his hand, each feint pulling Ahriman's guard and footwork apart. Their swords did not even touch. Sanakht ducked a blow, spun and slammed a kick into Ahriman's torso. The impact juddered up Sanakht's leg as Ahriman lifted from his feet. Sanakht spun back and cut Ahriman as he fell: once, twice, three times. Blood sprayed through the dark, splashing the passage walls with a soft patter. The severed hand clattered to the floor a second later.

Ahriman skidded across the smooth stone towards the sealed doors to the Athenaeum. Sanakht walked forwards, sword spinning in his grip. Behind him the growing glow filled the tunnel mouth.

Ahriman tried to rise again. Blood glossed his robes and armour. The stump of his right hand pulsed liquid into a growing pool. A razor line between the chest and lower torso plates was weeping thick, red runnels. Another wound grinned across Ahriman's lower back. None of them were kill wounds, at least not ones that would kill fast.

'Do you ever wonder why I saved you?' asked Sanakht. 'On Sortarius, when Khayon broke the pact, do you wonder why I stopped him?'

'You...' rasped Ahriman, 'were loyal.'

'I never believed in the Rubric, Ahriman. How could I believe in what I could not understand?' Sanakht felt the smile form and fade on his face. He bent down, and released the seals of Ahriman's helm. The face beneath was ashen pale, and gleaming with sweat. The pupils in Ahriman's eyes grew and shrank as they tried to focus. Sanakht stared back. 'But I believed in you.'

Sanakht looked to where the power sword lay amongst the spreading pool of Ahriman's blood. He picked it up and stood. He looked down at Ahriman.

'Your life was mine from the moment I saved you,' said Sanakht. 'Every moment you have lived since then has been mine. The futures you dream of are not yours. They are mine, and they end here.'

He dropped the sword next to Ahriman's remaining hand.

'Stand up. Take the sword.'

Ahriman shook his head.

'Sanakht…'

'Stand up! Stand up, damn you. Take the sword.'

'I knew,' said Ahriman.

Sanakht did not move. He could not move. Ahriman looked up at him, then closed his eyes and shook his head. 'I have always known.'

Sanakht felt the words punch through him. He stared at Ahriman, sword in hand, able to move but frozen. Ahriman coughed and blood wetted his lips. He looked again at Sanakht, and maybe there was supposed to be sorrow in those blue eyes, but Sanakht felt cold spread through his blood under their gaze. 'I brought you here,' said Ahriman. Behind Sanakht the glow of approaching light brightened in the tunnel mouth. 'I brought you all here.'

Ignis saw the Grey Knights unfold from the lightning of their teleportation. Five figures, their armour silver white and black shadow in the flash of light. He opened his mouth to give Credence a command, but too slow. The Grey Knights fired. His eyes saw the muzzle flare. A part of his brain that would never stop until he was dead read the angles of flight, and the heat pattern of the bolts igniting as they kissed the air. That same part of his brain began a calculation which would never complete but whose outcome was certain; he was going to end here.

Credence's fist hit Ignis and shot him through the air. The bolts exploded against the wall of the crucible behind where Ignis had stood. Ignis hit the floor. The Grey Knights charged, still firing. Credence turned its shoulder plates into the wall of fire. Explosions rang off its armour. Piston-driven legs tensed under the impacts, then stepped forward. The cannon on the automaton's back opened up with a stuttering roar. Each shell was the size of a clenched fist, their sigil-etched tips heavy with explosives. A Grey Knight vanished as three shells reduced his head and torso to a tangle of ceramite splinters and pulped flesh. Credence shifted stance and the gun raked fire into two other Grey Knights. One fell, his legs blown from beneath him in a cloud of bone splinters and shrapnel. A third spun back, the left side of his body a ruin of silver and wet red. Twin jets of flame spat from Credence's fists, and cooked the flesh of the dead warriors inside their broken armour. The surviving two Grey Knights did not hesitate. The air around their blades shimmered, keening with sharpness.

Ignis pulled himself to standing and shrugged the lightning claws free from the backs of his fists. The blades lit with a whipcrack of static. Anger cut sharp in his mind. It was not supposed to have happened like this, it was so nearly perfect and now it might all become nothing.

The two Grey Knights reached Credence. The automaton shuffled back, torso twisting to bring its weapons to bear. The Grey Knights spun their blades down and hacked into

Credence's leg pistons. Hydraulic fluid gushed out, and hissed to vapour on the Grey Knights blades. The automaton shuddered to its knees.

Ignis charged towards the pair. One of them turned to meet him, its halberd a spinning blur. He could hear the warrior's mind singing sharpness into the blade's edge. The other Grey Knight raised his sword, point down, above Credence's carapace. Ignis raised his claws as the halberd whipped towards him.

It was a fast blow, beautifully fast, but its beauty was predictable. Ignis's crossed claws caught the blade. Light exploded from the touch. Ignis ripped the claws apart and felt the halberd blade shear into fragments. He rammed the claws forwards and the tips punched deep through hard armour and into flesh. He wrenched them back. The Grey Knight fell. Ignis heard Credence give a blurt of machine code, and saw it try and twist to strike its executioner. The last Grey Knight stabbed down with his sword. Ignis roared as his claws sliced out. He was still roaring as he slashed again and again, and the Grey Knight became shreds of sinew and ceramite.

He blinked. His orange armour was washed with blood. Red meat and silver fragments lay heaped at his feet, steaming and smoking into the reeking air.

Credence gave a clatter of binaric.

'No,' said Ignis, breathing slowly. 'That will not be necessary.'

The automaton hissed static and slumped to the deck.

Ignis let out a slow breath and nodded.

Ignis shook himself. Alarms were blaring through the ship. He let his mind ripple out. There were more Grey Knights, more inside the hull of his ship cutting their way through to the engine decks and reactor levels. That was not good. That was decidedly outside of what should have been happening.

+Ahriman?+ He shouted the question into the warp, but no reply came. He wondered what else had not gone as intended. He refocused his mind and saw that most of the pattern remained in the warp. The renegades were tearing themselves apart, their ambition, and spite, and treachery pouring into the Great Ocean as they bled and died under each other's guns. Beyond it, under the star-pierced sheet of space, the storm rose in the warp. The pattern called to it in a voice of subtle numbers, invisible geometry, and inscrutable calculations. All it needed now was a final catalyst, a rod to call the lightning.

As his mind touched the pattern it seemed to pull at him, demanding to be set free. But was it the right moment, he wondered. Was this the right or the wrong time? Then he shrugged.

'As good as any,' he said. The fire just needed one last spark to light it, one last moment of ritual and sacrifice. He nodded to himself. He reached his mind out to the ships that filled the void with their fire. Treacherous and vile each of them, but some would answer.

+This is Master Ignis of the *Word of Hermes*. All who hear

obey this command… +He paused. The moment gathered around him, awesome and terrible in potential, an atrocity waiting to become a revelation. +Fire on the *Sycorax*.+

'I knew,' said Ahriman again. He could feel the blood pulsing out of him even as his body fought to clot it. Sanakht had cut well. Not so deep as to kill, but deep enough to bleed him of strength. The silver was there too, scattered through his chest, cutting deeper with every suck of breath and beat of blood. The pain was a muted scream held inside a wall of his will. Worse though was the presence of the deadening minds just behind the door to the Athenaeum. He felt so weak, as though his body had been cut in two. He buried both lights of agony deep down and continued to hold Sanakht's stare as he spoke. 'I knew what you planned. You are here because you chose this path, but I allowed you to walk it.'

Sanakht was shaking his head.

'No,' breathed Sanakht. He was shaking now. 'Not even you, not even you could–'

'I made this moment, Sanakht. Your treachery is your own, but you walked here on a road I made for you to follow.'

'No.' Sanakht shook his head again. 'You have no weapon left but lies. Your fleet is burning, Ahriman, your allies are dead, you bleed and will die with one more stroke of my sword.'

'Then why do you hesitate, old friend?' said Ahriman.

'Think, how could I not know you would betray me, and if that is true, how could you succeed if I did not help you?'

'Ignis–'

'Is my creature, not yours. I knew of him, and Hemellion, and those whose loyalty could easily be transferred to another.' Sanakht rocked back, and Ahriman heard the breath hiss from his lungs. 'My fleet burns, but only with a fire that will consume the treacherous. It is a fire that will carry from this moment into the future. A storm is rising, Sanakht, and it rises at my command.'

'Hemellion…' Sanakht's face was pale, drained of blood. 'Kadin… Carmenta… the *Sycorax*…'

Ahriman thought of the figure swathed in her red robes, flesh withering around the tubes binding her to the ship which ate her mind. He saw Kadin rise from the blood tank on chains.

'*You won't let me die*,' Kadin had said. '*You don't have the strength.*'

He heard Carmenta, her voice brittle with pain and crumbling control.

'*There are other voices in here with me*,' she said. '*They are getting stronger and I am getting weaker. Soon I will be gone, and they will remain.*'

He thought of the fate he had seen for Kadin, dead on a rusted deck, his head severed under Sanakht's sword. He thought of Hemellion, the one-time king's hate shaped by Sanakht until he walked onto the bridge of the *Sycorax* with a blade in his hand.

He sank the thoughts beneath his will.

'Sacrifice must have meaning,' he said. 'It is the price for salvation.'

Sanakht's mouth worked to form words. His eyes were wide with shock and rage. He looked like a wild animal that had just felt the snare tighten around its leg.

'Why,' he formed the word between slow breaths, 'am I here?'

'Because I need you to serve our Legion one last time. I need one of our blood and brotherhood, one who can become what our Legion needs. You chose yourself, Sanakht.'

Sanakht looked down at the spreading pool of blood, then at the bloody-edged sword in his hand. Ahriman saw the question without needing to hear it.

'I had to be certain,' he said. 'I had to be sure.'

'The others will turn on you,' snarled Sanakht. 'Our brothers will not trust you, after what you have done, and if I fall here.'

'But you will not fall here, brother,' said Ahriman. 'You will rise. None beside Ignis know what I have done, and none of them will. You saved me before, and now you make another sacrifice. That is what they will believe.' He paused, coughed and tasted his own blood bubble from his lungs. There was not much time left.

Sanakht was still. Ahriman watched him and waited. He saw him again as he had been, brilliant, and loyal and blind.

'I am sorry it was you who had to stand here, brother,' said Ahriman.

'No,' spat Sanakht, and his sword rose in his hand again. 'You have no power here, and you will die here, now.' He lunged forwards.

The Grey Knights came out of the tunnel behind Sanakht with a spray of bolter fire.

The world was shaking. Astraeos ran for the doors to the landing platform. Behind him, the fortress of his brother-hood was dissolving and crumbling as fire and lightning ate its stone. In front of him Thidias and Kadin ran, their bronzed armour oily red in the inferno light. Behind him the clatter of booted feet blended with the din of battle. A flash of stark white light flooded the passage behind him. An instant later the blast wave lifted him from the ground and slammed him down. Liquefied rock pinged off his armour as he pushed himself to his feet.

'Well met, my friend.' Astraeos froze as he met the blue eyes. Ahriman stood above him, unarmoured, clothed in blue and silver robes, his face still and emotionless. He smiled. Nothing else moved. Dust and glowing gob-bets of stone hung in mid-flight, the shadows cast by the flash of the explosion unmoving on the stone walls. The ground was still shaking, rumbling as though growing to a quake.

'You…' began Astraeos.

'I am not here, Astraeos, wherever here is for you.' He

paused and the smile faded from his face. 'And neither are you.'

Astraeos looked around at the motionless shrapnel and light of the explosion. An armoured figure hung in the air on the edge of the blast wave.

'Memories,' said Astraeos. Ahriman carried on with no sign of having heard.

'If they took you and broke your mind then whatever you place at the core of your being will be where you are now.' Ahriman turned his head, though his eyes did not focus on the scene around him. 'This is a moment of definition for you, something that formed you and made you as you are now, the last point and lowest ebb. And if you are here so is this gift.'

Astraeos let out a breath that he knew was not real.

'You knew,' he said, shaking his head, blinking at the stilled memory of his brotherhood's last moments. 'You knew I would be taken. You knew they would strip my mind...' His skin was tingling.

'You are wondering if this is what I intended all along, if I abandoned you to death and torture.'

Astraeos turned away, his gaze meeting the frozen eyes of Thidias, twisting as he ran towards the doors.

'You did, though, didn't you? You wanted them to know where you were going, and you wanted them not to question how they knew.'

'I will not pretend that what has happened will not have played out to my advantage, but it was not a certainty.

Nothing is, Astraeos. It was merely a possibility that I prepared for.'

'Why?'

'You do not remember why because you could not be allowed to. That memory and others wait for you beyond this one, buried behind a moment you do not wish to move past.'

'Why?' growled Astraeos. Ahriman's blank face turned to speak to the air.

'There are advantages in the Inquisition's coming. Draw one's enemies together and they will destroy one another. But that is not why you, or I, are here now.'

Ahriman paused. A sound like distant thunder filled the silence, and the ground and walls shook. No other part of the scene moved.

'It was your price, Astraeos, this possibility, and this gift hidden in the puzzle box of your mind. I could not deny you after what I asked of you, and what you have done.'

The thunder came again, louder, closer. Astraeos felt the sensations of the memory grow faint as the figures around him dissolved into cold blue light. Only the image of Ahriman remained, still staring towards some lost horizon.

'If you live, then you will be amongst them. You will be amongst the forces of the Inquisition who destroyed your brothers.'

'What was the price I demanded of you?' asked Astraeos. His throat felt tight.

Ahriman's head turned to Astraeos. He smiled sadly.

'Revenge, Astraeos. The price was revenge.'

The world shook, and he wakened to the gun-roar of the *Sigillite's Oath*.

XIX
AWAKENING

The doors rolled wide, and the figure which wore Maroth's skin pulled itself from the lift shaft. The shadow-filled bridge fell away from it. Gravity had failed across most of the ship. Beads of blood and oil floated like polished stones in the monochromatic gloom. Other things drifted through the space too, corpses mostly, dead from fire or the pressure changes that rippled through the darkened *Sycorax* like a god shivering. Fires burned across the bridge, glowing in spheres as they ate oil and promethium.

The figure pushed off with its borrowed hands, and spun down the bridge. The *Sycorax* shook around it with a sound as familiar as the beat of its heart. Someone was firing on the ship. Beyond the bridge's viewports light strobed from bright blue to angry red. The chamber lurched around it as the explosion twisted the ship in space.

Maroth... Maroth... Maroth... The name gargled and chuckled at the edge of its awareness, seeping from the flesh it inhabited. It had come here because the first truth of the universe was that nothing was insignificant, and what was about to happen needed the trappings of ritual.

It spun around a dead cogitator tower and saw the command throne. A robe-wrapped corpse drifted past, and it felt its body's flesh shiver with change inside its armour. The armour over its back cracked. Wings unfolded with a snap of shearing ceramite. Viscous fluid sheened the iridescent feathers. It paused, and steadied itself on a towering bank of machinery. Then its wings creaked to their full span and beat the air. It could feel more change trying to press into the flesh of its host. It had to wait, had to control the bleed of its essence into the real. Too much too fast and it would burn this body to liquid, and then this fragment of its being would be forced back into the warp. It could not allow that. It needed to be here, it needed to be close, so that it was ready.

It pushed off again, and glided towards the command dais. The figure of Carmenta floated above her throne, tethered in place by the cables linked to her flesh. Her hood had fallen back, and the slit in her throat smiled beneath the red lacquer mask. Close to her, the torn limbs and tattered flesh of a dead man hung in the air. A foot pirouetted lazily, glinting with the silver shackles of one of the Thousand Sons slaves. Hemellion: the human had been torn apart by machine claws. It noticed a hand, severed at the wrist, its fingers still clutching a crescent of sharpened metal.

It reached out and gripped the throne. Its fingers grew to claws and it cut through the cables holding Carmenta to her throne with a single swipe. She floated up, limbs slack and waving. For a second she looked almost as though she was alive and falling not up, but down into the drowning embrace of dark water. But she was dead, and the flicker of life was just an illusion. Another explosion rocked the ship. Somewhere a still-functioning alarm began to wail.

The figure settled onto the throne, the wings at its back furling behind it.

Yes, this was the right place to wait. This was as it should be.

Slowly it reached out with its clawed hands and peeled Maroth's hound helm off as though it were rotting cloth. The face beneath changed even as it met the still air of the bridge. Flesh flowed, bloated and withered, eyes vanished then reappeared. A crown of horns rose from its temples, curling as they grew. Out beyond the towering viewports a warhead exploded, stuttering white light through the bridge. The creature saw the light, and felt the threads of destiny twist tighter.

'Biorhythms rising.' The dead machine voice welcomed Astraeos back to consciousness. Tremors ran though him. The ship was shaking to the drumbeat of its guns and the breath of its engines. His muscles clenched. The bands of metal around his body holding him to the slab bit into his flesh. Blankness filled his sight. The link to the servo-skull, which had allowed him to see during his interrogation, was broken. He was blind, his world a cocoon of touch and sound. Alarms were sounding somewhere in the distance. The needles embedded in his flesh trembled. His hearts were racing in his chest.

'Neural overload detected.'

Close by he could hear the hum of the tech-priest floating closer, and the rising tone of bio-monitors. Somewhere further away he heard the Seraph guards left by the inquisitors shift under their ragged wrappings. His mind reached automatically for the warp, and found a cold wall of ice. There was no way out.

Something was coming closer. He could hear the wheezing sigh of the tech-priest's breath pump. Memory shivered down his nerves. Seeds of knowledge cracked open in the core of his mind, and grew, blooming through his mind and body. The warp could not answer his call, but that was always a possibility, and one that they had prepared for. The tech-priests watching over him knew he had woken. He heard a click of metal fingers on control keys. The needles twitched in Astraeos's flesh as they prepared to dump sedative into his blood.

'Neural storm detected.'

'Hidden behind this last memory is a gift,' said the echo of Ahriman.

The last seed in his mind opened.

Astraeos convulsed. His muscles bulged. The metal bands across his chest and limbs bit deep. His hearts beat faster and faster. The chime of the bio-monitors was a stuttered scream.

'Bio-rhythms critical,' said a machine's voice.

Astraeos gasped. His hearts were twin hammers in his chest. The tech-priest was almost beside him. He felt his hearts beat once more, and stop. His body slumped in the restraints.

The bio-monitor alarms silenced. In his mind everything became still, a bright whiteness. The tech-priest paused, as the silence grew second by second. A high dead tone rose from the machines beside Astraeos.

'Total bio-neural failure.'

In the empty possibility of his suspended mind he heard the machine voice, and felt the touch of robes as the tech-priest leaned over him. Instruments extended with a low metallic click and electric whine. He could almost see the chrome and brass probes extending towards him. Something pricked his skin, stabbing deep. He did not move, he could not move. He was a last thought stored in a prison of flesh.

The tech-priest was leaning closer, oil-thick breath hissing from its mouth. Astraeos heard the whir of augmetic eyes focusing. Metal fingers touched his arm.

'Life signs nil.'

The probes dug deeper into his skin. He heard a puzzled click of binaric. Everything was slowed as though held back behind a dam of stored seconds. The tech-priest's joints hissed as he leaned even closer. Fabric brushed the back of Astraeos's right hand.

The suspended stillness of his mind and body shattered. He twisted his hand, grabbed the tech-priest's robes and yanked him off his feet. The adept fell across Astraeos, scrabbling, burbling panicked machine code. Astraeos clamped his grip closed, and yanked his head up. The plate and cables bonded to his scalp ripped free. He felt blood run down his face.

The Seraphs had sensed something was wrong. They were moving, ragged cloth swishing, bare feet thumping on metal.

The dried flesh and machine-grease stink of the tech-priest filled Astraeos's nose. The collar around his throat stopped his rise, but it did not matter. They had muted his mind, bound him and taken his weapons. But he still had teeth.

'Life signs nil,' droned the bio-monitors.

The tech-priest thrashed. Astraeos twisted his head and bit down.

Blood and oil gushed into his mouth. Electricity burst across his gums as he bit deeper. The tech-priest was twisting and thrashing, gurgling in gasps of static. Astraeos's teeth cut through cogs, and into flesh. Sensations burst into his awareness as his body ripped information from the meat. Fear, malformed logic and machine data poured into him in a rushing mess of impressions. With panic came the tech-priest's desperate thoughts of the sedative and control restraints set into his wrist.

'Life signs detected.'

The sound of the Seraphs' accelerating steps rang on the decking. The dead numbness surrounding Astraeos's mind tightened. The tech-priest was shrieking now, a single buzzing note of panic.

Astraeos shifted his grip on the tech-priest's arm, fingers feeling for keys and switches on the metal limb. He found one and pressed. Something in the slab beneath him clicked and began to whir. A new alarm began to sound. The dying tech-priest twisted. Astraeos's grip almost broke.

'Restraint release process stage one activated.' The machine system's voice was almost lost beneath the blare of overlapping alarms.

His fingers fumbled at the wrist controls. He heard a series of pneumatic thumps from close by as aggression drugs were dumped into the Seraphs' bloodstreams. His fingers found the keys on the tech-priest's wrist again. He heard a crackle of activating power fields, and a wet snarl as the first Seraph leaped at him. He depressed the keys. The restraints snapped back into the slab.

He rose, throwing the tech-priest's corpse from him. Cables and tubes pulled free of his flesh in a shower of blood and sparks. He was still blind, still locked into a world of sound and touch, but he was free. He heard the last paces of the Seraph's charge, and dived aside.

A mane of energised cables whipped past him. The empty

slab shattered. Astraeos hit the floor in a crouch. The Seraph was close. The buzz of its power lashes raised the hairs of his skin. He could hear its feet move as it twisted to strike again. He stood, and lashed a kick into the space where he knew it must be. His foot hit muscle, and he felt something break beneath the impact. The Seraph staggered, snarling a tongueless cry. The sound of two more sets of running feet rose against the peal of alarms. He ran to meet them,

The air sang as the Seraphs' weapons lashed down towards him. He leapt. The shaking deck vanished beneath his feet, and he was twisting through a world made real only by sound. He knew that the Seraph he had kicked was already rising from the floor, ready to dive after him. He knew that the other two Seraphs were beneath him, their momentum driving them forwards even as their strides faltered. He had seen their kind before, in what seemed now like a life lived by someone else. He could almost see them, faces hidden by visors of beaten metal, the tatters of their robes fluttering from muscled, hunched bodies, the stumps of their arms trailing lightning-sheathed whips.

Then he landed and the moment ended. He grabbed the closest Seraph as he came down. Instinct screamed at him to let go, but his hands clamped shut. He felt skin and muscle tear as he yanked the Seraph off its feet. It writhed, blood sheeting down its muscle. Astraeos's hand found its head, locked around it and wrenched back. Vertebrae separated with a gunshot crack.

The second and third Seraphs were on him. He thrust the corpse of their kin at them. An energy whip ripped the dead Seraph in two. Warm liquid burst over him. He could hear the two Seraphs hissing. He spun the split body of the dead Seraph into the source of the sound. The energised whips on the corpse's arms hit meat with a jolt of discharging lightning.

Silence. Astraeos went still. It was not true silence; alarms still trembled through the air and the deck still growled to the rhythm of distant battle. It was the silence of transition. For a long drawn-out instant Astraeos's mind remained shackled, its thoughts cycling within his skull. The dead Seraphs twitched at his feet. Their psychic deadness vanished, and the warp returned. It almost overwhelmed him.

He dropped to his knees. Ice formed on his skin and vaporised in fire. His thoughts tumbled. Rage, elation and sorrow spun and snagged through him. He could hear voices calling him, telling him to let go, to let his mind free. Ghost hands pulled at his limbs, and claws plucked his skin. His will cut off the sensations like an axe. His mind hardened, focused. Thoughts formed and exploded outwards, found the warp and remade the real.

He began to walk forwards. Tongues of flame formed in his footprints, and licked up his body. His flesh tingled as wounds closed. Needles and cables fell to the floor as his muscles smoothed over puncture marks. He could feel time flowing around him, thick as tar. The Inquisition and their servants would know now that something was wrong, that he was free. That was good, it suited his purposes.

The metal hood clamped to his head glowed with heat and sloughed away in molten scabs. His face blistered as fresh skin and sinew grew. The fire drained into his eye sockets, spiralling around points of darkness. Sight returned. He looked out at the world through the pulse of flames, and saw that it had changed. Colours bled from every angle, swirling like ink stirred into water. Ghost impressions, too faint to see clearly, shifted through the air.

He turned his head. The chamber spread out from the slab that had been his bed, and the machines that surrounded it. Empty darkness crawled at its edges, spilling up walls that glowed with burning wards. The flames of other minds moved beyond that barrier; he could see them pulse and shimmer, seemingly in time with the drone of alarms. They were coming for him.

He kept walking, his pace quickening with every step. There was no gap between the fire without and the inferno in his skull. A sphere of blue light formed in front of him, growing, curling tendrils of white and orange heat. The globe of light leaped forwards from Astraeos when he was three paces from the chamber's slab doors. It struck the metal. Warding words etched in silver and gold flared and liquefied, drooling down the portal as it blackened. The sphere melted into the door like a sun sinking below the sea at sunset. It blew outwards in a spray of metal, and Astraeos walked through the molten ruin.

* * *

Cendrion fired, and saw the rounds punch the swordsman back off his feet. The threat rune marking the tumbling figure flickered amber then held red. Beside him came his brothers, behind him Izdubar and his fellow inquisitors followed. The silence of psychic deadness surrounded him as he ran forwards. He fired again, and beside him his brothers' guns rose in chorus as they charged. He blinked as a wave of nausea blurred his eyes.

Immobile suits of armour with high-crested helms filled the passage before the door. Threat runes spun in amber above the Rubrical as he looked at them, but it was the two figures before the doors that were his focus. The figure he had just hit was not moving but there was another, and he was rising to his feet. Cendrion could see blood-spattered armour and the stump where the warrior's right hand had been. The red targeting rune pulsed above the warrior as it stood and turned to the door at its back. It had a pistol in its remaining hand.

'Ahriman!' shouted Izdubar, and the figure glanced back at them as he placed a hand on the centre of the circular door. Cendrion fired and bolts hammered into Ahriman's back. He slammed into the door, chunks ripping from his armour's backpack, sparks crawling from the exposed fuel core. He did not fall, though. He pushed and the doors, the doors that had no key, opened.

The chamber beyond the door was circular. Niches of rolled parchments and stacked books lined the curved walls. At the centre of the circular chamber a lectern of iron and brass rose from the black glass floor. A figure sat atop the lectern. It had been a man once. Cendrion could see that at a glance, but its humanity was now just a shell of dry, translucent skin and wasted muscle. Cataract-clouded eyes stared down from sunken eye sockets. A single arm moved across the roll of parchment on top of the lectern, writing in a stuttering blur. A circle of nine figures in grey robes surrounded the lectern. Silver masks with one eye hid their faces.

This was the secret Izdubar and his comrades had kept chained here, a conduit into the mind of a fallen demigod. This was the Athenaeum of Kalimakus. Ahriman stood on its threshold, seemingly frozen.

Cendrion ran forward, still firing. Rounds ripped into Ahriman, flaying his armour to splinters. Ahriman staggered, almost falling, but somehow remaining upright. The grey figures pressed closer to the lectern. He looked at the grey-robed circle for an instant then raised his pistol.

'No!' screamed Izdubar. Ahriman fired. The burst of explosive rounds turned the grey figures into clouds of fire, blood and splintered bone. The psychic deadness vanished. The withered man on the lectern looked up, jaws working to shout with a tongueless mouth. Ahriman's shot hit the withered man in the mouth and blew his skull to vapour.

A long, delayed instant filled Cendrion. Then the warp crashed back like a storm tide. Blue fire burst into the air around the lectern at the chamber's centre. Turquoise flames rushed up the walls and spilled over the floor. Cendrion saw it in his mind as well as with his eyes. It looked like a flock of birds rising into the sky, their feathers burning as they flew.

Ahriman turned to face them. The pistol dropped from his hand. Beside and behind him Cendrion heard the immobile suits of armour come to life with a clatter of arming guns.

XX
SORCERY

Fire danced in Ignis's mind as death cradled Apollonia. There was not even the semblance of order now. In his mind's eye a dozen torpedoes hit the *Sycorax* and blew out a chunk of hull the size of a city. Debris rode on the fire wave. Thousands of bodies burned and tumbled beside the shredded stone and metal. The ship was taking some killing. Beyond and around it ships spun and died. In the warp the storm wave was cresting.

He was holding it all in his mind now, feeling the ratios narrow. They were running out of time. The storm had to break and it had to break now.

The *Word of Hermes* fired again. Lines of lance fire sliced into the open wounds in the *Sycorax*. Ignis heard things that had lived in the ship's bones begin to shriek into the warp. The storm answered. Blossoms of livid light spilled into the darkness between blazing ships. Rainbow lightning crackled across the darkness.

But where was Ahriman? No matter, the pattern of ruin could not be stopped now. In front of his eyes the *Sycorax* began to crack and burn.

+Brothers,+ his thought voice roared into the storm, and found the minds he called. They were all Thousand Sons, all brothers to him and Ahriman, and while the rest of the fleet had torn itself apart they had remained untouched. They had not known why, but they had Ahriman's orders, and now they answered Ignis as one. He called them and they began to converge on the *Word of Hermes*.

Ignis turned his thoughts to the ship and found the shivering mind of Silvanus the Navigator.

+Look to the warp, Navigator. The moment approaches.+

'There is no way out. There is no way out,' moaned the Navigator. Ignis had a flash vision of the man curled against his cell wall, hands covering his head. 'They are coming.'

+I command you,+ sent Ignis, but the Navigator pitched his head up and screamed.

'They are coming!'

Ignis felt the storm force rising, felt the elements of the pattern slip towards alignment. He reached deeper into the warp and realised that he had been wrong. It was not the storm that the Navigator had seen.

The first Imperial ship broke from the warp with a flash of tearing reality. A second later the sisters of its fleet followed.

* * *

The Grey Knights came for Astraeos as he broke through a door into a high chamber of vaulted stone and polished granite. Statues looked down at him from the bases of great pillars, their faces set in cold marble and their armour tarnished bronze. Braziers hung from chains which stretched from the roof, and the smell of incense clung to the air. Skulls stared at him from brackets on the walls and from crystal-covered niches in the floor.

There were four Grey Knights. The first Astraeos knew of them was a shiver in the air like a sudden gust of wind. Then they were there, their shining presences looming out of the warp. They charged across the chamber, armour moving like slab muscle, bolt-rounds spitting from the guns on their wrists. Astraeos's kine shield snapped into existence around him. Explosions filled the air in front of him, but the Grey Knights had been fast, very fast. A bolt ripped his shoulder to bloody shreds and pitched him from his feet. Chunks of his bare muscle tore from his bones, blood misting the air around him as he fell. The wounds were already closing as his blood spattered the floor.

He hit the ground, rolled and came to his feet as the Grey Knights cut through his kine shield with a synchronised shrug of mental force. The telekinetic shield imploded with a blink of lightning. Astraeos reeled with the impact, and had time to leap back as the edge of a sword sliced down towards his head. They were all around him, cutting towards him from every angle. Golden nimbuses of light grew above the Grey Knights, flowing together as their powers joined, feeding each other, caging him between them. The warp was singing with high clear voices. Time slowed to a greasy crawl. The instants that were about to be, and the instants that would be, became one. A halberd spun up and sliced down so fast that it was a circle sheet of white light.

Astraeos's mind spiralled up into the chains holding the braziers high above, and shattered them with a thought. The cages of coals fell, broken lengths of chains lashing behind them. The first brazier struck one of the Grey Knights in a roar of twisting iron and spilling embers. Time blinked back into full flow. The Grey Knight struck by the brazier reeled back, shards of red coal cascading down silver armour. Astraeos ducked closer to the staggering Terminator. The blades of the other Grey Knights sliced through air.

The other braziers hit the floor in explosions of sparks and shattered stone. Astraeos caught the severed lengths of chains with his mind before they touched the ground. Frost crystals glittered in the air. The chains whipped around a Grey Knight's halberd and flicked up his arms. The chains flashed with heat. Astraeos saw the Grey Knight's mind begin to react a second too late. A glowing tip of chain hit the red crystal of the Grey Knight's eyepiece, and punched through into the eye and brain beneath. The Grey Knight fell, blood turning to steam as it gushed over the hot links of chain.

The three remaining Grey Knights brought their storm

bolters up as one and fired. Astraeos leapt. The warp flowed through muscle and fibre. Heat and shrapnel lashed his back as he landed and spun. Fire-edged blood scattered from him as his mind snapped the chains taut, pulling the halberd from the dead knight's grasp. The weapon spun, a blur in the air around Astraeos's glowing form. Lightning spat from the three remaining Grey Knights. Astraeos's mind grasped the crackling arc as it formed, and yanked it out of being. The lightning vanished.

Astraeos snapped the halberd out. The blade was cold, its psycho-active core quiet, but it was still sharp. It struck the lead Grey Knight on the helm. His head turned just before the blade struck. The edge bit into the forehead plate, gouged upwards and slammed into the helmet's crown. The chain and blade yanked back, and the helm was wrenched from the Grey Knight's face. Astraeos saw dark eyes in a scarred face. He faltered. In his head he saw the fortress of his Chapter crumbling in fire.

The Grey Knight tore the remainder of his ruined helm from his head.

The air was shimmering around Astraeos, weeping liquid light and colour. He could hear sounds crackling like burning leaves of parchment. Louder but more distant, the voices of Cadar, Thidias and Kadin were shouting over the sound of the sky falling in fire in an unchangeable past.

The fire of his memory formed in the air, black-edged and red-cored. It shot towards the Grey Knights, spreading out as it grew, and the fire swallowed them. Astraeos felt a formless roar break from his mouth.

The fire drained away. Astraeos heard his cry of triumph die in the air. The Grey Knights walked from the flames, silver armour stained red and streaked black by the flames that soaked into it like water into sand. They seemed to move slowly, as though they were walking to a different beat of time. Their golden auras were flowing together, overlapping, becoming one. Astraeos felt a breath form in his throat. The spinning chains and halberd were moving in stopped-time rotations.

Golden wings unfolded in the air around the Grey Knights, first two, then more and more. Astraeos watched the shape grow in slow slices of seconds. It was a thought form, a projection of a mind on the fabric of the warp, but this was like nothing he had ever dreamed could exist. It was not one mind but many, the powers and wills of all three Grey Knights unified and harmonised. As he beheld it Astraeos found the one thought in his mind was of an idea old before the stars were conquered.

An angel, he thought. *An angel of execution.*

A single high note rang in his ears.

Time in the real world stopped. The chamber bled to the edge of his eyes, and the warp was all there was, more real than real.

The Grey Knights' thought form rippled, white light shivering from its edges.

Voices, both old and new, poured into his mind.

We are not made by our blood, said a voice at the centre

of his thoughts. It was cold, calm, like a steel blade. He knew it very well, but still it seemed strange, as though it belonged to another person. It was his voice, speaking from his past. *We are made by our oaths.*

Astraeos's mind rose into the warp. The angel's thought form dived.

Astraeos's thought form took shape as it flew. For a second it was like the shadow of a bird, its beak and eyes a flash of cold light. Then that brief shadow was gone. A serpentine body of smoke and fireglow stretched into the warp. Scales of silver ice flickered into existence. Wings of bone and fire spread behind a long saurian head.

But when all others are broken, one oath will always remain.

Astraeos roared, and flame greeted the descending angel.

The oath to defy defeat.

Fire burst across the golden feathers, and spun away in glinting spirals.

To defy to the last.

The angel struck.

Astraeos's thought form shattered.

The Rubricae fired as one. Crawling blue fire burst across the Grey Knights as they ran towards Ahriman. The flames ran together, flashing white hot as the Rubricae continued to fire. Ahriman rose into the blazing air. Behind him the Athenaeum chamber roared as the inferno grew.

The warp fire engulfed Ahriman. He felt it flow over his armour and skin. He felt the runes etched in his armour twist, felt his bones judder inside his flesh. His mind was tumbling away from his body, burning and melting like a ball of wax in a furnace. The bloody silk of his robe whipped in the gale as the fire reached up to cradle him. Tendrils of flame wormed across his body, writhing across the stump of his arm and the gouges in his flesh. Flesh bubbled up in the wounds, before armour spread across them like liquid. It felt like breaking the surface of water after going to the edge of drowning. Sensation and light whirled through his mind as the warp fire prickled the edge of his thoughts. Part of him just wanted to let it race through him, to let its currents lift him. There were voices rushing from the burning chamber, whispering in the voices of lost friends and dead brothers.

'Listen to us,' they said. 'Listen to all we can tell you of what was and what will come.'

He shut the instinct away, pushing it deep within. He needed calm now. It came, and with it he felt his mind spread through the aether. Patterns of thought amplified. He looked at the reformed flesh of his hand as the armour hardened over it again. He lifted his fingers to his mouth, and wiped the half-dried blood from his lips.

The Rubricae marched from the flames before the door, blue armour cast black in the stark light. Ahriman reached down with a thought and pulled the crumpled form of Sanakht into the air with him.

Blackened figures broke from the blazing corridor behind Ahriman. He felt Cendrion's sword as it cut through a Rubricae. The split armour fell to the ground. A high-pitched wail stabbed into Ahriman's thoughts. The armour began to judder and dissolve into grey dust.

The rest of the Rubricae turned to fire at Cendrion, but he was already moving, already hacking two more down. Beyond him Ahriman saw Izdubar break from the fire, and with him more Grey Knights.

He reached out with his mind and yanked the Rubricae and Sanakht through the door into the Athenaeum chamber. The Grey Knights surged forwards. Ahriman slammed the bronze door shut. Its edges glowed, fusing to the stone. The Rubricae hit the flame-covered floor with a clatter. Ahriman turned to look at Sanakht, still held above the ground by his will.

Sanakht's skin was pale, but his eyes were open. Behind him the pillar of blue and golden flames at the centre of the chamber roared as it sucked in air. Ahriman could see nothing else with his mind, just the rushing infinity of knowledge pouring from the warp into reality, looking for a vessel.

'The Athenaeum is not a book, brother,' said Ahriman, his true voice rising above the rushing air. 'It was not the books of Kalimakus, it was Kalimakus himself, his link to Magnus. It is a river of knowledge, ever seeking for a way into the world. It consumes all those who dip their minds into its water. But a son of Magnus could perhaps be a strong enough vessel to last longer. That is the fate treachery bought you. You will become the Athenaeum, my brother.'

'Always teaching,' sneered Sanakht. He began to laugh. 'Everything you try will fail, Ahriman. That you do not know why only makes you more the fool.'

Ahriman's jaw tightened.

The laughter died in Sanakht's throat.

'Do not say that you are sorry,' he said.

Ahriman shook his head.

'More than you will ever know,' said Ahriman, and sent his brother into the heart of the fire with a thought.

The Imperial fleet spread out as it closed on Apollonia. Dozens of vessels churned the void as they dropped from the warp. Most were warships summoned by the power of the Inquisition. They bore new names for this service, names that spoke to the intent of their purpose. *Wish of Purgation*, *Seventh Judgement*, *Damnation's Answer*: if they survived this battle their crews would go to the fire, and their hulls would be reconsecrated under their old names. But for now they existed only as the tools of the Inquisition's judgement.

Amongst them ships of three Chapters of the Adeptus Astartes broke from the aether together. The *Immortalis* was a daughter of the Jovian forges bound to the Black Consuls; beside her rode the *First Oath*, battle-barge of the Praetors of Orpheus, and the vast Brazen Claws battle-barge *Sunderer*. Called by old oaths they moved forwards as the fleet spread to their sides.

Ignis watched the scene play out in his mind, and across

the lenses of his helmet. The Imperial ships began to fire
into the already scattered remains of Ahriman's fleet. He
started to count vessels, and calculate arcs. The fires of
battle brightened. The ships of his Thousand Sons brothers were close now, clustered around the *Word of Hermes*.
It was the renegades, the scattered ships of the mongrel
warbands that took the opening salvoes. Some of the ships
broke away and raced towards the Imperial fleet, bleeding
and firing ragged broadsides as they went to their deaths.

Silvanus was right, there was no way they could reach the
system edge now, no way they could drop to the warp. No
way out, no way at all.

Ignis shivered, and looked to the *Sycorax*. Impossibly it
still held its shape even as it burned and fresh explosions
ripped through its structure. Space was rippling close to
its hull, bulging and smoking with sickly light as the warp
pressed through the thinned skin of reality. The ship was
a pyre, and the storm was rising to meet its death. Ignis
reached out his thoughts to the Thousand Sons ships
which had gathered close. He gave the order and the ships
fired on the *Sycorax* as one.

Astraeos saw his own body quiver and start to fall. It moved
with the slowness of a jammed pict-feed. The three Grey
Knights were still, their silver armour shining golden light
across the rubble-strewn floor. He saw all of this as though
looking down from a great height as the scene grew distant beneath him. His mind was a thousand spinning

fragments of pain and emotion. The angel thought form was everywhere, melting his will, shredding it into scraps.

He could not think clearly. Everything was a jumble of sensations. Memories flicked around him like tarot cards tossed into the air. He was not even aware of time or the past or the present any more. Some small flare of clarity spluttered as images ripped into smaller and smaller pieces.

I am being torn apart, the lone thought said. *My existence is being shredded, and the scraps burned.* He had not stood a chance, not really, not with all the arts that Ahriman had taught him, or the need for vengeance boiling through his soul. A splinter of pain lanced into his fading thoughts, sudden and vicious in its urgency. His last thought spun on in confusion. The pain came again, like a barbed hook tugging into flesh.

Why has this happened? The question rang clear in his thoughts. *Why has all this happened?* He remembered his home world burning, and the inquisitor shaking his head.

Why had his Chapter died? They had kept their oaths, but the Imperium had broken theirs and slaughtered them as traitors. That unanswered question had driven him for so long, carrying him to the Eye of Terror, and into the service of Ahriman. Why had it all happened? What reason had the Imperium had to kill his brothers? How had it begun?

He saw it then, the answer that had eluded him, that made no sense unless you accepted the broken logic of the warp. He knew why his Chapter had died.

He understood how fate had unfolded and heard its laughter.

He cried out, and the scream was silence. The pain and rage were beyond even the agony of his soul ripping to shreds. There had been no hope, not for him, not for his brothers. There was nothing left, not even the comfort of the lies he had believed.

'Ahriman,' he said, and heard the bitter name come from his lips. Vengeance, yes, there was still vengeance to live for.

+Astraeos,+ said a voice in his mind. It sounded very distant but familiar, as though it had always been there. +Astraeos, my son. I am here.+

+What are you?+

+I am waiting.+

And within him a connection made long ago emerged for the last shreds of his soul; it came as though summoned, it came like an answer.

The bond, the link to the creature bound by Maroth, the daemon he had bound to his will once but never called on again.

He touched the connection to the daemon.

But it cannot answer, he thought. It was locked away on the *Sycorax* behind silver doors and wards. Even as that thought formed he felt something respond, something that called in a voice of brittle ice.

+Call me and I shall come.+

The angel thought form was slicing through the last pieces of him. It was not separate from him now, it was the universe.

Call me and I shall come… the words lay in the last scrap of his awareness, black as a fall into night, sharp as a razor. He could see his true body, slumped on its knees amongst scattered embers.

+I call you to me,+ he said, with voice and thought.

The creature on the throne of the *Sycorax* looked up. Light exploded through the bridge. The crystal of the viewport shattered. Fire and molten shards billowed inwards. Then the air was rushing around it, pulling debris towards the vacuum. The creature sat unmoving on the throne.

It could feel the bond to Astraeos now, snapping in the winds of the warp like rope whipping in a gale. The bond had been made in ignorance, but it had been made willingly. Soul bound to soul, will to will.

A chunk of twisted metal spun into it from above with bone-breaking force. It felt the shock of impact as the metal sliced into its shoulder. Blood showered from it in strings of wet globes which burned as they spun away. It did not move from the throne – it could not. It needed the end of its host and the call of the one it had waited for to occur together.

The bridge was a spinning blur. Its flesh and armour was flowing together, setting into bronzed chitin and glowing soft flesh. A wash of glittering energy spilled through the bridge. A spar of girder shot through the burning wave and transfixed its chest to the throne. The skin of its skull blistered. Flesh began to melt from its bones. Black liquid bubbled between its glass teeth. For a second the flesh of its face settled into a single twisted mass of scar tissue above a ragged slit of a mouth. Above the smile a single bright blue eye looked out.

'I call you to me,' Astraeos's voice echoed from all around.

A salvo of macro shells hit the last remains of the *Sycorax* and turned the world to bright oblivion.

The ghosts of bloody feathers were falling around Astraeos as he opened his eyes. He looked down at his hands. Fire burned beneath the smooth skin, then blinked to nothing. He looked up. The barrels of a Grey Knight storm bolter looked back at him. It fired. He felt the fragments and fire slice through the air. He stopped them. A sword flashed towards him, its edge running with lightning. The blade slammed into the floor. Astraeos looked down at the blade. He stood a metre from where it had struck.

He looked back up. The Grey Knight tried to wrench the blade up. His armour would not move. The air around the warrior was glowing; he was sweating frost and blue light as he strained. The wards woven into the ceramite were keening under the psychic pressure. The Grey Knight's arms started to move. The sword started to rise.

Astraeos felt a stab of pain in his eyes. The Grey Knight's armour imploded with a wet thump.

There were three more Grey Knights on the floor, one dead, the other two unconscious from the psychic feedback of their thought form's destruction. Astraeos turned away from them. He had to leave. He had to be far away from what was about to happen. It would take time to prepare, vengeance always did.

'Ahriman,' he said, and shadows formed in the wake of the word. Yes, it would need time, but time and fate were on his side.

He closed his eyes. When they opened again they were fire. He raised his hand. The air shivered and then split. Astraeos looked into the tumbling madness beyond and stepped through.

Ahriman watched as Sanakht rose in the pillar of flame. To his mundane eyes the flame-shrouded shape still looked like Sanakht, still the slim lines to the face, still the silver-worked blue armour, still the slight crease at the edge of his mouth and eyes which hinted at mockery or laughter. But to his second sight the figure was not Sanakht. The inferno drained into it. It was a void, a shadow cast by an absence, an outline of a figure with wings and arms and curled horns. It had no size but it seemed both to tower beyond the confines of the chamber and to be small, as though it was shrunk by vast distance. It was not a living thing any more, it was a point in the universe where knowledge converged and bubbled to the surface of reality. It was not Sanakht; it was the Athenaeum.

The Athenaeum hung in the centre of the suddenly silent chamber. Then it fell to the ground in a clatter of ceramite on stone. It lay on the floor, body held in a seated position by its armour, head lolling in the collar. Its eyes were cataract white in the dead skin of its face. Ahriman started forwards and then froze. The Athenaeum's lips were quivering as though it was trying to remember how they worked. Fire-cast shadows appeared on the walls, but there was no fire.

'And the Wolves come,' it said in a dry corpse voice. 'They come out of the night. Red are their axes, and their dreams and wishes are for blood and frost. The black-clad son of the thousand...'

Words tumbled from its mouth. Ahriman listened to them, hearing things that he understood and more that he did not.

'...the path, the path, the path written in the blood of red suns, the path...'

He moved closer, extended his mind and hand towards the Athenaeum.

'...the ashes of Prospero are the embers of the new flame...'

He was just a step away. He held his mind still. His thoughts brushed forwards as light as a breath. His fingertips touched the polished blue of a shoulder guard. Sanakht's head rolled up and back. Ahriman stared at the Athenaeum, and the shadow it cast in the warp. He could not look away. He felt his mouth open, and the slightest tremble move his tongue.

'Ahriman,' said the Athenaeum.

His hand and mind snapped back as though he had tried to touch something hot. His mouth and throat were dry.

'Yes,' was all he could say.

'All things draw to a point, and the sins of the past and future create a new darkness.'

'What… what is close?'

'Focus is blindness. We create our own enemies.' Its head lolled back and it began its drone again.

Ahriman looked down at the Athenaeum, and felt a sudden shiver of uncertainty.

A dull *crack* filled the air, then another, rattling through the stillness like a chaingun. Stone fragments tumbled from the wall beside the door. He spun around, reaching out with his will even as he felt the telekinetic force strike the door again. Cracks spiralled across the glass-smooth stone.

Thunderheads reared in the warp. He felt the surge of vast currents roll around him like the waves of a storm-darkened sea. His Rubricae had turned towards the doors, their guns rising. A thought pulled his helm from the bloody floor. A broken horn on the right temple reformed as it settled over his head. He reached out with his mind and pulled the body of the Athenaeum up. It was time to leave.

The door blew out of the wall and spun through the air towards Ahriman. His mind met it. The door burst into glowing dust. The Rubricae were firing through the ragged breach in the wall. Blue and red flames flashed in the dust cloud.

Cendrion came out of the murk. In the warp he was a single tongue of white flame. Cracks were still spreading from the broken doorway. Chunks of stone fell from the ceiling.

Five paces separated Ahriman and the Grey Knight.

Ahriman tilted his head. A slowed slice of time spread between them.

Five paces.

He took a breath, felt it soak into his muscles.

His left heart beat once.

Cendrion flew forwards, sword rising. Flame poured from Ahriman. The silver of the Grey Knight's armour flashed to white heat. Ahriman reshaped his will. A whirl of shadows rose around him, beating with a thousand dark wings. Crow voices screamed in his mind.

Four paces.

Cendrion rammed a blunt spear of mental force at Ahriman. He met it and spun its power into his own. The shadow birds around Ahriman flew faster. Izdubar and a cluster of other armoured humans broke into sight. Gunfire buzzed towards him. He unmade the rounds in flares of light. They kept coming.

Three paces.

Ahriman held the thought of the beating wings, pouring himself into each one, feeling his mind and body become like smoke. Cendrion's sword was a splinter of sharpness and sunlight above his head. He could feel the pressure in the warp building and building.

Two paces.

Ahriman vanished, and in his place a cyclone of shadow and carrion cries roared. Chunks of stone ripped from the floor. Cendrion leapt, spinning his body into the turning wind, sword slicing.

One pace.

Cendrion's sword cut through the spiral of shadow. The mass of wings parted like a slit sheet of silk. Ahriman felt the pain of the cut, felt the Grey Knight's will pouring into the blade. But he was ready. The Grey Knight was strong, strong in ways that he had never imagined, but he was like his sword, a weapon, and that focus made him blind. Ahriman focused his whole mind for an instant. Cendrion's sword shattered. Silver fragments spun through the air.

He felt the Grey Knight's shock. He almost smiled. Then the flock of shadow birds tore through Cendrion. Wards woven into the silver armour held and then cracked. Splinters of ceramite tore into Cendrion's muscles. A wall of telekinetic force lifted him from the floor, spinning his bulk like a dry leaf. Polished plates buckled and tore. Ragged edges of metal punctured his flesh. Bones in his chest and arms shattered. Warning chimes sang from around his collar. His flesh burned as warding runes melted on the inside of his armour. Liquid silver dripped from the Grey Knight as he fell.

Ahriman pulled his dispersed mind back together, feeling the substance of his body flickering back into reality.

He looked down at Cendrion.

His right heart beat once.

XXI
STORM BREAK

The killing salvo hit the *Sycorax*. Plasma conduits ruptured. Fires raced through her machine decks and blew plates from her aft hull. Then the fire found a primary reactor core. The explosion ripped the ship in two. A disc of blue-white fire razored outwards. Clouds of gas spread in a flower of furnace light. The two halves of the ship twisted in different directions. Half-melted cliffs of honeycombed metal crawled with flames as pockets of gas and fuel ignited. The front section exploded first as munitions held close to its forward guns cooked off in a kaleidoscopic display of overlapping detonations. The aft of the ship lasted a little longer, turning over slowly like a fire-blackened mountain tossed into the heavens. Then the warp drives sucked it into a single bright point, before blowing it outwards. A sphere of glittering, metallic sand pattered against the larger chunks of debris. The scream of the *Sycorax*'s death became silent, like a voice cut off by a knife across the throat.

The battle seemed to hesitate for a second as the great ship died. The curtains of warp flame trembled. Volleys of macro-cannon fire stuttered in mute fury. Ships drifted for an instant, course correction forgotten.

A line of lightning appeared in the empty space where the *Sycorax* had been. It shone like a razor slit in a black veil, lengthening slowly then faster. Impossible cries rolled through the vacuum. Crew screamed in the guts of ships. Globes of blood formed in the void, flowed together, split apart. The line widened, buzzing between colours.

The slit of light touched the *Wish of Purgation* as it thrust at the head of the Imperial fleet. The warship shone, rainbow colours sparkling over the pitted metal of its hull. Dazzling splinters broke from it like shattering crystal. The ship held its shape for a second and then collapsed, its angles folding into each other, as though nothing had ever been there.

The warp storm boiled through the widening tear.

Vapour the colour of skinned flesh spilled into the vacuum. Vast faces, rolling eyes and smiles of teeth congealed into being, divided, shrank and divided again until thousands of shapes were tumbling in the void. The shapes twisted and began to scramble through the vacuum towards the light of the battle. The writhing ball of daemons reached the heavy cruiser *Damnation's Answer*, and swarmed through its hull into the air-filled decks within.

The crew began to die, flesh running from their bones at the daemons' touch. Its weapons began to fire at random as hallucinations danced in the gunners' minds. Its engines still burning, it slewed through its own fleet like a drunken madman.

Ships fired back. Macro-cannon rounds struck shoals of daemons and churned them to foaming blood and fire. The battle-barge *Sunderer* turned into the tide spilling towards it, and sawed through it, defence turrets and macro batteries lighting its hull with a cloak of explosions. The other two Space Marine vessels held course. Locking their firing grids together, they burned through the clouds of ectoplasm, and bore down on the ships clustering close to the moon.

Ignis felt the pressure of the storm release in his mind, and saw it swamp the last of Ahriman's fleet that they had sacrificed to create this symmetry of destruction. The alignments of number and angle were there, beautiful in their purity. It was done. The pattern was complete, and this moment, this perfect moment of birth was like the touch of sunlight after night. He shivered and turned his awareness back to the world around him. He stood in the high Navigation cupola. At his feet Silvanus Yeshar wept.

+Turn towards the moon, full power to engines,+ he broadcast, and knew that each of the Thousand Sons ships would obey.

He heard Silvanus's despair as he brushed the Navigator's mind.

'No way out, no way out, no way out…' said Silvanus, over and over again. Ignis sent a jolt of will into the Navigator.

+Look,+ he sent.

The *Word of Hermes* and its clutch of ships were pointing towards Apollonia now, engines thrusting them towards the black surface of the moon.

'No way out…' wept Silvanus as he crawled into the *Word of Hermes*'s navigation cradle.

+Look,+ Ignis sent again. Silvanus looked, staring out with all three of his eyes. He gasped.

Ahriman looked up from Cendrion's broken form. Three paces from him a fissure split wide, stone collapsing into the opening. A sulphur-yellow glow pulsed through the cracks in the walls. He took a breath, and tasted burning hair and copper. The moon was breaking apart. The Athenaeum had been at its heart for so long that it was like a keystone in an arch, but now the Athenaeum was gone and the warp was crushing its hiding place. Sickly light poured through the web of gaping cracks. Grey Knights began to fall or to launch themselves from the crumbling floor.

He reached out and called the Rubricae. They came, firing as they ran. The Athenaeum floated close to him. He reached out a hand and grasped its armoured collar. His fingers tingled with the contact. It was still speaking, droning on with Sanakht's mutilated voice. The final step awaited them.

+Are you there?+ he called. +Ignis?+

'Ahriman!' The cry made him look around. A gun looked back at him. Izdubar stood before the lightning-lit smoke, pistol aimed. His finger closed on the trigger. The gun spat fire and silver. Ahriman's mind brushed the round as it came from the barrel. It was cold. His mind slid away from it. The warp creaked around him. He could feel the Grey Knights' minds linking, energy and will following between them as they came forwards. He watched the round spin on its tail of flame. To his mind it was a hole cut in the warp-saturated universe. It was death if it struck, sure and certain.

The silver round was a swelling black dot in the eye of his mind.

+We are here,+ came Ignis's voice. It sounded distant, like several voices shouting at once above the crash of breaking waves.

+Guide me, brother.+

Stillness: as though the entirety of existence had stopped. Sound and colour and shape split into tatters. The walls of the floor and chamber bulged outwards. The silver round struck Ahriman's armour. The world vanished. Everything was rushing past him, through him, and he knew that all that was holding the storm from tearing him apart was a single thought linking him to the call of his brothers.

The moon of Apollonia imploded. Cracks spread out from its heart as its substance dissolved into the warp. The dark hole at its heart sucked inwards as the black rock crumbled.

The curve of the moon reversed, became a concave pit, and then snapped back. It broke apart. Ghost light fountained up from fissures, sickening auroras looping far out into the dark. Then it seemed to explode backwards, burrowing through the storm like hot water through snow.

The storm carried Ahriman, rolling him in its fingers. Leering faces swam past him, smiling at him with rotting teeth. Great voices roared and chuckled at him. He let it take him, holding all the while to the distant presence of familiar places and the call of his broher's voices. The Athenaeum remained with him, the collar of its armour clamped in his hand. He saw geometries etched into reality, each one pulling at him, calling to him like a light guiding a ship to harbour. He focused on them. The curtain of reality parted before him, and he tumbled through into a circle of etched sigils.

Ignis looked down at him. His orange armour was grey with frost, his eyes gloss red with haemorrhaged blood. He just looked at Ahriman, black pupils swelling and shrinking in his blood-drowned eyes. The patterns of ruin hovered around him, spiralling and iterating into new forms even as Ahriman looked at them.

+You have it,+ said Ignis, and looked at the Athenaeum still gripped by the collar in Ahriman's hand. Ahriman nodded and stood.

+Bind it in a tower for now. Only I may see it.+

+And what do we say of Sanakht to the others?+ asked

Ignis, looking at the motionless body on the ground, its lips moving but its eyes staring blankly at nothing.

+What we agreed, that he took this burden for the future of the Legion.+

Ignis looked up at Ahriman, the geometric tattoos spiralling into new patterns across his forehead. Ahriman held Ignis's gaze for a long second.

+How many of our Legion brothers are still with us?+ asked Ahriman.

+All but one ship.+

+The other vassals?+

+Fed to the flames.+

Ahriman nodded once, and turned away.

+The Imperial fleet still has strength enough to stop us.+

Ahriman turned back, and reached his mind out to listen to the storm roar of the warp.

+Do you hear that?+ he asked. Ignis cocked his head, then frowned. Ahriman nodded. +The Wolves howl.+

The Wolves came from the storm-churned warp. *Hel's Daughter*, *Storm Wyrm*, *Crone Hammer* and *Death's Laughter* crashed into the battle sphere, the bow wave of their exit seeming to shake the stars in their settings. They poured fire ahead of them, splitting the assembled ships like a burning axe blow. Shields shimmered and blew out. Hull armour distorted and ran like fire-touched wax. The storm tide rolled across the barrier of reality, sucking back briefly before crashing down again. The fires of battle blinked from one colour to another. There was no order to the battle now, no lines or formations, just a twirling mess of ships and torn light. Daemons swarmed, whooping as they rode the death waves of ships, cackling even as some were swallowed by the hungry currents.

Boarding torpedoes ripped from the snouts of the Wolves ships. The Imperial fleet turned its eyes and guns towards the newcomers and greeted them with scattered fire. The torpedoes slammed into hulls and the warriors within were loosed from their harness. Creatures of dented armour and twisted flesh spilled into the bowels of Imperial ships, axes rising and falling, clawed hands ripping into any flesh they found.

Grimur felt the shudder of the boarding torpedo as it prepared to loose from *Hel's Daughter*. At his side Sycld shook and coughed blood onto the deck as the torpedo tensed in its breech.

'The silver craft,' hissed the Rune Priest between wet gasps. 'It is the exile. Silver like the snow under a storm sky. Silver of the new moon on water. Silver…'

Grimur said nothing. In his helm he was staring at the battle fires that greeted him. There were ships already burning, already dying in the storm break, but more remained. All would soon be black bones and carcasses of metal. They had found their prey: the end of the hunt was close, it was a blade swing away.

Beside him Sycld was shaking in his harness, bones rattling and jumping against his armour.

'The dream is here, it is here. Silver…' The words were a bared-teeth groan. Grimur could feel muscles bunching inside his armour. He could not stop it. There was blood on his tongue. His teeth were cutting his mouth as they lengthened. He gripped the fragment of red iron armour at his neck.

'Silver are their tears. Pull them down to the red ground, mix their bones with the mud, let the ocean swallow their bones.' White and blue arcs of storm lightning were running up and down the babbling Rune Priest, and hunger and rage radiated from him like cold from a glacier.

Part of Grimur thought of calm, of forcing the wolf within back into the dark. But there was no point, they were running over snow, beneath the moon and the dome of darkness, and the blood of the prey was salt and iron on the air. It was the end of oaths long kept. He let go, and the howl rose through his throat. Around him his brothers howled, and the battle howled back.

Cendrion was still conscious when the strike forces flashed back into existence on the *Sigillite's Oath*. He saw it through the eyes of his brothers, as his true vision faded to smudged red and black. They appeared in the teleport chamber, twenty-eight Grey Knights and four humans. Dirty smoke rose from their armour, as residue from the flash teleport. Izdubar ripped his helmet free. Beside him the crone stood unmoving in her exo-armour. Erionas was waiting for them, his mane of cables locked into ports in the chamber's walls.

Izdubar's face was a pale mask, veins ticking at his jaw and temple.

'We still have strength,' said the inquisitor lord, biting off the words as though they were pieces of bitter fruit. 'They cannot break out. Gut every last ship, then we can search the ashes for his corpse.'

Erionas's face twitched around, his silver eyes dancing with projected data. A look of panic was spreading across his face.

'Lord Izdubar…'

'That makes no sense,' said Malkira, acid voice booming from her armour's external speaker. Izdubar turned to her. 'If Ahriman has what he came for he should run, try and break out.'

'My lord…' Erionas's voice was a high whine.

She is right, thought Cendrion as he heard the words through the haze of his wounds. *But they are missing something. We are all missing something.* The warp was roaring in Cendrion's mind, rattling his fading thoughts with rising fury. His projected awareness began to slip, the image of the inquisitors growing dim as his senses seeped back into the mess of his broken body. He could hear something, a psychic noise which rose over the storm. It was a howl. 'He would have planned a way out,' said Malkira.

'Lord!' shouted Erionas. Silence fell as every eye turned to him. Cendrion felt his grip on consciousness break.

Erionas opened his mouth to speak as the first boarding torpedo hit the *Sigillite's Oath*.

A tongue of flame plucked a brother from Grimur's side. The stink of sorcery was rank in his mouth. He was not seeing the enemy, not really; his mind was dancing with scents: blood, ozone, offal. He roared, fangs wide, and brought the grinning edge of his axe down on the sorcerer's head. Armour broke beneath the blow, scattering splinters and shards of lightning. The sorcerer's corpse was falling, but Grimur was already moving, breathing the smell of the blood as it misted the air. Another sorcerer came at him, fast, very fast, blade singing with light. He swayed out of the way without breaking stride, and struck back and down. The head of his axe took the sorcerer's right leg from beneath him. He looped the axe up and took the falling warrior in the throat. The axe sheared the top of the helm off and another corpse went down to feed the Underverse with its blood. Beside him Sycld was speaking even as he moved between the dead, words broken by the lash of lightning from his staff and the crackle of ice as it spread through the blood of the dead beneath his feet.

'The dream is no more,' rasped the Rune Priest, pointing forwards, fingers splaying to send a whirl of broken shards and shadow towards a cluster of red-robed humans. His eyes were rolled back into his head, his skin ice white. 'The moon rides red in the sky, and its tears are silver.'

Sycld was in the grip of the dreams that had led them here.

A blow struck him and spun him from his feet. He had not seen it coming, had not seen the warrior that struck it. He fell, seeing a shape in vast Terminator armour loom above him. Sorcerous fire washed from the Terminator, and the great sword in his hand, tinting the silver of his armour the colour of forge fire. He remembered Prospero, and the smell of flesh charring in armour as the Thousand Sons had turned their witchcraft on Grimur and his brothers. The sorcerers had worn crimson then, but now they were creatures of silver that glittered like the flanks of the glass pyramids on that now-dead world.

The sorcerer's sword was descending. Grimur sprang up, turning the blow with the flat of his axe and ramming its edge into the sorcerer's eyepieces. Crystal and silvered ceramite shattered. Blood kissed the axe's field and cooked into smoke. Grimur let go of the axe with one hand and grabbed the ruined front of the sorcerer's helm. Claws ripped from the tips of his fingers and tore the helm from the sorcerer's head. The face beneath was a mask of blood and white exposed bone.

The sorcerer twisted away, still alive and somehow still able to see. Grimur leaped, his claws closing on the sorcerer's skull and ripping it from the collar of the armour. He landed on top of the silver giant as it hit the ground. He paused, feeling the race of life in his veins. Around him the pyramids of Prospero burned again in his memory.

He raised his clawed hand, looking at the blood drooling from the broken skull. This was victory unfolding around him, victory and release. Ahriman would not survive, for they had run him and his kin down. He wanted to touch that realisation, to know his victory through his dead enemies' eyes.

He opened his mouth and let the blood of his enemy touch his tongue. Ice and heat shuddered through him. The sorcerer's last sensations and thoughts unfurled in blurred tatters in his awareness. He went still, seeming to shrink, breath coming slow and shuddering from his bloody lips. He looked around, blinking, eyes focusing and refocusing. Slowly he stood.

He turned his eyes to Sycld. The Rune Priest seemed to feel his lord's gaze, and turned his head at the same moment.

'The path, the red path beneath the moon,' croaked Sycld. 'We are there, we are at the dream's end.'

Grimur looked at the Rune Priest, at the ghost light crawling over his staff. He looked down at the head of his own axe and the blood thickening on his clawed hands. He thought of all that he had done to reach this point, and all the things that he had allowed or caused to be done.

We followed dreams. And we never asked who was their master. The prey that runs may run from fear or to draw on the hunters. Revenge, he thought, *is an axe with two smiles.*

He looked into Sycld's blank eyes. The Rune Priest had gone still as though propped up on a stake.

'I...' he said. 'I can't see it any more... the scent, the dream path... I...' His voice cracked, faltered and became something else.

'Wolf,' said Sycld's mouth, but the voice was a hollow rumble. 'The thread of your fate is yours again. No longer will my dreams guide you. You may live, or you may fall, and I will care not, but I wish you to know one thing. I want you to remember it until your soul goes back into the pit of night.' Sycld's mouth twisted into a smile as though pulled by strings. 'I want you to know that you have served me well this day. That truth is my thanks.'

Grimur stood, silent, hunched and bloody in his patched and battered armour. Then he brought his axe up. Sycld shuddered and opened his mouth to speak again. The axe fell.

Silvanus kept his eyes shut, all of them. He pressed his hands over his face, and did not move. It did not help. He could still see. He could see the warp. It shone on the other side of his fingers, lighting his veins and bones. And it was angry. He knew that with a certainty that frightened him because he did not know how he knew.

+Navigator,+ the voice in his skull called: Ignis. He would not answer. He would not do what they asked. He would not look, he would not.

+Navigator.+ The thought voice roared in his skull. Bright motes of light burst in his mind.

'No,' he moaned. 'No, please.'

+Navigator, you will heed our will.+

'No,' he moaned again, and felt bile rise with the words. His teeth felt wrong in his mouth, and the vomit taste was sweet on his tongue. He was suddenly aware of the loose flaps of skin on his face and between his fingers, the red veins bright in the light of the warp. 'No,' he whispered.

+Silvanus.+ The voice was like cool water. Silvanus stopped moaning. He felt the defiance in him rise and break. His hands fell from his face. His eyelids were closed, but the folds of skin over his face made it seem as though they were just two shut eyes amongst many.

He opened his eyes. Vision filled his tri-ocular awareness. The chamber walls were simply a sketch of substance, the ship a ghost, and the souls within it made of light that changed colour with every beat of their hearts. He breathed, focusing and trying to calm the twitching in his face and hands.

He raised his gaze. The black vortex, which had formed where the moon had vanished into nothing, spun before his eyes. It was like looking into a lightless tunnel. Storm winds ringed it, spiralling down into its core like water draining through a hole. The *Word of Hermes* was poised on the edge of that vortex, and beside it a clutch of other ships.

'That is where we must go?' he asked.

+Yes, we will pass through the storm.+

'And then?'

He waited, feeling Ahriman's presence still at the edge of his thoughts.

+Then we begin the path back to where this began.+ Ahriman's thought voice paused. +We return to the Planet of the Sorcerers.+

EPILOGUE

Leaves of crystal crunched beneath her feet as she crossed the summit of the tower. Ahriman did not look up at her approach, but kept his eyes on the transparent sliver of mirror lying on a plinth of black marble.

'You have rebuilt it,' she said. 'Or should it be you have rebuilt yourself?' He straightened. The cloth of his robes caught the warm wind, and pressed itself against his skin. The shard of mirror winked the deep blue of the sky back at him. 'This *place* is different,' she said.

'Everything changes,' he said. Carefully he picked the piece of mirror up between thumb and forefinger. He gazed into the still surface for a long moment, and then tossed it up into the air. The shards of crystal on the floor followed it in a cascade of colours. A tree formed in the air, its trunk a rainbow, its branches a swaying pattern of reflected light.

He looked down from the tree. The palace of his memory extended away and down around him. Towers of rippled black stone and silver rose like half-burned candles from a web of bridges and stairs. Some were brass, others jade, others verdigris-dusted bronze. Domes and cupolas sat like blisters amongst the reaching fingers of the towers. Here and there the white marble of the original palace could be seen peeking out from the new. The whole now resembled something grown rather than built, a vast coral reef of stone and metal, which sprouted new structures even while he watched.

'You will fail,' she said, her voice closer behind him.

'So you have said before,' he replied and turned.

Iobel stood before him. She had shape, but it was like a charcoal sketch pulled into three dimensions, a blur for a body, limbs that bled into nothing, a face formed by suggestion and shadow. She turned, and appeared to look out over the memory palace.

'You did not try to find me.'

'I have found you now,' he said, and shrugged. 'What need is there to hunt you through my own mind?'

She smiled.

'You don't know how I am still here, do you? Have you ever thought how much of your mind now exists beyond you, out there in the warp?' He watched her but said nothing. 'I have walked the edges of your psyche, Ahriman. There are parts of you which are not wholly yours any more, parts which think and dream outside of your skull.'

She looked back at him, her eyes two smudges of shadow under the sun. 'I am here with you now and forever, sorcerer. I live in the shadow of your mind, and until you fall I will walk with you.'

He turned away from her, and started down a flight of stairs which spiralled down from the tower's summit.

'You will fail,' she called to him, but he did not respond. 'I have seen the insides of your knowledge, I have walked your thoughts. Even with the Athenaeum you will fail. The Crimson King will oppose you. Time itself will defy you. You are alone. Kadin, Carmenta, Astraeos – everyone gone, all spent to take you closer to ruin.' Ahriman kept walking, descending through the towers and storerooms of his past. High above him Iobel's voice called after him. 'Only enemies and betrayers remain to you now, Ahriman.'

The waking was slow and filled with pain.

Cendrion, Cendrion, Cendrion… his name beat softly around him, like a reminder left for him to find as he returned from sleep. His limbs were dull aches, both numb and brittle at once. Shocks ran up and down his nerves, while blackness filled his eyes. He reached out with his mind as soon as he was aware, and found the minds of his brothers present but distant.

+What is happening?+ he asked them, but they did not reply.

He tried to wake further, tried to move, but could do neither. He waited.

Sight returned, sudden and sharp in its brightness. He tried to blink, but could not. Static fuzzed across the monochrome vision of a chamber hung with thick cables and chains. Inquisitor Izdubar stood in front of him, a patient expression on his thin face. The crone Malkira and the glass-eyed Erionas stood at his shoulders.

'He has woken?' asked Izdubar, glancing to someone that Cendrion could not see.

'**Where. Am. I?**' Cendrion heard his own voice echo through the chamber like metallic thunder. Izdubar looked up at him again.

'Titan,' said Izdubar. 'The Hall of Ancients.'

Cendrion understood then. The knowledge shivered through his body which was now no more than a broken foetus curled inside the iron womb of a Dreadnought sarcophagus. The pain in his limbs was a ghost, a scrambled sensation that now related to nothing at all.

'**How. Long?**' he asked.

'Eight years since Apollonia, seven in warp travel, one in preparation,' said Erionas, with cold precision.

'**Ahriman?**' he growled.

'Escaped with a few vessels.' Izdubar paused, his tongue poised on his teeth. 'And with the Athenaeum. Only the *Sigillite's Oath* returned from the battle. Ahriman had... allies that attacked us and gave him a chance to dive back into the storm.'

'**The. Storm...**' he began, the words forming ponderously.

'We cannot hope that it destroyed him. He planned for

it, and the allies that rode on its winds,' said Malkira. Cendrion thought that she had withered even further in the time since he had last seen her.

'Allies?'

'Space Marines taken and twisted by the warp,' said Erionas. 'They fled after Ahriman dived into the storm. We recovered bodies, though. The creatures bore the mark of Russ.'

'The. Wolves. Of. Fenris?' Cendrion growled, half in shock, half in anger.

'A remnant perhaps, or a diseased offshoot.' Izdubar tilted his head. 'Perhaps.'

'Our eye has turned on the sons of Russ,' said Malkira.

Cendrion let the thoughts and information flow around him. He kept feeling the tug of unconsciousness, like a hand trying to beckon him down a dark set of stairs. He shut it out, and asked the question that above all others he now needed answered.

'Why. Have. You. Woken. Me?'

'Because it is not only the inheritance of Ahriman's saviours that we have discovered,' said Erionas. 'The gene-samples taken from the traitor Astraeos, before his escape, have been identified, as has the Chapter that created him.'

'Chapter?'

'Oh, yes,' smiled Malkira. 'He is not of the ancient breed of traitors, but of a Chapter that lives now, and still claims loyalty to the Imperium.'

Izdubar looked from the crone back to Cendrion.

'I know I have asked much of you, but now I must ask more of you and your brotherhood.'

'What. Is. Your. Will?'

'Their home world, and every one of their kind must burn, Cendrion. You will lead the execution of that sentence.'

Cendrion looked back into Izdubar's thin emotionless face.

'As. You. Will. It,' he said.

The warriors watched the sorcerer as he walked between their lines. The polished bronze of his armour shimmered under the dirty light of the fires. Blue and green stones set amongst etched patterns of feathers and claws winked in the low light. A helm covered his face, its surface smooth and featureless except for a single blue gem set into its forehead. A serpentine amulet of azurite, brass, and copper hung from his neck. The silver staff in his hand tapped on the stone floor in time with his steps. Some amongst the warriors stirred as the sorcerer passed, their hands brushing their weapons as though half in temptation and half in threat. The sorcerer paused in his procession, his head turning slowly to look at the stirring warriors. Stillness formed under that gaze. After a second the sorcerer continued, his tread unhurried.

When he was at the foot of the altar he stopped and looked up at the three figures who stood beside a wide bowl in which yellow and red flames danced. Each of them wore armour that bore the echo of Prospero in its lines. The heads of serpents, hawks and jackals looked out from carved armour plates, and high crests rose above slit-visored helms. They watched the sorcerer for a long moment, not moving.

'I am Calitiedies,' said one. 'These are my brothers, and this is our circle of warriors.' Calitiedies paused, and his eyes flicked to the armoured figures lining the temple's tiers. 'You come before us bearing the marks of ancient lore on your armour, and knowing the words of passing from ancient Prospero.' Calitiedies blinked slowly, and the air became taut. Beside him the flames in the wide bronze bowl dimmed and shrank. Throughout the temple weapons armed with a roll of metallic clatters and the shiver of energy fields. 'But you are not of our blood, and you have never seen the skies of Prospero. Who are you, that you can come so before us and hope to live?'

The sorcerer looked around slowly, as though taking in the temple and all its occupants with brief interest.

The fire in the bronze bowl exploded upwards, flames writhing blue as the light drained from the air. Calitiedies began to move, but the voice stopped him in mid-step, and the invocation forming in his mind died before it could complete. The voice was not loud, but the air quivered at its sound.

'I am Astraeos,' said the sorcerer, 'and your oaths will be mine.'

ACKNOWLEDGEMENTS

As ever this book owes much of its shape and existence to many people:

To Liz, for, well, just about everything really.

To Graham McNeill, for all the chats about the XV Legion, past and future.

To Aaron Dembski-Bowden, my Brother in Darkness, for all the long conversations about the nature of the warp, time, Black Crusades and the Rubric.

To the Black Library editors, for shepherding this insanity into being.

To Ead Brown, Colin Goodwin, Trevor Larkin, Andy Smillie, Greg Smith and Chris Wraight for their encouragement and feedback.

And all the rest.

This one's yours, guys.

ABOUT THE AUTHOR

John French is a writer and freelance games designer from Nottingham. His work for Black Library includes a number of short stories, the novellas *Fateweaver* and *The Crimson Fist* and the novel *Ahriman: Exile*. He also works on the Warhammer 40,000 role-playing games. When he is not thinking of ways that dark and corrupting beings can destroy reality and space, John enjoys making it so with his own Traitor Legions on the gaming table.